WHITE GHOSTS

THE RUSSIAN TREASURES SERIES

BOOK TWO

ELVIRA BARYAKINA

Translated from Russian

by Elvira Baryakina and Simon Geoghegan

This book is a work of fiction. Any references to historical events, real people, or real places are used fictitiously. Other names, characters, places, and events are products of the author's imagination, and any resemblance to actual events or places or persons, living or dead, is entirely coincidental.

ISBN: 978-1-7325840-2-0

For Pavel Mamaev

1. THE REFUGEES

1

December, 1922

Shivering in her worn-out black coat and astrakhan hat, Nina Kupina paced the rusty low deck of the refugee steamer, cramming English verbs into her head: "Come, came, come; see, saw, seen; win, won, won."

For several weeks now, two thousand Russian souls had been killing time in the Shanghai harbor, trapped on their ships bearing the faded banners of a state that no longer existed—the Russian Empire. But the Shanghai authorities still had no idea what to do with them. The representatives of the Chinese part of the city, the French concession, and the International Settlement had expressed sympathy for the refugees who had fled the Bolsheviks after the brutal civil war in Russia, but no one wanted these homeless and penniless foreigners on their territory or on their hands.

Just to be on the safe side, they had sent a Chinese

battleship to keep the refugees in their sights. It was a sensible precaution. In the depths of their despair, the Russians might easily launch an attack on peaceful Shanghai. Their holds were brimming with arms: they had enough to start a small war.

Father Seraphim, a man built like a bear, with cannonballs for fists and a bushy beard, approached Nina.

"The parents' committee wants to arrange a Christmas celebration for the kids," he said. "Can you draw us a Christmas tree on the wall next to the mess hall? We have to arrange some semblance of normality for the children during the holiday."

He gave Nina a piece of charcoal, and she went up to the crowded upper deck, lit by the weak winter sun.

The low, flat shores of the Huangpu River were powdered with snow. The roofs of the ancient watchtowers with their corners curved skywards were silhouetted like black paper cut-outs against the pink-grayish evening sky. All sorts of ships swarmed past the anchored refugee flotilla—swift moving junks with carved sterns and sails like dragons' wings, soot-blackened coal barges, and white ocean-going liners. Shanghai was so near yet so far. Everybody had the right to go ashore, it seemed, except the Russians.

The men on board, for the most part former White Army officers and soldiers, were grinding rice delivered by Shanghai charities, using improvised homemade hand grinders. Their wives and daughters were doing their laundry. Drying shirts and pants, draped over the ship's gun barrels, flapped in the icy wind. From the stern came the sound of keening: a woman had died of pneumonia and her friends were preparing her for burial.

Nina found an area on the wall where the paint was not peeling and began to draw. Suddenly she heard the voice of her husband, Klim Rogov, floating from the opened porthole. Nina hesitated for a moment but couldn't resist the temptation to eavesdrop.

Klim enjoyed great authority among the refugees as he had spent some time in Shanghai when he was younger. In the evenings, he invited people to the mess hall and imparted his knowledge to them. Nina had pretended not to be interested in these meetings. When you've sent your husband packing, it's awkward to rely on him for priceless information concerning your future.

"According to official documents," Klim said, "China is an independent state, but in fact, it's a colony of the Great Powers—Great Britain, France, Italy, the United States, and Japan. The Chinese have suffered defeat in every war they have fought against them, and the victors have made them sign unequal treaties that have made the Great Powers masters of the country. The whites barely consider the Chinese human and despise them so much that they call their Chinese male servants "boys," even the elderly ones, and give them numbers—Boy One, Boy Two, Boy Three."

Nina peeked furtively through the porthole.

The audience listened attentively, hanging on Klim's every word. They were dying to escape to Shanghai from their floating prison, yet the very idea terrified them. Few of them knew any foreign languages, and most of the men had never pursued any trades other than military service. The women were in an even worse position, especially those who had only been raised to be mothers and wives. Nina was one of them.

Klim looked tired, his thick dark brows knitted, his broad shoulders oddly hunched, but he made an effort to be upbeat and untroubled about their current position.

"Sooner or later, the officials will let us into the city," he said. "Our steamers are in such a bad condition we can't sail any further. I doubt our fellow Christians will let us die here before their very eyes. Who would want two thousand vengeful ghosts coming to visit them at night?"

Nina stepped back from the porthole, feeling uneasy. Here, on the ship, she could at least count on a meal, but she didn't have the faintest idea what would be awaiting her once she arrived in the city. When she had separated from Klim, she had had a plan to find herself another, more established husband. In her previous life before the revolution, she could dazzle and enchant men and had therefore relied on their help and generosity. But recently Nina had realized that at twenty-five-years-old, she was severely hampered by her less than glamorous condition. Once Klim had told her that she would make an ideal Swan Princess, with her large grayish-green eyes and pointed face framed with dark curls, but being a princess in rags and without a kingdom was not a safe bet for her.

In fact, the only valuable thing Nina had was a revolver she had removed from Klim's possession when she had decided to break up with him. The last thing she needed was for him to put a bullet through his brains.

Nina had tried her best to draw a nice Christmas tree on the wall but it had ended up looking more like the tip of a barbed harpoon. It felt as if everything she tried her hand to these days turned into a brutal and ugly mess.

In Vladivostok, just before the refugee flotilla's departure, she had contracted typhus and, in her delirium, had imagined herself living under a bridge, rummaging through rubbish dumps for food. She had convinced herself that this would be her destiny if she didn't leave Klim. Who needed a Russian- and Spanish-speaking writer in Asia? Klim's English lacked refinement, and his knowledge of Shanghainese was only good enough for haggling with market traders. Both of them knew that he wouldn't be able to find a good job in Shanghai.

"I'm sure we can work something out," Klim had tried to reassure her. "I started from scratch in Argentina and ended up becoming a reasonably good journalist."

She hadn't listened. "I can't wait for you to get back on your feet."

But the longer the refugees sat on their ships, the less enthusiastic Nina became about her decision. There was no way she could find anyone better than Klim. He was smart, enterprising, talented, and trustworthy—nobody could compare to him.

What if the typhus had driven me crazy? Nina thought. She had heard that the disease had a debilitating effect on people's nerves and decision-making faculties. Half of Russia had come down with the typhus, and perhaps that was the reason why the country had been wracked with so much cruel and irrational behavior.

She peeked into the porthole again. Klim drew a rough map of Shanghai on a piece of brown paper and explained to his listeners where the markets, the railroad station, and the Russian Orthodox church were located.

I should wait until this meeting is over and go and talk to him, Nina thought.

But would he find it in his heart to take her back? In his place, she would never have forgiven a man for leaving her in the lurch. It had only recently occurred to Nina that Klim's life in Vladivostok had in many ways been harder than her own. Not only had he been responsible for supporting the two of them, but he had also had to nurse her through her illness as well. How could she be so ungrateful?

Finally the meeting ended, the audience poured out onto the deck, but Nina missed her chance to speak to Klim. He had swiftly passed her by, and pretending to be looking in a different direction he had dropped his map of the city at her feet. Nina picked it up and studied it for a while.

Had Klim done this on purpose? He knew that there was nobody else on board who could help her find her feet in Shanghai.

2

When dusk fell, the Chinese fishermen lighted round paper lanterns on their sampans anchored by the pier.

They lived on their boats, sleeping in cramped cabins fashioned out of boards and reeds, cooking their food in small sooty pots.

The other refugees had long gone to sleep, but Nina was still pacing the empty deck. Jiří Labuda, a former Czech prisoner of war, approached her. He was a short, scrawny, gray-eyed young man with bright red hair and countless freckles peppering his nose. His right hand had three fingers missing.

"If you like, I could light your way back to your cabin with my cigarette lighter," he said. "It's already dark in the corridors, and you might trip."

Jiří was always trying to please Nina, and it kept her diverted. She had rescued him from the angry officers who had accused him of stealing bread. They had decided to hang him to make an example, but Nina had shown them bread sacks chewed through by rats, and the officers had let Jiří go.

He had told her he had been a cellist and seemed destined for a brilliant musical career, but when the Great War started, he had been drafted into the Austro-Hungarian Army. Wounded and captured, he had spent three years in a prisoner-of-war camp, where he learned Russian. Somehow he had ended up with the White Army flotilla, and now Jiří didn't have a clue where he was headed and why.

"Let's go to sleep," Nina told him, but he didn't move, staring intensely into the darkness behind her back.

She turned and shuddered at the sight of a large junk approaching their ship. It had a carved dragon on its bow, and its Chinese sailors were lit an eerie red by the onboard lanterns as they bustled about on deck.

"Missy, guns! Me wantchee guns," shouted one of them, dressed in a bowler hat and a quilted Chinese jacket.

"What does he want?" Nina asked Jiří, perplexed.

He shrugged. "They seem to be speaking English, but I can't figure it out."

The sailor made a gesture as if he was firing with his finger and then pulled a banknote from his pocket.

"I think he wants to buy a gun," Nina guessed. "Ask him will a revolver do? I have a revolver."

It would be nice to sell it and get some money, she thought.

The sailor fanned his fingers out on both hands.

"He needs more than one gun," Jiří said.

"How much then? Ten?"

"More, more!" the sailor shouted.

The captain of the refugee ship came out on the deck, accompanied by the sailors on watch. "What's going on here?"

"This man wants to buy guns," said Nina excitedly. "Let's sell him something from our arsenal and get some money."

The captain looked at her as if she was crazy. "The Great Powers have imposed an embargo here: it is prohibited to import any arms into China. If they catch us selling guns, they'll deport us immediately."

"How much cash have you got?" Nina asked quietly. "I don't mean worthless paper rubles, but real money, dollars, that you can actually buy something with."

The captain frowned. "I don't have the right to trade these arms. They are not my property."

"But you do have the right to sign off anything that has gone out of service."

After a moment's hesitation, the captain invited the Chinese on board.

"Come on up, but don't make any noise," he said. "Our passengers are already asleep."

The first to appear over the side was a fat man wearing a fashionable hat and an unbuttoned leather coat.

"Good evening," he said in French.

Nina was delighted. She knew some French and would be able to talk to the guests.

The fat man kissed her hand. "Oh, what secret treasures are hidden on this boat! Don Jose Fernando

Burbano at your service, ma'am."

Two Chinese followed him, the one who had initiated the negotiations, and another one, a huge, terrifying one-eyed man with a hideously burned face.

Nina offered them her services as an interpreter, but Don Fernando declined saying that this was no business for a woman.

"Does anyone know English here?" he asked.

Jiří raised his hand enthusiastically, like a student in a classroom, and Don Fernando patted him on the shoulder. "Come on then, Redhead, let's see what you've got for us."

The captain told Nina to go to her cabin, but she held her ground and resolutely followed the men down into the hold. She had calculated that if she sold her revolver to Don Fernando, she might get five or even ten Chinese dollars for it.

The sailors took turns spinning the handle of the dynamo torch while the captain showed Don Fernando his wares.

"We have rifles made in Russia, Mills Bomb hand grenades, handguns, gun sights, and periscopes," Jiří interpreted, and Nina was surprised that she could understand some of the English.

The haggling went on endlessly. Finally, Don Fernando's patience ran out. "You're in no position to make any bargains," he barked at the captain. "You should take what you're given and be grateful."

One-Eye handed him a small abacus, and the Don began snapping the beads to and fro.

"Cartridge shells, twenty boxes; Mosin-Nagant rifles, dreadful old crap. I bet half of them are out of service. Sixteen caskets, plus the grenades . . . Sixteen hundred dollars for the lot, and I won't give you a copper more."

Jiří interpreted his words: "He's only offering six hundred dollars."

Nina instinctively wanted to correct him: *Sixteen hundred means one thousand and six hundred—*

But the captain had already offered the Don his hand. "Well, to hell with you. Just take everything away quickly and get out of here."

Nina's heart was thumping.

"You pay the captain six hundred dollars," she said to the Don in French, "and I'll collect the rest of the money. But we need to be discreet about it."

Don Fernando looked at her, and a knowing smile lit up his chubby face. "As you wish, ma'am. Come over to my junk, and we'll settle matters there."

Nina watched the sailors and deckhands shift the crates from one vessel to another, her whole body trembling with fear and excitement. If her fellow refugees had learned what she was about to do, she would be tried and punished in accordance with martial law. However, if she succeeded she would have the money that she and Klim needed to get settled in Shanghai. She would ask for his forgiveness, tell him she had a mental breakdown, and they would make up.

When the last crate had been transferred to the junk, Nina quickly jumped onto the gangway connecting the two ships.

The captain grabbed her by her elbow. "Where are you going?"

Nina gave him a forced smile. "I want to sell my revolver to Don Fernando. I don't have any money left."

The captain let her go, reluctantly. "Don't stay there too long."

But as soon as Nina jumped down onto the junk's deck, a searchlight from the distant patrol ship flashed in the darkness, and a voice boomed over the river, speaking in English through a loud-hailer. "Don't move! You are under arrest!"

A moment later, Don Fernando's men had pulled up the gangway, and the anchor chain clattered.

"Wait!" Nina cried, but nobody paid her the slightest attention. Sailors ran to their stations on deck, the sail filled above her head, and the junk moved irrevocably away from the refugee ship.

"Miss Nina!" a frightened voice called out to her.

She turned her head and saw Jiří sitting on the deck, holding his travel bag.

"What are you doing here?" Nina asked.

"Don Fernando promised to take me to Shanghai," Jiří whispered. "I'm sick of wasting my time on that rotten steamer."

There was a gunshot, and the searchlight from the patrol ship shone straight at the junk's deck.

"Damn it!" Don Fernando roared in the darkness. "Drop the anchor! That's Captain Eggers. I'll have to talk to him."

3

Don Fernando made a courtesy visit to the patrol ship, returning only at dawn, drunk and in high spirits.

"Let's go home," he told the deckhands. "Captain Eggers and I had a talk. There are no hard feelings."

Shivering with fear and cold, Nina sat next to Jiří on a coil of cables, not daring to attract the attention of the smugglers.

There's no way I can get back to the refugee ship, she thought in panic. *What if these smugglers rape and kill me? Well, it would serve me right—I'm always asking for trouble.*

A Chinese pilot stood impassively on the high, painted stern, moving the heavy steering oar with considerable effort. The timbers shivered above Nina's head, and the moist air smelled of seaweed and smoke.

"We're lucky to be the first into Shanghai," Jiří said quietly. "Do you realize what will happen once the city becomes inundated with all these penniless refugees? The Shanghailanders will come to hate us as intruders. We need to settle in as soon as possible before our accents turn us into pariahs."

"What are you going to do in Shanghai?" Nina asked.

"I don't know . . . Maybe we should try to find a homeless shelter."

Don Fernando lurched unsteadily around his newly acquired weapon crates.

"Hey, ma'am, come over here," he called to Nina, pulling a wad of banknotes out of his pocket. "Here's a thousand dollars. Count it. It's all there."

Nina looked at him in amazement. She wasn't expecting the Don to keep his word.

"I don't know what's come over me," Fernando sighed. "Perhaps I have gone soft and taken a shine to you, with your pretty eyes shining like little stars. Hey, One-Eye!" he called his sidekick. "I'll go take a nap. Wake me up when we get there."

Nina hid the money in her pocket. She still couldn't take in what had happened. *I've got a thousand dollars, and I didn't have to lift a finger to earn it.*

Things weren't looking too bad, after all. With money in her pocket, she would be able to start a business and find Klim as soon as the other refugees got ashore. She would probably be able to get his address at the Russian Consulate or the local Orthodox church.

Nina moved to the junk's bow, a carved dragon head jutting proudly above her. She felt the fresh sea breeze on her face as the junk skipping at a good clip over the waves.

The closer it got to the city, the more wharves and warehouses she could make out along the embankment. Billboards with exotic slogans in English were on display above their tiled roofs: "Buy Great Wall cigarettes," "Tiger Balm—the best remedy for all illnesses." Smoke-stacks, factory shops, building cranes . . . The river was packed from bank to bank with boats of all shapes and sizes. One-Eye took up a position next to Nina and began shouting at the other boats through a megaphone.

Soon a large steel bridge appeared on their starboard side, surrounded by enormous buildings capped with domes and adorned with towers and columns. The streetlamps on the promenade were still alight and were reflected in the countless windows around.

Nina looked at One-Eye, puzzled. "Am I really in China?"

He grinned. "This is Band, this where the International Settlement works and lives. China is a bit further upriver."

At last, the junk moored up to one of the piers. The disheveled Don Fernando emerged from his cabin, scratching his belly.

"You should get a passport for yourself," he said to Nina genially. "People in your line of business need documents."

"How much does one cost?" Nina asked.

"Three hundred Chinese dollars."

"For a fake? Don't be ridiculous."

Don Fernando shrugged. "Well, as you wish. Let me kiss your pretty hand goodbye?"

Nina put her hands in her pockets. "I'd rather you told me what the best hotel in Shanghai is."

"The Astor House. Why?"

"Just curious."

4

Nina and Jiří crossed the gangway onto the promenade and froze, stunned by the sight of the shiny cars parked along the snow-covered street.

"I've never seen so many cars in one place," Nina whispered.

Brown smoke curled from chimneys; large buses forged their way through swarms of rickshaws, single-seated passenger buggies pulled by Chinese men dressed in quilted jackets and pants, and canvas shoes. They would pick up the thin shafts and start to jog, easily outstripping the heavily laden single-wheeled carts.

Despite the early hour, the sidewalks were already crowded. White gentlemen in expensive coats with fur collars were buying newspapers from Chinese boys who yelled in English: "Breaking news! Soviet Russia is now called the Soviet Union."

Chinese clerks wearing almost identical blue coats and black satin caps hurried to their offices and shops. Workers were working hard removing Christmas wreaths tied with red ribbons from street-lamp posts. Unlike Russian Orthodox Christians, who celebrate Christmas on January 7, Shanghai's Catholics and Protestants had already celebrated their feast thirteen days earlier.

A detachment of black-bearded horsemen in blue coats and red turbans galloped by.

"Those are Sikhs," Jiří told Nina. "I read that the British brought them over from India to police their colonies."

They heard a little bell jingling as a street peddler pushed his cart with a steaming brazier piled high with pots, bowls, and teapots.

Jiří gave Nina a pleading look. He was evidently very hungry.

"Don't even think about it," she said sternly. "Today we will be breakfasting at the Astor House."

"Are you out of your mind?" gasped Jiří, "We are illegal immigrants. The police will catch us there for sure."

"A fancy hotel is the last place they'll be looking for illegal immigrants."

Nina boldly headed toward a row of parked rickshaws. "Astor House!" she called.

Several men immediately ran up to her. "Here, Missy! Come with me, please!"

Pretending that she was not in the slightest bit embarrassed, Nina climbed into the cart, and the rickshaw puller, a young man in a torn quilted jacket, covered her lap with a leather lap-robe.

Nina turned to Jiří. "Are you coming with me or

not?"

He hesitated. "I can't ride a cart pulled by a human being."

"Just arrived in Shanghai?" the rickshaw man asked him in broken English. "People power is good! People need food. I bring money to my family."

Jiří resignedly waved his hand, got into the cart, and they drove on along the elegant promenade.

Shanghai was lit up with the morning sun. Tram bells rang, horns blared, horseshoes clattered, and Nina's head spun from the sheer din of it all.

Suddenly she noticed a Chinese girl walking with a very strange gait, followed by another and then another. Instead of normal feet, they all seemed to have tiny hooves wrapped in embroidered shoes.

It took Nina a while to construct her question in English, and when the rickshaw stopped at an intersection, she asked: "What's wrong with these women? Why do they have such small feet?"

"Here, all girls have their feet bound," the rickshaw man said, wiping sweat from his forehead. "We don't want their feet to grow; it's ugly."

"How come?" Nina said with indignation. "Your women can't even walk normally, let alone run."

"That is how it should be. Otherwise, the wives would run away from their husbands."

Nina frowned, remembering Klim. She was going to get a room in the best hotel in Shanghai, and he had been left behind on that stinking ship.

There is nothing I can do about it now, she thought.

The Astor House doorman was baffled by the shabby appearance of the white guests.

"We have just come back from a hunting trip," Nina told him in French. "To Swan Lake."

Reluctantly, the doorman ushered them into the brightly lit lobby.

"I'd almost forgotten that these sorts of places

existed," Nina murmured, gazing at the crystal chandeliers and marble floors.

Paying no attention to the porters gawking at her, she went straight up to the reception desk.

"Hello! We need two adjoining rooms. For a month."

The receptionist blinked at her in confusion. "But that will be a hundred and fifty dollars, ma'am, and I'm not sure you're going to be able to—"

"Do you need a deposit?" Nina pulled out a wad of cash from her pocket, which made the receptionist even more flustered.

"Oh no, ma'am, no deposit necessary. Here, in Shanghai, we pay with chits; we'll send you an invoice later. I hope you enjoy your stay."

"He didn't even ask for our passports," Jiří whispered when they entered the elevator.

"Our white skin is all the passports we need," Nina replied. "Klim told me that they even offer loans on a white man's word of honor. Although I'm not sure that's going to last for much longer."

The bellboy led Nina and Jiří past stained-glass windows and sumptuous mahogany-paneled walls to a gallery that wound its way around a large ballroom. Downstairs, under a huge glass roof, an orchestra played next to tables covered with pristine white linen.

Nina stopped to look at the dancing couples. Half of the ladies had their hair cut short, and they wore dresses with belts that were fastened at the side to accentuate their hips. *Wow!*

"What kind of music is this?" Nina asked Jiří.

He shook his head. "I don't know. I've never heard anything like it before."

"And you call yourself a musician?" Nina teased. "Oh, we're hopelessly behind the times."

The bellboy informed them that the music was known as jazz, and that the event going on downstairs was *tiffin*— a kind of late second breakfast complete with cocktails and dances.

He turned the lock on one of the polished doors. "Monsieur, madame, welcome!"

It was a little chilly in the room, and it smelled of lavender soap. Nina put her hat on the neatly made bed, threw the curtains open, and laughed. "Jiří, I love this city!"

5

After a luxurious bath and breakfast, they decided to go shopping.

Nina was awe struck by Shanghai's wealth and modernity. She observed the well-heeled crowd promenading down Nanking Road and gasped at the staggering dresses on display in the giant shop windows. The trees had been trimmed, all the sidewalks had trashcans, and dashing traffic policemen stood at the road crossings, waving on pedestrians with their batons.

To all intents and purposes it was a European city, with the exception of the Chinese shop signs, rickshaws, and pedestrians carrying ducks in cages or bundles of cabbage on bamboo yokes.

It now seemed strange to Nina that she had ever been so afraid of emigrating. What was there to miss about ill-starred Russia? Shanghai was a city where you could live life to the full.

While she and Jiří were roaming the Wing On department store, Nina wanted to laugh and cry with happiness. To think that only yesterday she hadn't even had enough thread to sew a button, and now she could buy herself whatever she wanted: an American photo camera or a set of fine porcelain cups from Japan, or a fine British leather purse, or even a fountain pen with a golden nib. Everything was available if you could afford it, without even waiting in line, and the prices were ridiculously cheap.

Clerks in gray gowns heaped silk on the counter, cut a little nick into the weightless fabric, and then tore it in a perfect line the rest of the way. "Bye-bye makee me pay," they said. "Mee send chit."

They didn't ask for money in the shops, either; it was enough just to show a hotel card and sign for the purchase.

"Jiří, wake me up!" Nina moaned. But Shanghai had completely benumbed his senses as well.

They returned to their hotel completely different people: well-dressed, refreshed, and with a gleam in their eyes.

Nina led Jiří to the big mirror that stretched from the floor to the ceiling.

"This is the real us," she said, "and this is how we should always remain. We've been under a curse, but now it has been lifted forever."

Jiří glanced at his crippled hand and quickly hid it behind his back. "Yes, you're right. Most likely."

6

That evening, Nina lay in bed reading the menu from the French restaurant as if it were the most delightful novel. "Capon fillet and chestnut mash. Roasted pheasant in a sauce of woodcock mince, bacon, anchovy, and truffles. Mandarin fish aspic with wild saffron rice. Oh Lord, have mercy on us!"

Her feet ached from the shopping marathon, and she hadn't quite found her land legs after the long days spent at sea. Shopping bags and boxes were spread all over the floor—'a woman's basic necessities' as Klim used to call them.

Thinking of him made her feel uneasy. He would probably be devastated when he learned how she had escaped from the steamer.

There was a quiet knock, and Jiří appeared in her doorway, looking like a choirboy with his neat new haircut

17

and his full-length terrycloth robe.

"I'm sorry to intrude on your daydreams," he said. "But I have a question. How do you plan to pay for all of this?" He pointed at the shopping bags.

"I'll think of something," Nina replied breezily. "I can put an ad in the newspaper: 'Impeccably bred young lady available to entertain and hold court with the cream of society. One hundred dollars an hour. Satisfaction guaranteed."

Jiří snickered. "I've just read a very similar ad in the newspaper. The young ladies providing this service in Shanghai are geishas from the Japanese settlement, and they're paid a miserly two dollars an hour."

2. THE HOUSE OF HOPE

1

At the age of fifteen Ada Marshall had become an orphan. Her American father, who was contracted to an Izhevsk factory in Siberia, had been killed right at the start of the revolution, and Ada's Russian mother had died from pneumonia on the refugee ship.

After her mother's body had been buried at sea, Ada had found a hiding place for herself behind the large crate containing the life jackets, and it was there that she had created her own little world, complete with a red blanket on the floor and the stack of books that her mother had been carrying with her ever since they had left Izhevsk. Ada had stayed cocooned there for weeks, while the refugees negotiated with the Shanghai authorities.

Finally, the Russians were allowed to go ashore, but they had to leave all their weapons behind, and the ships had to remove themselves from Chinese territorial waters.

The news stirred joyfully throughout the ship.

"Come with us, poor child," Father Seraphim said.

"I'm not going anywhere," Ada whispered in fear. She

had no idea what she was going to do in Shanghai.

"Well, suit yourself," the priest sighed. "The ships will go to Manila soon, and it's a long way from there to Russia. How are you going to get back home when the Bolsheviks are finally toppled?"

Ada had no reply.

Soon the only people on board were the volunteer sailors. Ada wandered about the empty corridors trying to decide what she should do now.

Several times she encountered Klim Rogov, who had also refused to go ashore at Shanghai. Nobody could understand why his wife would leave such a kindhearted, strong man who knew some English. There could only be one possible explanation for Nina's betrayal: that funny little Czech man, Jiří Labuda, had been pretending to be poor and desperate when in fact he had a large sum of money, and that was how he had managed to seduce Klim's wife.

On the rare occasions when they met, Klim and Ada would look askance at each other, carrying on their separate business in silence. Neither was in the mood to talk.

2

One morning, as Ada came up on deck, she saw Klim climbing over the ship's side and beginning to descend a rope ladder down to a sampan. An old Chinese man dressed in a quilted jacket and a ragged woolen hat was waiting for him in the boat.

"Where are you going?" Ada gasped.

"I've decided to go to Shanghai after all," Klim said.

Ada looked around her at a complete loss. It now finally dawned on her that she really would be the last passenger left on the ship.

"Wait, I'm going with you!"

Ada returned to her nook, folded her red blanket and

tied up her books with a piece of twine. They were heavy and cumbersome, and she was in two minds whether she should take them or not. But they were her only memento of her former life, and in any case, it would be sad to live without books in Shanghai.

As Ada lowered herself into the boat, she lost her balance and nearly fell into the water. Fortunately, Klim managed to catch her. She felt a strange feeling coursing through her body as his strong hands saved her from her fall.

He told her to sit down on the straw mat next to his knapsack and a big battered samovar. The old man started moving his wide oar at the stern, and the sampan headed upriver.

"Do you have any relatives?" Klim asked Ada.

She shook her head. "No. I mean, yes, I have an aunt in America. My mom gave me her address and some money. I'm going to write her a letter."

Waiting for Klim to say where they were going, Ada gnawed a fingernail on her thumb that was protruding through a hole in her mitten. *What's going to happen,* she thought, *if this man abandons me when we reach Shanghai? Where am I going to go then?*

She regarded him furtively—his frowning brow, his stubble, and his dark hair that was rebelliously peeping out from underneath his newsboy cap.

"Why have you decided to go to Shanghai?" Ada asked.

"Yesterday, I had an epiphany when I was in the galley," Klim said. "It occurred to me that a person's life is rather like a sack of potatoes, and each day is like a single potato. It's up to us what we do with each precious day that has been allotted to us. We can make something tasty, or we can throw it in the trashcan to rot. It didn't make any sense to me to carry on rotting out there on the ship."

Ada smiled. "But what if the potato has already been spoiled?"

"A smart person will figure out how to put it to good

use." Klim pointed at a boat with a huge fetid barrel on its deck. "Do you know what that is? The Chinese take the excrement out of their chamber pots and make fertilizer out of it for their fields. All the local vegetables are grown using it."

Ada shuddered at the very idea and decided that she wouldn't be touching any Chinese food.

The old boatman was planning to take his passengers to the luxury waterfront once the sampan reached Shanghai, but Klim told him to go further.

Upstream there were warehouses and factory shops next to unimaginable hovels made out of old broken boards and billboards. Brown smoke floated over the thatched roofs, and laundry hanging to dry on bamboo poles was stiff with the frost.

The boatman maneuvered the sampan next to a lopsided pier. Sleepy fishermen with makeshift rods sat on the shore while their dirty-faced womenfolk cleaned huge copper cauldrons next to them.

"You mentioned that you had some money," Klim said to Ada.

She frowned. "Why do you ask?"

"I've told the boatman that I'll give him my samovar as a fee, but it's worth a lot more than twenty cents. I have no money on me, so it's up to you whether we keep my last remaining possession or not. Personally, I think a samovar might come in handy for us."

Ada's heart leapt. Klim had said "us," and that implied that he wasn't going to abandon her.

She readily pulled a knitted moneybag out of her pocket. "Here, I have some Chinese dollars that my mom gave to me."

Klim paid the boatman and took Ada along the crooked noisy street lined with two-story houses. The ground floors were occupied by shops with the floors above used as apartments.

Ada stared open-mouthed at the tiled roofs, the

windows latticed with thin red slats, and the vertical boards with strange hieroglyphs painted on them.

"What are they?" she asked Klim. "Shop signs?"

He nodded. "The Chinese write from top to bottom, not from left to right."

Peddlers were selling watermelon seeds, sunflower seeds, and sugar cane. Mountains of pickled cucumbers and carrots lay on the stalls along the road. Women were grilling something on their sooty braziers—it looked suspiciously like grasshoppers or even scorpions.

"Good gracious!" Ada kept gasping, as she marveled at the rickshaws, palanquins, and carts with huge wheels. Two young Chinese men were carrying an enormous bale hanging from a bamboo pole. In order to keep time, they shouted in unison: "Aya-hah! Aya-hah!"

A bus, packed with people, roared past, a policeman blew his whistle, car brakes squealed, and shaven-headed monks in orange robes climbed out of a huge shiny automobile.

Ada's head was spinning. Where had she ended up? In Asia? In Europe? This city was an incomprehensible mix of all the world's cultures and historical epochs, dating from the Middle Ages to modernity.

"Where are we going?" Ada asked plaintively. She felt that she was about to collapse from exhaustion.

Klim stopped and gave her a serious look. "Please, don't be scared but . . . we're going to a brothel."

"Excuse me?"

"We need to look around and learn the news."

Should I run away? Ada thought. She looked around and suddenly noticed the familiar face of one of the women who had been with them on the ship. She was sitting on the ground next to a shop, bowing low to every person entering and exiting it. She was begging, but no one was giving her any money.

3

Klim brought Ada to a small courtyard behind a two-story brick building. A rusted bicycle frame lay in a pile of litter; somebody's drawers drooped morosely on a washing line.

Klim approached the porch and hammered on the flaking door.

"Martha, open the door," he shouted in English.

Ada cautiously looked around. She was about to enter a brothel. The shame of it!

They heard footsteps, and a blue eye appeared at the peephole. "Who is it?"

"Martha, don't you recognize me?"

The door flew open, and a petite and voluptuous woman with paper curlers in her hair threw her arms around Klim's neck. "You're back!"

What a dressing gown she had on! Ada had never seen such a robe in her whole life. It had a dragon on the back, and its hem and sleeves were trimmed with fur.

Klim and Martha embraced each other. "How are you doing, my lovely?" he asked.

Ada gave him a puzzled look. Has he gone blind? His friend's face was puffy, and she had a large nose and a double chin.

"Come on in. It's cold out here," Martha said, shivering, and led her guests into the lobby.

Ada followed Martha and Klim upstairs, her face blushing and her heart racing. The walls were papered with striped wallpaper, the stairs were laid with carpet, and a dusty chandelier made of different colored glass hung from the ceiling. *So this is what brothels look like*, she thought.

Upstairs was a large elegant room with a green grand piano, a gramophone player, and velvet sofas. Clients had evidently been carousing there recently, and the maid hadn't had time to sweep the floors and take the dirty glasses away.

"So where have you come from, Mr. Rogov?" Martha asked, scrutinizing Klim's shabby outfit. "Just out of jail?"

"Just out of a civil war."

"I bet you came out of it decorated?"

"Of course. The Order of the Legion of Refugees and the broken Purple Heart."

"Did you come with the Russians? Sit down and tell me all about it."

Klim told her his story and those of a number of mutual acquaintances they both knew. Ada was sitting next to him, embarrassed, holding her blanket and books close to her chest.

Oranges and cookies were sitting in a dish on the round table in front of her. *It would be nice of Martha if she offered us a treat,* Ada thought. It must have been five years since she last had a cookie, and she had only ever seen oranges in pictures before.

But Martha was busy talking and complaining about the Russian refugees who were ruining her business.

"I used to get a good price for a white girl," she said. "Now anyone can just go to the Russian Consulate and choose any sweetheart they want. There are hundreds of them. All a man needs to do is to take a frightened little chick to a café, order a muffin, and the poor thing will be happy to do anything for her shining new Prince Charming."

"I need a job," Klim said. "I don't have two pennies to rub together."

Martha shook her head pensively. "It's difficult with jobs now. The Chinese are ready to do anything for ten cents a day. And now we have your Russians on our hands. Only a nice-looking girl can get a job in certain establishments." She glanced at Ada. "Who is she?"

Klim frowned. "Her mother died, and she has nowhere else to go."

"How is she going to support herself?"

"I can teach English and French," said Ada, blushing.

"Let me have a look at you." Martha stretched her hand to undo Ada's coat.

"Don't touch me!"

Martha started to laugh. "She's going to teach French—to whom, may I ask?"

"Give her a job as a taxi-girl in the Havana," suggested Klim. "We used to have dancing parties on our ship, and I think she's a very good dancer."

Ada froze. "What is a 'taxi-girl'?"

"A paid dance partner," Klim explained. "There are a lot more men in Shanghai than women, and all the bachelors hang around the restaurants. They don't have their own girlfriends, so they dance with taxi-girls. There's no prostitution involved."

Klim stood up and undid his jacket and took off his scarf.

"Come on. Let's show off your talents."

Trembling, Ada placed her blanket and books on the sofa and approached Klim.

"If Martha gives you an offer, take it," he whispered in Russian. "It's a difficult job, but this way you might earn a living."

Martha wound up the gramophone, and the strangled melody of a tango poured from its flaring horn. Klim pulled Ada to him by the waist, and again she experienced that novel flush of sensation caused by the close proximity of an adult male. His breath was too hot, his eyes were too ardent; it was as if in a split second Klim had fallen in love with her.

She readily anticipated his every move. If there was one thing you could say about Ada Marshall, it was that she loved to dance.

"Oh, my girl! Bravo, bravo!" Martha said, clapping her hands. "She's very good indeed."

"Then get her something to wear," said Klim, releasing Ada from his embrace. "She must have grown out of this dress three years ago."

26

"I'll find something for her," Martha replied and ran into the next room.

Panting with excitement, Ada sat down on the edge of the sofa. She didn't dare look Klim in the face. What had happened between the two of them? While they had been dancing, he had been so *gentle* with her.

Ada looked at him out of the corner of her eye. It was strange: now, there wasn't even a hint of the passion he had shown on the dance floor. His face betrayed nothing but indifference and fatigue.

Martha returned with two dresses on hangers. "I won't let you try them on—you clearly haven't had a bath for ages. I'll just hold the dress up to you."

Ada obeyed, silently.

"So, this one will be alright and this one will do, too," Martha said. "Do you have shoes? Show me your foot."

She gave Ada a pair of expensive, but slightly worn shoes and announced that she would give her a dollar and a half a day and deduct the cost of the dresses and the shoes from Ada's salary.

"I'll skin you alive if the girl runs away with the dresses," Martha warned Klim.

"Where's she going to run?" he replied glumly. "Back to the Bolsheviks?"

"You brought her here so you're responsible for her. Where are you staying?"

"We haven't got anywhere yet."

"Ask Chen—he rents rooms and speaks English." Martha scribbled Chen's address on a piece of paper. "Now go—I need to get my beauty sleep. Make sure that the girl is at the Havana at seven tonight."

Klim gallantly kissed Martha's hand and headed towards the stairs. Ada followed him, with a sigh. *No oranges today*, she thought.

As Ada was about to go, Martha grabbed her by the shoulder. "If you're a virgin, I beg you, don't sleep with anyone without letting me know first," she whispered,

27

giving Klim a meaningful look. "I could get you the sort of client that you could only dream of."

4

After a long search, Klim and Ada found a three-story building, a bizarre U-shaped hodgepodge of classical European architecture and Chinese poverty. The last time its walls had seen whitewash must have been well into the last century, and its latticed gate was bent, as if it had been hit by a truck. Above it, a plaque read in Chinese and in English: "The House of Hope and a Burgeoning Career."

"Well, with a name like that, we can't go wrong here," Klim chuckled.

Ada followed him into the inner courtyard, a grim enclosure of gray walls and windows, each adorned with caged pet birds. The rectangle of sky overhead was cross-stitched with bamboo poles festooned with washing. In the center of the yard under a ragged straw canopy stood a stove. A dark-skinned woman in a quilted vest over her long shirts was busy cooking.

Klim asked her something, and she made an incomprehensible din, pointing at a grand but dilapidated old entrance with a door knocker in the form of a lion's head.

"Wait for me here," he told Ada and went off to negotiate with the landlord.

Please God, help us find a room! Ada prayed silently. To get a job and a place to live in one day would be incredible luck. *I wonder where Klim met Martha?* she thought. *Surely, he wasn't using her services when he used to live here?*

A sudden recollection of their tango sent shivers down Ada's back. What would she do if Klim were to make advances towards her? The very idea made her blush, and she hugged herself, as if in self-defense. Oh, what a horrible thought! But on the other hand, maybe it might be quite nice to drive a grown man crazy with passion for you.

Klim emerged from Chen's apartment. "It looks like we've agreed on a price: we pay ten dollars a month and get a room and boiling water in the dorm kitchen. I've told the landlord that you are my concubine; otherwise he wouldn't let us stay together. The Chinese are very strict when it comes to moral standards."

Now even Ada's ears were flushing with embarrassment.

Klim laughed. "Don't worry, no one's going to check."

5

Chen, a stooping Chinese man with a long thin pigtail, led them upstairs on squeaking wooden steps.

He didn't stop at the third-floor but took them even higher.

"We're in the pigeon-loft," Klim said to Ada.

"Please, please," Chen repeated as he pointed to a low cracked door.

Behind it was an unheated cubbyhole that smelled of damp wood and was only a tad bigger than a train compartment. A stove fashioned out of a metal barrel and labeled *Kerosene* stood in one corner, and a bunk bed, made out of boards and bamboo poles, was positioned by the wall.

"Where's the lavatory here?" Ada asked.

"Chinese houses don't have sewage systems," Klim explained. "Everybody uses night pots with lids. Early in the morning, they put them outside, and the night-soil man collects them and then returns them clean."

"So there's no bathroom at all? How are we supposed to wash ourselves?"

"You can lug water up here, heat it up, and wash yourself. Or you can go to the river. But I wouldn't recommend it: it's full of cholera."

"Are you going to bring water up here?"

"I'm going to use the public bathhouse."

While Ada was spreading her blanket on the top bunk and arranging her books along the wall, Klim procured some wood chips to heat the samovar and, taking several cents from Ada, went to get some food. He came back with a packet of boiled rice and six little sticks beaded with something brown.

"What is it?" Ada asked suspiciously, remembering Klim's tales of Chinese fertilizer.

"These are frogs' brains. They're a real local delicacy," said Klim, laughing at Ada's look of horror. "Just kidding. I've got no idea what it is."

The Chinese food was too greasy and not salty enough, but Ada ate all of it ravenously.

"Mr. Chen swore to me there are no bedbugs here, and that's the most important thing," Klim said as he shook the remnants of the rice into his palm. "The first time I came to Shanghai, I ended up renting a bedbug colony. It got so bad that in the middle of the night I sought shelter in the landlord's shed and ended up falling asleep on what I thought was a trunk or a chest. In the morning, I was woken by the landlord screaming his head off at me, 'You dirty blasphemer! How dare you sleep on my grandmother's coffin!'"

Ada smiled. Today had really been her lucky day: she had found someone who could protect her, got a job in a restaurant attached to a brothel, had to pretend that she was someone's concubine, and to top it all, she had eaten *frog's brains*. If only her school friends in Izhevsk could see her now!

6

Once it had got dark, Klim escorted Ada back to Martha's.

There wasn't a single light in the back lanes and alleys, but the main shopping streets of Shanghai shone with huge electric signs and billboards.

"It's so beautiful!" Ada whispered, looking around.

Klim was surprised, too. He didn't remember the city being like this the last time he was here. Everything had changed—national flags, automobiles, fashion, and signs. Martha had told him the tea company that he used to work at no longer existed; it had been replaced by a riding accessories store. The little red-tiled house where Klim used to rent a room was also long gone.

He would have to start all over again.

Dressed in her new clothes, Ada felt like Cinderella going to the ball. She was terrified and exhilarated at the same time, keeping up a constant stream of nervous chatter.

A fifteen-year-old shouldn't be working as a taxi-girl, Klim thought grimly. But there was no chance of her finding another job, and without money, Ada would be doomed to starve for a couple of days and then start walking the streets.

Reluctantly, Klim told Ada the rules of the Havana. "While the taxi-girls sit at the designated tables, their customers buy fifty-cent tickets at the box office and then choose a girl to dance with. If the client is very unpleasant, she is entitled to refuse him, but if she's too picky, she'll end up earning nothing. After a dance, you should ask your client to buy you some wine and snacks. You'll get a commission from the proceeds."

"What if I'm offered an alcoholic drink?" Ada asked.

"Try to make sure that he buys you a different bottle for yourself. The waiter will bring you weak apple cider, but will charge the client as if it were champagne. If the client insists on pouring you a drink from his bottle, be sure to only take small sips. Just try not to get drunk, otherwise you'll never be able to dance through the night. If it all gets too much, and you can't handle it any more, take your shoes off. It's a sign you're tired."

"How do you know all this?" Ada asked, surprised.

"I used to have a friend who worked as a taxi-girl."

"Where is she now?"

"Went up in the world: got married."

Klim's first love, a Chinese girl named Jie Jie, had come to Shanghai from Canton, a big city not far from Hong Kong. There, in the south, they didn't bind girls' feet, and Jie Jie had been free to dance. She had been so good that Martha had made an exception and offered her a job, even though the Havana was meant to be a strictly "whites only" establishment.

Klim had fallen in love at first sight. He would spend all his money on dances with Jie Jie and then walk her to her house in the morning. He would even get into fistfights with the sailors, if they ever dared to insult his "chinky" girlfriend.

When his employer, a chronic racist, had found out Klim wanted to marry an Asian, he had banded together with his friends to send the "black sheep" out of China. The Shanghai ex-pats perversely believed it was their duty to protect the purity of the supreme race, and they were prepared to do everything to prevent the very idea of interracial marriage.

Klim had been kidnapped and taken to the port, but the Russian steamer had already left, so they had thrown him on a ship to Buenos Aires instead. That was how Klim had found himself in Argentina. He had worked like a dog just to save enough money for a return ticket—first in a printing shop, then at a newspaper. He would write Jie Jie passionate letters every day, promising his sweetheart that he would soon return and take her to Russia. But one day he received a telegram from Martha saying that Jie Jie had left Shanghai with some rich merchant, becoming another adornment in his considerable harem. She had never learned that Klim had become one of the best journalists in Argentina and had even been well received by the president.

Klim had thought he would never forget her, but life

had proved him wrong. He had met Nina, and it had started all over again—the glow in his eyes and the delightful mess in his head. But he had lost that woman as well, to the horror of the civil war and to typhus that had shaken her mental state.

At the Havana, Klim escorted a trembling Ada to the dressing room and then went down to the restaurant hall. It was already packed with tourists and sailors from the Great Powers. Two huge bouncers at the door made sure that no Asians or blacks, except servants, would be allowed onto the premises.

An orchestra was playing a foxtrot. Waiters in white jackets scurried around the tables. They were working for tips to buy their own dinners and bent over backwards to please their customers.

The Havana had changed too, Klim noticed. Now beer advertising illuminated with electric lights hung above the tables, where before there had been gas lamps. The brick walls were freshly plastered and painted with murals, and the stage had been remodeled. Only the smoky wine cabinets remained the same with their rows of assorted bottles, cloudy mirrors, and a gilded little god of luck sitting on the top shelf.

The taxi-girls emerged from the back rooms and ceremoniously sashayed to the tables. Ada was the last one to come out. The other girls had blackened her eyebrows, painted her lips with bright red lipstick, and dolled up her hair with a rose. Immediately, two British sailors rushed up to Ada with their tickets. Slightly taken aback, she squinted, searching for Klim. The manager efficiently sidled up to her and sorted out which of the two men should dance with her first.

The music started, and Ada disappeared into the merry crowd.

"Tell your girlfriend she's welcome to our club," Martha said, taking a seat next to Klim. "I've already got a lot of clients asking after her."

"She's just a kid—" Klim began, but Martha interrupted him.

"So what? I wasn't even thirteen when I became a taxi-girl. Are you going to sit here guarding her all night?"

Klim nodded.

"Don't worry, nothing will happen to her," said Martha, laughing. "I've already told everyone that your little chick doesn't work upstairs . . . for the time being."

7

Dawn was breaking just over the horizon. Smoke was rising from the chimneys, and the roosters were crowing. The first hawkers, carrying churns and baskets on their yokes, hurried through the streets.

Ada held onto Klim's arm, limping slowly. Her feet were blistered and bleeding from the new shoes that Martha had given her.

"Thank you for waiting for me," she stammered in a drunken voice. "There was a time when I used to think, 'What do I have to live for? What future do I have?' But I'm not so scared when I'm with you. We'll figure things out somehow, right?"

Back in their room at the House of Hope, Ada collapsed on to Klim's bed and immediately fell asleep.

He remembered how he had danced with her yesterday, imagining that he was holding another woman in his arms. Thank God for the tango! When you dance, you can be anyone you want to be, and with anyone you want to imagine. When the music stops, reality returns, but it's all worth it just for those few minutes of escape.

Klim covered Ada with her blanket and went over to the window, which offered a peculiar view of grand palaces on the left and a shanty town on the right. A dilapidated tower dominated the crossroads between the two. Covered in inscrutable hieroglyphs, it reminded him of the ancient stone signpost in the Russian folk tale that directs the hero on his journey towards happiness or doom.

It would be good, Klim thought, *if someone could tell this traveling knight which road will lead him safely to his Swan Princess.*

But what would be the point? Even if he were to meet Nina now, what could he possibly say to her? I love you? Apparently, this was not enough for her. Before the knight could dream about his Princess he needed to heal his wounds, polish his armor, and procure a decent steed.

3. OUTSIDERS

1

RECEIPTS AND EXPENDITURES

Klim Rogov's Notebook

Shanghai's pawnshops are making a killing out of us Russians—the refugees have no choice but to pawn what few valuables they have. Wedding rings, fur coats, icons, and even their baptismal crosses are all exchanged for a song.

The Church of the Holy Epiphany, the only Russian place of worship in Shanghai, has become a temporary refugee camp, where people live in makeshift tents and huts made out of plywood. The stench, noise, and dirt hangs like a pall over the enclosure around the church. Father Seraphim ladles soup from a large cauldron; a queue to his mobile kitchen stretches across the churchyard and disappears up the street. The refugees use a chemist's scale to weigh tiny bars of laundry soap, one minuscule piece per person. There are queues for everything: queues to use the bucket to fetch water and queues to dry laundry on the washing line.

A local neatly-dressed business owner, keen to cut back on his labor costs, appears at the gates. "I need ten men at the slaughter-house to help load discarded guts. Anyone interested?"

The crowd rushes to their benefactor. "Me! Me! I am!"

The refugees have to go to Chinese public bathhouses where the second floor is for the rich, the first floor for the poor. The hot water from the second floor pours downstairs through a wide stone-lined gutter, and the poor wash themselves with it, picking up all sort of skin diseases in the process.

Everybody is desperately trying to make ends meet. Women who set themselves up as fortune-tellers were the first to start earning. Their services are in huge demand among their fellow countrymen. Divination and clairvoyance are prohibited on the territory of the International Settlement, but the colonial authorities can't do anything about the Russians because they are stateless and come under Chinese jurisdiction, and according to Chinese law and custom, fortune-telling is an honorable occupation.

Starting from scratch is the most difficult thing for the exile. No one cares that you used to be a successful journalist, or a general, or a well-known politician. Life hurls you back down to the first rung of the ladder, back with the inexperienced and the young, who, incidentally, are much more adept at picking up the local language and customs. But you are no longer eighteen; at your age, you should have at least a few accomplishments to boast of. If you really have nothing to justify your years in this world, your value depreciates, as does your esteem, not only in other people's eyes but in your own.

All of us Russians, including myself, hate Shanghai with an impotent rage. Deep down inside, each of us believed that we had some God-given right to a certain status in China, at least as a sign of respect for our race and the fact that our country had once been one of the Great Powers. But in reality, we are now the lowest of the low in China's social hierarchy. Like all fallen gods, the Russian refugees are not even granted mortal status and certainly no forgiveness. Our place is to dwell out of sight in hell.

In search of a miracle, I visited all the English-speaking editorial offices in the city, but the doormen didn't even let me in. The Russian accent is a curse. Before I can even get a sentence out, the door is slammed in my face: "No Bolsheviks in here!" How am I meant to convince them that I'm not a Bolshevik? It requires time and effort to find out who is White and who is Red, and it's really much simpler to sling every single one of these Russian tramps out on their ear, just in case.

I was lucky enough to find a temporary job and spent several days working for a furniture workshop. This involved sawing hard teak wood using an enormous eight-foot, two-man saw until your muscles are screaming for respite. As soon as one man begins to lag, the owner kicks him out and replaces him with a fresh Slav(e). Nobody bothers with sawmills here when the manual labor is so cheap.

However, I'm slowly learning to survive in Shanghai, too. If I'm lucky enough to earn a silver coin, I have learned not to spend it immediately but exchange it for a larger number of copper coins. That way, after scampering around the city for hours, I can usually find a money changer that offers good rates and end up making about ten cents for my pains. For me, this is the difference between dinner and hunger. Ten cents can buy you a princely feast of noodles or sugar-roasted nuts. But you always have to keep your eyes open: those scumbag street hawkers sometimes add sand to the food to make it heavier.

If it's been a particularly bad day, I can get by on a couple of pickles for seven coppers or go to the French Catholic nuns who give out carrot soup if you can put up with their interminable sermons.

This is how all the unemployed live in Shanghai. The only way to earn more than a dollar a day is through crime. Some burgle apartments, others work as racketeers providing "protection" to the local small traders.

2

The stuffy dressing room was filled with taxi-girls preparing for the night ahead: getting changed, applying their make-up, and curling their hair. Any outsider might have been forgiven for thinking that they were speaking some sort of secret language, but Ada had already started to grasp their slang.

The best clients—young, rich, daring men—were known as "dragons." Ugly but well-heeled ones were called "gold mines," and the ladies on their arms "gold miners." Boring men, who didn't know how to dance properly, were known as "toe crunchers," and men without money were called "false alarms." "Locksmiths" was the name given to guys who put pieces of metal in their pockets to make them jingle so you'd think they were loaded.

Dark-eyed Betty, the wild and beautiful queen of the Havana, burst impetuously into the dressing room.

"Martha has told the cloakroom assistant to lock up my coat," she cried indignantly, "so I won't go running off to town with any of my *goldmines*."

Ada watched her in admiration, not daring to say a word in her presence. Betty's dress was red, with a side slit that reached right up to her thigh. Her lipstick was crimson and utterly shameless.

The manager barged into the dressing room without knocking. The newer girls squealed, covering their naked bodies.

"Hey, you, the Russian girl!" he barked, indifferently. "The Madam wants to see you."

Ada made her way upstairs to Martha's little office. The walls in the room were covered with porcelain plates showing pictures of various cities: Paris, Vienna and Florence. Martha was collecting them.

"Sit down," she said, motioning to a brocade armchair. "The Municipal Council wants me to give details of all the people working here. What's your full name and address?"

Ada told her.

"Nationality?"

"I'm an American."

Ada had been to the American Consulate three times, hoping to secure some documents, but an evil-looking Marine wouldn't even let her past the door. "Do you have a passport?"

"No."

"Then beat it, lady."

"But my father is from Texas, and I have Auntie Clare—" Ada protested each time.

"I said, scram!"

Martha wrote "Russian" in the box designated for nationality.

"Are you married? We'd better say yes. Hadn't we?"

"Klim and I are only renting a room together and—"

"That doesn't matter," Martha interrupted. "Now, down you go and get back to work."

Ada plodded dejectedly downstairs.

She had no one in this city, apart from Klim, and she wanted to put their relationship on an even footing for herself and for everyone else they met. But in reality it was all a big mess. She was sharing a room with a man who was eighteen years her senior and who was neither her husband nor even a relative.

Klim would walk her to the Havana every evening and always be at the entrance to meet her in the early hours after her shift was over. He took care of her, made her laugh, and taught her simple magic tricks, a skill that had provided her some decent tips. But at the same time, he acted towards her as if they were no more than good friends.

One day he mentioned to her, "Ada, there's an orphanage in Xujiahui, and they have taken in some Russian girls. Do you want to go there? At least, they'll teach you embroidery. The drinking and the tobacco smoke in the Havana really isn't good for a girl of your age."

"Well, it was you who brought me there," Ada said, frowning. She was upset at the idea that he might be trying to get rid of her.

The other taxi-girls taught her to value herself for her feminine qualities, and she copied the tricks they used to win over their customers. But despite her efforts, Klim had not been tempted by her charms.

Sometimes Ada would change out of her clothes in front of him, waiting to see if he would say or do anything. But he would just sigh and silently go out into the corridor, leaving her seething with anger.

Who did he think he was? Some fine gentleman, who didn't believe that she was worthy of him?

Ada decided to take a different tack. Once, while he was asleep, she crawled into his bed beside him. Then, intoxicated by her daring and debauchery, she placed her hand lightly on his thigh. Klim woke up instantly, shoving Ada onto the floor.

"Are you crazy?" she yelled, rubbing her bruised elbow.

He sat up on his bed and crossed his arms over his chest. "Ada, stop it! You would come to hate me, if anything were to happen between us."

"I already hate you!" Ada spat back and started to cry. "You don't love me."

"Ada, you have your whole life ahead of you to learn about these things. You'll find the right person and get married in your own good time."

"To hell with you! I've sent a letter to Auntie Claire. She'll invite me to America and send me some money. And you'll be stuck here to rot in the House of Hope forever."

3

Klim got a job at a tannery, which consisted of a few sheds standing next to a mountain of garbage and slimy waste. The land all around had been burned by the chemicals they used; the pools, where the pig hides were soaked, gave off an evil smelling gas, and the stench was so bad, that it would make anyone who wasn't used to it retch.

The tannery owner told Klim and the other workers to drag the hides out of the pools and scrape off the semi-decomposed bristle on them. It was hard to imagine how this slimy, foul smelling skin could ever be transformed into a pretty handbag or an elegant pair of shoes.

Lime dust filled the air, obscuring the sun and covering the workers' faces and clothing with a fine white powder. The pale figures moved around like ghosts in a hellish pall of smoke and fumes, waving their hooks, dragging stacks of hides, and carrying heavy barrels filled with dyes on their shoulders.

The Chinese workers laughed at Klim. "You've finally become a real white person."

"Have you taken a look in the mirror yourselves recently?" he snapped back.

That evening, when everyone was lined up in front of the cashier to get their day's pay, a shiny car appeared at the open gates, and a white lady stepped out. She was young, tall and slightly stooped, with a long narrow face and light-brown almond-shaped eyes. She was dressed in a small French beret, Oxford suede shoes, and a checkered suit that didn't really become her, even though it was obviously expensive.

The stench was so overpowering that she visibly flinched. The workers roared with laughter.

"Does anyone speak English here?" the lady asked in a loud voice.

Nobody answered. The Chinese looked at her as if she was completely mad and asking for trouble.

"I'm a journalist," the lady introduced herself. "I work for the *North China Daily News,* and I'm planning to write an article about the children working in this tannery."

Klim watched her silently. Had she just said "journalist"? He had almost forgotten that such a profession ever existed.

He pointed at a gang of grubby-looking boys who were sitting near the fence. "Those are the characters you're looking for."

"Oh, thanks!" she said delightedly. "Could you—"

"Who let you in?" the tannery owner yelled in broken English, running up to her. "Get back to your settlement and stop sticking your nose in around here! This is our territory and none of your business."

"Yeah, right!" the workers echoed in Shanghainese. "Go away!"

The lady took a step back. "But I wanted to—"

"Get out of here!"

She hastily got back into her car to a chorus of cat calls and whistling. The driver started the engine, and they drove away in a cloud of dust, clods of dirt following in their wake.

Annoyed, Klim frowned at the jubilant workers. At one point, he really thought this might have been his lucky break to meet a fellow journalist from an English language newspaper. He might have been able to help the lady as an interpreter—his Shanghainese had improved significantly over the last few months. Apparently, it wasn't to be.

Klim received his pathetic wages, went out of the gate, and walked along the road lined with the huts of the poor. The coolies, their faces red with effort, pushed big carts with three or four women sitting on them. The women were match factory workers whose feet were so deformed that they had had to hire carters to drive them to and from work.

Old men played mahjong on their porches, little children watching by their sides. There was a slit in the rear of the children's pants, and if they needed to relieve themselves, they would squat and do their business right in the middle of the road.

Klim's whole body was numb with fatigue. The lime dust was still tickling his throat, and the skin on his face and neck felt as if it was on fire. *Another month of this work,* he thought, *and I'll be a prime candidate either for asthma or tuberculosis.*

A car horn blared behind Klim, and the lady journalist's car stopped right next to him.

"Get in," she said as she opened the rear door for him. "I'll give you a ride."

Klim stared at her in amazement. "Are you sure? I'll only dirty your car—" he began, but the lady waved her hand dismissively.

"Don't worry, the servants will clean it up. My name is Edna Bernard. What's yours?"

Klim introduced himself.

"So, I was right in guessing that you're a Russian," Edna said. "Where are you going now?"

"To the French Concession."

"Great. You can tell me what's going on with the children in your tannery on the way."

When was the last time I rode in a car? Klim thought as he took the rear seat next to Edna. It must have been at least several years ago, when he had been given a ride on a half-broken boneshaker belonging to a White Army official. Edna Bernard had a brand new Buick with a polished dashboard, shiny door handles, and comfortable leather seats. *I bet she has no idea how the leather on these seats was made,* Klim thought, smiling to himself.

He told her that the children working at Chinese tanneries were set the job of stretching the skins out to dry. Each hide had to be nailed to a wooden board with a dozen nails to prevent it from wrinkling. It was not a very difficult job, but the children had to work at it from twelve to fifteen hours a day, seven days a week, constantly breathing in the lime dust and the poisonous fumes.

The children were supposed to get seven dollars a month, but very few of them ever received their full salaries, since the owner would fine them for the most insignificant misdemeanors. Daydreaming or dozing during working hours would cost them five cents, going to the toilet without permission twenty cents, and any homesickness or crying would set them back as much as a dollar. The owner had lied to their parents, telling them that the children would get sixty dollars and three changes of clothing during their apprenticeship. In reality, all he and his foremen did was rob and beat them.

"Few of these factory kids will ever make it to their twenties," Klim said. "And those who do will be illiterate, angry, and hard-bitten adults."

"But how do *you* manage to survive there?" Edna asked, shocked.

Klim shrugged. "The same way everybody else does."

The chauffeur drove them to Avenue Joffre.

"I still have to pay a visit to the silk factory and then to the match factory," Edna said. "I want to investigate what's going on there. Will you go with me?"

Klim shook his head. "Mrs. Bernard, my work starts at six in the morning."

"I'll pay you. How much do you want? Five dollars? Ten?"

Klim made five dollars a week maximum, but for Edna this sum was nothing, a trifle.

She gave him an advance, and they agreed to meet the next day at nine in the morning at the same place.

4

When her article about the Chinese factory children was published, Edna received one hundred and fifty letters from her readers. This was a bumper response for her.

She was commissioned with a new assignment to write an article on refugees, and she and Klim spent several days in the markets and shanty towns, talking to the Russian immigrants.

Previously, the poor had not been particularly eager to tell Edna about their troubles. They either saw her as a false friend who was only pretending to be kind, or rather as an eccentric who was sticking her nose into other people's business.

But with Klim, things were different. He was observant, able to get in with the people, and he had an eye for details that gave Edna's reports a vital element of spice.

With the money she paid him, he bought a new outfit for himself, complete with a hat and canvas shoes, and he took on a new lease of life.

"What were you before the revolution?" she asked him one day. "A Tsarist officer?"

"You'll never guess," he replied. "An Argentine journalist."

He recounted his story to Edna, not mentioning Nina, of course.

"If your English was up to scratch," Edna said, "and you could provide the editors with letters of recommendation from your previous employers, you wouldn't be unemployed for a single day. Let me think how I can help you."

4. AMERICAN LAWER

1

As soon as the Shanghai authorities had allowed the refugees to go ashore, Nina started looking for Klim. But he had never registered himself in the Russian Consulate, and when she went to the Orthodox church, she met some ladies who knew her from the refugees' ship.

"Look at that shameless woman all dressed in fur!" they spat at her. "How dare you step foot in this church, you hussy? Where's your Czech lover boy?"

What should I do now? Nina thought, at a loss.

Her money and confidence were dissipating rapidly. Initially, Shanghai had almost seemed like a fairy tale to Nina, but she was soon hit with a sobering dose of reality. Time was passing, and she still hadn't come up with a single good idea about how to make a living. For all her fine clothes, Nina found it difficult to slip into the glittering fast stream of connections, opportunities, and wealth that the city had to offer. Firstly, she was a woman, and a woman, according to the established order of things, shouldn't be involved in business. Secondly, she was a stateless person with no start-up capital; and thirdly, she didn't have much of a head for business.

Jiří was convinced that Nina would soon fritter away all her money and turn to petty crime, while he would end up drinking himself into an early grave. He was angry at his own impotence, and even more angry with Nina—for trying to do something about their situation, thus emphasizing his lack of courage and application.

"Let's open a cinema?" she proposed. "We could rent a place and hire benches and a projector."

"You'll spend your whole time haggling with the censor committees," Jiří said. "Each district of Shanghai has its own and each of them will insist on censoring your film themselves."

But Nina was not about to give up.

"Why don't we try to win a municipal order to repair their roads properly? You've seen how they fix the pavements here: if a cobblestone comes lose, they call in a gang of coolies who fill the hole with clay, and it only lasts until the next rain storm."

Jiří looked at her pityingly.

"You'll never get into a business like that; it's much too lucrative. Clay is free, the coolies' labor costs less than a dollar a day, and the local authorities pay a lot of money to have their roads repaired. The contractors bribe the city fathers with huge sums and deliberately do a poor job so they'll be asked to fix it again at the earliest opportunity."

Sometimes Jiří's resignation and pessimism irritated Nina so much that she was on the verge of throwing him out altogether.

She went to the bank to ask about a loan, but being a Russian did nothing for her credit status. The bank teller refused to even speak to her. "We reserve the right to refuse service to stateless people," he said curtly and closed his window.

Nina was becoming increasingly despondent. *I just can't cope with it by myself,* she thought. *Should I look for a new husband?*

Hoping to put her plan in motion, she ventured out to join the elite throng at the Astor House tiffin room but it never worked out. Nina couldn't understand what she was doing wrong. In her silk and pearls, she looked better than any other woman in the room; men were quick to invite her to dance, but none were keen to ask for a second.

She would storm back to her room, mad with rage. "They're all crazy there," she complained to Jiří. "At first, they listen to me in polite silence and then all they want to do is run away."

He laughed. "I know exactly what they're thinking. Men like their women to be funny and carefree, but you behave like an evil sucker . . . No, no . . . That's not right. What's the word for that creature that drinks other people's blood in Russian?"

"A mosquito," Nina replied crossly.

2

Nina didn't dare to go back to the Orthodox church, and Jiří advised her to go to the Catholic one instead.

"You'll be fine as long as you do the same as everybody else," he reassured Nina, and so she agreed.

St Ignatius Cathedral was the tallest building in Shanghai, and every day tour guides would bring visitors there to admire its twin spires and stunning stained glass windows.

The sound of the organ and the smell of incense were welcoming, but when Nina entered the cathedral, she discovered that it wasn't a mass that she had come to but a funeral.

Feeling deflated, Nina sank down on the nearest pew, her prayerful mood gone. The coffin, decorated with wreaths, seemed to be a bad omen to her.

Nina heard somebody puffing up the aisle, and a fat man in a leather coat came and sat next to her.

"Oh, what a coincidence!" whispered Don Fernando, kissing Nina on the cheek without even asking her permission. "Do you know the man in this coffin? He was my closest friend, Augusto."

Without a shadow of sadness on his face, Don Fernando began to tell Nina how Augusto had failed to listen to his advice, involved himself in other people's business, and ended up with a knife in his back. Nina had a sneaking suspicion that the Don had had a hand in this.

She listened to him in silence. The irony of it! The only person in the whole of Shanghai who was genuinely glad to see her was a local gangster kingpin.

A thin old man sitting on the bench in front of them turned round and put his finger to his lips to remind them of the coffin, but Fernando gave him such a withering look that the poor man quickly moved to another pew.

"How do you like Shanghai so far?" the Don asked Nina. "Are you prospering? Or still finding your feet?"

"You were right," she said almost inaudibly. "I do need documents."

"No problem. Do you want a Spanish passport? We'll get it sorted right here, in Zhabei."

"I'm not interested in fakes," Nina interrupted. "I need a genuine proof of identity, that will persuade a bank to give me a loan."

"Oh well, that'll be at least three hundred dollars."

"Why so much?"

"Because Shanghai is infested with refugees from all over the world. Without a passport you won't even be able to get into a library. The consuls here don't want the risk of issuing a passport to every adventuress that comes running to them."

"So, legal papers are in great demand?"

Don Fernando grabbed Nina's hand. "Let's go outside. I don't want to disturb the relatives of the deceased."

They went outside and sat on a bench in the churchyard.

"Only the documents from decent European and American countries are valued," Don Fernando explained to Nina. "For example, with a Belgian passport, you could get a visa to any country in the world. But it's better to be a citizen of one of the Great Powers, with their extraterritorial rights."

"What are they?" Nina asked.

"Extraterritorial rights are the rights that the white people of the imperial powers enjoy. Let's say you're a British citizen, then the Chinese authorities won't be able to touch you, and you can only be tried by a British Consul. The same goes for the French, the Americans, and one or two other nations. The Russians also used to have these rights, but they frittered them away when they had their revolution."

For a while, Nina was deep in thought. "Is there a Czechoslovak Consulate in Shanghai?" she finally asked.

"Cze . . . what?"

"I mean Czechoslovakia—it's a new country. It used to be a part of the Austro-Hungarian Empire, but after the Great War it declared independence."

Don Fernando pushed his hat to the back of his head. "Never heard of it, and I'm pretty sure there isn't a consulate. There's a lot going on now in Europe at the moment, so I don't imagine your Czechoslovaks are going to be arriving in China any time soon."

"Then I'll set up a Czechoslovak Consulate myself," Nina declared. "And produce and sell passports. What will I need for people to take me seriously?"

For a moment, Don Fernando was at a loss for words. "You are joking, right?"

"No. If you can forge me a passport, then you can easily sort me out with consulate papers and stamps. It will all seem perfectly feasible and legitimate. After all, why shouldn't a small new republic wish to protect its citizens in China? If no one here has ever heard of Czechoslovakia, then no one will question the validity of my enterprise. I can provide a genuine Czech Consul who can talk about whatever you desire: politics, culture, or history."

"You'll almost certainly be thrown into prison," Don Fernando said with confidence. "But, you know what? I admire your guts. If you're going to do this, you'll need to talk to a proper lawyer, and I know just the right one. His name is Tony Aulman. He's saved me from all sorts of trouble on many an occasion."

"What sort of trouble?"

"Criminal, of course."

"Is your Aulman an expert in international law?"

Don Fernando started counting on his fingers. "He knows International Law, Maritime Law, the Code Napoleon, every single one of the decisions handed down by U.S. Supreme Court, all the laws of the forty-eight American states, the Law of the District of Columbia, and even the Philippines. What's more, he's a great horse rider, which is essential if you want to be a Shanghai lawyer."

"Why?" asked Nina.

"Because most of the local judges are crazy about polo, and if a lawyer can play well, he'll have all the right connections."

3

Don Fernando hired two rickshaws and ordered the rickshaw boys to take him and Nina to Peking Road.

"I always thought that men do big deeds out of courage, but women out of despair," he roared over the racket of the street. "If you want to witness a truly heroic act, then scare the living daylights out of a lady."

Nina didn't answer. The Don had been right: if her scam was discovered, she would end up in a Chinese prison, which was tantamount to a certain death for the likes of her. But she was desperate and she had no "Plan B."

The offices of Aulman, Bormann and Pevzner,

Attorneys at Law were located in a stunning five-story building with an elevator. Without even knocking, Don Fernando barged straight through the reception and into one of the offices, beckoning Nina to follow him.

"Allow me to introduce the best lawyer in Shanghai!"

A short, neatly dressed gentleman with a curled mustache was standing on his desk, hanging a scroll on the wall. Two Chinese clerks in European suits were assisting him.

"Don Fernando, is that you?" he exclaimed, jumping off his desk.

Standing before them was Tony Aulman. In excellent French, he explained that his Chinese clients often brought him valuable presents for successfully resolving their difficulties: ancient calligraphy, poems, and artwork. Naturally, his clients wanted to see their gifts on display, but the office lacked the wall space to show them all. So, every day they had to re-hang these works of art depending on who was coming.

Aulman motioned his visitors towards two wide oxblood armchairs.

"What can I do for you?"

Nina felt like an unfaithful wife at a venereal clinic. She was trying hard to pretend that she was a respectable lady but still had to admit her sinful deeds.

Aulman listened to her, showing no surprise, as if confidence tricksters dreaming of making money out of fake passports were frequent visitors to his office.

"It shouldn't be a problem to set up a consulate," he said. "We'll draw up a fake state decree of foundation for you, but the permission documentation will be genuine. We can get it done at the Chinese Foreign Affairs Office. How long do you think you'll last?"

"As long as luck allows," Nina replied, growing a little bolder.

Aulman twisted his mustache thoughtfully. "Your problem is that you're claiming a piece of someone else's pie. All the other consulates will immediately start digging around to find out who you really are and what you're really up to. I'll give you some advice: stay away from passports and deal in liquor instead."

Don Fernando slapped his thighs. "You're absolutely right!"

"What do you mean?" Nina frowned.

"The customs here take a duty of ninety-five dollars for a crate of champagne," Aulman explained. "But consulates have the right to purchase alcohol duty-free—for social events, of course. If you were to order ten crates, you'd be able to make a considerable mark up."

"Surely the customs people will get suspicious," Nina said. "It'll be hard for a small consulate to justify ten crates of champagne, even in a month."

"If it was only you and your staff drinking it, no doubt. But if the Czechoslovak Consul was arranging small receptions for important personages, then no one would start counting exactly how many bottles his guests have got through."

"I'll sort out the champagne business," Don Fernando said, "but the parties and receptions will be your domain, ma'am. Do we have a deal?"

Nina was completely taken aback; she never dreamed that events could take such a sudden and dramatic turn.

"How am I going to arrange the parties?" she asked. "I don't know anyone. No one would come."

Aulman showed her a framed photograph standing on his desk. It was an image of a pretty blond woman with dimples on her cheeks.

"I'll introduce you to my wife, Tamara. She'll figure everything out."

They agreed they would all have shares in the business. Nina's job would be to negotiate with Jiří and arrange the ceremonial side of things, the Don would establish relations with the local liquor dealers, and Aulman would provide the documents and connections with the Chinese civil service and bureaucracy.

Out on the street, Don Fernando blew a kiss to the sky. "I owe you one, Holy Virgin!" Then he turned to Nina. "You have no idea how lucky we are that Aulman decided to join us. With him and his connections, we risk nothing. What's more, he has very deep pockets."

"Then what does he need us for?" Nina asked. "If he's so rich, a few hundred dollars more or less won't make any difference to him."

"It's all because of his wife. She used to be the first grand lady of Shanghai, but a year ago she fell from her horse and broke her spine. She's bored to death sitting at home, and it would appear Aulman has decided to keep her busy and entertained with your scam. His wife loves dressing-up and organizing social events. Besides Tamara is Russian, so you'll have much in common."

"Have you ever met her?" Nina asked. "What's she like?"

"Oh, she's a great woman," Don Fernando said reverently. "Can you imagine it, a woman paralyzed from the waist down, and yet her husband is so in love with her that he doesn't even go to brothels."

4

Nina reached the Aulmans' house at seven in the evening. A quiet servant appeared at the gate and led her down the red sand-dusted pathway. The heat of the day wreathed the lawn in steam, and the birds squabbled in their roosts for the night.

Nina felt nervous. What if Tamara didn't take a liking to her? Jiří had been right when he had said that Nina often put people off. Nobody wants to be around a woman who has obviously lost her moral bearing and has no concept of right and wrong.

If you want to make friends and charm people, Nina told herself, *you have to be witty and carefree. Be amusing and try not to offend anyone.*

Jiří had screamed his head off when she informed him about her plans to make him a fake consul.

"You're going to rake off all the cash," he cried, "but if anything happens, it'll be me who goes to jail."

Nina had told him that if he didn't agree, he could start packing. It had been blackmail, pure and simple—where could he go? Who needed a musician with missing fingers?

"You give me no choice," he had said, sullenly avoiding her eyes. "I'll be your consul."

But I have no choice either, she told herself for the hundredth time.

The wide windows of the Aulmans' house were open, and behind the mosquito nets, Nina could see a brightly lit room with a grand piano, bookcases, and low oriental-style sofas.

Three boys in scout uniforms were building a fortress on the carpet.

"What are you doing?" yelled one in English. "Can't you see that's meant for the roof? It'll all fall down now because of you."

"It won't! Mom, tell him!"

Under the grand piano a pair of elegant Russian borzoi wolfhounds were gnawing at either end of a huge bone.

The servant showed Nina into the house. "This way, please." He bowed, letting her into the room.

Tamara was sitting in an armchair, propped up with embroidered pillows. Small, brightly colored parakeets were fluttering about in their cages on each side of her.

"Nina Vasilievna? Nice to meet you!" Tamara said, greeting her guest by her patronymic in the traditional, respectful way.

"And what's your patronymic?" Nina asked, returning the courtesy.

"Please just call me by my first name," Tamara replied. "I'm so used to it here—I've become completely *shanghaied.*"

Her hair was not blond but white, and her young face looked emaciated; the dimples on her cheeks were gone. Tamara's blue silk dress emphasized her turquoise eyes, and her wrist was adorned with a string of pearls that looked very expensive.

"Go along and play outside," Tamara told the boys. "Roger, would you mind taking the dogs out with you as well? They've already made a mess of the carpet. Would you like some coffee, Nina Vasilievna?"

Tamara asked lots of questions, and Nina told her all about herself in much the same way as Klim used to—making light of herself and her circumstances. One would have thought there had been no misfortune in her life, just a series of funny adventures. Had she fled the length of Russia from the Bolsheviks? Oh yes, it had been an unforgettable trip! All the way, Nina had been on a diet of bread and water—quite the rage among refugees at that time. And as for the dirt, well, they do say that taking a mud bath is very good for the complexion. She had shared her cattle truck with the cream of society: professors from Moscow University, officers from the General Staff, opera singers, and leading members of the nobility. Everyone had been very kind, crushing the lice from each other's bodies and cursing the revolution in the politest and the most cultured way.

Tamara was thrilled with Nina's story. She had arrived in China twenty years previously, with her father, who had a job with the Russian-Chinese Bank, and now she only had a very vague idea about what was going on in Russia.

"Do you speak English?" Tamara asked.

"A little," Nina admitted. "But my Russian accent is a real handicap."

"You must think of it as a cute little quirk that makes you stand out from the crowd. My friends are fine with my accent."

Well, they would be, wouldn't they? Nina thought. If you lived in a luxurious mansion and had a husband like Tony

Aulman, you'd be accepted if you had three heads and spoke Martian with a forked tongue.

"Tony told me about your venture," Tamara said. "We have a house near the race course, and we can rent it to you for a nominal fee. There's plenty of room there for the balls."

"What do you mean by 'balls'?" Nina asked, surprised. "I was thinking that we'd mainly be organizing small receptions."

"It's much more interesting to play big," Tamara replied with a smile. "While I was listening to you, I came up with a great idea. We can introduce you as a Russian countess, who has come from Europe to visit her cousin, the Czechoslovak Consul. To honor your arrival, you'll arrange a fancy dress masquerade, and the theme shall be: *High Society in One Hundred Years Time*. I read in the newspaper that somebody has brought a new material to Shanghai, called 'cellophane,' all the way from Switzerland. We could use it for futuristic costumes. I'll foot the expenses and you'll make a start on your champagne sales. Now all we have to decide upon is the guest list."

Tamara took a pencil and notebook from the table next to her armchair and began to write down some names.

"The Smiths are out of the question," she stated matter-of-factly. "They're good friends with the British Consul, and we should steer clear of officials for the time being. We'd be wiser to invite the McGraths. They're not interested in politics at all." She looked up at Nina and smiled playfully. "Lucille McGrath claims to be my best friend, but I haven't seen her here for two months. I think she needs to be taught a lesson or two."

Nina realized that Tamara was very angry with her friends. She was no longer on their guest lists, and they had started to visit her less and less. Apparently, Tamara had decided that she could be a social lioness again through Nina, and at the same time get back at her disloyal friends by fooling them into thinking that a couple of refugee con artists were European aristocrats.

Nina had secretly hoped that she and Tamara would become soul mates, but that was out of the question. Tony Aulman was *hiring* Nina in order to divert and cheer up his wife.

I have no other choice, Nina repeated to herself. *My main goal now is to get my foot in the door, and then we'll see how things turn out.*

5

As soon as Tony Aulman got back from work, dinner was served. It turned out to be a boisterous and fun affair. Tamara showed the boys how to catapult peas with their spoons and make ballet dancers' legs out of their napkins. Tony had almost lost his voice after a three-hour deposition at the court, but he ate with a huge appetite and laughed more than anyone at the antics around him. He was in high spirits and recounted the day's case with great humor.

The police had raided a warehouse packed with counterfeit records that had been worth over twenty thousand dollars. Tony explained that the Chinese would forge and illegally copy practically every product that had ever been advertised in the press, from cough medicine to sheets of music. He was representing the interests of the affected companies and had hired several sleuths to snoop around the Chinese warehouses. Then Aulman would either settle the case in his client's favor, with a big payout, or demand the destruction of the fake goods.

"How can you tell a legal copy from an illegal one?" Nina asked.

"We look at the labels," Tony explained. "The Chinese typesetters don't speak any foreign languages and often they put the letters upside down or mix up the word order. Another giveaway is a lack of spaces between words or punctuation marks. When my sleuths find a forged item in a store, they will pose as a big wholesaler and discover who the manufacturer is via the entire chain of suppliers."

"Why don't the police carry out the investigation?"

Tony and Tamara exchanged knowing glances and laughed.

"Because the purpose of holding any official position in China," said Tamara, "is to provide for yourself, not the public. If you don't give the police a bribe, they won't lift a finger for you."

"What if the counterfeiters provide them with an even bigger bribe?"

"In that case, we ask Don Fernando to intervene," said Tony. "He knows how to resolve that sort of issue."

Nina recalled Fernando's innuendoes at the funeral earlier that week. So that was why Aulman was friends with a murderer and a gangster.

Throughout the entire evening she observed Tony closely. It was clear that he really adored his wife and that his entertaining stories were largely meant for Tamara's amusement. He didn't wait for the servants to pour her orange juice, preferring to do it himself, and assiduously made sure that she wouldn't get cold sitting in a draft. For the first time in her life, Nina was looking at a man who was successful, strong, and wealthy and utterly loved a woman regardless of her health and beauty. The impression was strange and delightful.

When the maid announced the arrival of the taxi, Tony accompanied Nina to the porch. It was dark outside, and the servants had lit a garland of Chinese lanterns along the driveway.

"Thank you," Tony said quietly, shaking Nina's hand. "I'm so glad Tamara has met you. I haven't seen her so cheerful for a long time."

Nina felt confused. "It's my pleasure."

Klim had once told her that the most important things in life were to be loved, to be healthy, and to be capable of doing good deeds. Tamara could only boast one of these three—the love of her husband and children, but this didn't seem to be enough for her to be happy.

Nina had nothing but her health, and if tomorrow she were to break her spine, she would have no one willing to take care of her.

5. THE BLUE EXPRESS

1

RECEIPTS AND EXPENDITURES

Klim Rogov's Notebook

Edna led me into the holy of holies—the editorial office of the *North China Daily News*. Some people call this paper and its staff the "imperialists' mouthpiece," others a "bunch of blundering idiots in rose-tinted spectacles," while others still simply dismiss it as a "sniveling, liberal rag." But one thing is certain: the *Daily News* is the most popular, influential, and prestigious foreign newspaper ever created in another country's territory.

Alas, its editor-in-chief, Mr. Green, didn't believe that I was the sort of reporter he needed. Having been introduced and then ushered out of his office, I heard him explaining to Edna that I couldn't write English fluently, and that he wasn't going to hire a special editor just for my sake.

"If the man doesn't have the necessary skills," he said, "he has to work as a courier, not a journalist."

"I'm fine with that," Edna replied. "Enroll Rogov as a courier, and he can work as my personal assistant."

Her husband regularly paid for ads in the *Daily News*, so Mr. Green wasn't about to argue.

I do my best to pay Edna back. Previously, it used to take her half the day to run around the city and find a good story, and then the other half to write it up on her typewriter. But now we share the work: I bring her material about horse auctions, pickpockets on trams, illegal fight clubs, and the like, and Edna turns this raw material into clever, witty articles.

Shanghai journalism is very competitive, and the true sign of a successful hack is to have your articles copied and published by the Chinese press without your permission. It's a big honor. As they say, plagiarism is the highest compliment, and at the moment, Edna is getting more compliments than any other journalist in Shanghai, which makes me feel very proud as well.

Once I was on the payroll, I told Ada that now it was my turn to pay for the room. She hopes and prays that I won't lose my new job. She thinks that I work in paradise because I have the chance to meet the local celebrities every day. They never return my greetings, though, but that doesn't bother me terribly.

What I want more than anything else is to work on my own. I have tried my hand writing an article about the Street of Eternal Happiness, which is the name of a few blocks down the Foochow Road. Rich Chinese men come there to visit the sing-song girls who sell the illusion of love for an hour or two. Neither the purveyors or consumers of this temporal happiness seem to see the irony in the street's name.

I was sure that I had written a decent article but by

the time Edna had finished with it, it was covered in red pencil.

"You have what it takes," she said, "you have a great grasp of the necessary details and emotions. But your grammar is terrible. I don't know what to do about you."

For me, it's obvious what I need to do—practice, practice, and more practice. I stay back at the editorial office well after working hours and write endless copy. First, I read someone else's article and then try to copy it from memory. It's tough and sometimes I feel desperate, but I keep telling myself that genuine talent will always triumph regardless of the failure and lack of progress on the way. Looking on the bright side, I'm beginning to make some real improvement on my verbs, and there was a time when I thought I'd never master the mysteries of English grammar.

2

Mr. Green said that he would raise Klim's salary, if he took over the responsibility of corresponding with the Chinese subscribers who used the *Daily News* to practice their English. Half of all the mail coming to the editorial office contained questions regarding English vocabulary or grammar.

When Chinese subscribers received polite answers to their enquiries, they would be extremely pleased and provide the best sort of word of mouth advertising that the *Daily News* could hope for.

Klim had had no time to deal with the mail during the day; instead he would come to the editorial office well before office hours.

One morning he had no sooner sat down at his desk when the door flew open, and Mr. Green burst into the room.

"Where's Edna?" he asked abruptly. "Still in Canton?"

Klim nodded. Edna had left a week ago for the South,

hoping to organize an interview with the local Chinese nationalists.

Mr. Green went to his office but soon returned.

"Rogov, have you heard the news? The *Blue Express* has been captured by a gang of bandits. Three hundred passengers have been taken up into the mountains and among them are a lot of wealthy and reputable foreigners."

Klim whistled in surprise. The *Blue Express* was the pride of the Chinese railways. It had recently been purchased from the United States to ensure safe and convenient communications between Peking and Shanghai, and tickets for it were so expensive that only rich businessmen and government officials could afford them.

Mr. Green began telephoning someone.

"I need to send a correspondent to Shandong Province," he yelled into the receiver. "Michael is on leave, and Edna is in Canton, so you'll have to go instead. You need to get to the town of Lincheng. They already have a situation room there for the hostage mission . . . So what if there are bandits? . . . Do you think just because they've attacked one train, they're going to attack them every day? You don't fool me, you're just being a coward!"

After several similar calls, Mr. Green hurled the receiver back into its cradle.

"Rogov, what time is it?"

"Five minutes to seven."

"Damn it! The train leaves in two hours, and I still have no one to send to Lincheng."

Klim's heart started pumping fast. What if this was his chance, a real opportunity to show his true colors?

"I can go to Lincheng," he said.

Mr. Green looked at Klim with irritation. "And what experience do you have?"

"Well, I've been through a war and I'm definitely not going to run away at the first sound of gun shots. Just ask Edna if I have the ability to sniff out and report back a good story—"

"I know, I know!" Green interrupted testily. "Well, we don't have time anyway. Take my car and go to Yates Road. I hope the stores are open. Get yourself a decent suit and go to the station immediately. Tell the shop to send the chit to the editorial office. As soon as you get to Lincheng, send me a cable."

Having received his long-awaited press ID from Mr. Green, Klim ran headlong down the stairs.

3

A hastily assembled train was to take journalists, military experts, and officials to Lincheng. The railroad car shook slightly as it passed the peach orchards and the first shoots of rice peeping up through the water-flooded paddy fields.

Klim still couldn't believe his luck. That morning he had been a nobody answering inane correspondence in the office, and now he was a reporter for a respectable newspaper, the owner of an elegant gray suit, a hat, and a second-hand silver watch with an inscription on its cover: "To a great sharpshooter."

Klim stepped out into the corridor and met Ursula, a petite, dark-eyed correspondent from the New York-based *International News Service*. They chatted for a while about mutual acquaintances and agreed to pool their resources.

"Do you think it's possible that the *Blue Express* has been taken over by Bolsheviks?" Ursula asked. "I visited Russia recently and interviewed some of the new political leaders there. Their ultimate goal is to start a world revolution and impose their Soviet system on every country on the globe. They told me that China is a particularly weak spot for the capitalist West, and that if there was a rebellion against us here, it would be a huge blow to the Great Powers."

"I don't think they would be stupid enough to attack a

train with foreigners on it," Klim said.

But Ursula was convinced the Bolsheviks were capable of anything. "I'm so worried there's going to be another great war."

Very casually, she put her hand on Klim's shoulder, and he couldn't help but smile. Apart from Ada's teenage advances, he couldn't remember the last time a woman had flirted with him. It seemed so long ago that it belonged to a past life.

Evidently, a new white shirt and a smart silk necktie could do wonders for a man.

4

With its steep slopes, impenetrable forests, and low clouds looming over its forbidding mountains, Shandong Province looked a wild and inhospitable place.

The local officials showed the press the wreck of the *Blue Express* and told them what they knew about the attack.

At 2 a.m., the engine driver had spotted suspicious shadowy figures on the tracks ahead. He tried to hit the brakes, but it was too late—the rails had been sabotaged. The train flew off the rails and came to a stop at a precarious angle. As its sleeping passengers fell from their berths, their luggage tumbling down on their heads, shots were fired, and soon horses' hooves and a war cry could be heard. The security detachment aboard the *Blue Express* had been the first to realize what was going on and made a run for it, while the attackers smashed the car windows with the butts of their rifles.

The bandits then jumped into the compartments from their saddles, throwing passengers and luggage onto the sidings. Barefoot and dressed only in their night clothes, the hostages had been led up into the mountains. The looting had carried on all through the night and well into the next morning. The Governor had sent officials to investigate the incident, but the only information they had discovered so far was that the attackers were local.

As Klim made his way through the bullet-scarred railroad cars, he noticed a piece of glass in a broken window, covered with dried blood. Next to it, on the wall, were smeared bloody handprints; someone had tried to escape but never made it.

The journalists were taken to Lincheng, a small town surrounded by high walls.

Dazed soldiers and officials rushed around the dirty crooked streets. Local elders with their brown faces furrowed with deep wrinkles sat on the porches of their huts and followed the unwelcome visitors with their bleary eyes, their sunken mouths emitting clouds of evil smelling tobacco smoke.

Klim cabled Mr. Green a telegram describing the accident and the initial reports provided by the local officials. The garrison at Lincheng had already sent a detachment to the rescue, but the soldiers had been unable to approach the hostages because the bandits were using them as human shields.

At the telegraph office, Klim bumped into Ursula, and she told him that a representative of the American diplomatic mission, Roy Anderson, had arrived from Peking and been put in charge of negotiating the hostages' release.

"Where is he staying?" asked Klim.

"In his railroad car. All the inns in town are packed. Mr. Andersen is promising to hold a press briefing tomorrow, at eight in the morning."

Klim and Ursula wandered around the town, trying to find somewhere to stay. Eventually, some Italian journalists were persuaded to let the lady spend the night in the wagon they had rented. There was no room for Klim, so he went back to the station.

Campfires were blazing everywhere; some people were arguing near one of them, others were singing around another. Local traders offered firewood, tea, and cold rice for sale. Even the shelter under the railroad cars was occupied. Klim took out his flashlight and spotted a gaggle of small children snuggled up next to one another among the wheels.

His torchlight slid over a footboard, and he caught a glimpse of a lady's shoes and silk dress decorated with red poppies.

Good God, it was Nina!

She covered her face with her hand. "Turn that light off, please," she said in English.

"Hello, my dear," Klim said.

Nina shuddered. "You?"

Klim turned off his flashlight. First, a white dress emerged from the darkness, then Nina's face, framed by her tresses of curls. A miraculous spirit had descended down to this godforsaken corner of the earth.

At a loss for words, each waited for the other to say something.

"There's no electricity in my sleeping car," Nina said finally, "and the attendant has run off somewhere."

Surprised at his own composure, Klim offered her his hand. "Let's go find your car attendant."

She didn't push him away. She took his arm while descending the steps.

Klim followed her at some distance, listening pebbles crunching under her feet. Other cars still had electricity, and Nina appeared like a vision in the golden squares of light they shed on the siding, and then just as quickly she disappeared in the darkness. Klim breathed in the cool air filled with Nina's perfume.

How could this meeting be possible? He felt wave after wave of hot flushes roll over his body. His heart was pounding, and his face was covered with an incredulous grin.

"Do you have some business in Lincheng?" he asked.

"Yes," Nina replied without turning her head.

"Where do you live now?"

"In Shanghai."

"How do you keep yourself busy there?"

"With this and that."

Nina didn't want to talk about herself, and Klim had no right to expect detailed answers. The only thing he could do now was simply look at his wife and shudder at the exhilarating realization that nothing had changed. He still loved her as much as ever.

"Let's forget the attendant," Nina said suddenly. "I only wanted to read a little before going to sleep, but it's too late now anyway."

That's it, Klim thought. *The miraculous spirit will now disperse into the ether.*

"Where are you staying?" Nina asked. "If you want, we can go to my compartment."

"Will Jiří mind?"

"Do I have to ask his permission?"

They returned to Nina's car, and Klim switched on his flashlight to help her find her compartment in the dark corridor. He was still waiting for this dream to be interrupted with the appearance of Nina's sleepy lover or her mocking words: "I'm sorry, I only invited you in as a joke." But nothing of the sort happened.

She turned the bronze door knob and pushed the door to the side. "Come in."

It was a first-class compartment with a shade covering half of the window, a single bed with rumpled bed clothes, and a useless lamp over the headboard.

"You can put your suitcase on the top shelf," Nina said. "The couch is all yours."

Klim hung his jacket on one of the hangers and loosened his necktie. Good God, why had Nina invited him in?

"You can turn the flashlight off now," she said as she put her knee on the bed and pulled down the window shade.

The darkness was so dense that it felt as if they were surrounded by nothing but an endless and eternal void.

So many months had passed, yet the rustle of Nina's dress and the collected evenness of her breathing were as familiar to Klim as ever. He knew by the sound of her movement that she removed her comb from her hair and slipped off her shoes.

"Did you get a good job?" Nina asked.

"Yes."

"And where exactly do you work?"

"You know, with a newspaper," said Klim involuntarily echoing her terse answers.

What could he say to Nina? That he was listed at the paper as a courier and shared a room in the House of Hope with a fifteen-year-old girl? That all these months, he had been wandering around the city, peering at the faces of passersby in the vain hope of catching a fleeting sight of his wife?

He could sense Nina standing in front of him—his darling, invisible, and inaccessible wife. What was the point of deluding himself? She would never come back to him.

"We should get a divorce," Klim said flatly. It was better not to wait for Nina to broach the subject.

"Have you already found someone else?" she asked.

"Marriage is like a house; if you're not using it, you should either get new tenants in or knock it down completely and build everything up again from scratch."

Klim could hear the floor creak, and Nina's silk skirt slide against his knee. She was so close that he could feel her breath on his temple.

"Our marriage certificate is lost," Nina said, "so the only way we could get a divorce would be to get married again."

Klim could not stand it anymore. He pulled Nina close to him, making her sit on his lap. She shrieked faintly: "What are you doing?" but he pressed her head against his shoulder and kissed her on the lips.

The window shade turned red with a pulsating glow; the people outside had poured new fuel onto their fire and started chanting a barbaric, incomprehensible song.

Klim's head was full of jubilant horror. *I don't care anymore. What will be, will be.*

His hand travelled along the Great Silk Road—down to Nina's waist and then her thigh, tightly sheathed by her dress. At first she grasped Klim's hand as if not wanting him to go further, but then she let out a short gasp and started to unbutton his shirt.

6. THE DIVORCEES

1

Tony Aulman had been right: the documents for the fake consulate weren't difficult to arrange. All it took was a well-aimed bribe and an official-looking letter to the Foreign Affairs Office, and very soon one of the houses near the Tibet Road got a brand new polished plaque with the legend "The Consulate of the Czechoslovak Republic" engraved on it.

Nina was forbidden to mention the horrors she had experienced during the Bolshevik Revolution to anyone.

"In your situation," Tamara said, "it's not only senseless, but also harmful to seek sympathy. People are only able to feel sorry for you if they can imagine themselves in your shoes. You don't clutch your head every time you hear about a hurricane in the West Indies, do you? Well, likewise, don't expect any degree of compassion for your suffering during the revolution in Russia."

"The real reason people don't sympathize with us is because they know so little about us," Nina said with vehemence. "And I can tell them a lot about what's happened—"

"And your guests will decide you are one of the losers who lost their country to the Bolsheviks. The gentlemen

73

from the Shanghai Club are convinced that if they had found themselves in the same position as your White Army officers, they would have seen off the Bolshevik riff-raff in a couple of months."

"Anyone can win a war from the comfort of the smoking room in a gentleman's club," Nina said. "I'd like to see how these 'armchair heroes' would have fought without reinforcements, ammunition, or transportation."

"And how do you think you are going to disabuse them of their puffed-up illusions?" said Tamara, smiling. "Believe me, you'd be much better off telling them tall stories about European aristocrats. That is a topic that is always in demand."

Tamara had kept a lot of old Russian magazines from the pre-revolutionary era, and Nina spent hours studying the descriptions of diplomatic receptions and opening nights in Imperial theaters. Then she would rehearse them to herself in front of a mirror, using her newly-acquired English.

The High Society in One Hundred Years Time masquerade was a great success. Thanks to Tamara's advice, Nina was judged by all to be a consummate and brilliant hostess. The Chinese government was missing customs duties for ten crates of champagne, and soon Don Fernando had given Nina her first share in the profit.

"Not bad for a party girl, heh? Keep dancing, and we'll have ourselves a good little business."

A couple of weeks later, Nina invited her new acquaintances to a Masquerade of Lookalikes, which was also a great success. Among the glittering array of guests were three black Florence Mills cabaret singers, two mustachioed Thomas Beecham orchestra conductors, four Mary Pickford Hollywood actresses, and one revolutionary Leon Trotsky who pestered the ladies by demanding that they give him their "bloody diamonds."

Before each party, Tamara would set Nina an assignment to work on a special anecdote to drop into a conversation or to flirt with this or that gentleman. Tamara took infinite delight in making fools of her former friends.

Everything was going smoothly, but Nina felt no joy at her success. She was Tamara's 'kept woman.' Nina's white house, her furniture, and dresses all belonged to the Aulmans; her guests were Tamara's friends, not hers. Worst of all Nina wasn't even mistress of her own past anymore. On Tamara's advice she told everyone that for the entire duration of the civil war in Russia, she had had been living in a grand hotel on Lake Geneva.

Thanks to an endless whirl of social events, her consulate was scarcely ever out of the limelight, and Nina shuddered at the thought that sooner or later, her cover will be blown.

"Do we really need to keep up the facade of the consulate for our parties anymore?" she asked Tamara. "Why don't we keep the events going but just quietly close the consulate down?"

But her mistress rejected the idea outright. "Don Fernando sells your liquor to the Governor's assistant. If there is no consulate and no cheap champagne, Tony will lose a very valuable friendship."

Nina had got into the habit of wandering around antique shops. For her, beautiful trinkets were symbols of wealth and represented a confidence in the future. At Rue Montauban, she would buy smoke-colored watercolors, porcelain, and lacquer boxes, and the finest embroideries and perfume bottles made of green and white jade at the stores on the Broadway. Soon Nina's house began to resemble a museum but it did not feel like home at all.

2

One day, Nina came to visit Tamara and noticed a new photograph on her bedside table. It was a picture of Tony Aulman and a blond gentleman wearing a yacht club sweater. The man was in profile, and Nina was immediately struck by his high forehead and chiseled jaw.

"Daniel Bernard is one of the most amazing people I've ever met," said Tamara. "Did you know that China joined the Great War on the side of the Allies, and under that pretext, it confiscated the property of German and Austro-Hungarian citizens? The poor Germans were herded like cattle into barracks, and when the Spanish flu epidemic hit, our 'patriotic' doctors refused to lift a finger to help them. Only Mr. Bernard showed any decency and organized a temporary hospital for the sick. He is a Czech by nationality, and his nation had suffered from Austrian and German oppressors for centuries, but it didn't stop him from being human and helping them in their misfortune."

"It would be nice to meet such a person," Nina said. "Let's invite him to my party?"

"Daniel is currently out of Shanghai," Tamara replied.

For no apparent reason, Nina's acquaintances also began telling her about Mr. Bernard, and she learned that he was selling tea and Chinese art to Europe. His erudition and sophistication were combined with a number of manly passions, such as sports, politics, and hunting. He was an avid reader, a successful entrepreneur, and a keen philanthropist.

The more Nina learned about Daniel, the more often she would glance at the picture on Tamara's bedside table. A strange chain of coincidences seemed to be bringing them together, she thought. She had come up with the Czechoslovak Consulate idea, and Daniel was a Czech. He had gone to Europe soon after she had arrived in Shanghai, as if deliberately to give her time to get herself back on her feet. He was a friend of the Aulmans, and she would have every opportunity to meet him through them. Nina had an inkling that her mistress wanted to bring her and Daniel together, and, for now, she was fine with the idea.

When Nina learned from the newspapers that Mr.

Bernard was among the hostages on the *Blue Express*, she immediately called Tamara.

"What do you think will happen to him?" she asked, shocked at the thought that her fragile hope for personal happiness might be crushed.

"The Chinese will buy their relatives' freedom, and the representatives of the Great Powers will negotiate the release of their subjects," Tamara said unemotionally.

There was no one to stand up for Daniel Bernard, a Czechoslovak national.

Nina announced to Jiří that they were going to Lincheng. "We have to save your countryman."

"Are you out of your mind?" he cried. "What can we do for him? And why?"

"Get ready, I said!"

Nina couldn't wait for the Chinese authorities to eventually see through their scam or for Tamara to get bored of her little games. Daniel Bernard seemed to offer Nina's her best chance to take her destiny into her own hands.

At Lincheng, all she found was chaos and filth, and they learned that hostage release negotiations could often run for months.

"I knew that our journey would be completely pointless," Jiří kept saying.

I really have lost my mind, Nina had to admit. *There is no Daniel Bernard. I must have imagined it all.*

She spent a long time moping in her compartment, convinced that her life was essentially over. Her past no longer existed, she had no control over her present, and the only realistic future that awaited her was a Chinese prison and not some imagined romance with a rich handsome stranger.

Just when Nina thought things couldn't get any worse, the electricity had failed. But as she descended the steps of her car, she was met by a man she had never imagined she would see again.

3

Klim woke up and discovered that Nina had moved to her bed; the couch had been too narrow for the two of them.

Outside, in the world beyond the window shade, bustle, voices, and the snorting of a steam engine could be heard. The sun was shining and the morning was in full swing. But here, in the cocoon of the compartment, a gentle restorative twilight still reigned.

Klim leaned on his elbow and drank in the sight of his sleeping wife. What incredible and improbable circumstances had thrown them together?

Strong, stunning, and impossible, Nina hadn't changed an iota. The shadow of her eyelashes flickered imperceptibly, and the skin on her neck and rounded shoulder shone like a dusky and ethereal pearl.

Klim looked around him. Someone had paid for Nina's luxury compartment, her perfume and outfits. Most likely, she had had a fight with her sugar daddy and decided to cheat on him to get her revenge. Meeting Klim had just provided her with the perfect opportunity. What role could he ever play in her current life? An occasional guest lover? The ring on her finger alone cost more than he could earn in six months.

Klim glanced at his watch and hurriedly started to dress. It was five to eight, and he was in danger of missing the meeting with Roy Andersen.

He took his suitcase from the luggage rack, slipped out of the compartment, and stopped for a second in the middle of the corridor. *Should I wake Nina up?* he thought. *No, let her sleep. We can talk when I get back, and then what will be, will be.*

He went out onto the platform and squinted in the bright May sun. People were rushing past in one direction as if hurrying to see a house on fire.

"Have you heard the news?" Ursula cried, rushing up to him. "Daniel Bernard has managed to escape from the bandits."

"Edna's husband?"

"Come quickly. He's just about to recount his story to the press. He's very fair, and his face became so severely sunburned that the bandits thought he had contracted a dangerous disease. So they left him for dead in the forest."

There was a huge crush of people by the station building, but the guards were only letting journalists in. Klim entered the waiting room where a blond man was sitting in a dense circle of photographers and reporters. Daniel Bernard was dressed in dirty striped pajamas, someone else's coat had been thrown over his shoulders. His face was a livid red, and the skin on his nose and forehead was peeling in small white scales.

Daniel Bernard was dead on his feet: he had been wandering the mountains for two days before he met a search party of soldiers who finally brought him to the station.

"The bandits lined us up in rows and drove us into the mountains," he said. "But with three hundred of us, they had bitten off more than they could chew. We didn't have any food or water supplies, and many of us didn't even have shoes. The gentleman who was walking by my side knew the local dialect, and he overheard the bandits talking about letting the women and children go free. To their way of thinking, men are much more valuable hostages and can command much higher ransoms."

Ursula was too small to be able to see Daniel from behind the scrum of other reporters. "The authorities have tried to provide the hostages food and water supplies through envoys," she cried from behind the reporters' backs. "Did anything get through?"

Daniel shook his head. "The bandits threw everything away except the canned stew. They thought that the food might contain sleeping drugs."

"Do they have any political demands?" Klim asked.

"No. These villagers haven't become robbers because of politics. It's purely out of desperation. The local peasants have five to eight children and live in utter poverty because they have no land rights. The bandits are young men who can only provide for themselves by robbing others."

At that moment a short plump man with a doctor's bag under his arm rushed into the room, barging through the crowd. "Ladies and gentlemen, my name is Dr. Piper and I must insist that you leave Mr. Bernard alone immediately. He needs medical attention and rest."

Klim and Ursula went off to the telegraph office to send their cables, but there was a huge queue, and they ended up waiting for hours.

"Edna is so lucky that her husband has managed to escape from the bandits," Ursula kept saying.

Klim nodded, but he was thinking about something else. What if he was to offer Nina a fresh start in life? Would she agree? What if she had meant it when she had said that they couldn't get a divorce?

After sending his telegram, Klim raced back to the station, but when he reached the platform, he didn't recognize the place. There were only empty freight cars on the tracks.

"Where is the Shanghai train?" Klim asked a young Chinese dressed in a railway uniform.

He looked at him over his round glasses. "I'm sorry, sir. It left a long time ago."

4

A woman always knows when intimacy with her becomes very special for a man and when he is overwhelmed with happiness just because he has had a chance to hold her in his arms. That was what had happened between Nina and Klim that night, and she was surprised that he had disappeared, without saying a word to her.

She was sitting by the window, waiting for him, but an hour passed, then another, and another—and still Klim hadn't shown up. There could only be one possible explanation: he had wanted nothing but to teach Nina a lesson and show her what she had lost.

How could she have doubted Klim? In less than a half a year he had settled in Shanghai and, apparently, was making a much better job than his ne'er-do-well wife.

There was a knock on the door, and Nina sprang to her feet.

But it was only Jiří. "Daniel Bernard has just escaped from captivity," he said, excitedly. "He'll be traveling to Shanghai on our train."

Utterly crushed, Nina sank back down on the couch. She no longer gave a damn about Daniel Bernard.

The attendant appeared at the end of the corridor. "Ladies and gentlemen, the train will be leaving in fifteen minutes. Please, have your return tickets ready."

Nina looked at her watch. It was half past one. Klim was not about to return. He had, after all, said that he wanted a divorce.

"Are you all right?" Jiří asked, looking into her eyes.

"Let's just go home," Nina replied, barely audible.

5

Every now and then, Jiří would knock at Nina's door and tell her about Daniel Bernard. First, he went to the dining car, and then the train master visited him, and after that—

Nina couldn't stand it any longer and rushed to the open smoking area at the end of the last car, just to have a chance to be alone.

The wheels clattered rhythmically, and the wind eddied over the vast green fields of sorghum. Nina stood, clutching the handrail, and wept silently.

Eventually, her remorse gave way to anger. "We'll see who wins," she whispered. "And boy, are you going to regret it."

The doors parted slightly. Nina turned her head and recoiled as a man with a red scaly face stepped into the smoking area. To top everything, this was the "prince" she had been dreaming of—Jiří had already told Nina about Daniel's misadventures in the forest.

Daniel lighted his cigarette, and he and Nina stood in silence for a while. From time to time, she gave him a puzzled look. In real life, Mr. Bernard was an angular, disheveled man with a rather abrupt way of moving. He constantly shrugged his shoulders, and the hand that held his cigarette jerked upward every now and then.

He had been sneaking secret glances at Nina, too.

"You know, you have a remarkable complexion," he said. "I've really never seen anything like it before."

Nina looked at her reflection in the glass door and gasped: her face was as filthy as a chimney sweep's. The handrail she had been clutching had been smeared in soot, and she had soiled her face while wiping away her tears.

"Why didn't you tell me earlier?" she asked. "Do you have a handkerchief?"

Daniel smiled. "I do, but I daren't give it to you. If you end up transforming yourself into a beautiful woman, I'd never be able to summon up the courage to talk to you. As things are, I think we rather complement each other. After all red and black do go rather well together."

Nina was confused. Was he laughing at himself or her?

"We'll just have to pass ourselves off as 'a pair of rough diamonds,'" Daniel suggested. "Have you ever heard the story of the Imperial Seal of China?"

"Do you really have no one else to talk to?" Nina said, frowning.

Daniel shrugged. "I think I'd rather converse with you than the train master. He's so dull, he could bore a man into an early grave. So I fear you have little choice but to listen to my story: A long time ago, a man called Bian He found a piece of jade in the hills and brought it to the king. Alas, the poor man was soon chased out of the palace without a word of thanks for his pains, his lump of jade tossed after him in contempt. When the king died, his younger brother ascended the throne, and Bian He repeated his long journey but again to no avail. Only the third king recognized the value of the treasure laid before him. Out of this stone, he ordered that a special ritual disc be made, known as *bi*, the symbol of the sky. It was so beautiful that it became an object of envy throughout China. Other rulers coveted it, and to obtain it, armies and even cities were lost. Many wars were waged for it and much blood shed for its sake. Long centuries passed, and the disc happened to fall into the hands of Qin Shi Huang, who turned it into the Heirloom Seal of the Realm. From that time forth, whoever possessed it was granted a mandate of power from the Heavens to rule the Empire. So the moral of my story is: Do not rush to reject a thing that might at first appear unsightly."

Daniel was clearly referring himself, but for Nina it was another hint of her inability to see true value in people and things.

"What happened to the Seal afterwards?" she asked.

"For more than a thousand years, it passed from generation to generation, and then it disappeared under mysterious circumstances. The only thing that is certain is that the last two dynasties ruled without the Seal, and it all ended up with the collapse of the Empire."

Daniel could talk endlessly about porcelain manufacturing, ancient scrolls, and China's great libraries reduced to ashes by successive waves of barbarian invaders. His stories were so fascinating that Nina had even forgotten about the soot on her cheeks.

Two hours seemed to pass like a minute in his company, and she was amazed how quickly Daniel managed to win her over with his charm, wit, and erudition. She had always had a soft spot for self-confident, well-educated men with a delicious sense of self-irony.

But there was more to their meeting than just that. They were both in sore need of the balm that good company could provide to smooth over their recent troubles. Nina was desperate not to be left alone with her thoughts about Klim, and Daniel, it appeared, was just grateful to be alive and not brooding on the murders, the suffering, and the long hours of marching through the mountains. Now he could just smoke his cigarette and chat with a random fellow traveler about history and culture.

They agreed to have dinner together. Nina went to wash her face and came to the dining car a transformed woman.

"If the bandits hadn't taken all my luggage," Daniel said, "I would have made more of an effort to make myself presentable too. I had a remarkable German gas mask in my suitcase that I found at a flea market. I think it would have been just the thing to wear to dinner in polite company, considering the state of my face at the moment."

Tamara was right: Mr. Bernard was an extraordinary man.

6

All the way to Shanghai, Nina and Daniel were almost inseparable, and they enjoyed every minute of each other's company.

What if we are really fated to be together? Nina thought in dismay. She couldn't imagine him as her lover, but she kept telling herself that his burnt face would heal up and that she'd get used to his strange gestures.

Finally, the train arrived at the North Station, and the passengers poured out onto the platform. Steam escaping from under the platform billowed onto the passengers' feet. The crowd buzzed, the engines whistled, and the porters jostled from all quarters trying to attract the attention of their customers.

Nina had forgotten all the words she had wanted to say to Daniel before parting. He was silent, too, fiddling with her visiting card.

"It was a great pleasure meeting you—" he began, but at that moment a young lady in a checkered suit ran up to him.

"You're alive!" she cried, throwing her arms around him.

Nina stared at her in amazement. Who on earth was this woman?

Daniel's face didn't betray the slightest emotion, as if he was at a business meeting.

"Edna, let me introduce you to Miss Nina Kupina. Nina, this is my wife, Edna."

Nina was appalled. In her wild imaginings it hadn't even occurred to her that there might already be a Mrs. Bernard.

Edna greeted Nina and immediately forgot about her existence. "Come on, the car is waiting for us," she called to Daniel.

He followed his wife without a backward look, while Nina watched them go.

"Did Mr. Bernard forget to tell you that he was married?" Jiří asked as he stepped off the footboard of the railroad car. "How very ungentlemanly of him! But then I suppose *you* weren't in any great hurry to tell him that you have a husband either?"

"One day I'm going to get rid of you for good, you clown!" Nina hissed through her teeth.

But Jiří only laughed. "You'll just have to accept it. I'm the only man who is truly worthy of your rank. And unlike these fickle princes of yours, I'll never abandon you."

7. THE BAR ROOM BRAWL

1

In the past, no white girl in Shanghai would have agreed to dance with a Chinese man, but with the arrival of the Russian refugees, all that changed. Speaking English was not a mandatory requirement to work as a taxi-girl, and hundreds of immigrants flooded the docks and port's bars and taverns. These young women were able to provide for a whole family by dancing foxtrots and tangos and sweetly whispering the only English phrase they knew into their client's ear: "Darling, just one small bottle of wine, please." They didn't care who they danced with as long as they got paid.

Young Asian men were burning with curiosity to learn about Western ways and were especially fascinated by riotous dance parties. Restaurant owners were quick to realize that there was a killing to be made by allowing Chinese men to dance with Russian girls.

With the bottom falling out of the market, things weren't going so well at the Havana either, and Martha reluctantly ordered her doormen to let in people of all race and color.

"Our business is going to the dogs," Betty said indignantly. "Does the Madam seriously think that any self-respecting white woman is going to let herself fall into the arms of an Oriental?"

Betty was Brazilian, and her credentials as a pure bred

"white lady" required a serious stretch of the imagination, but no one was in a hurry to take issue, let alone offend her. Betty's left hook was legendary.

She bluntly refused to dance with the "chinks," and Martha was forced to accept the situation. Betty was popular with the regulars, and it would have been unwise to argue with her.

Martha told the rest of the girls to stop being so picky, but they secretly persuaded the manager to send all the Chinese men Ada's way. She was too young to know how to stand up for herself, and she couldn't even complain to Klim because he had been out of the city for a number of days now.

It was only on Fridays when the U.S. Marines received their pay packets that Ada was given a break. The Asians knew better than to go to a bar commandeered by the Americans for the night.

Initially, Ada had hoped she would meet a nice officer who would fall in love with her and take her away with him to the United States. She had heard rumors that a great Russian beauty from the Black Eyes restaurant had ended up marrying the captain of a battleship. If she could land herself a big fish like that, then why couldn't Ada?

Martha overheard her talking about her plans and soon brought her down to earth. "American officers never marry taxi-girls," she said to Ada. "The sailors and Marines might promise you the moon but they're not allowed to marry anyone without their superiors' permission. If you want to get married, you should look for a rich old-timer. The uglier and balder he is, the better. They're the type of men who are usually ignored by women. If you surrender to their advances they'll be so overjoyed they'll happily propose. You could even get them to make their will out to you. Then, all you've got to do is put up with your catch for ten years or so, and when he dies, you'll become a rich and merry widow."

Listening to Martha made Ada shudder.

2

This particular Friday had got off on the wrong foot from the very beginning. The Italian sailors from the cruiser *Libia* were in town, and they had old scores to settle with the Americans. The taxi-girls had been nervous from the very outset: What if their clients started fighting again?

Ada hadn't been invited to dance by a single customer, and she sat at the bar, nibbling sunflower seeds and watching an Italian sailor dancing with Betty. He circled her like a predator, while the beaded threads from her dress spun around her like a fan of shimmering water.

Ada couldn't help but notice an American corporal slumped heavily on a table nearby. He was chain smoking and very much the worse for wear. Whenever any of his companions addressed him, he would start grumbling like an old bulldog. He had been dancing with Betty at the start of the evening, but when the Italians arrived, she had switched her allegiances to them. Now, the other Americans were teasing the corporal about it.

I'd better tell the manager to call the doormen and get this guy out of here, thought Ada.

The manager was talking to a young Japanese man and pointing at her. Judging by the fan of dance tickets the Japanese held in his fist, this was a punter who had money to burn.

Ada assumed a dignified air.

Making his way to her, the Japanese accidentally bumped into the corporal. The American grabbed him by the lapels and shoved him with all his might towards Betty and the Italian officer. Everybody sprang to their feet, and the music stopped with only the drummer continuing to beat out his rhythms oblivious to everything going on around him.

"Call the police!" Ada shrieked, but no one paid her

attention.

The Italian moved Betty out of harm's way, sent the Japanese sprawling across the floor, and took on the corporal. Taxi-girls squealed, Marines rushed over to break up the fight, and several Italians ran in from the street to join the fray. Ada peeked out at the Japanese, who had jumped to his feet, and saw him pulling a revolver out of his pocket.

The sound of the shot was so loud that it made Ada's head ring. She expected the Italian officer to fall to the floor, with a bullet wound to his chest, but he just kept on punching the American on the floor.

A split second later, Ada felt a searing pain in her left ankle.

"She's been hurt!" Betty screamed, but Ada didn't understand who she was talking about. Faces started floating around her, and she passed out.

3

On the way to the hospital, Martha cursed the Japanese and their idiotic habit of carrying guns around with them all the time.

"Well, at least he hit you and not one of the customers," she said to Ada. "If that had happened, the authorities would have shut us down without batting an eyelid."

Ada nodded, sobbing. She was shaking not so much from the pain, but from the horrific realization that several minutes ago she could have been killed.

A bald doctor with a monocle on a string stitched up and bandaged Ada's leg. "No bones broken," he said breezily. "You'll be fine in a month."

Ada gasped. "But how am I going to dance?"

"No dancing for you," snapped the doctor. "You need to stay at home and rest, unless you want to lose that leg of yours."

"Great," Martha muttered, cursing under her breath.

She took Ada to the House of Hope and helped her up to her room.

"Where's Klim?" she asked.

"I don't know," Ada said. "He left two weeks ago and didn't even say where he was going."

"If the police come here, tell them you caught your foot on a nail," Martha said over her shoulder as she made her way down the stairs.

For a long time, Ada just sat in the dark. Not only was she now unable to go out to buy groceries, she couldn't even fetch boiling water from the kitchen. Hopping up the stairs on one leg with a hot kettle was not an option, and even emptying the night pot was an impossible task. Ada was overwhelmed by a sick feeling as she calculated how much it would cost her to pay the neighbors' kids to do it for her.

She tried to put a little weight on her injured leg but nearly collapsed. It was so painful!

That's it, it's over, she thought. *I can't work and soon I'll die of hunger. In a week or so, Chen will come to collect the rent payment and discover my corpse under this blanket.*

Ada lit a candle and took a crumpled paper icon from under her pillow.

"Lord, please, help me!" she whispered.

After she had had her fill of praying and weeping, she tried to climb up on to her top bunk, but even this was beyond her. She fell asleep exhausted on Klim's bed.

4

The next morning, Ada was woken up by the sound of a loud argument coming up from the street. Betty, resplendent in a full skirt and red jacket trimmed with exotic tropical bird feathers, was standing at the gates of the House of Hope. Chen hadn't wanted to let her in, but she gave him such a roasting that he soon retreated with his tail between his legs.

Betty marched upstairs to Ada's room, flung the door open so that it banged against the wall, and stopped at the threshold.

"So, you're ready to dance with any Oriental in order to pay for this bird cage? You're a bigger fool than I thought."

She walked over to the table and placed canned meat, biscuits, and smoked sausage onto it. "This should keep you going for a while. The other girls and I have decided to keep an eye on you until you get better."

"Thank you!" Ada whispered, deeply touched.

Betty sat down on the stool and took out a cigarette.

"Now you listen to me. It's not safe for you to be penniless in your situation. You need to seize the day, while you're still young, and start working on the second floor. I know what I'm talking about. I had a hard time too, when I first arrived in Shanghai. I used to work as a waitress on a steamer, but was fired for soliciting the passengers. The captain told me that I'd die here but he's not the first person I've proved wrong in my life."

Ada looked at her with such pitiful eyes that Betty couldn't help laughing.

"I'm only wishing the best for you, you silly girl! Men like beautiful, bold, and flexible women. Can you do the splits? No? Then you'll need to start practicing. Here's another trick that always works as well—"

Betty flicked her cigarette out of the window, took off her hat, and proceeded to do a handstand, her skirt slipping down over her head.

Ada stared in silence at Betty's black silk stockings and white cami-knickers trimmed with blue ribbons.

"What do you think?" Betty asked from under her skirt.

"Very impressive," Klim said, peering in from the door.

Ada gasped, while Betty calmly planted her legs back

down on the ground, stood up, and straightened her hair.

"Hello, lover boy. We've been waiting for you." She gave Ada, crimson with embarrassment, a congratulatory pat on the shoulder. "Just look at your handsome boyfriend with his fancy new suit and tie! Well, love birds, I have to go now, but you, Ada, have a good think about what I was saying to you earlier. Your boyfriend could disappear any moment, leaving you high and dry and without a friend in the world."

"I've told her a hundred times that you're not my boyfriend," Ada said hotly after Betty had left.

Klim sat down beside her on the bed. "What's wrong with your leg?"

Ada told him all about the shooting at the Havana.

"I'm really sorry," he said, lowering his eyes. The expression on his face suggested that he held himself personally responsible for what had happened. "I have some good news, though. I was promoted at work, and now I'm going to get thirty dollars a week. After that, I hope I'll be getting even more."

Ada couldn't even imagine having so much money. "Does this mean we're both out of the woods now?" Her lower lip started shaking. "Betty tried to persuade me to become a prostitute, and for a moment I almost thought I would agree."

Klim frowned. "You must promise me that you'll never do that."

"And you must promise you'll never leave me on my own for so long again. You do love me, don't you?"

"Well, how would it be possible not to?"

As if he was afraid that Ada would throw herself on his neck, Klim got up and walked to the window.

"You know," he said pensively, "sometimes I think that if we weren't so foolish, we might be happy together. But we'd need the moon to fall into our laps. You're dreaming about America, and I would need— Well, it's not important. Forget it."

"You're the only fool around here," Ada snapped. "Are you going to remain faithful to that worthless wife of yours for the rest of your days? She cares about you about as much as she cares for last year's fashions."

"Thank you for your kind words," retorted Klim and he stalked out of the room.

Ada hurled a pillow after him.

5

RECEIPTS AND EXPENDITURES

Klim Rogov's Notebook

Thanks to my reports from Lincheng, the sales of our newspaper have doubled, and Mr. Green has officially taken me on as a journalist. As a member of this exclusive little club, I now have my own desk, mailbox, and press card. The smug expression on my photo reminds me of the soldier who's just enlisted for the army on a recruitment drive poster: "He's Happy & Satisfied. Are You?"

So, this is our news:

Edna has returned from Canton, and her story about the local nationalist governor named Sun Yat-sen caused a great stir. He has far-reaching plans to unite China which was divided up among all sorts of warlords and kick the white ghosts, as the Chinese call the expatriates from Europe and America, out of the country.

Sun Yat-sen's political party, the Kuomintang, was denied recognition by the Great Powers, and he has found a new ally in Soviet Russia. Moscow has not only promised him funds to keep up the good fight against imperialism, but also political and military advisers.

Here, in Shanghai, some people find the news from the South a source of amusement, and some are genuinely scared. As for me, all this is a far cry from what really preoccupies me.

I still feel the touch of Nina's soft hands on my skin.

My wife weighed my heart up in her palm and tossed it carelessly into the trash can, and I now have an uncontrollable urge to find her and demand an explanation: What was it then between us that night on the train? I still don't understand a thing.

Ada has persuaded me to rent a two-room apartment on the floor below our old one, and now we have our own kitchen, but still no electricity, though. Ada's wound has healed up, but I have dissuaded her from going back to the Havana and promised that I would provide her with a small allowance.

My good intentions will end up being my downfall. The first thing Ada did with her money was to buy provocatively lacy knickers, and now she spends much of her time learning to do handstands, with the obvious intention of trying to seduce me. I spend much of my time these days hiding from her in my room, but she is constantly banging on my door, demanding that I hold her legs. "You wouldn't want me to fall and break my neck, would you?"

Despite her age she is only too aware that I'm no saint. I constantly have to remind myself that Ada is little more than a silly infatuated child, and I definitely don't want to have another sin on my conscience.

Today we made a deal: she swore that she would stop pestering me, if I found her a job. I forced her to agree that the moment she breaks our agreement, I will immediately take away her allowance and move to another apartment. Ada gave in but on condition that our agreement will only be valid until she comes of age. She is convinced that in a year I will forget about Nina and be looking to marry again—a successful, caring, albeit mildly grumpy potential husband.

I feel as if I'm standing at the cinema box office; I

really want to see the *Fair Lady*, but the only tickets available are for *The Extra Girl*.

6

Klim bounded into the apartment with the news that he had found a job for Ada. Mrs. Edna Bernard needed a competent and well-organized person who could keep her library in order.

"Be sure to mind your p's and q's," Klim told Ada, "and whatever you do, don't mention a word about the Havana. Edna is a member of the Moral Welfare League, and she would never dream of employing someone who used to work as a taxi-girl."

Ada had heard the other girls mention the League: it was largely made up of rich ladies on a crusade to rid China of prostitution. They would regularly publish damning articles in their church bulletins, organize propaganda meetings, and even picket the Municipal Council. But no matter how hard these upstanding and well-meaning ladies fought against vice, they achieved little or nothing. Unknown to them, most of Shanghai's legislators were regular patrons of the city's brothels.

Klim explained to Ada how to get to the Bernards, and after a delightful ride on a tramcar, she reached a quiet leafy street, where she saw nobody except a Chinese gardener trimming hedges.

Ada looked in wonder at the follies with their towers, weather vanes, and gates decorated with cast-iron curlicues. She felt as if she had entered into some fairytale kingdom, and that sooner or later someone would chase her away. Mere mortals evidently didn't belong here.

When a young servant let Ada into the house, she almost panicked. There were statues in every corner, the walls were decorated with paintings, and huge fans the size of windmill sails spun from the ceiling.

Goodness me, Ada thought, *what do these people do to earn the money to buy all this?*

The servant ushered Ada into a cramped studio, bowed, and disappeared. The mistress's appearance shocked Ada to the core. Mrs. Bernard's hair was twisted into a bun and fixed with a couple of pencils instead of hairpins. Her hands were smeared with ink, and a black telephone wire was coiled around her bare foot. She was sitting at a desk and talking on the phone.

Mrs. Bernard made a sign for Ada to wait. "We have established a rescue fund for the hostages from the *Blue Express*," she yelled into the receiver. "The bandits have requested two million dollars in ransom, but we have found a middleman who has negotiated a smaller amount."

Finally, Mrs. Bernard hung up and turned to Ada. "Miss Marshall? Klim Rogov gave you glowing references. What can you tell me about yourself?"

Ada had never been good at talking about herself. What did people expect her to say: "I'm a pretty, kind, and bright . . . modest sort of girl"?

Thankfully, Mrs. Bernard asked the questions, and with a little expert coaxing Ada told her all about her childhood and her odyssey from Izhevsk to Shanghai.

"I'm so sorry to hear you've been through so much, and at such a young age," Edna said. "But if you work hard, you'll be fine here."

She took Ada to a large sunny room filled with boxes of books. Books were littered all over the floor and piled precariously on the chairs. Some of them had been carefully stacked on the shelves, while others had been hurriedly stuffed into bookcases.

"Your task is to make a detailed catalog of all these books and arrange them so that they'll be easy to find," Mrs. Bernard said. "I can pay you twelve dollars a week. Is that alright with you?"

Ada nodded, stunned. She tried to find the right words of gratitude, but the telephone rang again from the studio, and Mrs. Bernard rushed off to answer it.

"You can start right now," Ada heard her calling from the corridor.

Twelve dollars a week—a princely sum. And Ada was going to earn it for the pleasure of sorting out books in a stunning library.

With trembling hands, she picked up the first book, then the second, and the third . . . To be honest, she was surprised and disappointed at the Bernards' taste. The library was filled with a hodgepodge of different topics that ranged from *Agriculture in Central China* to *The Industrial Revolution in Great Britain*. How could this couple possibly be interested in such dull topics?

Ada spent the whole morning repairing torn book covers and replacing missing pages. By twelve o'clock, a neat-looking Chinese lad knocked at the library door.

"Hi! My name is Sam, I'm boy number five," he introduced himself. "Our cook, Yun, told me to invite you down to the kitchen for lunch."

On their way, Sam told her that there were five Chinese boys, three maids, two grooms, a gardener, a laundress, a dishwasher, a chauffeur, a kitchen boy, a housekeeper, and a messenger boy all serving in the house.

"And all this for a family of two people?" Ada asked.

"It's good to have a lot of servants," Sam said proudly. "It shows that you are rich and can afford to invite lots of guests over. Did they hire you part- or full-time?"

Ada shrugged. "I don't know. But I'd like to stay here."

"Then find yourself extra work, and when you're done with the books, try to persuade Missy to keep you on. But don't go taking on other people's work. If they start hating you, they'll drive you out within a week. Not long ago, Yun fell out with one of the maids. He ended up putting special herbs into her food, which made her gassy. It became impossible to be in the same room as her, and Missy had to discharge her."

"I really have no intention of stealing anyone else's job—" Ada began, but Sam reassured her that she had nothing to be afraid of.

"Just be nice to everybody and you'll be fine."

He took Ada to the small kitchen, not the one that was used for cooking the masters' food, but the one with a whitewashed Chinese stove and a brood of blackened pots huddling in the corner.

A warped and grease-stained image of the kitchen god, the patron of the hearth and household, stood in a wall niche. Yun, an old man with a copper-colored face and a gray beard tucked into the collar of his jacket, was busy at the chopping board. He took an onion out of a basket and had it cleaned and sliced into translucent rings in a trice. The staccato of his chopping knife resembled the sound of a sewing machine.

Most of the servants had already had their lunch and had returned to their duties, leaving the kitchen boy to clean their plates. As Sam and Ada entered the kitchen, Yun ladled them bowls of soup with yellow noodles.

"May I have a spoon?" Ada asked timidly, looking down at the chopsticks that had been placed next to her bowl.

"No, you can't," Yun cut her short. "Learn to use chopsticks, like everybody else."

Frightened out of her wits, Ada sat next to Sam, trying to pick up her noodles with her chopsticks.

"Praise Yun's cooking," Sam whispered.

"Mmm, this is lovely!" Ada said. The noodles were delicious, but it was fiendishly difficult to pin them down with the chopsticks.

She tried lifting her bowl to her mouth, like Sam, but this was even worse, and she ended up spilling half the soup down her dress.

"Here comes the second course," said the kitchen boy.

Yun took a round basket from under the table, picked up a fork with a long handle, and used it to pull out . . . a live snake. In one deft movement, he cut its head off and skinned it.

The oil in the frying pan sizzled, flames shot up from the stove, and a cloud of steam enveloped the portrait of the kitchen god. A minute later, Ada was presented with two pieces of perfectly fried meat on her plate.

"Now, eat!" Yun ordered.

She stared at her plate, feeling more dead than alive.

"You'd better not upset the cook," said Sam.

At that moment footsteps came echoing from the corridor, and a man in a riding coat entered the kitchen, his pith helmet under his arm.

"Here, Yun, can you give me some apples?"

Sam stood up and bowed to him. "Good afternoon, Mr. Bernard."

Ada was dumbfounded: only a few weeks previously, she had seen this man in the Havana. He had caught her attention because his face had been unnaturally red, but now he looked fine.

"Are you going to spoil your horses again?" Yun muttered, filling the pith helmet with small yellow apples. "White people are nuts, riding horses in the midday sun or chasing golf balls all day long."

Mr. Bernard crunched an apple. "Stop grumbling. It's for a new horse I bought, but it's wild and needs to be tamed."

"And we are taming your young librarian here," said Yun, pointing to Ada.

Mr. Bernard turned to her, and she realized that he had recognized her, too.

"What have you given her?" he asked, looking at Ada's plate. "Chinese rat snake? Yun, give her a break. Don't torture the poor girl."

"Me? Torturing her? It's one of the finest delicacies in China!"

Mr. Bernard winked at Ada. "If he gives you any more of that muck, just ask him for tea with *milk* in it."

"It's barbaric to pour milk in tea!" Yun screamed. "You might as well pour it into beer."

"I can eat your rat snake," Sam whispered to Ada after the master had left and Yun's back was turned.

She nodded silently. Her heart was trembling. What would happen now? Would Mr. Bernard kick her out?

As Ada made her way back to the library through the gallery surrounding the courtyard, she noticed two grooms holding the reins of the black horse below while Mr. Bernard tried to coax it towards him with an apple. The trick didn't work, though. The horse looked at him with wild rolling eyes and kicked out in all directions.

Mr. Bernard noticed Ada. "Come over here," he ordered.

Her heart almost bursting out of her chest, Ada descended the stairs to the court yard.

"What an exceptional breed," said Mr. Bernard, approaching Ada. "These horses are caught in the Mongolian steppes, and when they come to Shanghai, it takes at least four months for them to get used to good fodder. Out on the steppe, they eat nothing but dry grass and don't want to try anything else."

Mr. Bernard took off his dusty gloves and threw them into his hat.

"Your name is Miss Marshall, isn't it? You know, my wife would be furious if she were to find out where you used to work."

"Please don't tell her," Ada pleaded. "Otherwise, she might ask how you know me, and it would become obvious that you've been to the Havana."

Mr. Bernard laughed. "That's true. Well, in that case you'd better get back to work, hadn't you?"

Back in the library, Ada collapsed into an armchair. She had been so brazen with her new master on her very first day at work. It was almost as if she had been blackmailing him: "If you don't betray me, I won't betray you."

But Mr. Bernard hadn't seemed to be offended. Betty was right: men like bold spirited girls.

8. CHASING AFTER ANOTHER WOMAN'S HUSBAND

1

Daniel Bernard never sent Nina his visiting card and hadn't even bothered to call. She had learned that there was to be a banquet celebrating his safe return home, but she and Jiří had not been invited.

Nina couldn't understand what he was playing at. Had he merely been dallying with her on the train to break up the boredom of the long trip? It was as if Destiny was deliberately mocking her.

Tamara had invited her over a couple of times, but Nina had refused, pretending she had a migraine. She couldn't stand the idea of discussing her failures with anyone. But Tamara was persistent. She mentioned Nina's reluctance to Tony, and he went to see her directly.

"Have you and Tamara fallen out?" he asked. "I hope you understand that this sort of anxiety is not good for her in her condition."

Reluctantly, Nina went to the Aulmans. She had expected an interrogation about Daniel Bernard immediately, but Tamara never mentioned him and gossiped instead about Shanghai's newly-opened movie studio.

"You should invite a cameraman to your next party," Tamara said, "and get him to film all the guests. They would love it."

She continued to elaborate on her idea, but Nina wasn't listening. Finally she couldn't hold herself back anymore. "Why were you so keen for me to meet Daniel Bernard?" she asked.

Tamara raised an eyebrow. "Daniel Bernard?"

"Please don't pretend that you weren't. You wouldn't stop talking about him, and I know you wanted me to go to Lincheng. Why didn't you tell me he's married?"

Tamara stared at Nina incredulously. "This is ridiculous—"

"You set everything up," Nina interrupted. "You even planted his portrait on your dressing table here." She pointed to the photo on Tamara's bedside table and then tailed off. The photograph was a portrait of Tony, not Daniel. Nina could now see that Daniel's presence was largely incidental.

"You seemed to be interested in Daniel, so I told you all about him," Tamara said calmly. "The rest is purely speculation on your part."

Nina was speechless. Was this some kind of a practical joke? Or had she really blown the whole incident out of all proportion?

"I might be able to help you," Tamara said, "if you tell me what happened. But if you feel uncomfortable, let's forget about it."

Brushing over the episode with Klim, Nina told Tamara all about her trip to Lincheng, her chance meeting with Daniel, and then his refusal to continue their acquaintance.

Tamara listened, her face growing gloomier.

"I think Daniel really did like you," she said. "But I'm also sure he made inquiries about you and found out that you and Jiří are impostors. I told you not to do anything without consulting me first. Daniel is a Czech national. He constantly visits Europe and spends a lot of time with the diplomats in Shanghai. He must be well aware that there is no official Czechoslovak Consulate here."

"But I was so sure that you wanted me to meet him," Nina protested.

"No, I didn't, and you've been very foolish."

Nina lowered her head. There was no point in arguing.

"You need to lay low and forget about Mr. Bernard," Tamara said. "You're never going to catch him anyway. He's married to the daughter of the Police Commissioner, and he would never leave her for a Russian adventuress."

On her way home in her recently purchased Ford, Nina was deep in thought.

"I have a license to drive in the International Settlement," her chauffeur said, "but if you want to go to the Chinese city, we'll need a different one."

Nina nodded absentmindedly. She was convinced Tamara had wanted her to see Mr. Bernard again. "I think Daniel really did like you," she had said teasingly to Nina. But again, it was impossible to be sure what she truly meant. Tamara was a master at hiding her intentions.

Nina herself was not about to give up on Daniel that easily. She didn't want her whole future depending on the good grace of a man she barely knew. Even though he was married and a serious relationship with him was out of the question, she could nevertheless try to turn his head, and then he wouldn't dare harm her.

2

Every now and then, Nina met the Bernards at mutual friends' houses, at theaters, or at concerts. Daniel's face had healed, but Nina had to admit that he looked much more handsome in Tamara's photograph than he did in real life.

Daniel would greet Nina and then do his utmost to avoid getting into conversation with her. Nevertheless, she would catch him giving her the occasional furtive glance, and that was encouraging.

In order to gauge her chances of success, Nina gathered various bits of information about Edna and soon discovered that she was educated, fearless, and smart.

Mrs. Bernard couldn't stand anyone belittling women and questioning their intelligence. At one dinner party Nina heard Daniel saying that it was all very well allowing women into the work place but they were totally incapable of creating anything truly great.

"Yes, your mother is ample evidence of that," Edna said.

Many at the table were outraged at her boldness, but Nina was secretly delighted that Edna had so publicly taken her know-it-all husband down a peg or two. After all, he had been the first to cast aspersions at their sex.

Feminine wiles, with their secret, soft power and a woman's ability to play on men's weaknesses were an alien concept to Edna. She preferred a relationship based on reason and rational agreement rather than tumultuous passion and unpredictable emotional turmoil.

"Let the man think," Nina's mother had always told her, "that he's the head of the family and in charge of everything. But you must be the 'neck' turning the 'head' in the direction that suits you." And this was exactly what Nina was planning to do.

She persuaded Jiří to invite Daniel out to lunch and to steer the conversation towards the events in Lincheng and particularly the journey back to Shanghai.

"Find out what Mr. Bernard really thinks of me," she instructed Jiří. It provided him with a perfect opportunity to make fun of her, but he still agreed to meet Mr. Bernard. To Nina's great relief, Daniel accepted the invitation, and on the appointed day, she restlessly waited for Jiří to return with the news.

One way or another, I'm going to land Daniel, Nina thought excitedly. *And then we'll see what that arrogant Mr. Rogov has to say.*

Jiří arrived back late, drunk and mellow.

"What took you so long?" Nina asked.

"I do beg your pardon, Madam Excellency, but we were busy reminiscing about Prague."

"Did Daniel say anything about me?"

"Yes. He told you to go and find the ninth son of the dragon."

"What on earth does he mean by that?" Nina frowned.

"I have no idea. Perhaps it's some kind of Chinese riddle."

Nina went to see a recent acquaintance, an old antique dealer by the name of Gu Ya-min, and asked him about the ninth son of the dragon.

"He's referring to Jiaotu," the old man replied, pointing at a bronze door handle cast in the shape of an animal snout with a ring in its mouth. "Jiaotu doesn't like to be disturbed and keeps uninvited guests out of the house."

Nina was furious. Albeit politely, Daniel had just told her to go to hell.

In response, she sent him a traditional Chinese watercolor of a fish jumping out of the water against the background of a distant gate standing in the middle of a river. She was sure that Daniel knew the legend of the silver carp that had overcome a great waterfall called the "Dragon's Gate" and thus turned into a dragon itself.

3

Every 4th of July, Shanghai's American expatriates would celebrate U.S. Independence Day. In the Public Garden long rows of tables were laid out with perfectly starched white tablecloths under striped awnings. Next to them stood souvenir stalls and barbecues selling food, merry-go-rounds for the children, and a huge stage with a podium for the U.S. Consul General and the Chairman of the Municipal Council, who were due to address the gathering.

The heat was so intense that the air seemed to tremble overhead. The enticing aroma of vanilla ice-cream and grilled meat mixed with the bitter smell of the gunpowder smoke that hovered over the well-dressed crowd. The sound of gun shots and cheers could be heard over the booming music of the brass band.

In the shooting range, Nina was aiming at a paper target. After she had hit the bull's eye five times in a row, the owner of the shooting arcade doffed his hat. "I've never seen anything like it, ma'am."

Nina handed him back his rifle and headed for the door. She knew that Daniel Bernard had been watching her, but she hadn't so much as glanced at him. He would have to make the first move.

"Nina, wait!" Daniel called when she was out in the street.

She pretended to be pleasantly surprised.

"How nice to see you again. How are you?"

"Very well, thanks."

They stood in the middle of the crowd looking into each other's eyes.

"Do you always find your target?" Daniel asked.

"If I thought I was going to miss, I wouldn't bother going hunting," Nina said.

He clasped both her hands in an intimate, sensual, almost imploring gesture. "You've had your sights on me in the last couple of months. What do you want of me?"

Nina freed her hands and gave Daniel a reproachful stare, as if he had suggested something indecent.

"I'm just looking for some advice on Chinese art," she said. "A friend of mine has an unusual collection of antiques. He's an old man now and wants to sell it but has no idea how to go about it."

Daniel had such a distraught look on his face that it

was all Nina could do to stop herself laughing.

"Well, you must let me see the collection," he said. "Name a time and a place and we must meet."

Suddenly Edna rushed up to them, hot and bothered.

"Have you completely lost track of the time?" she said to Daniel. "Everyone is waiting for us in the Administration Booth."

"I'm terribly sorry," Daniel said to Nina and tipped his hat. "You'll have to excuse me."

Nina clenched her fists. Edna had come at just the wrong moment. But on the plus side, it was clear that Daniel had succumbed to the inevitable and that the idea of another woman entering his life had taken root in his mind. The rest would be a matter of time.

4

He called Nina two days later, and it was a while before she managed to locate the receiver of the telephone standing on her bedside table.

"Hello!"

"Good morning," Daniel said. "Do you still want to show me those antiques?"

Nina pressed her hand to her forehead. The previous day, she had held a Spanish masquerade at her house and had been dancing flamenco until the small hours. Now her head was still buzzing from the excesses of gathering.

"Let's meet up in couple of hours," she said.

"Agreed."

She pulled herself out of bed and looked at her triptych vanity mirror. *Goodness gracious!* Remnants of make-up were smudged under her eyes, and her hair was a total mess. But worst of all she had a horrendous hangover.

"Qin!" Nina called to her *amah*, the Chinese maid. "Could you bring me a glass of seltzer water and ice, please?"

5

Daniel met Nina at the entrance of the antique market. It was packed with tourists, sightseers, and art collectors, all wandering around the numerous tents and stalls. The air was thick with the scent of old wood and incense sticks smoking in front of small shrines and altars. Inscrutable dealers sat deep in the cave-like interior of their stalls, surrounded by mountains of colorful bric-a-brac and nonchalantly cooling themselves with fans. Every now and then a heated dispute would break out over the provenance or price of an item. The vendors would invoke the gods and ancestral spirits as their witness, a deal would eventually be agreed on, and a couple of old chairs or a temple bell would pass from one hand to another.

Nina led Daniel along a line of stalls that seemed to have every imaginable item for sale: pots, statues, palanquins, lanterns, vintage embroidered clothes, implements of torture, fortunetelling bones with century-old predictions, and even images of Zigu, the goddess of the privy, to whom people would pray for good luck in their family matters.

Gu Ya-min's antique shop took up two-floors of a creaky old house, rickety ladders leaned against the shelves on its walls, and light shone in through its colored-glass windows. The owner, who appeared at least a hundred years old, had become so shrunken and dark with age that he looked more like one of his own ancient teak carvings than a living human being. Even in the height of summer he felt the cold and would wander around his shop in a quilted coat and felt slippers.

Gu Ya-min gave Daniel a long searching look and asked Nina who he was and what he wanted. After introductions were made, he agreed to show Daniel his collection.

"A lewd and licentious man lost these items to me at cards," the old man said, heading for the back room. "He told me they were worth at least three thousand *taels* of silver, but I can't even get a yuan for them. It's against the law for me to sell them."

The dark, hot, and stuffy back room was cluttered with boxes that reached right up to the ceiling. Nina pushed aside a carved screen and opened the window. She had been hoping that Gu Ya-min would leave her on her own with Daniel, but instead the old man sat down on a stool, resting his hands on the intricately carved head of his stick. "Be my guests," he said.

Nina had hatched her plan to lure Daniel to this room a long time ago, but now her hangover and nerves had thrown these well laid schemes into complete disarray. To make things worse, Gu Ya-min followed her movements with a disapproving look, as if fathoming what was on her mind.

Daniel opened a cardboard box and pulled out a smaller one covered with silk. Inside was a jade disc depicting a beautiful smiling girl lying on nine chrysanthemum petals, her naked body gleaming and her eyes closed in ecstatic abandon.

Daniel glanced at Nina but said nothing. He took a porcelain bracelet out of a different box. It was decorated with a painted garden along with a pagoda and humpbacked bridge. On the other side of the bracelet was a playful looking woman with a high coiffure. Her gown had slipped open revealing her breasts, and its red belt slid over her stomach disappearing between her thighs.

In the next box there was a fragment of a mammoth tusk covered with carvings of nude figures enjoying every possible sensory delight.

"Do you know how much this thing is worth?" Daniel asked Nina.

"No idea," she mumbled, rubbing her aching temples.

"This collection could be sold for a very large sum of money. Not here but in Europe."

Gu Ya-min suddenly dropped his head on his chest

and began to snore, his gray mustache quivering in time with his breathing like a pennant in a light wind.

"If Gu Ya-min tries to send these things abroad," Nina whispered in Daniel's ear, "he could be accused of selling pornography and end up in jail. That's why I turned to you: the old man needs advice on what to do with this stuff."

"What if you were to send the collection under the protection of one of your diplomatic bags?" Daniel said. "You could avoid customs by sending it through your Czechoslovak Consulate. You know there's a lot more money in illicit antiques than in illicit champagne."

Nina went cold. Daniel had twigged her little scheme after all.

"You're a dangerous man," she said hesitantly.

Daniel laughed. "If I was so dangerous, would you have invited me here on your own?"

"I can explain—"

"Don't bother. You'd be better off helping me to make an inventory of these treasures."

They sorted through the remaining boxes together. There were albums with brass corners and prints that smelled of spices, sets of painted fans depicting the most unimaginably debauched scenes, porcelain figurines, and laced puppet figures for the shadow theater. Daniel looked at them in the light while recounting the plots of the famous Chinese medieval stories in an excited whisper. But all Nina could manage to do was to nod and smile stiffly.

Daniel showed her a scroll yellowed with age, depicting a samurai writing thin columns of characters on the thigh of a naked Japanese lady.

"Do you want me to translate it for you?" Daniel asked.

I slept all night on your kimono sleeve,
Your delicate aroma preserved in its folds.

Before the dawn, the curtain swayed.
Your dew-grass footprints barely seen.

Gu Ya-min woke up suddenly and looked reproachfully at Nina and Daniel.

"Forget about these footprints," he grunted and pointed at a big box with his stick. "You'd be better off having a look in there."

Daniel opened the box and pulled out a saddle with a sharp peg sticking out of the middle of it.

"What is it?" he asked in surprise.

"A very useful thing," Gu Yamin said with a smile. "It's a donkey saddle for adulterous wives. The philandering hussy is placed on top of the peg by her cuckolded husband, and then the donkey is goaded into a gallop."

Nina pulled Daniel's sleeve. "Let's get out of here. I need some fresh air."

He accompanied her out into the street. "I didn't know you were so impressionable. Did you not realize the old man was just teasing you?"

Nina nodded, fanning herself briskly. Hot and cold flushes coursed up and down her body, and the thick pall of sweet-smelling incense that hung over the street was making her feel nauseous.

"If you agree to bring the collection to Europe," Daniel said, "I can make enquiries to see if any of my clients would be interested in buying it."

"Thank you," said Nina. "But I'm afraid I really have to go now."

"Have I done something wrong?"

"No. Bye."

Nina disappeared around the corner. If she had stayed with Daniel a minute longer she might have been sick right in front of him.

Even on her return home, it was a while before Nina managed to get over her nausea.

What on earth was it? she pondered. From the very first

moment of their meeting, it was as if her body had felt a physical revulsion for him.

However, when Daniel called her again, Nina agreed to meet up. The only omens she ever chose to believe were those with a prediction that she approved of.

9. JUST GOOD FRIENDS

1

Nina had been hoping to rekindle the bond and intellectual kinship that she and Daniel had enjoyed back on the train, but instead they fell into a strange and exciting game of feigning indifference towards each other.

Daniel was nothing Nina had imagined. After visiting Gu Ya-min's treasure chamber, he decided that there was no need to be a perfect gentleman in her presence. He spent much of his time with her now making scabrous and unflattering comments about other people and made no pretense of the fact that he found Nina "really rather attractive."

"Thank God I'm a cynic and a misanthrope," he told her, "and I have the good sense not to have an affair with you."

"It's me, not you, who has the good sense here," Nina said. "I prefer to steer well clear of cynical married misanthropes."

Pretty soon she figured out that Daniel didn't love Edna.

"The Chinese believe that it's a great virtue if a woman has no talent," he said. "Unfortunately, Edna is crazy talented."

"What are you complaining about?" Nina asked, surprised.

"Because I can't bury her talent in the ground. When I come home at night, I always find my wife inspired. When the muse starts hovering over Edna's shoulder, she forces her to rattle away on her typewriter until two in the morning."

"Have you tried buying a trombone and rehearsing in the next room?"

"I wish it would help, but during the Great War, Edna lived in London and soon learned to ignore even the bombs and sirens."

It was obvious that the problem was not Mrs. Bernard's talents. Her mother had died at childbirth, her father was a tough, uncommunicative man, and Edna had become accustomed to finding solace in the church, eventually becoming a religious prude. For her, everything related to sex was ugly and sinful, and she believed that a man and wife should "keep their minds and bodies pure." Daniel had deemed it unwise to explain his feelings on the matter or try to persuade her otherwise, and it had all ended with his banal and sordid little trips to the brothels.

"Alas, the woman I married is a complete cold fish, as unfeeling, flat, and one-dimensional as a flounder," Daniel sighed.

He had a weakness for lively, sensual women, and Nina shamelessly took advantage of it, constantly teasing him but not allowing him to get too close. Daniel returned the compliment by making fun of Nina's dream of one day having a legitimate income. Every time she shared her latest business idea with him, he couldn't resist the pleasure of cutting her down to size.

"For goodness sake," he told her, "why are you so eager to engage yourself in men's business? I can see the point of Edna's writing—she has a gift after all—but what do you have to offer?"

These "jokes," as he liked to call them, drove Nina up the wall. After each put-down she would promise herself that she would never discuss her business ideas with Daniel, only to seek his opinion again at the first opportunity. She felt too insecure too be alone with her dreams.

However, it was impossible to win approval or praise from Daniel.

"You're such a nitpicker," Nina raged after another put-down. "You're constantly putting me in the shade."

"I'm just protecting you from sunburn," Daniel said, shrugging. "You do want to be treated and regarded as a white lady, don't you?"

Still, he willingly helped with Nina's consulate business and gave her good advice on financial matters and how to keep her scam a secret.

He had photographed each item from Gu Ya-min's collection and sent the pictures to his friends in Europe, who were expert collectors and antique dealers.

"If you manage to strike a deal, you can keep the commission," he told Nina.

She was certain that Daniel had a crush on her, because he would often talk about her femininity, which he found impossible to resist.

"Thank God, you don't realize its power," he said.

"Sure I do," she protested.

"If you did, dabbling in something as banal as business wouldn't even occur to you. Can you imagine anything more absurd than Botticelli's Venus with a briefcase under one arm and an abacus under the other?"

"But she's butt naked."

"And she carries it off very well. People should stick to where their talents lie."

She felt that the inevitable would soon happen: Daniel would divorce Edna and ask Nina to marry him. But she was uneasy about her own divorce. Klim and Nina had had a church marriage and that wouldn't be so easy to dissolve. Besides that, Chinese law favored men, and if a husband refused to let his wife go, there was nothing she could do about it.

Should I pretend I've never been married to Klim? Nina thought. *He can't prove we're married without any documents. And anyway, there is no way he's going to find out in this huge great city.*

Just to be on the safe side, she asked Tony what the punishment in China was for a woman found guilty of having more than one husband. The answer was more than a little alarming: ninety lashes with the bamboo cane.

2

In summer 1923, not much was left in Nina's memory besides fights with Daniel, reconciliations, and crazy flirtation. She had hoped to keep their relationship a secret, but Daniel told her from the very beginning that he was not going to sneak about in the shadows. He didn't care what Edna or the rest of the world would think of him.

Whenever Nina began to worry—"People will see us!"—Daniel laughed at her. "How old are you? Thirteen? What are you afraid of?"

"You know perfectly well," Nina snapped. "I shouldn't draw attention to myself."

Daniel assured her that as long as she was under his protection, she had nothing to fear. It seemed as though he didn't realize how vulnerable Nina was, and there was no persuading him otherwise. He didn't risk anything, but Nina had lost a lot: the ladies who had been happily attending her parties now saw her as a potential danger to their marriages and a bad example for their teenage daughters. Increasingly, Nina started receiving cards with polite notes: "Unfortunately, we can't come to you tonight."

Jiří believed that Nina had gone crazy, getting into an

affair with Daniel.

"You'll destroy both of us!" he yelled at her. "Do you want Tamara kicking us out of her house? If Daniel hasn't proposed yet, he won't do it."

That made Nina scared. "Daniel can't live without me."

"Don't flatter yourself. His father-in-law is a police commissioner, and Mr. Bernard isn't such a fool as to upset him."

I should make Daniel choose, Nina thought again and again. *This situation can't continue indefinitely. Let him either marry me or leave me alone.*

But the thought of her victory was equally frightening to Nina. She was attracted to Daniel not by passion but by her desire to arrange her future. She always found something annoying about him—the tobacco smell or his irritating laughter. When indignant at something, Daniel would roll his eyes, and his pupils disappeared under his upper eyelids. When Nina was a child, her mother had told her about a "white-eyed monster" who comes to naughty children and carries them into the woods. Now that was Nina thought about when she was looking at her Mr. Right.

What if I'm unhappy staying with him? she thought. She knew that he was capable of leaving her behind if she lost her "feminine charm" or simply did something he didn't like. She couldn't expect eternal love from him, similar to Aulmans'. He was not that type of a person.

Anxiety made Nina ill; she felt weak, suffering from headaches and nausea. Sometimes it was so bad that she was unable to leave the house.

3

Everything was clarified in the beginning of September, and not in the way Nina had hoped.

After Japan had had a major earthquake and Edna had gone to Tokyo for her newspaper, Daniel called Nina and asked her if she wanted to visit the Chinese City.

But the heavy rain interrupted their walk, and they found shelter under the archway at the entrance to the spice shop. Daniel took off his jacket and put it around Nina's shoulders. They stood quietly in the moist dim, listening to the sound of the rain and inhaling the pungent herb aromas coming from the door to the shop.

"Should we run to the car?" Nina suggested.

She felt Daniel was looking at her in a new way, with annoyance and impatience, as if he had missed the target while hunting.

"Aren't you tired of pretending to be bashful school children?" he said and suddenly pulled her to his chest. "We both know how it ends."

Nina didn't expect him to be so straightforward. She tried to wriggle herself out of his hands.

"Do you want to get warm holding me like this? I'll give you your jacket back, or you'll crumple my dress."

Daniel didn't listen to her. "God is my witness, I'd tried to stop it before it was too late."

He ran his hand over her breast, and Nina, hardly realizing what she was doing, slapped him across the face. "Don't you dare!"

Daniel stepped away from her.

"What the hell—" he began but didn't finish and got out from the archway into the rain. A moment later his car speeded past her.

Stunned, Nina watched it disappear. *Did he dump me just like that?*

4

It took a long time for her to find a rickshaw, and Nina reached home only when it was already dark. Her dress was soaking and her teeth were chattering from the cold.

Now what? she thought in panic. *But it's not my fault! Daniel should blame himself for what happened. Who told him he could paw me about as though I'm a hooker?*

While Qin was preparing a hot bath for her, Nina paced in her bedroom. She prayed incoherently, then threw things on the carpet or twisted her fingers, deliberately trying to hurt herself.

What if Daniel spills the beans about her fake consulate? Oh no, he's not that sneaky.

I should calm down and develop an action plan, Nina told herself. *Nothing is yet lost. Tomorrow Daniel will call me, we'll make peace and forget about this stupid incident.*

"Your bath is ready, Missy," said Qin as she appeared in the doorway.

Nina took her clothes off and descended into the lavender-scented water.

"Today I went to the temple on Babbling Well Road," Qin said. "I lit red candles and burned joss sticks for Guan Yin goddess, so your labor will go easily."

Startled, Nina stared at her. "What labor? What are you talking about?"

A smile spread across Qin's round face. "Oh Missy, you don't have to hide from me. Do you think I haven't seen anyone pregnant before? You'll have a baby on the Chinese New Year, so you too should go to the temple and asked Guan Yin to give you a son."

5

Nina rushed into Tamara's room, pale and untidy.

"What's wrong?" Tamara gasped.

Nina collapsed on the low stool and pressed her knees to her chest as if something was burning her from inside.

"It's all over," she whispered, looking up at Tamara, her eyes full of tears. "Daniel left me. This morning I've got this—"

She handed Tamara his business card.

"I'm going to Guangdong province for a few months," he had written on its back side. "Take care of yourself."

"I don't get it—" Tamara began.

"That's not all," Nina said in a shaky voice. "I'm . . . I'm pregnant."

Tamara was silent for a while, trying to realize what had happened.

"I don't want any children!" Nina sobbed. "Maybe you know a doctor who . . . well, who can—" Her thoughts were scattering. "I should have guessed long ago. Oh, I'll poison myself!"

"There, there . . . " Tamara felt so sorry for her that she was about to cry too. "You'll be fine. How far along are you?"

"Five months."

Tamara scrutinized Nina's belly. It had just slightly rounded. "Keep the baby," she said firmly. "I have no other advice for you. Children are the best thing in the world. An abortion could result in infertility or some nasty complication."

"But how will I explain the child to everyone?" Nina moaned.

"We'll figure something out. Promise you won't make any rash decisions."

"All right," Nina replied almost inaudibly.

6

In the evening, Tony brought Tamara an orchid in a glossy pot.

"It's for you. Now kiss your victorious husband. I won in court, in polo, and on the stock exchange."

His head had a special smell, but it was so delicate that Tamara could feel it only on her first breath.

"Nina visited today," she said. "What do you think of her?"

"She's lovely." Tony raised his smiling eyes. "Let's have a chess match after dinner? If you win I'll be amazed. Today I'm feeling as lucky and shrewd as Odysseus."

Love and tenderness, thought Tamara. After all, it was very flattering that he, the best of husbands, was totally uninterested in the most fascinating of women.

"Nina's pregnant," Tamara said.

"Really? Who's the father?"

"Daniel Bernard, who else? And he immediately left for Guangdong province in order to bear no responsibility."

The news was such a shock for Tony that he lost a game of chess after all.

If you are enjoying *White Ghosts*, please leave a review on Amazon and Goodreads.
Your feedback is very important for the author.

THANKS!

10. THE POLICE CAPTAIN

1

At first Ada had been terrified that the Bernards would fire her, but it turned out that nobody gave her checkered past much thought. Her salary was so insignificant and she herself was so quiet and inconspicuous that it never occurred to Edna to check up on her background.

Mr. Bernard's books had long been catalogued and placed in order on the shelves and cabinets, and now Ada's job was to be on call as and when she was needed to find and bring a relevant book from the library.

Following Sam's advice, Ada came up with an additional task for herself. She would go to bookshops, copying the names of new titles, and then report them back to the Bernards. Sometimes they would choose a book or two, but more often they would tell Ada to use her own initiative and order the books herself. Naturally, she would always choose romantic novels, which she would read and then retell to Sam.

He would listen to Ada with great interest and then share the latest household gossip with her.

"Did you know that Yun has opened a secret cookery school?"

Every day boys aged ten to fifteen would climb through a hole in the fence and come to the servants' kitchen to study Yun's culinary arts.

One time Sam and Ada hid behind the garage and spied on Yun's students handing him small envelopes.

"Those are the fees for his lessons," Sam explained to Ada. "He gets a dollar apiece. Twenty boys mean twenty dollars. I wonder why Yun needs so much money?"

Every now and then Ada and Sam would split the cost of a lottery ticket and dream about their winnings.

"What would you do with your share?" Ada asked.

"I'd buy myself a library and hire you to manage it," Sam replied in a serious voice.

Ada laughed. "That's never going to work because I'm going to America."

They studied the globe, looking for San Francisco, Los Angeles, and New York.

The only fly in the ointment was Edna's father, Captain Hugh Wyer. Once a week, he would visit his daughter and proceed to terrify everyone in the house. Only Mr. Bernard was unafraid of the captain, but even he detested spending any time with the old man, and as soon as Wyer's car appeared in the driveway, he would take to his horse and gallop away.

More than anything, Captain Wyer loved to "instill order." He would go around the rooms, finding the tiniest faults and chastising the servants accordingly. Ada had been on the wrong end of a tongue lashing several times for a misplaced book or a creaking window frame in the library.

Sam called Wyer "the rotten fish."

"He ruins everything he touches. If we win the lottery," he told Ada, "I'll hire thugs to kill him."

2

That week, as usual, Captain Wyer appeared at the Bernard's at eight o'clock sharp. The lobby trembled and thundered under his heavy hobnail boots; the mirror reflected his tall figure in its habitual khaki jacket. Boy Two bowed and took the captain's cane and pith helmet.

"Breakfast! Now!" barked Wyer. "And tell your master and mistress I'm here and waiting for them."

The kitchen was thrown into complete pandemonium as the frightened kitchen staff dropped dishes and rattled pans to meet the order in the allotted regulation time. Ten minutes later on the dot, Boy One served up deviled kidneys, sizzling fried sausages, bacon, mushrooms and eggs, grilled tomatoes, and triangles of perfectly brown toast, delivered on an immaculate silver service.

When Sam served the coffee, his hands shook so much that the lid of the coffee pot rattled.

"Are you drunk, or just a gibbering idiot?" exploded Wyer, giving Sam the evil eye. "Get out of my sight, you imbecile!"

Having pronounced sentence on Sam, the captain then summoned Ada for interrogation. "Where's Mr. Bernard?"

"He went on an expedition to the province of Guangdong," she said, avoiding the old man's gaze. "He's looking for a supplier of rare teas."

"Has he gone completely mad? What kind of daft expedition is that?"

"I . . . I don't know, sir."

"The bounder," Wyer muttered. "Alright, I'll deal with him later. What's the news here?"

Ada wished there was something she could say but she could not think of anything.

The captain hurled his napkin onto his plate in his impatience. "What a driveling little fool! Can't you even string a sentence together?"

Finally, Edna entered the dining room, much to Ada's relief.

"Here she is!" cried the captain as he offered Edna his dry, yellowish hand.

She greeted her father and asked Sam to give her some coffee.

"Ms. Marshall, would you mind going to see if we have any letters today?" she asked.

When Ada came back with the mail, the other servants had already vacated the dining room. She hesitated at the door, not knowing whether she would be scolded for interrupting Captain Wyer, who seem to be talking about something important.

"These hussies are ruining good English families," he said, rolling his eyes. "Last week, there was a petition doing the rounds of the Shanghai Club to have every single one of these Russian jezebels expelled out of China for their loose moral behavior."

"Then you'll have to expel a lot of the English men as well," Edna replied. "Let's face it, their moral standards aren't exactly exemplary either."

"So you've found out, have you?"

"I've found out what?"

"That your philandering husband has gone and made Nina Kupina pregnant and left you to deal with the mess."

Edna recoiled visibly as if her father had slapped her. "That can't be true," she said in a barely audible voice, but her father wasn't listening.

"Daniel has no children with you, and it won't bode any good if he has an heir on the side. What if he decides to adopt the baby? What will happen then is that this Russian whore's bastard will inherit all your property."

Ada backed away and quietly slipped away from the dining room door.

3

Klim had been held up at work, and Ada waited impatiently for him at their apartment. She was eager to tell him the news about Nina's pregnancy.

Finally she heard keys turning in the door, footsteps, and the sound of something heavy being dragged along the floor. Ada ran out into the hallway and saw Klim pulling a large crate into their apartment.

"What is it?" Ada asked.

"A Victoria gramophone," Klim announced cheerfully. "Where do you think would be a good place to put it? Do you want to have it in your room?"

He dragged the crate to Ada's room and pulled a gleaming polished box out of the straw packaging.

"It's a beauty," he said. "See, the horn is neatly stored inside, and all the mechanical parts are made of nickel."

"How much did it cost?" Ada asked.

Klim waved his hand dismissively. He took a brand new record out of its envelope and started winding the Victrola's mechanism.

"Is *señorita* dancing?" he asked with a smile.

The sounds of a tango rumbled from the depths of the Victrola, and Ada put her hand on Klim's shoulder.

"Do you make enough money to pay for toys like this?"

"Who cares about money when you can tango?"

Ada leaned towards him. It was lovely when he brought all sorts of curious presents, and even better to have him all to herself to dance with.

Later, they had their dinner together in the kitchen. Ada had baked an apple pie, and it had been the first time the recipe had worked out. Klim was drinking tea from his recently purchased painted cup and was telling Ada about a story he had picked up about the rivalry between two dance halls in the French Concession. The owner of the first one had hired men to release a bag full of snakes onto his competitor's dance floor. The second man had got back at him by hiring thugs who just sat in his rival's premises spitting chewing tobacco all over the dance floor.

Ada listened politely but in the end she couldn't restrain herself any longer.

"Did you know that your wife is going to have Mr. Bernard's baby?" she asked. "But as soon as she got pregnant, he just left her."

Ada expected her words to make Klim furious, but he just shrugged.

"Everybody in our editorial office knows about it. A lot of people are jealous of Edna and happy to spread rumors like that around. They are saying that's what happens to a woman who concentrates too much on her work and not enough on her family."

Klim was much more worried about Edna's wounded pride than his own, and he had spent a long time taking the gossipers to task for showing pleasure in a colleague's misfortunes instead of standing by her.

"But what about you?" Ada asked. "Nina has cheated on you as well."

"Who cares? We weren't together for more than a year."

Klim told Ada that he had to get up early tomorrow and excused himself from the table, without finishing his tea.

"Whatever you do, don't tell anyone that Nina and I were married," he instructed Ada. "It would be better for both of us if Edna knows nothing about it."

4

RECEIPTS AND EXPENDITURES

Klim Rogov's Notebook

It might have been easier if Daniel Bernard had been a complete stranger to me. But we've shaken hands on many occasions at Edna's. The world of white Shanghai is a small one.

I don't fully understand why I'm so ashamed of Nina. We have nothing to do with each other anymore. Nevertheless, I still feel like a man who has donated his last coins to a church only to find out that the priest has squandered everything on drink.

I'm trying not to think about what has happened, but my desk is close to the door, so I can hear every word coming from the corridor and the smoking room where people are discussing the minutiae of Edna's misfortunes.

I started to avoid her out of embarrassment, the woman I owe my very survival to. She is perplexed by my behavior, unable to understand what's going on. It's hard enough when your loved one betrays you, but even more so when it seems that everybody else is turning their back on you. But I can't master my feelings. The sight of Edna, broken and gloomy, causes me to recall the craziest things from my childhood. I still remember the smallest details of the scenes that my father used to make if my mother so much as smiled at a younger or better-looking man. A bit of my father's envious green blood would appear to be flowing in my veins as well, and it takes me a great effort to stop myself from . . .

Well, I'm not going to put to paper some of the notions that come into my head at times like this.

Now that everybody knows who Nina is, it's not been difficult to track down her address, and yesterday I went to negotiate our divorce and put an end to this vile farce of a marriage.

It turns out my wife is living in a white mansion with a perfectly clipped lawn in the front yard. She's managed to acquire all the material things that she always dreamed of, but it would appear that all her well-laid plans have come to nought now that she is pregnant and no longer of any value to her sugar daddy lover. Alas, even the most gregarious and gorgeous courtesans don't remain in a powerful man's affections for long.

I wonder what will happen to my "sing-song girl"? Who will take care of her now?

While I was standing there looking at her house, a black Ford with bright white lights and yellow wheels came out of the gate, and I spotted Nina's face in the car window. I don't know if she saw me, or maybe she chose not to recognize me. Anyway, we never did meet.

For months I have been trying to work out what it was that brought Nina to Lincheng. Now it's all as clear as day to me. She went there for the sake of Daniel Bernard. But if that's the case, why did she bring me back to her compartment that night? I'm afraid I'll never get to the bottom of it.

I keep trying to accept that Nina will soon be giving birth to another man's child. Even though I have no rights over her any longer, it all appears to be some kind of sacrilege to me, a gross violation of the most basic laws of life. Now it seems incredible to imagine that at one time, little more than a couple of years ago, we were lying in each other's arms thinking up names for our future children. I wanted to call our daughter Katya after my mother, and if we had a boy we would have called him . . .

But there's no point writing any of this now. I'm only rubbing salt into my own wounds.

5

In his heart Klim's was dying to find someone to pick a reckless fight with, it didn't matter who. Being employed to write the newspaper's regular column on the city's criminal underworld, he didn't have long to wait for an opportunity to let out his pent-up frustration.

A police team in plain clothes had surrounded a house with a sign in English and Chinese saying: "Magic Cloud Pharmacy. Reliable remedies for all ailments."

The pharmacy's owner was not there, and Klim was waiting for him on the corner of the street, along with the head of the Drug Enforcement Division, Johnny Collor, and his assistant Felix.

Felix, a tall, dark-haired and hook-nosed young man,

had been a former Russian cadet.

"What foul weather!" he grumbled, shoving his reddened hands into the pockets of his great coat. "But who's complaining? This is much better than having to hide in barrels on the docks in the summer heat. The sun roasted us from above, and the mosquitoes were biting our butts from below. It was a whole fortnight before I could sit comfortably again after that operation."

Johnny peered around the corner.

"Here's our pharmacist," he whispered excitedly, pointing at the elderly Chinese man climbing up the pharmacy porch.

Short and stocky, Johnny resembled a gray-haired fox terrier, ready to lunge for his prey's throat. His eyes were shining, and he was constantly reaching for the holster under his jacket.

"Don't give any quarter, boys," Johnny warned Klim and Felix. "The pharmacy belongs to the Green Gang. Those bastards won't hesitate to put a bullet through your brain."

He looked at his watch and raised his hand. "It's time!"

Klim ran behind the policemen into the pharmacy and stood squinting under the bright light of a lamp. The policemen searched the place as calmly and efficiently as if they were on a training run. Glass crunched under their shoes, and the air was filled with ashes from a raked-up oven.

Klim looked around the cluttered rooms. Along the walls there were dark red cabinets with lots of drawers. The shelves were crammed with sealed pots, and on the table, next to the brass weights and writing implements, lay a large white doll studded with long needles. Its body was covered with lines showing the flow of *qi*, life energy.

Klim heard the sound of heavy boots on the stairs.

"There's a safe in the bedroom on the second floor, sir," cried Sergeant Trots.

Johnny had the pharmacist by his lapels.

"Ask him where the keys are," he told the translator.

The pharmacist started to babble something, spraying the policemen with his saliva in his terror. Johnny pushed him away in disgust.

"What is he saying?"

The translator pulled a sour face. "He doesn't understand a thing, sir. It seems he's from a different province and doesn't speak Shanghainese."

"The bastard's lying."

Johnny pulled a revolver out of a holster and shot the wall behind the pharmacist's back. The man gave a whimper and fell on the floor face down.

"Feeble people," said Felix through his teeth.

Johnny searched the pharmacist's desk. "Here are the keys. Let's go."

They went up the stairs. In the bedroom, a woman with two terrified children sat in the far corner of a big bed with a red cover on it.

"Clear them out," ordered Johnny, and the policemen quickly took them out of the room.

Behind the bed was a huge iron safe covered with an embroidered spread. A bronze candlestick and vases were placed on top of it. Johnny removed the spread and, after fiddling with the keys for a few seconds, finally had the safe open.

Klim craned his neck to see what was inside.

"Wow!" he whistled looking at the parcels piled up one on top of the other.

Felix pulled out a pen knife and cut several of the parcels open.

"It's Indian opium," he said after trying the dark sticky paste. "And here's some cocaine."

Johnny took a thick binder out of safe and called the translator over. "What are these papers?"

The Chinese glanced through it. "These are lists of suppliers, sir."

Johnny's eyes lit up. "Well, this should see our friendly

neighborhood pharmacist in prison for a while."

There was stamping on the stairs, and a boy of about fourteen burst into the room. He was hiding something under his green shirt.

"Grab him!" screamed someone from downstairs.

Sergeant Trots grabbed the youngster by his shoulder, but the boy took a revolver from inside his shirt and fired at him.

The sergeant, bleeding heavily, fell down the stairs. The youngster headed to the window and, crashing into Klim on the way, pointed his revolver at him.

This is it, Klim thought.

The revolver went off again, the boy yelped, and something heavy hit the floor.

A moment later Klim realized what had happened: Felix had hurled the heavy candlestick at the boy, breaking his wrist.

6

More police arrived on the scene followed closely by reporters and photographers. All of them wanted the full story from Felix, but he was too modest and left his boss to do the explaining.

"Felix Rodionov is that rare breed of man whose actions speak louder than his words," Johnny said proudly. "He came to our station hoping to get a job, but he was so emaciated that the commissioner was about to turn him down. However, I asked him, 'What can you do?' And he told me to try to attack him with a knife. What do you think happened? The son of a gun knocked the knife right out of *my* hand! If I've told you once, gentlemen, I've told you a thousand times: We shall continue to man our forces on the basis of race. The Russians are an asset to the force that the Chinese can never be."

Johnny then saddled up his hobby horse and began to hold forth on the perfidious Chinese and their numerous conspiracies against the ruling whites.

"More than two-thirds of our men are Chinese and Sikhs from India," he said warming to his theme. "The same could be said of the French Concession, but they have Vietnamese instead of Sikhs."

The reporters recorded his every word, and Klim who had heard his sermon many times before, went off to talk to Felix.

He found the young man sitting on a bench on the back porch, smoking and stroking a fat ginger cat at his feet.

"Thank you for saving my life," Klim said as he sat down next to him.

Felix sniffed. "My pleasure."

They got to talking. Felix had been an orphan from Omsk and had joined the cadets at a very young age. He and his fellow trainee officers had been among the first to be evacuated to Vladivostok and then to China after the outbreak of the civil war.

A Shanghai merchant had allowed the boys to stay in his house, and there they had lived in close quarters. Space had been so scarce that they had to take turns to sleep. It was hard to feed seven hundred teenagers, and the French Consul resolved to hold a lottery for the younger orphans, and that was how they raised funds. The majority of the boys dug graves and guarded warehouses for a living, and only a few, like Felix, had been lucky enough to find decent jobs.

"I really hope I'll get promoted to inspector one day," he said dreamily. "Inspectors get three hundred dollars a month and a paid vacation of seventeen days a year or, if you want, seven months every five years. But first I will need to distinguish myself."

"Do you have any ideas how you're going to do this?" Klim asked.

Felix nodded. "My friend works as a doorman at the Three Pleasures pub. He says that all the alcohol they sell there is bought duty-free and delivered by the local Czechoslovak Consul. I've suggested having him arrested a long time ago, but Johnny is reluctant to go there because it's a French protectorate. But the consul, Jiří Labuda, is a resident in the International Settlement, and therefore he comes under our jurisdiction."

"Who did you say?" Klim asked, stunned. "Jiří Labuda?"

"That's his name," Felix nodded. "If you want, we could track him down together. You'll get an exclusive for your paper, and I'll get my promotion. It's a great story—a respectable diplomat turned small-time crook."

Klim didn't know what to think. *What kind of people had Nina got herself mixed up with?*

"There won't be the slightest problem," Felix persuaded. "This Labuda is a sickly individual. One punch and he'll be done for. His driver won't be so easy. He's as big as an ox. But between the two of us, we'll be more than a match for them."

"Let's go hunting then," said Klim after a pause.

Felix beamed. "Good. I'll see you at the Three Pleasures tomorrow at seven o'clock."

11. THE HOUSE ARREST

1

As her pregnancy progressed, Nina stopped giving her parties.

Jiří was furious. "How are we going to pay our bills now?" he yelled at her. "You're no more a mother than I'm Napoleon. Have an abortion before it's too late."

Nina could have killed him on the spot.

"Don't ever talk to me about my baby again!" she whispered in such a cold fury that Jiří quickly retreated to the next room.

Don Fernando was also disappointed that Nina was bowing out of the liquor business and kept badgering her with new ideas for making money out of the Czechoslovak Consulate.

"I've got a brilliant idea," he said to Nina. "Why don't we ship liquor as a diplomatic cargo? They have brought in Prohibition in America, and the prices have gone through the roof. We can brew our own 'French wine' right here, in China, and smuggle it into the United States through

Canada."

Nina soon fell out with the Don as well. She felt that something amazing was happening to her, as if some immense tectonic shift was going on inside her body, and the idea of spending her time and energy on liquor seemed sacrilegious to Nina.

Her perception of the world was changing fundamentally. Street smells, such as car fumes, tobacco, and fried food, were all sickening to her, and the sight of homeless mothers with children would make her shudder with horror. Nina was incapable of thinking about anything except her baby. Her greatest pleasure was to visit the toy store or a workshop where they made adorable playthings for infants. The thought that caused her the most turmoil was the question of her child's citizenship. When the baby arrived, she would need to make sure that its documents were in order. But how was she going to do this? Would she really have to buy fakes? She was determined that there should be nothing false in her child's life.

The past and future took on a new meaning. Until recently, her fight with Daniel had seemed a complete disaster, but now she was glad they had broken up. *It would be quite something*, she thought, *if he were to divorce Edna and then find out about my pregnancy.*

Nina tried to shut Klim out of her mind. If she were to find him and tell him about their child, he was bound to assume that she was just trying to land him with someone else's baby. With all the scandal that had followed her friendship with Daniel, Klim was sure to assume they had actually had an affair.

Nina wanted her baby to be important not only for herself but for other people too, and she couldn't resist the urge to talk about it, if only to the servants. But they gave her such outlandish advice that she was left at a complete loss. According to them, an expectant young mother should never leave the house, wash her hair, or sew, and as for standing in the wind, well, that was totally out of the question.

Nina at least found some consolation with Tamara, who—thank God—had lost her interest in the parties and was happy to spend hours discussing matters relating to motherhood.

"I'm sure," Nina said, "everybody is critical of me for having a baby by an unknown father. There isn't a decent woman who will let me into her house anymore. Except for you, of course."

"You don't need anyone but me," Tamara said.

Nina thanked her for her kindness and at the same time thought that she was more reliant on Tamara than ever. There was no way Nina was ever going to find a husband now and she could forget about making money of her own with a baby to look after. The only role she could play from now on was to be Tamara's dependent.

2

"I want to buy something for Nina's child," Tamara said to her husband. "She and I will go to Yates Road."

Tony was horrified. "Is it safe for you to go that far? What if you slip a disk? You know how fragile your back is."

But Tamara was determined to take the risk, so he had a special chair made for her that two men could carry. He put an egg on its seat, chased the porters around the house several times, and only when the egg still remained on the seat intact was he satisfied. No automobile could have provided Tamara with such a smooth way to get around, especially on the Chinese roads with their cracks and potholes.

It was snowing when the servants took Tamara out for the first time that whole year. She squinted, laughed, and inhaled the cold air deeply.

"I can't believe how long I've allowed myself to be

cooped up in my own house," she said.

3

The English called Yates Road "Petticoat Lane;" you could find every imaginable type of undergarment there for all occasions and for all ages—from the cradle to the coffin.

The porters carried Tamara at a sprightly trot past the decorated shop windows. Behind her Nina rode in the Aulman's car followed by a number of servants pushing wheelbarrows that were to be used to deliver Nina's purchases to her house.

"Onwards to Mr. Bookers!" Tamara commanded imperiously from her chair. Nina's chauffeur nodded and slowly followed behind, ignoring the blaring horns of the impatient cars that overtook them. Nina, who was sitting in the back seat, could barely suppress her mirth as their procession seemed so comical to her.

The porters brought Tamara's chair into Bookers & Co., purveyors of the finest linen and maternity wear. While the servants and shop assistants made Mrs. Aulman comfortable, Nina wandered around the displays looking at satin blankets, canopies for cots, beautifully embroidered bedding sets, and silver rattles.

"I can't choose anything," she said, looking totally lost. "There are so many lovely things; it's making my head dizzy."

"You sit and have a rest," Tamara replied. "I'll sort everything out."

Shop assistants piled towers of baby's clothes in front of them to be inspected. Suddenly Nina gasped. The hem of her dress was wet, and an embarrassing puddle had formed on the floor under her seat.

"Your waters have broken!" Tamara exclaimed. "Quick! Get in the car!"

They didn't make it home. Two trucks had collided on

the corner of Weihaiwei Road, and the traffic had ground to a standstill. Nina's little girl was born on the back seat of the car. The chauffeur delivered the baby under Tamara's close directions from her chair, while the porters chased away curious onlookers.

4

The Three Pleasures pub was on a small street called Blood Alley. There wasn't a day that went by there without a fight, but the imperturbable Vietnamese police would only intervene if knives or firearms were involved.

Every evening Felix would leave his motorbike at the hitching post, instruct a Chinese boy to guard it, and together with Klim, would enter the pub—to wait for the Czechoslovak Consul to appear.

People sat around battered tables—sailors of all ranks and nationalities, Chinese generals without armies, and the usual lowlifes that inhabit any port. Sweaty girls with messy hair would try to sit on their laps, and every now and then a Malayan midget would appear from a dark recess and offer a pipe of opium.

"If you don't have enough money, I can sell you some opium water for five coppers," he would say enticingly to the pub's patrons.

Klim knew exactly how this opium water was produced. The Malayan would clean the unburned remnants from the opium pipes and boil them in water on the premises.

"This will give you a better high than the purest cocaine," the midget promised, and he made a grotesque face to portray the ecstasy his customers derived from his product.

Felix drank his beer and told Klim about his friends from the cadets. Recently, a number of them had started talking about returning home. They felt they were just wasting their time in China, while in Russia they could get a free education and perhaps become an engineer or a dentist. At least, that's what they had read in the leaflets that somebody had placed stealthily in the back porch of the Russian church.

"The police know who are printing these leaflets," Felix grumbled. "The Bolsheviks send their agents to Shanghai to lure the youngsters back home. The white emigrants are a real thorn in their side, and the Kremlin fears that one day we might gather our forces together and win Russia back."

"Are there many young people who believe the Bolsheviks?" Klim asked.

"Oh yeah, plenty. One of my friends returned to Vladivostok and promised to write to me regularly to let me know how things were going there. We agreed between the two of us that he would send me a photograph with his letter. If the picture showed him standing, that would mean that everything was fine, but if he was sitting down, then that would be a sign that all was not so well in the land of the Soviets. You know what kind of picture my friend sent me? He was lying prostrate on the floor."

5

After a couple of weeks waiting, Jiří Labuda finally turned up at the Three Pleasures, dressed in a silk top hat and a dark green coat with a beaver fur collar.

Klim watched the little Czech's reflection in the oblique mirror behind the bar. Jiří had a brief chat with a tall one-eyed Chinese man and asked the waiter for a beer. After nursing his drink for a few minutes, he quickly ducked into the corridor heading to the rooms at the back.

"Let's see what he's up to, shall we?" Felix whispered to Klim.

They swiftly passed a smoky kitchen and a number of closed doors. Female voices could be heard laughing behind them. There was a man lying on the floor next to the back door, either drunk or dead. Felix stepped over the man's legs and looked out.

"Follow me," he told Klim and ran back into the saloon. "Labuda has a car full of liquor."

They rushed out onto the main street, which was filled with drunken sailors, and nearly fell under the wheels of a Ford leaving the back yard. Klim stared at it in shock. It was Nina's car!

Felix untied his motorbike from the hitching post and jumped into the saddle. "Let's go!"

They drove down the street, deftly dodging trucks and horses. Klim's heart was sinking. Was Nina really involved in Labuda's scam? But how could she, when she was about to bring a child into the world? What was she thinking of?

In a few minutes, the Ford crossed the International Settlement border.

"We're going to catch that Labuda red-handed," Felix shouted excitedly. "The Czechs have no special rights here, so he's not going to get off that easily."

When the Ford turned into one of the empty streets near the racecourse, Klim realized that Jiří was on his way to Nina's.

The road was dark and deserted, and only the dimly lit windows of the richly appointed villas could be seen beyond the deep snow-covered gardens.

Klim leaned in towards Felix's ear. "We need to arrest Labuda right now. Otherwise, he'll take us to his buddies, and we might not be able to deal with all of them."

Felix nodded. He speeded up, passing the Ford, and blocked its path. Brakes screeched, and the car nearly skidded off the curb.

"Are you blind or drunk?" shouted the driver, leaning out of the car window. He stopped mid-sentence when he saw the police badge in Felix's hand.

Klim jumped off the motorbike and threw open the rear door of the car.

"By what right?" Jiří shrieked in fear.

Felix shoved his revolver right into Jiří's face. "What do you have here?" he asked, pointing at the cases piled on the seat.

"Nothing in particular—"

Klim took out a penknife, tore open the cover—and froze. The case was packed with rifle barrels.

"They're not mine!" Jiří whimpered. "They made me do it! It's all Nina's fault—"

Klim hit him hard on the shoulder. "Shut up!"

Felix's eyes glowed with excitement. "Do you have a license for these weapons? No? Then we'll have to take you down to the police station to answer a few questions."

He got into the back seat next to Jiří and put a gun to the terrified driver's head.

"Go to Nanking Road. And don't even try any dirty tricks, or I'll blow your brains out. Klim, could you take my motorbike to the station?"

The door slammed, the car pulled away and disappeared into the cold mist.

Klim stood in the street, looking after them. He was sure that Labuda would pin all the blame on Nina and she would be under arrest in no time.

6

Klim wasn't used to driving a motorbike, and it took him a while to get to the Nanking Road police station.

He saw Felix in the waiting room.

"You won't believe what a catch we've made," he said excitedly. "Johnny and I asked Labuda for his documents and the address of his superiors in Prague, and you know what? It turns out he's an impostor. He appointed himself as consul and fooled the Chinese officials to avoid paying customs duties on liquor."

"Where did he get the rifles?" asked Klim.

"He says the Germans gave them to him. But I'm sure he's lying. We don't have any German smugglers here."

Klim was relieved a little. It seemed that Labuda had said nothing about Nina so far.

"Labuda got hysterical," Felix continued, chuckling. "He was crying like a baby up there, hitting his head against the wall. We put him into the cell to cool down, and I reported everything to Captain Wyer."

Johnny Collor came up to them and gave Felix a friendly pat on the shoulder. "You deserve a medal, mate."

Klim was questioned as a witness, and when the papers were signed, Johnny sent him to the Commissioner's office. "Wyer wants to have a word with you."

7

The room was furnished with cheap furniture and portraits of kings and presidents of the Great Powers.

"Sit down," Wyer told Klim, pointing at a worn chair. "Are you the one who covers the Criminal Chronicle in the *Daily News*?"

Klim nodded. "Yes, I am."

Wyer had a cold and kept clearing his throat hoarsely.

"When you write an article about today's arrest, make sure to insert the notion that the suspect cohabited with a woman named Nina Kupina and that he's the father of her child. Am I clear?"

It was clear as day: Wyer wanted to save Edna's honor and put all the blame for his son-in-law on Jiří.

"Nina Kupina has just given birth, and we have put her under house arrest," said the captain. "During the interrogation, Labuda told us that she was the one who made him establish a false consulate. Don't forget to mention that too."

Klim's heart skipped a beat. Obviously, the captain was going to send Nina to jail. And the heroes responsible for making it all happen would be none other than Klim Rogov and Felix Rodionov.

"I need more details for my article," Klim said. "Can I

have a look around the suspects' house and speak to the guards?"

"Why?" Wyer frowned.

"My editor wouldn't accept my material without a comment from them."

"The man sounds like an imbecile," Wyer muttered, but he nevertheless obliged Klim with a note for the chief of the guard.

8

At Nina's house, Klim demanded to be allowed to speak to the prisoner, but the pot-bellied duty sergeant didn't even want to listen to him.

"Come in the morning," he said. "It's too late today."

Klim handed him his silver watch. "I need to talk to the prisoner *now*."

The sergeant weighed the watch in his palm.

"Well, you can try if you want, but I'd say she probably isn't in the mood for an interview at the moment."

As they entered the ransacked living room, the lower-ranking officers who had been playing cards promptly stood to attention.

"The suspect is in her room and all is in order, sir," one of them reported.

A baby's cry could be heard from the second floor, and without waiting for permission, Klim ran upstairs. He couldn't find Nina's bedroom in the dark, and it seemed to him that the baby's screams were coming from all directions.

Finally, Klim saw a door with a faint crack of light underneath it. He knocked and entered the room.

"What else do you want?" groaned Nina and fell silent, staring at him.

She was slumped on her bed—barely recognizable, disheveled and with dark circles under her eyes. A baby, its little face distorted from crying, was wriggling in her arms.

The room had been trashed by the police. The large rug lay in a heap on the floor; Nina's lingerie, papers, and bits of broken chair were strewn all over the place.

"Nina . . . " Klim called quietly.

She pressed her hand to her mouth and started to cry, her whole body shaking.

Klim looked at her, not knowing what to do. He took off his coat and sat down next to her, averting his gaze from the baby.

"I can't feed Katya," Nina said between sobs.

So she's called her Katya after all, Klim thought. *As we had decided.*

The girl butted her head against Nina's distended breast but was incapable of taking the nipple.

"Put something under her neck," Klim said. "It's difficult for her when you're holding her like that."

For a while, they fussed over the baby, every now and then exchanging angry whispers.

"Don't you see, you have to lift her."

"No, she's uncomfortable that way."

Finally, Katya figured out what was required of her, and Nina leaned her head back on the pillow. She was so tired she could hardly keep her eyes open.

"If they send me to jail, will you take care of Katya?" she asked.

"I won't abandon your daughter," Klim said flatly.

"She is your daughter as well."

That's all I need, Klim thought. *Now, she's going press gang me into her crew of "gullible" fathers along with Bernard and Labuda.*

"You don't have to lie me to get what you want," he said. "If I promise to do something I always keep my word."

"Get the hell out of here," Nina whisper, her jaw trembling. "If you don't believe me, there's just no point."

With great difficulty, Klim succeeded in mastering his emotions.

"Do you have a lawyer?" he asked.

Nina nodded. "Yes. His name is Tony Aulman. He's promised to help me and Jiří."

"Is it true that you and Labuda pulled that scam with the Czechoslovak Consulate?"

"I had no choice. We didn't have any money left, and I couldn't think of anything better."

"So you started selling guns?"

"What?"

Klim told her the story of Jiří's arrest, and Nina was stunned.

"I had no idea this was going on," she said. "We were only selling champagne and cognac, and I told Jiří to stop all operations until I had the baby."

"Well, then, he obviously didn't listen to you," sighed Klim. "Now Wyer wants me to write that the father of your baby is Jiří, not Mr. Bernard."

"Why didn't you tell him about the night you and I spent together in Lincheng? It is almost exactly nine months since then."

"Nina, stop it!"

"I know I've wronged you badly. But you surely aren't planning to take revenge upon me like that. After all, you did play your part in getting me pregnant."

"But did I?"

"You slipped out of the railroad car and never even left me a note. I was waiting so long for you!"

Klim had become so accustomed to being the injured party that Nina's words baffled him.

"I was late," he said with indignation. "You were the one who came to Lincheng for the fun of it; I went there because I had a job to do."

"What's taking you so long?" the sergeant shouted from the corridor. "My shift is almost over."

Klim rose to his feet. "I have to go." He picked up his coat and headed for the door.

"Wait!" Nina called him. "I . . . well . . . Thanks for

coming over."

Apart from the encounter in Lincheng, this was the first time in a year and a half Nina had made it clear that she appreciated her husband.

"I'll be back tomorrow," Klim said and left the room.

He walked quickly through the monotone city, trying to make sense of what had happened. His confusion gave way to hope. What if Katya really was his daughter? Klim was completely unprepared for this eventuality and had no idea what he should do about it.

He had always wanted children, but when he thought about them, he imagined that he would be well-established with a house of his own and a loving and unquestionably loyal wife. And now what? On the one hand, Klim could not remember with any certainty whether he and Nina had been careful that night, but on the other hand, only a very naïve person could take Nina completely at her word. She had proven many times that honesty wasn't her strong suit.

Yet despite all this, Klim was overwhelmed by a totally inappropriate, inexplicable joy. *Nina had come back into his life.* And if she had given birth to Daniel Bernard's baby, then so be it. Many people bring up children who aren't theirs, and the world hadn't stopped spinning on its axis as a result.

If only he could keep Nina out of jail! Klim lifted his eyes to the magnificent winter sky. Countless stars peeped over the roofs of the city like an audience at the Coliseum, waiting with bated breath for the outcome of the battle unfolding before their eyes.

12. TWO BABY GIRLS

1

Nina shuffled around the house in a delirious trance. Her body wouldn't obey her, and she had had to turn her life on its head in order to adapt to her house arrest and ensure that she and Katya had the basic provisions they needed.

Terrified, her servants had scattered to the four winds; her financial assets had been seized, and the police could barge into her bedroom at any time. The telephone had been confiscated, and Nina felt completely cut off from the world. She didn't even know what she had been accused of and what was going to happen to her.

How could Jiří have used my car and house to trade arms behind my back? she wondered. He had the courage and decisiveness of a mouse, and ever since Nina had known him, the most daring thing he had ever done was to tease and irritate her.

It must have been Don Fernando who had put him up to it, Nina decided. *Oh, I'll take him down a peg or two when I get out!*

Klim came to visit her again, and Nina could sense immediately that he didn't even want to look at Katya. He didn't hold the baby, didn't ask how she was doing, and every time Nina started talking about their little girl he tried to change the subject. Katya was not a blessing for him but a problem and his attitude hurt Nina deeply.

"Why are you bothering to help me?" she asked him. "If you think I'm lying to you about Katya, what do you hope to gain from having anything to do with us?"

"Nothing," Klim snapped. "Well . . . to some extent, it was my fault you're under arrest in the first place. We're separated now, of course, but you're still not a stranger to me. And you've just had a baby . . . So, now you understand and that's that."

But Nina couldn't understand a thing.

Tony Aulman was the next visitor.

"I have two pieces of news," he said, "one good and one bad. Which one do you want to hear first?"

"The good one," Nina said hopefully.

Tony brought in a smiling Chinese woman with a wrinkled face.

"She's a nanny," he said. "She'll help you out with the baby."

Nina didn't even want to hear about entrusting her Katya to a stranger, but Tony was adamant. "If you're exhausted and not getting enough sleep, you'll end up spouting all sorts of nonsense to the investigators and find yourself in prison."

Nina forced herself to hand over her little girl to the nanny.

"You can still feel the cold air on this woman's clothes," Nina moaned after the nanny had left the room with the baby. "What do you think is so funny?" she snapped at Tony. "Katya will catch a cold in no time."

Tony didn't try to argue or persuade her otherwise.

"I remember when Tamara gave birth, she got anxious over every little thing too," he said, smiling.

"What's the bad news then?" Nina asked.

Tony frowned. "Last night, Jiří died in his cell."

"What?"

"I was told he died of a brain hemorrhage."

Tony took Nina's shaking hand and looked into her eyes. "You'll probably think that what I'm about to say is the height of cynicism. But I think this is your only way out. You need to lay all the blame on Jiří's shoulders. You must say that he never told you about his shady liquor and arms dealings and that you had no idea that his Czechoslovak Consulate was a fake. Don Fernando is out of the city now and the chauffeur didn't have a clue what was going on, so the police have nothing to work on."

"I see," said Nina in a trembling voice.

Tony patted her on the shoulder. "Tamara and I will take care of Jiří's funeral."

"Thank you," Nina sobbed. "It's my fault: I forced him to become a consul."

"Jiří knew what he was letting himself into, so you can't take all the blame on yourself. Tamara asked you to call her as soon as you're allowed to use the telephone. She sends you her best regards."

2

RECEIPTS AND EXPENDITURES

Klim Rogov's Notebook

I didn't write the article about the Czechoslovak Consul's arrest, and Wyer called me demanding an explanation. Without further ado, I told him that Katya was my daughter and I wasn't prepared to assign paternity to the late Mr. Labuda.

I thought this turn of events would please Captain Wyer, but I've evidently misjudged him. He yelled at me so loudly that I had to hold the receiver a good foot away from my ear. He brought up my unfortunate nationality, my corrupted country, and my own vices.

"How much did she pay you to come up with this balderdash?" he asked.

The captain was so infuriated that I had ignored his orders that he failed to realize that my "balderdash" would now make his and Edna's life much easier. I didn't argue with him though and eventually hung up.

Soon after, Edna called me and proposed going for a walk along the Bund.

"My father has just informed me that you have recognized Nina Kupina's child as your own," she said, perplexed. "I'm grateful to you for this noble gesture, but you shouldn't have taken my husband's sin upon yourself. I'm afraid this won't stop all the gossipers. They'll just say that you're paying me back for my help. Do you at least know who this Nina is?"

I had no choice but to admit to her that the woman that had caused her so much pain was my wife.

"Why didn't you tell me before?" Edna gasped, and her face darkened. "Now I see what's going on. When you found out how rich my husband is, you deliberately put your hussy of a wife onto him. You cooked up this scheme to blackmail Daniel and make him pay you off to clear his reputation."

There was no point trying to appeal to her logic; Edna wasn't able to see things reasonably. She needed to find a scapegoat for her misfortunes, and, of course, she was too blind to see through her lecherous husband.

"My father warned me that you Russians are unscrupulous swindlers," she shouted. "But you won't get a penny from us. Daniel was right to leave the city."

On her return to the editorial office, Edna packed up her things and told Mr. Green she was quitting forthwith.

"Happy now?" she spat at me on her way out. "I did everything I could to provide you with employment and security, and now you've driven me out of the job I love. I could make a scandal and show everyone your true colors, but I'm so disgusted I can't even bring myself to be in the same room with you."

What was I supposed to say? That Edna was deceiving herself to cover up for her husband? That she was looking for an excuse to leave her job and crawl into a hole in order to avoid seeing or hearing anyone? Or should I have disavowed Nina and told Edna that we are estranged and that my wife and I have nothing to do with each other?

Unfair accusations make me angry, and I didn't feel like running after my accuser to justify my actions. I wrote a letter to Edna, but she didn't answer, and I'm not sure if she even read my explanation or just threw it away.

Perhaps, in other circumstances, I might have found a way to make peace with her, but I can't deal with this right now. I can do little to help Nina with her court case and my sense of powerlessness in the face of the blunt and clumsy legal machine is overwhelming me.

I wanted to talk to Felix about the investigation but I couldn't find him. Neither Johnny nor the other boys at the police station know where he is. They seem to think that he's gone on vacation. But how could he have left without saying anything to anyone?

Nina is incredibly lucky to have Tony Aulman on her side. He is a brilliant lawyer and has found an ingenious loophole in the law. It turns out that the International Settlement police don't have the right to initiate a case against Nina at all due to the fact that she has not committed any crime on its territory.

Tony believes that if he put some pressure on the judge who signed the arrest warrant, Nina will eventually be released. The irony of all this is that I, who have always condemned bribery and backroom deals, am now ready to worship the ground that Aulman and his connections walk on.

After a lot of trouble, I finally gained permission for Katya to be baptized, and brought Father Seraphim to Nina's house. In Shanghai, there are dozens of Russian priests without parishes, and they make some extra income by administering the sacraments as and when they are required.

Most of the time Father Seraphim has to work as a whipping boy at the Big World entertainment center. The audience at boxing matches gets great pleasure seeing their plucky Chinese fighters vanquishing such a huge "white ghost."

During the ceremony he was terribly ashamed of his beaten-up face, but I told him that neither Nina nor I condemned him for it. After all, he needs to make a living as much as the rest of us. However, Nina was not very happy about Katya being baptized by a gladiator priest with a black eye.

I had hoped that our shared concerns would bring Nina and me closer, but everything I do seems to upset her, and even if she doesn't say it to my face, I can sense it.

When I come to see her, I try to be as circumspect, businesslike, and serious as I can, feeling like a sapper trying to defuse an unexploded bomb. No matter how carefully I tread, an explosion could occur at any moment for the most trivial reasons.

When Nina learned that I was sharing an apartment with Ada, she hit the roof.

"You've done well for yourself," she said in a tone that implied that I was an incurable philanderer.

As with Edna, it was useless to appeal to reason, and the only answer I got to all my protestations of innocence was: "You must take me for a complete idiot." But at the same time, Nina wants me to believe that her relations with Jiří and Daniel Bernard were also completely innocent.

I can't imagine what Nina and I are going to do when she is finally released from her house arrest. Will she just turn to me and say, "Thank you for your help. But that'll be all now"? Or will she decide to try to make a go of it?

If she decides the latter, what we are going to do about Ada? She's too young to get by on her own, and if she were to live with us, I know that she would be unbearably jealous. Teenagers are a handful at the best of times.

Ada doesn't yet know that I have achieved a reconciliation of sorts with my wife. I've told her that I have a lot of work on and that is why I have been coming home late. I can't face telling her the truth. If I were to mention Nina and Katya, Ada would only try to persuade me that I'm going to be stuck in a loveless relationship with the mother of another man's child.

Babies often resemble one of their parents, and I wish I could find at least some of my features in Katya's little face. But unlike Nina and me, she is blonde, and no matter how hard I try, I can't dispel the image of Daniel Bernard's golden mane from my mind.

I'm constantly trying to convince myself that bloodline and paternity issues are of no importance to me. Whoever her father is, it's thanks to Katya that I now have a means of winning my wife back, and hopefully, one day getting my life back on track.

3

Mr. Green was visibly upset. "What's the matter with you, Mr. Rogov?"

Klim had promised to write an article about a gang of thieves that had been operating in the locker rooms at the Chinese baths, but he had come into the office empty-handed.

"This isn't like you," the editor-in-chief said. "Maybe you're not well? Or has something cropped up in your private life?"

Klim was looking over Mr. Green's shoulder out of the window. It was raining. The snow had melted, and the city had become gray and brown.

"Go home," Mr. Green said, "and don't show your face in here again until you've sorted out whatever it is that is bothering you."

Klim silently put on his coat, went outside, and got a tram.

Mr. Green had a point: Klim hadn't been able to concentrate on his work at all that day. Thanks to Tony Aulman's efforts, all the allegations against Nina had been dropped, and today the judge was due to revoke her house arrest.

Klim couldn't believe that finally the changes he had waited for so long were about to happen in his life. Yesterday he had bought a pram with a pink silk lining for Katya. Nina had been excited. "Now she'll be able to go for lots of walks."

"Don't think that I don't appreciate what you're doing," she had said to Klim on his way out. "I just have too much going on. Come back tomorrow. I should get back home from the court by eleven."

Klim jumped off the tram steps at the intersection of Nanking Road and Tibet Road. At the crossing he saw a large crowd gathered. Little boys had climbed street lamps and were calling to each other, "Oh! Wow! Look at that!"

The first thing Klim noticed was a set of long black skid marks on the road, then a broken pram with a pink silk lining lying on its side on a nearby waterlogged lawn.

A police officer in a raincoat cut through the crowd, shouting, "Are there any witnesses? Did anyone see what happened?"

"They were hit by a black car," a voice in the crowd answered.

"It didn't even stop. The nanny and the baby were killed instantly."

Klim came closer. The wind threw a fine drizzle onto his face. Reflections of the buildings in the puddles swam before his eyes, and then out of the corner of his eye, he saw two figures on the pavement. One big one and one small one. Klim already knew who they were, but could not bring himself to look at them.

4

RECEIPTS AND EXPENDITURES

Klim Rogov's Notebook

I feel like everything inside me is hardening and stiffening like brittle salt crystals.

There's nothing between Nina and me except our irreparable misfortune. Why do we need to see each other? What do we possibly have to discuss? The depth of each other's grief?

Nina is either completely hysterical or searching for someone to blame. When I came into the house she looked at me as if I was Katya's murderer. After all, if I hadn't bought that damned pram, Nina wouldn't have sent the nanny out for a walk.

"You don't even want my daughter to exist," she told me and then threw herself on the sofa sobbing. "I'm sorry, I'm sorry! I just can't carry on living like this. My life has no aim or meaning anymore."

And I, of course, mean less to her now than ever before.

5

There was a surprisingly large crowd at Katya's funeral—many just curious to see the infamous and disgraced Ms. Kupina.

Nina was too wrapped up in herself to notice anyone, let alone take offense. In the church and then at the cemetery, she stood apart from everyone else, a fragile figure with a thick black veil pulled over her velvet hat.

"Leave me alone," she repeated lifelessly whenever anybody came up to her to offer their condolences.

After the funeral, Klim took her to the House of Hope, so she wouldn't have to deal with all this "sympathy."

She entered the apartment and slumped down on a stool in the kitchen.

Ada stared at her with wide eyes. "What's that on your breast?" she asked, noticing two wet spots spreading on Nina's black dress.

Nina looked at her blankly. "It's the milk that should be feeding my daughter."

Hearing this, Klim felt crushed inside.

Evening fell, the room became dark, and Ada wanted to light the lamp, but it had run out of oil.

Klim rose. "I'll go and get some." He had to do something; he couldn't just sit next to Nina, slowly sinking with her into utter despair.

He grabbed his umbrella and went out into the street. Low chanting voices could be heard from the Buddhist temple on the corner, competing with the noisy street stalls parked at its gate.

"Fresh almond and lotus seed squash for sale!" the street sellers yelled. "Hot shrimp soup! Noodles! Rice noodles!"

It seemed to Klim that he could hear the sound of a baby crying over their shouts. *Now I'm beginning to hallucinate,* he thought.

"Flavored tea eggs! Pancakes! Watermelon seeds!"

Klim passed along the temple fence and almost tripped over a pile of rags lying under a streetlamp. Without knowing why he inspected the rags with the tip of his umbrella . . . and froze. It was a new-born Chinese girl with her umbilical cord still attached to her belly. She was no longer crying but jerked her little hands, blue with cold.

Klim looked around. The mother, of course, was nowhere to be seen. He knew that prostitutes and beggars often abandoned their unwanted children in the street in the hope that someone might pick them up. If no one did, then the baby wouldn't have long to suffer, an hour or two at most. According to the statistics, up to forty dead street children or abandoned babies were found in Shanghai every day.

Klim unbuttoned his coat and held the baby next to his chest as though she were a puppy.

It was a coincidence that bordered on the miraculous, as if the benevolent Chinese gods had taken pity on him and placed Katya's soul into a new body. She was not a white girl, but in the greater scheme of things, race and color were not really their concern.

He ran to the House of Hope, bounded up the staircase to his apartment. The light was on in the kitchen; Ada had found a church candle and placed it up on the shelf they used for dishes.

Klim grabbed Ada's apron hanging from a nail in the wall, put it on the kitchen table, and carefully took the baby from his bosom.

Nina watched in horror at the disheveled big-headed creature with its eyes screwed up into small slits.

"Where did you get it from?" she gasped. "Take it away!"

"It's too late," said Klim, panting. "In China, if you save someone's soul, you have to take care of it until you or it dies. The baby is hungry. Your breasts are swollen with milk. You'll feel better if you feed her."

"Are you crazy?"

"She's going to die!"

"Do you think you are going to replace my Katya with—*this*?"

Ada put her hands on her hips. "And you're very much

mistaken if you think I'm going to put up with a screaming child in my apartment. You should take it to a convent or an orphanage. The nuns will take care of it."

"The child will stay here," Klim said stubbornly.

"How are you going to feed her?" cried Ada. "You're at work all day long."

Without taking her half-mad eyes from Klim, Nina ran her hand over her breast. Her hands were shaking, but she nevertheless began to unbutton her mourning dress.

Ada howled in disgust. "It's probably covered in lice."

"And so were you when we first arrived here," Klim barked. "Now do me a favor, go to your room."

With an offended air, Ada stomped out of the kitchen, slamming the door so hard that the candle flame went out.

Nina sobbed in the dark.

"Do you really want to keep this child?" She sounded like a person on the verge of doing herself a mischief but still hoping for salvation.

"I don't know how we're going to do it . . . but if we don't—" Klim hesitated and avoided finishing his sentence.

He heard the stool scrape across the kitchen floor in the darkness. The girl mewled softly and smacked her lips. Klim sighed, relieved. Nina had chosen the path that led to life.

He found the matchbox and lit the candle. Nina was sitting with her eyes closed, tears streaming from under her lashes.

"There you go," Klim said, forcing a smile. "Now you're caring for her as well."

"This is an insult to the memory of my daughter," Nina said. "No one could ever replace her."

"I would never want her to replace Katya. But I believe she's been given to us to fill the gaping hole."

Nina was silent for a long time.

"It's my fault that Katya died," she said at last. "I didn't tell you, but three days ago, Wyer called me and told me to get out of Shanghai. He said, 'I don't care who the father of your baby is. People believe that she's Daniel Bernard's daughter, and I will not have you and her bringing disgrace down on my family.' I refused to leave, and then he rang again and said I would have no one to blame but myself for what was about to happen."

"Do you think that Wyer sent someone to kill Katya?"

"The car deliberately swerved onto the sidewalk, hitting the nanny and the pram. If I had been taking her out for a walk that day, it would have been me that died."

Nina buttoned up her dress and rose, still holding the girl.

"Let her stay with me for a while. I don't know what I'm going to do with all this milk."

Klim nodded slowly. He could hardly take in what he had heard.

6

Klim called for a taxi and accompanied Nina to her house.

He imagined that every driver coming towards them was an assassin sent to kill Nina.

"Be extremely careful," he told her repeatedly. "Lock the doors and close all the shutters. What if we really do have to leave Shanghai?"

"It's not going to be possible for the time being," Nina said. "You can only work at an English language newspaper or news agency, so our only options are Peking or Hong Kong. But we have to get there first and we don't have enough money."

Their situation was untenable: Klim lived from one paycheck to the next, and Nina's account had been frozen.

At her house, they put the baby into Katya's outfit. It seemed unreal to see her lying in the bed where only two days earlier their baby had been sleeping.

Nina started to cry again, and Klim hurriedly took her

out of the nursery.

"We're not going to give up," he whispered, hugging Nina's shoulders.

Klim was afraid that she would say that there was no 'we,' but she said nothing. Emboldened a little, he recited his reassurances like an incantation: "Everything will be alright. Everything will fall into place."

"It really doesn't matter to you, what child is lying in that bed," Nina said suddenly, with a tortured look in her eyes. "But why are letting me know about this now? Why now?"

Klim was taken aback. "I'm just trying to help you."

"Exactly!" Nina freed herself from his arms. "These aren't your sufferings. You're not sharing them with me, you're just another 'sympathizer.' You would never have brought me this Chinese girl if you had thought Katya was your daughter. As far as you were concerned, Katya was just my toy, and you really don't see the difference between her and this other girl lying in that nursery. You think that if one toy is lost or broken, you can always just get me another one."

"Why are you always so unkind and unfair?" Klim began. "I did it because I love you—"

"Hell no!" she interrupted. "You don't accept me for what I am, the same way as you didn't accept Katya. For you, I'm just a woman that you don't want to share with anybody else."

Klim felt as though his whole life had just collapsed in on itself.

"And who am I for you? Just a substitute for Daniel Bernard? If he hadn't left you, you wouldn't have given me the time of day."

It was a foul, insane, and meaningless fight. They hurled the most appalling accusations at each other, without any regard for the consequences.

"If you want my respect, earn it first," Klim said. "How can I accept you for who you are if you run around

161

behaving like a hustler?"

Nina gave as good as she got. "Great! Your wife is a whore, your baby a bastard. Can't you see that it's you who ruin everything you touch?"

"I promise I won't touch you ever again."

Klim marched off to the nursery. "If that's your attitude to the baby, I'll take her back. What sort of mother are you going to be anyway?"

Nina barred his way, her face contorted in a cold fury. "Get out of here and don't ever come back!"

Klim went outside and looked for a while at the glowing windows of Nina's house. His mind was in a state of dark chaos. Instead of comforting each other, they had said things that could never be forgiven.

Nina was right: his heart was drained of love. She would expect warmth and intimacy from him, and he would no longer be able to provide her with them. She would become indignant, and he would become ever colder and go deeper into his shell.

Previously, Klim had felt that one day they might break out of this vicious circle, or that at least they could try. But Katya's death had dashed the last of his hopes, and this Chinese baby wouldn't be able to help them.

I'm still going to keep the girl, Klim kept repeating to himself as he walked home. *If I wasn't able to love my own child, I'll love somebody else's baby.*

His despair gradually transformed into rage. Wyer had crushed Klim's life by destroying his daughter's. And he had done this without the slightest personal malice; the captain probably hadn't even given Klim a second thought. He had done it because he was used to solving problems with force and violence. Wyer believed that he could do whatever he wanted, and if that led to some foreign immigrants suffering, then so be it. After all, nobody had invited them to come to Shanghai in the first place.

As God is my witness, Klim thought grimly, *he's going to pay for this.*

13. THE SECRET MISSION

1

That evening when Klim went for the lamp oil, Ada told Nina what she had heard from the servants at the Bernards.

When Edna and Tamara were young, they had been best friends and both had fallen in love with Daniel, who had just arrived in Shanghai from Europe. He had ended up proposing to Edna, but the servants suspected that Daniel was more taken with her father's connections, than Edna herself.

Mrs. Bernard knew that her husband occasionally visited places of ill repute and, feeling powerless to stop him, she avenged herself on the city's prostitutes.

When she had been told that Daniel had got himself a mistress and made her pregnant, Edna almost gone crazy with grief.

"She hates you so much!" Ada told Nina with a sigh. "She calls you *that femme fatale.*"

"Oh really?" Nina smiled bitterly. "Well, I and your stupid Edna have a lot more in common than she thinks. But unlike her, I don't have money or an influential daddy to fight my battles for me."

Nina was more convinced than ever that her acquaintance with Daniel Bernard had been no coincidence. Tamara had clearly never got over her rivalry with her old friend, despite her own marriage being much more successful. In all likelihood, it was Mrs. Aulman who had spread the word about Nina's illegitimate child. Nina would have loved to tell Tamara to her face that she was partly responsible for the death of her daughter, but she couldn't afford even that luxury. Nina's house belonged to the Aulmans. Where would she go if she had to move? To Klim and Ada?

Besides, Tony had promised her he would get her confiscated savings back, and she could forget about them if she fell out with Tamara.

The next time Tamara called, Nina told her that she wouldn't be able to visit her. "I've adopted a Chinese baby girl that I found on the street, and goodness knows what people would think if they saw me breastfeeding her. Your reputation would be in tatters."

"What induced you to do such a thing?" Tamara gasped. "It's utter madness. You'll become a complete pariah in polite society. You'd have been better off adopting a monkey."

"It's a bit late to be worrying about polite society in my position, don't you think?" Nina said.

On the plus side, Nina's Chinese baby provided her with the means to escape from Tamara's suffocating custody without having to have an open fight with her.

2

The case of Katya Rogov's and her nanny's murders was pushed from one office desk to another until the investigating officer finally announced that the suspect had probably fled to the Chinese territory and it would be impossible to find him.

Nina tried to console herself with the thought that most women would have to deal with the death of a child at some time in their life, be it through miscarriage, abortion, or a fatal illness. But nothing made it any easier for her. Every night Nina dreamed of her daughter, only to wake up to the reality of having to take care of Kitty, the name Klim had given to his foundling.

Everybody who knew Nina thought that she had gone completely crazy adopting a Chinese baby. After all, it was clear from the outset that the girl would have a hard life: an Asian child would never be allowed into a good school for white children or completely accepted into white society. Kitty was destined to be like a zebra in a herd of horses, and with the handicap of Russian foster parents, she would never be a fully signed up member of Chinese society.

But Nina realized from the start that rejecting Kitty would mean losing Klim as well, and she couldn't face being all alone. She knew that there was no point arguing with him about the foundling. Nina had recognized that familiar stubborn obsession in his eyes: in the most difficult moments, Klim would make sudden decisions that would dramatically change his life, and no one could change his mind. This was what had happened many years ago when he had run away from home, after a quarrel with his father, leaving his family fortune behind. The same had happened when he had decided to stay with Nina in revolutionary Russia, even though he could have gone back to Buenos Aires and escaped all the hardship they had had to endure. These decisions had cost him dearly, but Klim had his own unswerving view on what was the right and the wrong thing to do.

Although Nina had told him to never come back, he still returned, bringing her money and looking after the baby to allow Nina to get some sleep. But now he treated her as if she was merely a wet-nurse for his surrogate daughter. Klim found it easier to act this way. Tired of its unwieldiness, he had deprived his love of its freedom, constraining it in a straitjacket like a psychopathic criminal.

Nina and Klim had reversed roles. It was she who now felt secretly jealous of the baby and performed her parental duties reluctantly, while Klim behaved as if there was no one in the world dearer to him than Kitty.

3

RECEIPTS AND EXPENDITURES

Klim Rogov's Notebook

Ada tries hard to convince me that no good can come from adopting a Chinese child and that I'm just wasting my time with Kitty.

I rather spitefully told Ada that she was just being jealous. "Did you want me to adopt you instead? But how could I adopt a girl who is constantly throwing herself at me?"

My not very subtle hint made Ada spit blood, and she started cursing at me, employing the entire range of choice language she had picked up while working as a taxi-girl.

Ada knows absolutely nothing about little children. Kitty has turned into a lovely baby. She has a round face, eyes as black as currants, a cute little nose, and eyebrows that look like little clouds. Not long ago, her first two bottom teeth came through, and she tries them on everything she can sink them into—from her own feet to a utility bill Nina had absentmindedly left on a chair.

It seems strange now to think that I could ever have been bothered that she isn't my flesh and blood. Who cares? Kitty radiates happiness the same way as a light bulb radiates light, and she always makes me laugh. She is a bundle of joy—and that is the best description I can find for my daughter.

Nina has fallen for Kitty's charm too, even though there was a time when just looking at our baby girl made her feel sick to the heart. Now Nina sings her lullabies, patiently spoons porridge into her, and talks to her in a hilarious way: "Who is this little girl? And where has she been today? Has she been with Mommy to hire some men to move the furniture around the house?"

Kitty stares at Nina wide-eyed and appears to understand her questions perfectly, answering them with a loud "Ah-ah-ah." The performance is so amusing that even the servants come into the room to watch.

While Nina and I have fallen in love with Kitty with surprising rapidity, our own relationship is nothing like as rosy. It's as if we are living in a movie: everything is black and white, and the actors have such a thick layer of makeup on their faces that their attempts to communicate with each other are reduced to the farcical and grotesque. The plot of our movie is also in black and white, and lacking in subtlety—the sort of primitive Western that the residents of Shanghai go mad for. The Fair Lady has been abused and is in distress, and the Lone Cowboy has sworn to avenge her no matter the cost. Don't ask me what good this vengeance could possibly do him or the Fair Lady; he has no idea himself. But his natural sense of justice won't allow him to tolerate the Sheriff's brazen actions. The villain must be punished.

Captain Wyer is a British citizen with all the benefits that his powerful imperial state can bestow on him. I have no official status whatsoever; I can barely stick my head over the parapet let alone demand justice. The only redress I can find is through spiteful articles that I publish as a freelancer in a Chinese student newspaper, which is happy to accept anything publicizing the corruption of local white officials. Nina told me that I ruin everything I touch, so now I'm going to try this theory out on Captain Wyer's reputation.

I have become a great expert on his life story. It turns out that as a young man Wyer was shanghaied out of his home city of London and brought to China. In those days, very few people went voluntarily because of the fear of fatal oriental diseases, so the merchant ships were often reduced to abducting unsuspecting young men in the ports. Once they were out at sea the poor wretch could complain as much as he liked, but no one was going to listen to him.

When the young Wyer arrived in Shanghai he jumped ship and joined the local self-defense unit, which later became the International Settlement's police force. At first, he sold opium himself but then he found he could make more money by taking bribes from the dealers. As he moved up the ranks of the new force, he was quick to learn the manners of his superiors and, like many other newly arrived adventurers, invented a socially acceptable past that had him adopted into the local elite. When opium was banned, he realized there were fantastic amounts of money to be made by fighting a phony war against the drug.

I still can't figure out the way this man's mind works and why he is trying so hard to soil his own nest. Even if he doesn't care about the city he is living in and his ultimate plan is to retire to a life of luxury back home in London, he must surely understand that his daughter has no plans to abandon Shanghai and that she would be left living in a city of drug addicts, gangsters, and corrupt officials of his own making.

I don't need to look hard to find material to ruin Captain Wyer's reputation with the Chinese. A simple translation of the speeches he openly gives at the banquets in his gentlemen's club is more than sufficient.

"Imperialism brings the backward peoples modern science, and the teaching of Christ," he says. "We have no choice but to use force against the Chinese because they are not willing to give up their ignorance and lack of hygiene. Why is a Chinese life worth no more than a couple coppers? Because that is its true price. A coolie has no valuable skills, and he is easy to replace. If he dies, no one will mourn his departure. Indeed, the people he shares his quarters with are only too grateful to have the extra space."

The student newspapers don't have a very large circulation, but each issue is stuck to public walls and fences and read by a large number of people. The students use a special varnish, which sticks the newspaper firmly onto board or wall masonry, and it's not easy to remove it. The authorities try to paint over these seditious articles, but within a couple of hours, a new sheet appears on a different wall around the corner.

Wyer knows that the Chinese harass him in the press, but he can't do anything about it. The entire local population hates him, including the policemen who work under him and carry out his orders. Unsurprisingly, they aren't exactly busting a gut to defend his "good name" either.

The irony is that Wyer himself has had a big hand in creating a society where any problem can be solved with a bribe. If he closes down one objectionable newspaper, it will only reappear a week later under a new title. The students have the money for it—partly from local patriotic merchants and partly from the Soviet government which hopes to shatter the corrupt colonial system.

Ten years from now, I'll be telling my children amazing stories about how I and the Bolsheviks worked together to kick the Police Commissioner out of Shanghai.

Although it's painfully presumptuous to talk about children in the plural at the moment. Children are hard to come by if, according to the script, the Lone Cowboy is not even allowed to kiss the Fair Lady. Like the films on show in the Shanghai cinemas, all content of the remotest sexual nature is censored out of our movie and there's little chance of it ever being restored.

4

The deeper I dig into Wyer's case, the more grisly the details that come to light.

He has created a small slave state in the International Settlement's prison. Every prisoner has a job to do: some weave straw mats, some sew uniforms for the police, and some carve tombstones.

The lower ranking guards earn good money supplying the inmates with opium, tobacco, food, and letters from home. The officers get even more in bribes from the inmates to avoid heavy labor and to arrange visits from wives or prostitutes. But the biggest money is made by the firms owned by Captain Wyer, which use the free labor provided by the prisoners to fulfill big contracts.

I was told that there is a pond behind the prison where the convicts wash the dirty tablecloths from restaurants. When I went to investigate, it turned out that they were being guarded by none other than Felix Rodionov.

He was sitting under a tree, watching the prisoners chained to each other, crouching on a jetty, green with slime, while beating wet tablecloths with laundry paddles. It was an eerie sight—all those unkempt heads with their matted hair, sweaty backs, protruding ribs, and gray, cracked heels.

Felix was delighted to see me. He told me that last

winter Wyer had seconded him to Hong Kong to learn from the local police there, but when Felix came back, he had been transferred to the prison staff. This certainly wasn't the sort of "promotion" he had been expecting, but he wasn't in a position to argue with Wyer. As an immigrant, Felix was grateful to have any job, no matter what it was.

I told him that I wanted to write an article about the prison system, and he provided me with a story of a Chinese woodcarver who makes decoy ducks that are almost indistinguishable from the real birds. The man has spent two years waiting for his case to be heard. He has no relatives to intercede for him, and he is illiterate and can't write a petition for himself. When the committee from the Municipal Council visits his cell, he tries to attract attention to himself, but the translator from the prison administration won't translate anything that might cast a shadow on his bosses. Captain Wyer loves duck hunting and has no intentions of parting with his woodcarver. He has ordered that the man should be kept detained for an unlimited period, but not hurt.

My article is translated and published in the Chinese student newspaper. I hope it'll engender wide public outrage, and the poor woodcarver will be rescued by his fellow countrymen.

5

Felix sent me a note: "Come. It's urgent." I thought he had a new story for me and rushed to meet him at his pond. But what he had to say exceeded all my expectations.

"Today our senior warden got drunk and blurted out to me that Jiří Labuda was strangled on Wyer's orders. I think that our 'Czechoslovak Consul' was planning to spill the beans on the wrong people and that was why he was sent to meet his maker."

It appears that Wyer sent Felix out of Shanghai on purpose, so he wouldn't ask awkward questions about his suspicions.

We wracked our memories to recall the complete chain of events that had led to Labuda's death. Wyer had initially decided to make a scandal out of the Czechoslovak Consulate case and told me to write an article about Nina and Jiří. But later he realized that this was not in his interests and had ordered Jiří's disappearance.

I had wondered at the time why Wyer had allowed Nina to remain under house arrest: he wasn't exactly known for his leniency or pity, especially to a woman who had led his son-in-law astray. The only logical explanation was that he didn't want to draw any attention to the false Czechoslovak Consulate. In a sense, Nina belongs to Shanghai high society, and if she had gone to prison, especially with a baby, reporters would have been eager to delve more deeply into her case.

Wyer had even been prepared to leave Nina alone if she agreed to get out of town, but she refused, and then the captain had arranged a car accident to get rid of Katya. Jiří Labuda's case was buried for good; the child who represented a threat to any legitimate heirs Edna might have was dead, and getting rid of Nina was just not worth the trouble as far as Wyer was concerned.

No matter how hard we tried, Felix and I couldn't figure out what kind of information Jiří might have had on Wyer. Apparently, his testimony was related to the weapons in the crates, so I decided to ask Nina if she could possibly guess who Jiří might be selling arms to.

When she heard my question, Nina turned white. "It's none of our business. For your sake and mine, please, don't go into it, or Wyer will destroy you."

Perhaps, from a pragmatic woman's point of view, Nina is right. She is prepared to accept life with all its injustice and not challenge the rich and mighty. But I can't do that. My male pride screams out for revenge.

Wyer has killed Katya, and if the authorities can't provide me with satisfaction, then I'll have to find it myself.

6

Two days passed, and then I got an unexpected message from Nina telling me that we needed to talk about Jiří. Like me, she hasn't been able to forgive or forget anything.

"I know a smuggler, his name is Jose Fernando Burbano," she said. "He used to be into weapons, and I think he and Jiří were trying to do a bit of business together."

Now that was a name from the past. I remembered Don Fernando from my early days in Shanghai. Fifteen years ago we had played cards together and enjoyed every moment of each other's company.

"Don't have any dealings with him without telling me first," Nina implored me when I told her about our previous acquaintance. And then she suddenly added: "I didn't even think that you were giving Katya a thought."

Like many unhappy couples, Nina and I often fail to see things that are obviously good about each other, instead choosing to concentrate on vices that end up being a figment of our imaginations.

Tomorrow, I'll give Don Fernando a visit and try to figure out what the link is between him, Jiří, and Captain Wyer.

14. LASCIVIOUS ART

1

The dazzling sun was shining over the river, which reeked of mud and machine oil; the merchant ships in the dock were nearly melting from the heat. The tackle creaked, the seagulls squabbled, and the sound of hammering could be heard as the riveters fixed the outer hull of a ship.

Klim reached the dock by sampan and ordered the boatman to take him to an overloaded junk with the inscription *"Santa Maria"* emblazoned across its stern in gold.

"Do you see the rope ladder hanging from the side?" Klim said. "I'll try to climb up it, then you wait for me here in your sampan."

The boatman nodded, but when Klim pulled himself up onto the lowest rung, right above his head he heard the sound of a revolver being cocked.

"Who are you?" a one-eyed Chinese asked quietly, aiming his revolver at Klim's forehead.

The boatman let out a gasp and began to row back to

the shore, leaving Klim hanging helplessly over the water.

"My name is Klim Rogov," he said hastily. "I'm an old friend of Don Fernando."

The one-eyed man glanced over his shoulder and shouted something in an incomprehensible dialect. Steps thundered on the deck above, and after a few agonizing minutes, Klim was allowed on board.

Santa Maria's deck was buried in crates and bales. Small birds fluttered from one perch to another, chirping and pecking at the sacking and shaggy hemp ropes.

"The master is waiting for you," One-Eye said, and he chaperoned Klim through the narrow passage between the crates.

Fernando was dressed in a hat, a dirty shirt, and pants that were rolled up to his knees. He was sitting under a canopy, eating a watermelon, his Chinese crew standing at a respectful distance to one side.

"Now, look who's here!" the Don roared as he threw the watermelon rind overboard and rushed to give Klim a hug. "Where on earth have you been all this time?"

"*En Argentina y Rusia,*" said Klim, smiling.

"Wow, you've learned to speak our language!" Fernando said, changing to Spanish. "Now tell me everything. Would you like some coffee? But not just any old coffee, this stuff is *instant*. It's made using the latest military technology."

The Don listened to Klim's story and cackled happily.

"Listen, can you translate technical documents into English?" he asked. "You can see how much stuff I've accumulated?" Don Fernando pointed at the crates on the deck. "Tomorrow morning I'm going to Canton, and half of my papers are in Russian which nobody there understands at all."

Klim shrugged. "I can try."

It would be good to provide the Don with a service, he thought, *and then ask him to return the courtesy.*

A Chinese boy brought them a binder, and Klim

looked through the creased pages covered with scribbles in pencil. It was a list of military equipment—grenades, artillery shells, gas masks, field telephones, etc. The list had been compiled using the old Russian spelling rules that had been common before the revolution.

"Where did you get all these?" Klim asked the Don.

"I bought it from your countrymen, the Cossacks. Their steamer, the *Mongugai*, lies anchored right across from the Wusong fortress at the mouth of the Huangpu River. It was the last White Army ship to arrive in China, and the authorities refused the Cossacks permission to go ashore. They're stuck on board, their engine room is completely ruined, and they have nothing to eat, so they're selling off their arsenal."

"And you're planning to resell it in Canton?"

Don Fernando nodded. "Something is brewing there, you know, so the demand for weapons is huge. Sun Yat-sen wants to levy taxes on the local merchants to pay for his military expenses, so the Chamber of Commerce has raised a local militia to defend themselves against him."

Don Fernando ordered his boy to bring Klim a pen, an inkwell, and paper.

"Sit down right here under the canopy and write. I used to have a Czech translator who was good at Russian. He wanted to get home, to Prague, but didn't have the money, so he agreed to help me for a share in the business. Unfortunately, he's dead now."

Klim couldn't help but smile: things were working out much quicker than he had anticipated.

"The Cossacks have been sitting on that ship for almost a year," Don Fernando said, lighting up a cigar. "The Chinese governor has demanded that they give up all their weapons for nothing, but they are worth at least a hundred thousand dollars. Naturally, the Russians have turned down his generous offer, and now the Chinese navy is holding the *Mongugai* at gunpoint until the Cossacks starve to death."

"What do the foreign concessions have to say about this?" Klim asked.

"The whites in Shanghai are pretending that they know nothing about the whole situation."

They're so greedy, they've lost their minds, Klim thought. *They're torturing innocent people for no reason whatsoever, and as a result, all these weapons will end up in Sun Yat-sen's hands for a song.*

It took Klim the whole day to finish the translation.

"Oh, I forgot about the Avro!" Don Fernando said as Klim handed him the final page. "The Cossacks offered me a brand new biplane, still in its original packaging. It's too big for the *Santa Maria,* and I won't take it with me this time, but I'll try to find a buyer for it in Canton. One-Eye, bring me the papers the Russians gave us."

Klim couldn't understand a word of the biplane specifications.

"I'll need a technical dictionary," he said. "I have one at home, and I could bring you the translation tomorrow."

"That sounds fine with me," Don Fernando said. "How much do you want for your services?"

Klim put the biplane's specifications into his wallet. "I'd like to interview you for my newspaper."

Don Fernando exchanged glances with One-Eye. "My! We have become popular all of a sudden. All right, tomorrow you'll get your interview along with my heartfelt thanks. But don't be late. We set sail at ten in the morning."

2

Tony Aulman called Nina and told her that he had succeeded in releasing the cash from her bank account.

"Come and take it," he said. "Your account is closed."

Half an hour later the driver brought Nina to Peking Road where she saw young Chinese men and women queuing at the entrance and up the stairs leading to the lawyers' waiting room.

"Who are these people?" Nina asked as she entered Tony's office.

"Actors," he sighed.

Tony explained that his client, a film company called Metro-Goldwyn-Mayer, had asked him to find a couple of indigenous people to play the main roles in their new motion picture about China. Tony had been very reluctant to take up the job. "I'm not a casting agency," he had told the film producers, but they promised to grant him the rights to show the films in China, and Tony had relented. After all, outside of America, Shanghai was one of the biggest movie markets, and the offer had been too tempting to resist.

"I've had enough of these actresses," Tony complained as he counted out Nina's money. "We placed an ad in the Chinese newspapers: 'Healthy twenty-year-old men and women required for casting, fluent in English, pleasant appearance.' And what do you think we got? The world and his wife! Pimple-faced old men, and women with bound feet who can barely walk. Hardly one of them speaks a single word of English. I don't know what they were expecting."

Nina put the banknotes into her purse, waved goodbye to Tony, and went out. *Thank God, I have cash now,* she thought. She hadn't taken a copper of Klim's money to spend on herself and was eager to buy something that wasn't just a necessity item.

On her way out of the building, she came across European woman selling cigarettes, magazines, and wall calendars featuring scantily clad blondes. The seller was Russian, of course: no other European woman would have demeaned herself by working on the streets.

Nina bought a ladies' magazine and started to flip through the pages. A new type of a cloche hat in the shape of a bell had come into fashion that season, the waistline on the dresses was still low, but the hemlines had risen markedly.

"Would you like a calendar?" the saleswoman asked. "White people seem to like them."

Nina looked up at her. "What about the Chinese?"

"They don't understand this sort of art. They think white girls are ugly."

A rickshaw stopped nearby, and a young Chinese lady stepped out on the road. She wore a crimson hat and an elegant gray dress complete with a garnet necklace. Her feet were a normal size, not deformed.

"Do you know who she is?" the saleswoman asked Nina. "Her name is Hua Binbin, she's an actress. Her first film was such a success, and she's such a celebrity that even the British newspapers are writing articles about her."

"What was it about?" asked Nina.

"The story is about a father who wants to marry his daughter to a wealthy official, but she disobeys him and runs off with a young student. This is a shocking storyline for the Chinese because love matches are unheard of. All their marriages are arranged by the parents."

"I'd like a copy of each of these calendars," Nina said. "And could you write on them which fashions are selling better and which ones are not selling at all?"

3

Back home, Nina spread the calendars on the floor of the living room and stood there, examining every detail of the fresh pink-cheeked faces.

What if she replaced these Western starlets with Chinese women like Hua Binbin? More and more Chinese women with short hair and modern, stylish dresses were turning up on the streets of Shanghai. If the Chinese people were taking up Western styles, then the demand and market for Chinese fashion calendars would be immense.

Nina tried to calculate how much seed capital she

would need to set up a publishing company. She would have to find models and artists, rent a studio, pay for the printing, storage, and delivery. It was going to be a fairly considerable sum. Nina's savings would never be enough, no bank would give her a loan, and she didn't want to ask Tamara for money. Where was she going to get the funds she needed?

She wracked her brains trying to come up with a solution and then slapped her forehead. Gu Ya-min, the antique dealer! He was the man who would help her find the money she needed.

4

On the way to Nina's house, Klim tried to work out how he could help the Cossacks trapped on the *Mongugai*. If they had been women and children, he could have written a heart-rending article to encourage local philanthropists to help the refugees out. But who needed several hundred more men who had been brutalized by war, idleness, and hopelessness?

Previously, Russian refugees had been able to eat at the soup kitchen in the Orthodox church, but this had been closed at the request of the Soviet Consul. The Peking government had established diplomatic relations with the Soviet Union and for the first time in history signed an equal treaty with a European power. For the Chinese, it was a very important event, and they were happy to indulge the Bolsheviks' whims—although this didn't stop Moscow puppeteers organizing revolutionary propaganda in China and helping the local communists and rebellious Sun Yat-sen down in the south.

The Bolsheviks didn't see anything remotely duplicitous in their actions. After all, the government in Peking was *bourgeois*, and according to their views, making a deal with the *bourgeoisie* was not worth the paper it was written on. The Bolsheviks were convinced that world revolution was not far off, and then all previous agreements and rules would become meaningless anyway.

Nina's black Ford caught up with Klim just as he was about to reach her house.

"Get in," Nina said excitedly as she opened the rear door. "I need to talk to you."

Klim sat down next to her. "What's up?"

"You'll probably say I'm crazy. And yes, I know it's a risk." Nina clasped her hands on her knee and looked askance at him. "I've been to Gu Ya-min's. He's moving north to live with his son, and he's offered me the chance to buy his entire collection for just a thousand dollars. I'm going to talk to him again now."

"Why do you need it?" Klim asked.

"It's worth at least twenty times that. Tony gave me my money back, and if I invest it into antiques, and then resell them, I'll have enough money to open a publishing company to print calendars for the Chinese market."

Nina told him she had already visited a dozen printing presses and warehouses and found out all she needed to know about prices, supply, demand, and volumes. She had neatly inscribed all these figures in the columns of an old dancing book, which had been designed to record the names of dance partners in the balls.

It had been ages since Klim had seen her so inspired. *I don't care what she does,* he thought. *The main thing is that she gets her love for life back again.*

"What are you smiling about?" Nina asked, looking suspiciously at Klim. "Do you think I'm not capable of running a business?"

Klim squeezed her hand. "On the contrary. Let's go and see that antique dealer of yours."

He decided not to tell Nina about his meeting with Don Fernando. There was no need to bother her about it just yet. Let her think about her new project and dreams.

5

Klim wasn't much of an expert on oriental art, but he immediately realized that Gu Ya-min's collection was worth a lot of money.

As he looked through the albums and figurines, Nina tensely followed his expression. "I know what you're thinking," she said nervously. "I won't be able to resell them because everyone will think that they're pornographic."

"You underestimate the secret admirers of the pornographic," said Klim. "I know a woman who keeps a brothel, and she has a lot of clients who are very rich and eager to get their hands on the exotic. If we promised her a decent share, I'm sure she would be able to sell all this stuff."

"How do you know her?" Nina frowned. "Have you used her services?"

Klim laughed. "I also personally know a number of drug traffickers and assassins, not to mention some women sewing ladies' underwear. But this doesn't mean that I've used all their services."

Embarrassed, Nina lowered her eyes. "If only you knew how frightening this all is. I feel like a captain of a ship who has set sail without a compass or navigation charts."

She gave Gu Ya-min the money and promised to bring a truck and porters so that they could deliver the collection to her home.

On their way, Nina became even more agitated. "What if we won't be able to sell it, and I'm left with nothing but thirty boxes of pornographic art?"

"You won't be," Klim said. "Tomorrow I'll go to Martha's and talk to her. Maybe she'll open an art gallery at her brothel and charge visitors a fee to view her exhibition."

He touched the chauffeur's shoulder. "Would you

mind pulling over and getting me some cigarettes?"

"Why did you ask him to do that?" Nina asked once the chauffeur had got out of the car. "Have you started smoking?"

"It wouldn't feel right kissing you with the chauffeur looking on," Klim said and pulled Nina towards him.

She put her warm, trembling arm around his neck, hesitated, and then kissed him—first barely touching his lips, and then with an intense girlish passion.

"Please don't leave me on my own anymore," she whispered.

"I wasn't going to—" Klim began, but Nina put her finger to his lips.

"It's just that sometimes you're so remote from me—when you go into yourself and can't even look in my direction."

Klim held her tight. "I'm not going anywhere from you."

The chauffeur returned and handed him a green packet of cigarettes with a red circle on the wrapper.

Klim winked at Nina, showing her the brand name. "They're Lucky Strikes. I'll keep them for good luck."

"Why don't you come back to my house now?" Nina asked.

The temptation was great.

"I really need to go home tonight," Klim said. "I have a translation to finish. Tomorrow I'll come to you after work, and you can tell me what you've decided about our situation."

"I already have."

"Mull it over again. If you change your mind and don't feel we can be soul mates, it doesn't mean that we can't be around each other."

6

Klim had never expected his life would change quite so

suddenly. He admitted to himself that all these months he had been shadowboxing with a woman who he thought was Nina, but was, in fact, a figment of his imagination. He had been exhausted by these phantom battles, like a soldier who no longer remembers or cares about the cause he is fighting for and wishes for only one thing—to throw his rifle down by the roadside and go home.

Klim guessed that Nina must also have rehearsed endless disputes with him in her head, finding hidden meanings in every word he uttered.

The only possible way we could get over it, Klim thought as he walked up the stairs to his apartment, *is to accept that both of us were just looking for the best solution in the given situation. It doesn't matter who was right and who was wrong in the past; there's a lot to blame on both sides.*

Ada came out from the kitchen to greet Klim.

"What are you so happy about?" she asked, wiping her hands on her apron. "Did you find a wallet full of money on the pavement or what? By the way, a courier from Mr. Green came over and told you to come into the office immediately. Will you go now or have your dinner first? I've cooked Chinese cabbage today."

It was half past eight. Why on earth would Mr. Green summon Klim to a meeting this late?

"I'll be right back," he said and went out into the street.

7

The tram was filled with merry people returning from restaurants. While making a turn, the tram driver hit the brakes and a drunk young woman with a bright lipstick fell face first into Klim's arms.

"I'm so sorry!" she mumbled, looking at the lipstick mark she had left on his lapel.

Klim swore under his breath. She had ruined his jacket. How was he going to get it clean before his meeting?

It was already dark when he reached the Bund, and

there wasn't a single light on in the recently-built editorial office building. *Perhaps the meeting is over and everyone has gone home?* Klim wondered.

The old doorman ushered him into the dimly lit lobby.

"Do you have anything for this stain on my jacket?" Klim asked.

The doorman gave him a jar with an impressive red inscription on its side:

SHINE

The miraculous cleaning fluid for all your home needs.
Flammable and harmful if swallowed.

In all likelihood Shine had been manufactured in a nearby basement out of rice vodka and ditch water, however there was nothing Klim or his jacket had to lose.

He went up to the sixth floor. It was all very strange: the editorial room was empty.

I guess Ada lied to me about the meeting, Klim thought. *She probably invited Betty over and decided to keep it a secret from me.*

Frustrated, he threw his jacket on his desk and poured some Shine onto the stained lapel. The fumes were so strong that he coughed. That was all he needed. It was unlikely the bad smell would be gone by the next morning when the typists came into work.

He heard footsteps coming from the corridor, and two burly Chinese men burst into the room.

"Who are you looking—" Klim began but stopped in mid-sentence as Captain Wyer appeared from behind their backs with a fat cigar in his mouth.

"Sit down," he ordered Klim. "We need to talk."

Klim rushed to the door, but the Chinese caught him, twisting his arms behind his back and forcing him to sit down at his desk.

Wyer's square jaw was moving slowly as if he was chewing on something.

"What's that smell in here?" he asked.

He opened the window, and a draft riffled the papers on the desks and swayed the lamps hanging from the ceiling, causing their shadows to swing along the wall like oversized pendulums.

"Did you seriously think those students would never betray you?" Wyer chuckled. "No Chinese would ever risk his life for a second-rate 'white ghost' like you."

He made a sign to one of the Chinese, and the man pulled a brown bottle out of his pocket.

"I'm a kind and God-fearing man, and I will not kill you," Wyer said, "at least, not immediately. I expect you're wondering what's in this bottle? Well, I'll tell you. It contains cholera water—a very apt cure for your impudence. Since you're so fond of writing all sorts of crap about me, you should find yourself expelling every ounce of it for the foreseeable future. I think that should teach you a lesson unless you croak from the diarrhea first."

Klim stared at the blue smoke rising from Wyer's cigar.

"Could I have a smoke first?" he asked hoarsely and pulled the packet of Lucky Strikes out of his pocket. "Damn, I forgot my lighter."

Wyer tossed him his matches. "Yes, you can, if it helps you to calm your nerves."

Klim struck a match and threw it onto his jacket soaked with Shine. The draft blew the flame up to the ceiling, the Chinese jumped back, and Klim darted out of the room.

"Don't let him out of the building!" Wyer yelled.

Klim dashed down the stairs, taking several steps at the time. He hit the heavy front door with all his weight and found himself on the Bund.

Pushing passersby out of his way, Klim ran towards the bridge over the Suzhou Creek.

"Stop thief!" he heard the voices behind his back. He looked back and saw the Chinese thugs chasing after him.

Narrowly avoiding a car, he crossed the street, but a Sikh policeman who was directing traffic on the bridge blocked his path, hitting him on the neck with his bamboo stick. Klim fell onto the warm road that smelled of iron. The policeman gave a shrill blow on his whistle, and the traffic stopped.

Klim quickly got back up onto his feet and rushed to the railing on the bridge. Down below was an endless stream of boats and sampans. Without a second thought, he jumped over the railing and onto a motorboat.

He hit the deck so hard that the boat almost capsized. The Chinese woman sitting at the stern gawked at Klim.

"Who are you?" she shrieked. "What do you want?"

"Stop or I'll shoot!" someone yelled from the bridge.

"Get out of here quick, or they'll kill us!" Klim shouted to the woman.

The boat jerked forward, and in a few seconds, they were in the middle of the Huangpu River, gunshots ringing out after them.

15. A FUGITIVE'S NOTEBOOK

1

RECEIPTS AND EXPENDITURES

Klim Rogov's Notebook

The boat woman took me to the *Santa Maria*.

When Don Fernando learned that Wyer's thugs were after me, he offered to take me with him to Canton immediately. Feverish after the chase, my head foggy, I didn't have much time for reflection. At the time, it seemed to make sense to me to disappear from the city and draw the heat from Nina, Kitty, and Ada.

I was worried crazy about what might happen to my girls. What would Nina do with Gu Ya-min's collection? How were she and Kitty going to survive while I was away? What would happen to Ada? What if Wyer decided to take petty revenge on them? But there was no way I could take them with me to Canton on a smuggler's boat that might come under fire from the patrol ships at any moment.

It was agonizing that I didn't have time to let them

know what had happened. In any event, Wyer might have had my apartment watched, and Nina would never have agreed to drop everything and make a break for it with the baby to consider. I could imagine what she must be thinking about me. She had told me a hundred times not to provoke Wyer, and now I'd gone and ruined everything again.

I can only hope that she's put two and two together and guessed that I had to leave Shanghai because I had no other choice. It's such bad luck to be finally reconciled with Nina only to lose her the very next moment.

2

The *Santa Maria* is three days into the East China Sea, and Don Fernando and I kill time playing cards.

I will have no means of supporting myself in Canton, and the Don has offered me a job as his interpreter. There are dozens of Russian military experts in Guangdong province, and Fernando wants to make friends with them to get orders supplying arms to Sun Yat-sen's army.

I can't stand the idea of playing a part in another civil war, but Don Fernando has no time for my protests. "You have no choice," he laughs at me. "By the way, why don't you learn some German while you're at it, since you're so good at languages? I really need a German interpreter."

According to the Don, Germany is keen to get involved in Canton's political affairs. The Germans were expelled from China, and now they want to get back in with the help of Sun Yat-sen. After the Great War, the victorious Allies forced Germany to disarm, but Berlin had no intention of giving away everything for free. Now they are trying to sell whatever they can, and are secretly bringing shiploads of the stuff to neighboring ports, which the Don then obligingly smuggles into Canton for them.

He told me that previously he used to register everything as "diplomatic cargo," but this loophole had been closed after Jiří Labuda's untimely death. I remember the little Czech saying that he had got his guns from the Germans, but so far I haven't been able to glean any more details from the Don. Despite our agreement, Fernando has refused to grant an interview or answer any of my questions. "We're quits," he told me. "I haven't charged you for your passage out of Shanghai, have I? And I don't think you're in any position to lay down the law with me at the moment."

We sleep in the open on the upper deck, and I always dream of Nina and Kitty. I wake up suddenly, as if I've been given an electric shock, and then watch the night sky through the gaps between the bales and crates. There are so many stars up there that it seems as if a huge luminescent deluge has been suspended in time and space over our little planet. At the moment these dreams and optical illusions are the only things that prevent me from plunging into oblivion myself.

3

As we passed Formosa Island, our ship caught the tail end of a typhoon. Every forty seconds a wave would hurl us down into the boiling abyss, the bulkheads were at breaking point, and a permanent foam danced over the greenish waves like a crowd of sea demons.

I don't even know how we managed to limp into Hong Kong—our junk was on its last legs. With such a sensitive cargo onboard, there was no way that we could just roll up to the docks. So we spent what seemed like an eternity stuck out at sea, waiting for Don Fernando to negotiate safe harbor with the right people in the city.

Bored and with nothing to do, I would spend hours observing everything around me through binoculars: the sea dotted with countless small islets, outcrops of rock covered with dense vegetation, and a string of ships waiting in line to be unloaded. The heat was so stifling that the air felt as if it had thickened into hot jelly. The humidity not only soaked into my clothes but through every fiber of my being.

I desperately wanted to go ashore to send Nina a cable, but the Don wouldn't stand for it. He was afraid that I'd spill the beans about his cargo, and customs would arrest the *Santa Maria*. He ordered his men to confiscate my money, including the not inconsiderable sum I had won from him at cards, so I wouldn't hire a boatman and sneak away. I should have known the old crook would double-cross me.

Finally, the junk was repaired, but Fernando was in no hurry to set sail. He'd heard that the Cantonese merchants were at complete loggerheads with Sun Yat-sen. He is convinced that the political temperature will soon rise around here and with it the price for illicit arms and ammunition.

We only got underway when the Soviet steamer, the *Vorovskoy*, entered the harbor. Like the Don, the Bolsheviks smuggle arms to Sun Yat-sen. Their documents claim that they're shipping an exceptionally large load of pianos, but in reality, the oversized crates and packaging contain machine guns and ammunition.

The Don decided that we need to get to Canton before our competitors, and so we sailed up the Pearl River, our Mexican flag fluttering gaily from our stern.

I had assumed that Southern China is a jungle kingdom but it's nothing of the sort. The forests along the coastline have long been cut down, and the land has been turned into uniformly square rice paddies. Flocks of birds fly over the patches of reeds. Sharp-horned buffalo watch indifferently as our junk sails by, small boys astride their humped backs, which protrude out of the water like semi-submerged rocks.

On our way to Canton, the *Santa Maria* dropped anchor at the island of Whampoa, the site of Sun Yat-sen's military training camp.

After long negotiations in Cantonese, of which I don't understand a word, we were finally allowed to go ashore.

"I have to talk to some Russians," Don Fernando said. "You'll be my interpreter."

I told him I wasn't going anywhere until he gave me my money back, and reluctantly the Don counted out one hundred Hong Kong dollars. "I ought to shove it down your throat, you stubborn old goat," he said. "I'm beginning to regret saving your worthless ass from Wyer."

Don Fernando had already visited Whampoa Island, and he confidently led me through the training ground packed with obstacle courses and dark-skinned cadets. They couldn't have been more than fifteen or sixteen years old and resembled a jamboree of innocent boy scouts in their short trousers, short-sleeved shirts, sandals, and red neck scarves.

I couldn't believe that these kids were about to be sent into battle. However, it's a well-known fact that teenagers make the most dedicated and unquestioning soldiers. A world-weary, experienced men would never rush to die for the sake of someone else's ideas, while an idealistic teenager can easily be convinced to sacrifice his life to change the world.

Their military instructors are the Red Army and German officers. They teach their cadets how to march in formation and shoot at straw dummies, and the political instructors fill the boys' heads with a heady cocktail of Marxism, nationalism, and half-baked patriotism—a perfect and explosive recipe to transform semi-literate young men into fanatical cannon fodder.

We had arrived at the island at the ideal moment. After another fight with the Chamber of Commerce, Sun Yat-sen had moved to Whampoa and was preparing his counter-offensive. The head of his military academy, Chiang Kai-shek, had learned that Fernando had brought weapons and summoned him urgently, and I stayed waiting for the Don in the shade of a banana tree. It was there that I met a young man by the name of Nazar, who had come from Moscow in order to complete an internship at the English-language Bolshevik newspaper, the *People's Tribune*.

Nazar is nineteen years old, fair-haired, rosy-cheeked, and as full of youthful energy as a spring lamb. I told him that I work for the *Daily News*, and for some reason, Nazar assumed it was a Soviet newspaper.

"We are so lucky to be here," he enthused. "Canton is now the main arena of our struggle against global capitalism."

When he told me that he was about to get a motorboat into the city, where he lives, I realized I wasn't going to get a better chance to escape from Don Fernando. I casually asked Nazar if he could take me with him, saying that I needed to find a telegraph office to send a cable to my wife. He agreed.

Canton was astonishing—but not in any positive sense of the word. From a distance, its slums are as unremarkable as anywhere else in the world. But it's only on closer inspection that you realize that this sprawling mass of planks, rags, and rubbish is floating on water, with boats filling the numerous canals and backwaters as far as the eye can see. I had seen people living on sampans in Shanghai before, but nothing quite on the phenomenal scale of Canton's floating neighborhoods. According to Nazar, this place is home to about two hundred thousand people. They use the river to wash their clothes, quench their thirst, and as a final resting place for their dead, even those who have succumbed to infectious diseases.

Nazar took me to Shamian Island where the foreign concessions and the telegraph office are located. However, we were met by a patrol as soon as we approached the landing stage. I tried to hail them but was given very short shrift when they heard my accent. "Are you Russian? Don't even think of landing or we'll open fire." Shamian Island is on total security lockdown following recent developments in the city, and anyone speaking with a Russian or German accent is treated as an enemy.

It was too late to look for another telegraph office, and since I had nowhere to go, Nazar invited me to stay the night in his Soviet dormitory.

We ended up taking a couple of palanquins. Nazar apologized profusely for this exploitative, imperialist mode of transport, but the sun had already set, and it was unsafe to walk Canton's streets at night. The locals here hate "white ghosts" so much that the Russians and the Germans have to wear an armband with a special insignia indicating that we are "friendly." These work quite well during the day but are no good after dark.

Nazar and I got into the carved booths, the porters then picked us up and ran, their wooden sandals clattering against the pavement.

Canton's streets are so narrow that in some places I could have stretched arms through the palanquin's open windows and touched both walls. I had a feeling that we were traveling through a catacomb and that there was no way out.

Finally, we reached a three-story building with a balustrade, located in a quiet street. This was the Soviet dormitory.

Nazar lives in a room furnished only with a portrait of Lenin, a painted Chinese cabinet, and floor mats with blue porcelain bricks, which the locals use instead of pillows. Supposedly, they're pleasantly cool to the touch when you rest your head on them.

The bathtub also made a big impression; it was a clay vat, half my height, but so narrow that you can only wash while standing.

Nazar gave me a piece of black sticky soap and a bottle of Lysol, the surest precaution against parasites.

"Put at least a tablespoon into the water," he said, "or you'll end up with scabies or maybe something even worse."

When I returned to his room, it was full of foul smelling, suffocating smoke, which emanated from a glowing cord twisted like a snake in a clay saucer.

"This is to keep the mosquitoes away," Nazar said. He had come equipped with a mosquito net but had put it in the closet before leaving for Whampoa Island, and now after a couple of days, it was covered with black mold. Neither Nazar nor I dared to touch it. Goodness knows what kind of pests it contained now.

We stretched out on our floor mats, and Nazar told me about the life and customs of the Soviet commune.

He seems to have two completely contradictory personalities that coexist within him simultaneously. One is a very sensible, intelligent young man who appreciates the benefits of civilization, the division of labor, and personal comfort. He is perfectly happy with the fact that the Soviets employ maids to clean the dorm rooms and do the laundry. He doesn't consider this to be exploitation of the working people in the slightest.

However, Nazar's alter-ego is not of this world at all. In this incarnation, he lacks any sense of irony or self-criticism whatsoever. He believes that private property should be banned and all exploitation nipped in the bud. This Nazar talks entirely in Soviet newspaper clichés. In his world, everyone who is poorly dressed is "an oppressed worker, looking with hope to their Soviet brothers." Every slightly better-dressed person is a "puppet of world imperialism," and every Russian immigrant can only be a "corrupt counter-revolutionary running dog constantly seeking to undermine the USSR."

I wonder which category I would come under if he knew my real identity. Probably, the "bourgeois toady, trembling with fear and impotent rage at the sight of the unstoppable rise of the Soviet Union's prestige and power."

Soon Nazar was happily snoring, but I couldn't fall asleep. I'm currently sitting at the window and writing my diary by the light of a candle stub.

There is a railroad nearby and trains rattle by every ten minutes. The cicada and frog choruses are in full song, and boat whistles float up from the river.

I have to admit that my life in Shanghai was paradise in comparison. I had a pleasant apartment that was marred only by Ada's occasional teenage antics. I could put my clothes in closets without worrying whether they would have rotted by the next day from the humidity. I had a decent job, I could see Nina and Kitty whenever I wanted—and I still had the nerve to be dissatisfied with my lot. It seems the Chinese gods have decided to punish me for my ingratitude.

I have no idea what I should do now and how long my exile will last.

4

Back in the dark ages when Moscow had barely been established, Canton was already a thriving city with a thousand years of history. It was from here that the great Sea Silk Route started from China to the Middle East. It was here that the Chinese built their great ships and the world's finest carvings in ivory, amber, and precious wood were created.

Canton is a city of craftsmen. The local men make embroideries of extraordinary beauty and the women the famous Cantonese shawls with their customary long fringes. This craft was brought here from Portugal and then exported back to Europe. The Chinese don't wear shawls themselves but are quick to spot a business opportunity when they see one.

In the Xiguan area, every street is devoted to a specialized craft—silver, embroidered shoes, brocade robes, or turtle shell combs. The second floors of buildings jut out over the sidewalks, protecting the lower floors from the sun, and the townspeople busily make their way along these shady passages, carrying iron rings with hooks for their purchases, a kind of alternative shopping bag.

There are stores with stained-glass windows and counters of polished wood. There are little shops, where the pork carcasses hang from the ceiling, covered with flies. On the ground along the walkways, there are barrels of fish and cages with frogs, snakes, chickens, and crickets. A little to one side, there are small sculptures of the Buddha with gleaming thin candles and incense sticks devotedly placed in front of them. The stifling wind sweeps away the fallen petals and charred pieces of paper, the debris of yesterday's offerings to the gods.

I wish I could share my impressions of Canton with Nina, but I daren't write to her openly. If Wyer is checking her mail, he would soon be on to us.

My cryptic cable to Nina read as follows:

The item from your order 070489 (the date of my birth) arrived safely and will be delivered to you once it has been through quarantine.

Nina is a smart cookie and responded immediately:

Take all necessary insurance and ensure that the item is safe and sound.

It was such a relief to learn that she has at least partially understood what has happened.

By exchanging cables full of allegories and allusions, we agreed that I would secretly return to Shanghai, and then we would move to another city.

Here in Canton, there are daily clashes between Sun Yat-sen's people and the traders who have been driven to their wit's end by his extortionate taxation. It usually kicks off with the sound of distant shouting, the roar of drums, and the clatter of wooden sandals on the pavement. Before long the whole street is filled with two opposing protest marches—one side holding banners of Karl Marx and Chinese nationalists, and the other portraits of the leaders of the Chamber of Commerce. Soon a fight breaks out, and the locals watching from their second-story windows make bets on which side will be victorious. Once the fight is over, they throw their winnings to each other—directly over the heads of the fallen fighters.

Then the police come and lead away those who haven't managed to escape, and within a few minutes the battlefield is flooded with small boys collecting up the junk, trampled portraits, and other debris that has been left behind.

I have decided to stay in Canton for another couple of weeks and will try to return to Shanghai in late October. I still have no idea where Nina, Kitty, and I will go. Since the Great War, there are migrants everywhere and, as a result, tighter borders, and I'm afraid we won't be welcomed anywhere. So far, we have only been able to stay here, in China, because the Peking government has neither the power nor time to deal with us immigrants.

Money is tight, and I'm very grateful to Nazar for letting me stay in his room. I asked how I might be able to thank him, and he replied that helping a fellow revolutionary in the struggle against global capitalism was more than enough reward.

I wrote an essay about the unrest in Canton and took it to the *People's Tribune*. They were very pleased with it and even gave me a reward: the third volume of the collected works of Vladimir Lenin.

"I'm so glad that you can write in English," said the editor, a sweet American girl who is besotted with socialism. "Would you like to make a weekly report about the rallies and demonstrations in the city?"

If they had been able to pay me, I would have been happy to write more articles, but I don't think I need another tome by Lenin. The one I already have is more than sufficient, and it's a bit softer than the porcelain brick that had been serving as my pillow.

5

No one in our dormitory asks the other about their past or present occupation because each has a secret mission or assignment from the Communist party, the Intelligence Agency, the People's Commissariat for Foreign Affairs, the Comintern, or the political police— the OGRU. They call themselves the "South China group," and they live a hard, isolated, and ascetic life— much like the warrior monks of centuries past. The only difference is that the Soviet government pays them a salary and lets them have families.

Westerners believe that the Bolsheviks are

materialists. But nothing could be further from the truth. Their lives are subject to strict rituals filled with hymns, sermons, and festivals. They resolve any issue with quotations from their holy books—the "Old Testament" by Karl Marx and the "New Testament" by Vladimir Lenin.

My neighbors are essentially good guys, and I could get along with them fine under normal circumstances. But my goodwill evaporates as soon as they transform into "revolutionary fighters," brutal crusaders who don't have an ounce of pity for infidel unbelievers.

Just as medieval fanatics were always looking for the snares of the Devil, the Bolsheviks are constantly on the lookout for the "web of conspiracies that are being hatched against the Soviet Union." In their minds, Satan is a fat gentleman dressed in a top hat and sporting a monocle—the malicious face of Imperialism. Satan has many servants in many guises, including us, the White immigrants, who "have treacherously switched to the camp of the enemies of progressive mankind." Their credo dictates that these evil forces dream of enslaving everybody, and if it were not for Lenin the savior, the world would long ago have sunk into darkness.

I found a rather curious map of the world hanging on the wall on the ground floor of our dormitory. The artist has painted the USSR red and depicted Moscow as a star which radiates bright rays of light to the rest of the world. All the other countries are colored black. It reminded me of those medieval maps made by crusaders, with Jerusalem at the sacred center of the world, surrounded by the kingdoms of Christendom, with the lands of the infidels banished to the outer darkness and oblivion.

While Westerners come to China to exploit it and make themselves rich, my neighbors the Bolsheviks genuinely want to sacrifice themselves for the working people of the future. They come here, to the other side of the world, to expose themselves to danger, hellish heat, mosquitoes, and deadly diseases, utterly convinced that all this suffering is worth it and that they are doing the right thing.

None of these modern "crusaders" speaks Cantonese, so how can they possibly know what the local people want? Who told them that the millions of the Chinese would like to be "saved" from the "Imperialist Satan" through violence and civil war?

Personally, I don't believe there will be any "triumph of the proletarian idea" in Canton—for the simple reason that there is no proletariat here. It is a city inhabited by artisans, fishermen, and traders. Here Marx's portraits are adorned with flowers as if he were a reincarnation of the Buddha, and much of the city looks as though it belongs in the sixteenth century rather than the twentieth.

It seems that the Bolsheviks don't realize that they are playing the role of the distant rich uncle at someone else's wedding. He might be sitting in the place of honor next to the bride and bridegroom, everybody might be listening politely and nodding in agreement at his words of wisdom, but the real reason he has been invited is to provide the lavish gifts. He will be quickly forgotten once the party is over and the bride and bridegroom are left to enjoy his generosity.

6

After a while a quiet young man, who claimed to be an administrative assistant, approached me and asked cautious questions about who I was and where I had come from. I just glared at him and told him not to intrude on my mission.

Fortunately for me, as far as the South China group is

concerned, the right hand doesn't know what the left hand is doing. There is a simple reason for this: telegraph communications with the Soviet Union are unreliable and very expensive, and many departments are only allocated funds to send ten to fifteen typewritten pages per year. It takes three to four weeks for a courier to reach Moscow, so if someone has made a request about me, it's going to be a long time before they get an answer.

But in the meantime, I need to prepare myself for all eventualities. I have to move out before someone finds my diary or figures out that the *Daily News* is not quite as "proletarian" as they first thought it was.

A later entry

I have come up with a brilliant idea: I'll mail my diary to Ada. Not to the House of Hope address, where Wyer's spies might intercept it, but to the Bernard's. I'll disguise the envelope to make it look like some publisher's catalogue.

I'll ask Ada to pass on my diary to Nina. This will be the best way to contact her and explain what has happened to me.

16. PILOTS

1

Nazar asked Klim if he would be able to write an article about the pilots living at the airfield on Dashatou Island. Sun Yat-sen's recruiters had hired them from all over Europe, and now Canton boasted the most multinational air force in the world.

"These pilots are real heroes," Nazar persuaded Klim. "They fly their machines without any reliable weather forecasts and navigate using the mountain tops and the railways. In fact, they don't even have any maps. Would you dare go up into the sky without a map?"

Nazar's biggest hero was Comrade Krieger, who was in charge of technical maintenance at the airfield.

Krieger was a German by birth but had grown up in Prague and received his engineering training in America. According to Nazar, Krieger had arrived in China during the Great War to organize the shipment of all sorts of goods to Germany and the Austro-Hungarian Empire. Later on, when Sun Yat-sen had started building his army, Krieger had joined his air force to help the Kuomintang and the communists to free the Chinese people from the warlords and foreign invaders.

"He's an amazing man," Nazar kept saying. "He not only built our airfield from scratch but has also learned to fly better than any ace. He is besotted with aviation. He thinks it is the future of warfare."

"Sounds impressive," Klim said. "Well, let's go and interview these flyboys."

2

It was raining when they got to Dashatou Island, and they had to run across the flooded airfield to reach the "canteen," which was little more than a long table and a couple of benches under a thatched canopy.

There were a dozen tanned pilots sitting at the table in overalls stained with motor oil.

"Always a pleasure to have the press here!" they shouted, and after exchanging handshakes with their guests, they gave Nazar and Klim the seats of honor that had been improvised out of a couple of aviation fuel barrels.

It was pouring now, and it was so dark under the canopy that it might as well have been evening already. The orderlies, soaked to the skin, brought in pots of rice and fried canned meat with vegetables. Banana leaves were used instead of plates and enamel army cups instead of wine glasses.

Konstantin the Bulgarian filled the cups with *baijiu*, a kind of Chinese rice vodka.

"To the victory of socialism!" he toasted.

They all drank and talked, interrupting each other—in Russian, English, and German.

Klim took notes in his notebook. The pilots were all from different countries, but their stories were surprisingly similar. They had been sent to the front straight from school and had quickly learned how to survive, how to laugh in the face of danger, and to value camaraderie above all else. They were fond of women but loathed the responsibility and curbs to their freedom that children and a settled life entailed. The humdrum conformity of civilian life bored them.

"What kind of a man are you if you're afraid of a fight?" the curly-haired Pierre from Belgium shouted. He had returned from the war covered in decorations but could never stick at a permanent job. He was forever getting into trouble with his bosses for arguing with his customers.

"What exactly are you fighting for here, in China?" Klim asked the pilots.

"For justice," said Richard the Austrian, and he began recounting a recent operation they had undertaken against some rebels who had mutinied against Sun Yat-sen: "I banked and strafed their truck. The fuel tank exploded, and the soldiers jumped out of the truck with their pants on fire."

The pilots roared with laughter. Here, in Canton, they were gods of war riding the clouds and wreaking havoc against the enemy.

"I can't wait for our Northern Expedition to start in earnest," Konstantin said. "But first Sun Yat-sen must destroy these 'paper tigers' from the Chamber of Commerce."

"I'm not sure that he can," Klim said cautiously. "The merchants' army has already taken Xiguan and won't allow the government troops and tax collectors to enter."

"Nonsense!" Nazar said, his cheeks flushed with vodka. "We'll shell them into submission. Chiang Kai-shek has already received the mountain guns he needs. The only thing that is stopping him is that the shells we received from Shanghai are the wrong size for the guns. Our men have to manually shorten each sleeve. But soon we'll show the rebels what for."

"Is Chiang Kai-shek going to shell his own city?" Klim

asked.

"Not the whole city, only those traitors in Xiguan."

A bedraggled and muddy basset hound came to join them under the canopy.

"This is Mucha!" Nazar yelled, laughing and trying to fend off the dog as it strove to lick his face. "Leave me alone, you smelly mongrel!"

A man wrapped in a military cape appeared out of the rain, and Klim stared at him dumbfounded, unable to believe his eyes. It was Daniel Bernard.

"Comrade Krieger, take your beast away!" Nazar said with a laugh, but Daniel didn't laugh with him.

"What is this man doing here?" he asked, pointing at Klim. "He is a spy. I've met him before in Shanghai."

3

They searched Klim and brought him to a dingy guardhouse. The walls were covered with damp political posters, the roof leaked in several places, and there were tins on the floor to collect dripping water. Two soldiers with Mausers stood behind Klim.

"Was it Edna who ordered you to spy on me?" asked Daniel.

Klim watched him rummaging through his belongings on the desk. "I had no idea that you were in Canton."

It was obvious that Daniel wouldn't want anyone in Shanghai to learn about his secret double life, and the only way to keep that secret would be to bury his old acquaintance in the nearest ravine.

Klim had great difficulty portraying a semblance of calm. "I was asked to write an article for the *People's Tribune*, and so I—"

His words trailed off as he heard Nazar giving a yelp from behind the wall. "I met him at the Whampoa Academy and thought he was Soviet. A-ah! Don't hurt me!"

Klim went cold. Thank God, he had sent his diary to Shanghai. If Daniel had found and translated it, Klim would have been summarily executed as an enemy of the revolution.

The rain turned into a full-blown storm, and the raindrops drummed into the tins. Mucha tried to enter the guardhouse, but Daniel shouted at him sharply, "Get out of here!"

He pulled folded sheets from Klim's wallet and went to the window to examine them.

"Avro 504," Daniel said, grinning. "And you said you weren't a spy. Were you sent here to figure out what kind of airplanes we have?"

"This machine belongs to the White Cossacks trapped in Shanghai," Klim said. "They asked Fernando Burbano to find a buyer for it, and I helped him with the translation."

Daniel looked up at him in surprise. "Is the Don in Canton? Finally!"

He went out on the porch and gave the soldiers some orders.

The scales finally fell from Klim's eyes. Fernando and Jiří knew Daniel and had been working for him. It had been Nina who had brought them together, and they had used the fake Czechoslovak Consulate as a front to smuggle arms to Sun Yat-sen. When Jiří had been arrested, he had started giving testimony against Daniel, and Wyer had killed him to shut him up. The captain was evidently not keen for rumors to get out about his German son-in-law helping the Bolsheviks and Chinese nationalists.

"Don Fernando can vouch for me," said Klim when Daniel returned to the guardhouse. "We have known each other for years. He'll confirm that I'm not a spy."

Daniel took the Avro specifications. "We'll find out soon enough."

When he left, the soldiers made Klim sit on the bench, tied his hands behind his back, and sat down at the desk to play cards.

Time passed unbearably slowly, and in the end Klim lost all hope. Even if the Don had not already left Canton, he would be sure to refuse to vouch for Klim. The old mercenary had no reason to save Klim's worthless skin.

Water overflowed from the tins on the floor, but the soldiers didn't even notice. They were totally engrossed in their game, slamming down their cards hard as though they were swatting insects.

Does Edna know what her husband is doing? Klim thought. *Probably not. She has lived with this man for years without having any idea who he really is. Nina was fascinated with the scoundrel too, and now because of him, she'll never know what has become of me.*

Finally Klim heard the sound of splashing puddles.

"You son of a bitch!" roared Don Fernando as he appeared in the doorway. "I'm soaked right through to my bones, thanks to you. The things I have to do to save your ungrateful neck . . . Do you think I have nothing else to do with my time?"

He strode up to Klim, grabbed him by the shirt, and pulled him up on his feet.

"Hey you!" he called to the soldiers. "Let him go."

His interpreter, a dark-skinned lad dressed in faded army shorts, said something to the soldiers, and they cut the rope on Klim's wrists.

"Thank you!" said Klim with emotion, rubbing his numb hands together.

Fernando kicked the tin standing on the floor.

"I should put a ball and chain on you and set you to work in the boiler room alongside the Chinese."

They went outside, and the Don's bodyguards offered them umbrellas.

"We are going to see Mikhail Borodin now," said the Don. "He's been sent from Moscow to be Sun Yat-sen's chief political adviser. You'll be doing the interpreting for me, and if you try to escape from me again, I'll personally break every bone in your body. Is that clear?"

"As clear as day," Klim nodded. "I owe you for this. Thanks."

"I gave Mr. Bernard my word that you would never return to Shanghai to spill the beans on him," the Don said as they got into a motorboat. "We're going to Vladivostok, my boy. The Bolsheviks want to export their revolution to China, and for us, it's an excellent opportunity to earn good money by exporting guns and human stupidity."

That was really bad news. But Klim decided that now was not the time to take issue with Fernando. The first thing he needed to do now was to get away from Daniel Bernard, and as far as possible.

The rain stopped, and a patch of bright blue sky appeared in a gap between the clouds.

"Why the hell did you run away from me in Whampoa?" Don Fernando growled. "I wanted to introduce you to some useful people at Sun Yat-sen's headquarters. Don't you realize what a big chance you missed?"

"I've spent five years in a civil war," Klim said. "And I've seen enough to last me a lifetime—"

"You were just on the wrong side," Fernando laughed. "If you had brains, you would have joined the Reds, not the Whites."

Their motorboat reached the shore, and Klim followed the Don and his bodyguards to the pier.

"Let's walk," said Fernando. "Borodin doesn't live far from here."

They went up a street flooded with water. There wasn't a soul around, all the shops were locked, and the windows had been shut tight with wooden shutters.

Klim thought he saw a black shadow flit across one of the roofs. He covered his eyes with his hand to look up and almost tripped over a dead body in the process. Nearby lay three more. The streams of water running along the pavement were red with blood.

"What the—" Don Fernando swore as he slipped on a piece of human gore.

"Boss, we need to get out of here," said one of the bodyguards, his face turning white.

They rushed into a narrow street with countless advertising panels and reed awnings covering the second-floor windows. Something moved further up the street, and they heard the bark of a machine-gun, its deafening echo reverberating as though they were at the bottom of a well. Shop signs were shattered into splinters, and Klim, Fernando, and the bodyguards tumbled to the ground.

Klim rolled into the gutter and covered his head with his hands. The rainwater flowing over his body riffled the shirt on his back.

The pavement steamed, and here and there the street was lit with golden pillars of light. In the distance, Klim saw soldiers with rifles. Judging from the blood-curdling cries, they were busy stabbing someone with their bayonets.

Fernando groaned loudly. Klim turned his head and saw the Don struggling helplessly in a pool of blood, clutching his thigh. His bodyguards were nowhere to be seen.

"Fernando, keep quiet and play dead," hissed Klim, but the Don was crazy with pain and was insensible to anything going on around him. His eyes bulged, and he bellowed, breathing heavily.

Every fiber of Klim's being was clenched into a ball of nerves. *They're going to kill us. I know they will.*

He crawled over to Fernando, grasped him under the arms, and dragged him into a niche in the wall where a large gilded statue of the goddess Guan Yin stood. He managed to squeeze the Don into the narrow space between the statue and the wall, but there was nowhere for him to hide.

"Sit here and try not to give yourself away," Klim whispered to Fernando, but the Don didn't answer. His eyes rolled back, and foam appeared on his ashen lips.

There was a splash of water and the clatter of wooden shoes. Somebody's hands pulled Klim out of the niche, and he hit his head on a big stone censer standing in front of Guan Yin. For a brief second a black shadow stood over him, a bayonet covered with blood flashed—and then there was a deafening rumble.

The last thing Klim saw was the face of the goddess Guan Yin moving rapidly towards him. *Why is she trying to kiss me?* he thought and passed out.

17. THE CHINESE ACTRESS

1

Despite her enquiries and desperate search for Klim, Nina had never learned what had happened to him that night. One thing was certain: he had got in trouble with the police. Ada had told Nina that they had come to their apartment and searched the place looking for him.

That was it. Now Nina was alone, only with the baby by her side, and no one was there to back her up.

Anxiety and uncertainty were wearing Nina out completely. She was too depressed to do anything, much less start a business. But the bills kept coming, and Nina was forced to think about her situation.

She had noticed an article in a newspaper about a group of Jesuits who were collecting donations for an art school for orphans. According to the article, the monastery orphanage had produced many brilliant artists, and now their works were in demand not only in China but all over Europe.

Nina came up with a crazy idea: What if she were to offer Gu Ya-min's collection to the Jesuits? Since they were engaged in the arts, they were bound to have connections with art collectors. Sure, the monks might hand Nina over to the police, but on the other hand, the church in China was not particularly famous for its rectitude. Nina had learned from Don Fernando that the monks were ready to trade anything from theater advertising to sausage skins if it meant income for their charitable works. Many of the gambling machines in the bars and restaurants of Shanghai were the property of the mission of Saint Francis de Sales. The Augustinians produced fake perfume, and other orders had no qualms about investing money sent by Mussolini for the promotion of the Italian language and the Catholic Church into real estate.

Nina tried to find out everything she could about the Jesuit monastery in the Siccawei district. It had been founded over sixty years before and had gradually become a city within a city. There were colleges, an observatory, a museum, a library, dormitories, hospitals, and several churches. The Jesuits were especially proud of their famous orphanages that took in more than four hundred abandoned babies every month. The mortality rate was very high, but those that survived were given an education and profession. Boys became carpenters or worked in the garden, while girls sewed, embroidered, or took up the fine art of lace-making that had been imported from Europe. Their life was hard but a life nevertheless. And the most gifted children could make a real career for themselves upon graduation from the art school, which was considered the best in China.

Nina went to Siccawei feeling like the bold little mermaid on her way to visit the sea witch. Leaving the car in the shade of a plane tree, she stepped up the hot porch steps with her heavy package under her arm and knocked on the entrance door. A young novice showed her to the office of Father Nicolas, a slender, white-haired monk dressed in a dark robe.

"Make yourself at home, please," he said in French.

Nina rather felt as if she was in a school headmaster's office. The room was filled with book cabinets, dusty stuffed animals, and there were maps rolled into tubes standing in the corner.

On her way to the monastery, Nina had decided that she would pretend to be a dispassionate art critic, but when she started telling Father Nicolas about her proposal, she became so embarrassed that she found it hard to look into his eyes.

"May I have a look at the things you've brought?" he asked.

Nina unwrapped the heavy bundle on the desk and gave Father Nicolas an intricately-carved piece of mammoth ivory.

He examined it carefully through his magnifying glass. "Do you have an inventory of your collection?"

Nina handed him several sheets of paper. "Yes, I do."

Without hurrying, he read through the list. Nina waited nervously for him to get to the item entitled "purple amethyst male reproductive organ," expecting him to send for the police in shock and outrage.

"I'll have to talk to the brothers," Father Nicolas said finally. "This is a delicate matter, but if the rest of your collection is of the same quality, then I'm sure we'll be able to come to an agreement."

Nina couldn't remember how she made her way back outside and got into her car. Had her plan really worked out? Her relief was so great that she wanted to laugh and cry at the same time.

For two weeks, Nina was on tenterhooks. What would the Jesuits decide? Would they come to a deal with her or report her to the police?

At long last, she got a call from Siccawei.

"We will accept your collection," Father Nicolas said. "Unfortunately, we don't have enough money to pay you in cash, but we can pay you in goods kind from our warehouses instead. Would you be interested in some lace collars or parasols? You are a business woman, and I'm sure you'll be able to sell them easily."

The wily old Jesuits had evidently guessed that she was in a desperate situation and were trying to palm her off with a load of old junk. However, she was willing to accept any product as long as she could sell it legally.

Nina came to Siccawei, and Father Nicolas showed her around the warehouses.

"The images of Jesus and the Holy Virgin are very popular," he said, pointing at a stack of freshly printed posters. "Everyone is praying for peace these days, and I'm sure you'll have no problems selling them."

Nina was struck by the quality of the posters. They had been beautifully painted, and the printing had been done on the finest paper.

"These were done by our students," Father Nicolas said. "We recently purchased the latest printing equipment from Europe, and we produce these posters right here, in Siccawei."

Nina asked if he could take her to the workshop. There, in a large, brightly lit room, were dozens of young Chinese artists. Only a few of them were drawing religious subjects; the others were busy painting shop signs, playing cards, menus, and movie posters.

A short, bowlegged Chinese man entered the workshop and returned to his easel. Nina looked at his work: the mustachioed general peering out at her from the canvas was so lifelike he looked as if he would bark an order at her any minute.

"Who is this artist?" she asked.

"His name is Shao," said Father Nicolas. "He borrowed a lot of money from us and had nothing to pay off his debt. So now he is working for us."

Back at the office, Nina agreed with Father Nicolas that she would "donate" her collection to the monastery, if the Jesuits were prepared to pay her five hundred dollars in cash up front, let her use Shao's and four other artists' services, and give her three months credit for printing. She was going to start her publishing business after all.

The papers were signed, and a dozen orphan boys followed Nina to her house where they took Gu Ya-min's boxes away for safe-keeping at the monastery.

3

Nina called Tony and asked if he knew any Chinese actresses who would be willing to pose for her calendars.

"Talk to Hua Binbin," Tony said. "She's an old client of mine—an educated, intelligent girl from a high ranking family."

According to Tony, Binbin, who had been forcibly married off to an old man, had committed the most heinous crime imaginable for a woman: she had run away from her husband to Shanghai and become an actress. The success of her first film turned out to be a mixed blessing for her. Binbin's relatives sued her for tarnishing the memory of the ancestors and bringing shame on the entire family. If Tony hadn't defended her, Binbin would have been forced to return back to her family and dealt with as they pleased.

"A woman's status in China is so low," Tony told Nina, "that her folks would probably have murdered her for disobeying their traditions. But we managed to come to an agreement. Binbin was forced to change her surname to

Hua and swore never to mention her relations with her well-to-do family in public."

Nina sent Binbin a note, and they agreed to meet at the Bund.

4

Nina arrived early. She was anxious and paced up and down next to the bronze lions at the entrance to the Hong Kong and Shanghai Banking Corporation. The lions' paws had been polished bright by countless passersby who had rubbed them for good luck. Nina couldn't resist the temptation to stroke the claws that were warm from the rays of the sun.

Please, God, let things work out with Binbin, she prayed silently.

Nina wondered how she should behave with this woman. *Should I treat her as an equal? Or would I be belittling my social position as a white lady?* It was absurd: Nina had been living in Shanghai for a year and a half and, apart from her servants and shop girls, she had never spoken to a single Chinese woman.

Cars thundered past, coolies unloaded barrels on the quay, and workers at a nearby construction site were driving in piles for the new customs building. Slowly and inexorably doubts began to creep into Nina's mind. Her enterprise was bound to fail. Binbin would either refuse to pose for her calendars or ask for a totally unrealistic fee.

"Hello," Nina heard a woman's voice behind her.

Binbin had a round face, thin eyebrows, and pale pink lips. Two black strands of hair poked out from under her cloche hat and curled in ringlets behind her ears.

Nina wasn't sure whether she should offer her hand or not. Perhaps the gesture would not be accepted? Tony had told her that the Chinese couldn't stand touching foreigners.

"Maybe we could go to the park to discuss our

217

business?" Nina suggested.

Binbin gave her a puzzled look. "Didn't you know? Dogs and Chinese are not allowed in the public parks here."

Nina felt embarrassed. She was afraid that Binbin might think that Nina had been trying to humiliate her on purpose.

They crossed the road and walked along the waterfront. Thankfully, after a while, Binbin had the tact and good grace to break the initial awkward silence.

"I don't know anything about Russia," she said. "Isn't it strange that our countries have such a long border, but even the most educated Chinese are unlikely to know more than two or three Russian cities."

"We also know very little about China," Nina replied cautiously. She felt relieved: it seemed that Binbin hadn't taken offense after all.

Soon the conversation turned towards the whites' perceptions of the Chinese and the Chinese perceptions of the whites.

"You never betray your feelings to the person you're talking to," Nina said. "We never know whether it's because you don't want to talk to us, have something to hide, or don't feel anything at all."

"In China, it's not appropriate to reveal your feelings to a stranger, especially in public," Binbin explained.

"I expect the whites seem terribly rude to you?"

"We understand that you're different."

When Nina described her idea, Binbin was delighted.

"I'm sure we can make money on this," Binbin said. "Colorful posters are the only decoration available for the poor. And how many of them are living here, in Shanghai, let alone the rest of China?"

Binbin only asked for five dollars a day. To Nina's great relief Shanghai's film industry hadn't yet started spoiling its actors with exorbitant fees.

"It's a deal," Nina said and, without a second thought,

shook Binbin's hand.

She froze, thinking that it was a very inappropriate move, but to her surprise, Binbin didn't recoil and returned her handshake heartily.

5

Klim's telegram came like a bolt from the blue, and Nina's spirits immediately revived. It didn't matter that they were separated by hundreds of miles and that their future was at best precarious. Nina didn't dare rail against her fate. He was alive!

They needed money to move to another city, and Nina threw herself into her publishing business.

She rented a small house on Babbling Well Road for her office and art studio. Binbin invited her friends to be models, and Nina had her artists on easel duty.

They didn't have much time. The calendar distributors usually gathered in Shanghai every November. They would meet up at the Green Lotus Tea House to examine drafts and set prices based on sales figures from the previous year.

Artist Shao, a grumpy pessimist, told Nina and Binbin that ten years previously somebody had tried selling calendars with Chinese models but it hadn't worked out.

"We're just wasting our time," he muttered, chewing the end of his thin brush.

But Binbin wasn't having any of it. "Times change! My first film came out in the middle of summer and they had to entice people in by offering them ice-cold wet towels. No one had ever made that kind of movie before, but we tried and we succeeded. The audience was given the option to ask for their money back in the interval if they didn't like the film. But there wasn't a single person who took us up on our offer."

Nina was pleased that Binbin had stood up for her project. She wanted her to be a colleague and also a friend.

They had a lot in common, but they had their cultural differences too. Nina was used to open exchanges of opinion, long working hours, and late informal conversation. But Binbin preferred a much more structured day and a guaranteed lunch at noon. Nina still couldn't decide whether Binbin was just trying to please her because she was effectively her boss, or whether she really did want the business to be a success.

Binbin quickly realized that Nina knew very little about her target market.

"Why did you ask that model to put her hands behind her head?" she asked.

"What's wrong with that?" Nina said. "I don't want her to sit as though she's in church."

"It's very important to keep everything decent. If the pose is too vulgar, the only people who will buy your calendars are drunken soldiers."

"Is putting your hands behind the head vulgar?"

"Of course. It's an inviting gesture."

They had disagreements on politics as well. Binbin was convinced that China needed a revolution to sweep away the warlords and the "white ghosts" who funded and protected them.

"You have no idea how it will all end," Nina said sadly. "Revolutions often start out with good intentions but always end in hunger and tyranny."

"Don't you think it's a tyranny that Chinese people living in their own country are not allowed to go to their own parks?" said Binbin.

They soon realized that it was better not to talk about these things if they didn't want to end up fighting.

After a lot of hard work, they had a dozen sample calendars ready by November, and the distributors from the Green Lotus Tea House agreed to give them a try. Nina and Binbin were so thrilled that they threw a party for the artists and models.

Shao cautiously tried one of the Russian pies Nina

offered him.

"The world has gone mad," he said. "People have no idea what they are putting into their bodies anymore, and they forget to pray to the spirits of the ancestors. There's no good can come of it," he muttered. However, he didn't a refuse a second pie.

The next day, Nina sent a cable to Canton:

The samples are on their way. Looking forward to seeing the provider to discuss our plans.

But she never got a reply from Klim—neither from this cable, nor the next one she sent.

18. THE DIARY

1

Daniel returned home, and Edna decided not to reproach him for his affair. They needed to make a fresh start, but things didn't go quite as she had expected. During the day, Daniel was always in a hurry, and he spent his evenings at the Shanghai Club where women were denied access.

Every day Daniel would insult Edna—not directly with his words but with his coldness and reluctance to spend any time alone with her. She could tell that he no longer felt at home in Shanghai. She could see it in everything he did—the way he talked to servants and the way he couldn't even remember where his neckties were in his own dressing room. Daniel wasn't even pretending to "visit Edna"—her house was no more than a temporary shelter for him.

Edna began to lose sleep over her predicament.

It was late. She had already gone to bed, but Daniel had still not returned from the club yet.

She was listening out for the slightest sounds from the street—the sound of a car parking, somebody's steps echoing along the pavement. Was it Daniel? No, it was only the neighbors.

Edna felt terribly thirsty. She pulled down her nightgown, which had rolled up around her armpits, and headed downstairs into the dining room. The house was as dark and quiet as an old cemetery. The carpets seemed as soft as moss, and the dark silhouettes of the heavy furniture looked like ancient tombstones.

Edna saw a man standing by the window and shrieked.

"It's me," Daniel said flatly. "Why aren't you asleep?"

She approached him and sat on the window sill. A night bird was chirping in the garden. The air smelled of cigarette smoke and damp earth.

Daniel moved into the shade where Edna couldn't see his face.

"Is there something you wanted to ask?" he said.

"Yes . . . I need your help," Edna hurriedly said. "It's about a bill. My friends and I are trying to impose a ban on child labor, at least within the International Settlement limits. But we're at a deadlock. "

"What are you talking about?" Daniel said, annoyed.

Edna knew that her words sounded out of place. Should they really discuss bills in the middle of the night? But what else could she say to her husband? Since his return home, they'd had little to talk about.

Daniel made a step towards the door, and she was afraid that he was going to leave.

"Did you know," Edna said, "that the owners of the silk mills make little girls pull the silk cocoons out of boiling water? These children have permanently scalded hands. The Moral Welfare League has initiated a bill prohibiting child labor, but the Chinese unions threaten to go on strike if our bill passes. It seems they don't want to do anything to better the lot of their own children."

Daniel took the matchbox from the mantelpiece and lit his cigarette. The orange flame illuminated his tired face for a few seconds.

"Did you know that these kids are often the only breadwinners in their large families?" he said. "Their parents frequently can't find work, so if you discharge the children tomorrow, they and their parents will starve to death."

Edna was taken aback. "And what's your suggestion? Leave things as they are? Let the children continue to be scalded with boiling water? Let them breathe in cotton dust in the factory shops? They don't play, they don't go to school, and if they die, other kids will immediately be sent from nearby villages to take their places. They don't have a single chance in life!"

"If you want these poor children to have a chance, you will have to create a society where their parents will be able to provide for them," Daniel said, sighing. "What kind of schooling are you talking about, for goodness sake? Here, in China, even adults have the most primitive education. Their most advanced idea is to take money away from the rich."

"Precisely!" Edna exclaimed. "If you do nothing, the poor will turn into communists. Our librarian, Ada, has a friend who lives in Canton. He sent her a letter in which he described how he lived among the Bolsheviks—"

"What's his name?" Daniel's voice sounded so strange that Edna got scared.

"I don't know. You should ask Ada. Why?"

Daniel threw his half-smoked cigarette into the fireplace and took Edna's hand. "Let's go to sleep. It's too late to be discussing such things," he said tenderly.

Edna looked at him, perplexed. A minute ago, he had been so distant and patronizing, and now suddenly everything had changed. He walked Edna to her bedroom and even kissed her goodnight.

He still loves me, she thought. *He's just tired and needs some rest.*

2

Betty met Ada in the street and invited her to have a

cup of hot chocolate in the café.

She took one look at Ada and demanded, "What's up? You look worried."

Ada admitted that Klim had left the House of Hope, and she could no longer afford to pay for her two-bedroom apartment. Time had passed, and the landlord had told her that he might have to start taking her household items to cover her debt.

In order to get Mrs. Bernard to increase her wages, Ada had suggested getting an aquarium. "I could take care of it for you," she had ventured. But Edna had no interest in aquariums or anything else for that matter. Her relationship with Mr. Bernard was going nowhere, and the gossip among the house servants was that most likely, he would get himself a mistress again.

Listening to Ada, Betty laughed and then said in a serious tone, "If that Mr. Bernard is such a womanizer, you should seduce him. Then he'll give you a raise and maybe some valuable presents as well."

Betty's idea had impressed Ada so much that from that moment on she could think of little else.

A couple of weeks previously, she had received a parcel from Canton with a sealed package inside it—Klim had asked Ada to pass it on to Nina. But Ada was in no mood to comply with his request. She missed Klim desperately. She had been so worried about him, and all he had written to her were a couple of lines ordering her to act as his messenger girl.

Ada didn't know how she came to open someone else's mail. She was just curious to know what Klim had sent to his wife.

Inside there was his diary, and when Ada started to read it, it reduced her to tears. Klim called her "an extra worry" and "an angry teenager."

Oh, it would be wonderful if Mr. Bernard were to fall in love with Ada. Then she would be able to thumb her nose at Klim and his precious wife. Nina would probably turn green with envy, learning that Mr. Bernard had forgotten about her because of his beguiling and lovely young librarian.

Of course, Ada didn't want to hurt Edna's feelings, but it was not as if the Bernards had a happy marriage anyway. It was much better that at least two out of three unhappy people find love.

3

Daniel Bernard was working for German military intelligence, and he had been greatly relieved when his Berlin command had ordered him to move to the hustle and bustle of Canton, away from the increasingly irritating Edna—and some other unexpected complications.

He had never considered returning to Shanghai, but his major supplier, Don Fernando, had been seriously wounded in Xiguan when the shells the Don himself had brought to Canton started pouring out of the sky. The surgeon said that Fernando would have to spend at least six months in hospital, and Daniel had to go back to Shanghai to re-establish his connections with other smugglers.

Daniel guessed immediately that Ada's friend from Canton was Klim Rogov. After all, it was he who had introduced her to Edna as a new librarian. Daniel was anxious to find out when Klim had sent his letter to Ada. If it happened after he had met Daniel at the airfield, it could jeopardize his entire operation in Shanghai.

Daniel watched Ada closely for several days and noticed that she had started wearing lipstick. As soon as he would leave his room, she would follow him out from the library and try to attract his attention.

"Mr. Bernard, did you check the new catalog from the bookstore?" Or, "Have you read Edmund Husserl's works? He wrote *Ideas Pertaining to a Pure Phe—Phenimore—*Oh, now I remember! *Ideas Pertaining to a Pure Phenomenology* *and to a Phenomenological Philosophy.* I have a feeling you'll enjoy it."

Out of mischief, Daniel began to tease the poor foolish child. Whenever he saw Ada, he would pass a weary hand over his eyes, sigh, and then abruptly turn his head away, as if her beauty were too overwhelming for him to behold. Without fail, Ada would blush and run back into the library.

One day when she was out for lunch, Daniel went into the library and found a blotting paper on the desk, covered with doodles of hearts, doves, and the letters "D. B." next to them.

4

Edna had decided to go to a meeting of philanthropists and had let the house servants go home early. From his window, Daniel watched Ada as she headed towards the gates and out of the house.

"My car, please," he told Sam.

Daniel caught up with Ada at the crossroads. She was trying to get into a grocery store but was surrounded by a gang of child beggars, no older than six or seven.

"No mama, no papa, no whiskey-soda," they whined, stretching their dirty palms towards her.

Clutching her bag to her chest, Ada backed away, frightened.

"Go away!" Daniel snapped at the children and pressed the horn several times. The little ragamuffins scattered.

"Get in," he told Ada, and swiftly she leapt into his car. "How on earth do you manage here in Shanghai if you can't deal with some street urchins?"

"They scared me to death," she said. "I heard they can bite you, and their saliva is full of rabies . . . What are you laughing at? I read an article about it in the newspaper."

"Do you want me to take you home?" Daniel asked.

Ada was taken aback. "Really? I'll be fine, you don't

need to waste all that fuel for my sake."

However, Daniel ignored her protestations and insisted that he give her a lift to her home in the French Concession.

All the way Ada was as excitedly as a schoolgirl who has unexpectedly been given the top grades in her class.

"Edna told me that you only get twelve dollars a week," Daniel let slip casually, once they had stopped outside the gate of the House of Hope. "How can you get by on such a small amount?"

Ada blushed. "Well, it's not much, of course. To tell the truth, I'm a bit worried my landlord will kick me out of here soon."

"Show me your bills," said Daniel.

He followed her to her modest but neat apartment, which smelled of faded flowers, and Ada showed him a big pile of menacing messages from the landlord.

Daniel glanced through them. "Don't you have friends or relatives to help you?"

"No." Ada frowned. "Before I had a roommate, Klim Rogov, but he left for Canton."

Daniel's heart skipped a beat. He had been right about Klim.

"I know that Mr. Rogov sent you some papers," he said. "May I see them?"

Ada's expression changed. "But—why do you need them? They're in Russian, and you don't speak Russian, do you?"

"I have business in the south, and it would be very useful for me to have the latest first-hand news." Daniel took a ten-dollar bill out of his wallet. "This will be your fee for translating it for me."

"I can't," Ada protested. "It's a private diary. Klim didn't send it to me but to Nina Kupina."

"What has she got to do with Klim Rogov?"

"The two of them were married back in Russia. But she never fully appreciated him—she seems to be like that

228

with all the men she meets."

Daniel took out his cigarette case, but no matter how hard he tried to get the lighter to work, his fingers betrayed him.

Ada obligingly offered him a match.

"So let me get this straight," Daniel said inhaling deeply. "You haven't given Nina Mr. Rogov's diary yet?"

"I didn't have time. I have so much to do at work, and—"

He counted out forty dollars. "That's more than enough to pay off your debts. Now translate for me what Mr. Rogov has written."

Ada looked at the money, then at Daniel, and nearly in tears she nodded her assent.

5

Ada was sitting at the open window, recounting to Daniel what was written in the small notebook with the worn corners.

Daniel listened to her, stunned. Only now did he realize what his acquaintances had been talking about when they had been dropping hints about some baby. Nina had had a daughter, and everybody had decided that Daniel was the father of the child.

As God was his witness, Daniel had had no intention of starting an affair with Nina Kupina. But this woman had attracted him like the mystical will-o'-the-wisp lights that lead travelers astray at night in fairy tale forests.

She had reminded him of the magical foxes of Chinese and Japanese folklore who could transform themselves into beguiling women. In China, they were known as *húli jīng* and in Japan *kitsune*. With their magical abilities, these vixens could fool men into falling in love with them. And woe to the man who failed to recognize the bushy tail concealed beneath her silk robe. Even if she were to reciprocate the love of a mere mortal, nothing good could ever come of it. Sooner or later the fox would reveal her true nature.

"What has made Nina and I so angry and suspicious?" Ada continued reading Klim's diary. "We have fenced ourselves in with barbed wire and minefields only to become the victims of the traps that we ourselves have created."

Daniel clenched his jaw and fists until they hurt. Then he tried exhaling to relax but to no avail. He was overwhelmed by an all-consuming, suffocating jealousy. How was it even possible for that man, Edna's courier or whoever he was, to dream about Nina?

Back then, in 1923, Daniel had tried to reduce his relationship with Nina to a game between two adults who enjoyed living in opulent style, engaging in ironic debate, and abandoning themselves to an all-consuming but obligation-free lasciviousness. But Nina's intentions had turned out to be serious, and this had discouraged Daniel. What had she seriously expected him to do? Marry her? The idea was too absurd.

He had realized all that but had waited for his orders to go south with a heavy heart. He could see his life being reduced to a shapeless lump like a festival marquee that has crumpled to the ground after its main pole has been snapped in a storm. No longer would he enjoy the almost excruciatingly painful anticipation of their trysts, or the furtive exchange of stolen looks or ambiguous, witty remarks, which he loved to recall at the end of the day.

On arriving in Canton, Daniel had tried to spend as much of his time as possible in the cockpit. He had slept six hours a day and eaten whatever came to hand. He had done everything he could to exhaust himself completely so that he would have no time to wallow in his fond memories. What was the point of regretting that which was beyond his reach?

Klim Rogov had made no mention of Comrade Krieger or the airfield in his diary. When Ada finished reading it, she wanted to put it back in the drawer, but Daniel wouldn't let her.

"Give it to me," he said.

Ada silently handed him the notebook.

"I'll increase your salary, so you can pay your rent," Daniel said curtly and left the apartment.

6

The Filipino women were hanging their laundry in the courtyard, and the tortured sound of a badly played violin was coming from the open window.

Daniel felt dizzy as if he had been poisoned. As soon as he got home, he locked himself in his studio.

So, the *kitsune* woman that had driven him crazy had given birth to another man's baby. A hatred for her flared up within Daniel and then as quickly receded. He reproached himself and then Nina, laughing hoarsely. Then he began to leaf through Klim's diary, tightly packed with its small Slavic letters.

I should kill that son of a bitch right away, he thought in impotent rage.

That evening, Daniel sent a cable to Canton demanding to find out what had happened to Rogov.

He couldn't work out why he felt such a strong resentment for Klim—there was nothing to be envious of. And yet he felt like an ugly freak who has been spurned on the dance floor by a beautiful woman for a handsome and inspiring tango dancer.

It was a mystery to him how he could ever have let another man have Nina. What had he, Daniel Bernard, been doing with his life instead? Serving Sun Yat-sen's cause at the expense of his own? Propping up a joke of a marriage with Edna for the sake of the ties that her brute of a father had to offer?

Daniel had desperately wanted to possess and take Nina away with him, no matter the cost. He was sure she had been ready to love him. Her pregnancy had been an irrelevance. She could always have had an abortion.

Daniel felt as though he had missed the greatest chance of his life. He was thirty-eight; all he had to look forward to was a civil war and, quite possibly, a senseless death, but he still hadn't experienced even the palest semblance of the love that Klim Rogov had enjoyed.

19. YIN AND YANG

1

Don Fernando replied to Daniel Bernard's telegram telling him that he had been with Klim Rogov when they both came under artillery fire and that the fugitive journalist had been struck on the head by a falling statue of the Guan Yin goddess. It appeared that the celestial forces had decided to come to Daniel's aid.

On his return to Shanghai Daniel had bought the Avro 504 from the Cossacks, and every day now, he went up in the air to spy on the movements of the warships on the Yangtze and Huangpu rivers. He made a point of flying over Nina's house on these reconnaissance missions. Sometimes he would see a woman's silhouette down below, and every time his heart felt as if it were falling into an abyss.

I'll get her back, he repeated to himself, but still he didn't dare visit Nina. After all that had happened between them, he was worried that she might not let him into her house.

He found out through Tony Aulman that Nina had started a calendar publishing business and that she had hired an actress named Hua Binbin to help. Daniel arranged a meeting with Binbin and learned that she was dreaming of shooting a film of her own but so far had failed to find any sponsorship. The issue of women's rights she was trying to address was too divisive, and the authorities could easily end up banning the movie, which would lead to financial losses for everyone involved.

Daniel found a way of inveigling himself into Binbin's confidence. He told his wife about the screenplay, and Edna immediately coughed up the money for the good cause.

Binbin didn't know how to thank the Bernards. Excited, she began preparing for the movie, working at Nina's publishing house in the mornings and rehearsing with her fellow actors in the evenings. Now, instead of the Shanghai Club, Daniel would go to see her on the set and make casual inquiries about Nina.

It seemed initially that Nina's business had been going well: the first print run had been sold out, and she had signed several contracts for advertising. She had told the artists to place the pretty girls in the center of her new posters, the calendars at the bottom, and the adverts with images of lavender soap, combs, and tooth powder in the corners.

Everything had been ready for printing, but the Jesuits had delayed sending Nina's order to the printing shop. It was paid for out of the debt they owed her, and other cash-paying clients were a greater priority. Meanwhile, having found out that calendars with Chinese girls were proving very popular, other publishing houses proceeded to flood the market with similar products.

"I doubt Miss Nina will manage to keep her head above water," Binbin confided to Daniel. "Recently, she hasn't been capable of doing anything. She's been waiting for a letter from somebody and is crazy with worry."

Daniel realized that he couldn't postpone his visit to Nina any longer.

2

At first Nina refused to receive Daniel. He stood in front of her house for a long time, wondering what to do. The ground around him was covered with a carpet of white acacia flowers, and Daniel absentmindedly drew question marks on it with his cane.

He heard a slight rustle above him, looked up, and noticed the curtain flicker in the second-floor window.

He raised his hat. "Good morning, Nina."

"What do you want?" she asked angrily.

"We need to talk. I know that you're on the verge of bankruptcy because of the Jesuits."

In the end, Nina let Daniel in, and he followed the amah into the house. There were no men's umbrellas in the stand in the lobby. Toy bricks, napkins, and rattles were strewn over the carpet. He could see the clear signs of negligence typical in houses where their owners have no time for their chores.

Nina was waiting for Daniel on the sunny terrace. Pale and tense, she sat on a wicker couch, a small black satin fan trembling in her hand.

The guest's armchair had been placed next to the garden steps, as far as possible from Nina, but Daniel chose to ignore his hostess's seating arrangements and sat on the sofa next to her instead.

"Tell me what's going on," he said.

Nina tried to put on a brave face, saying that she was perfectly capable of coping with her problems, but then suddenly dropped her mask and enumerated the entire list of disasters that had befallen her since their last meeting.

"The monks knew that I couldn't take them to the

court," Nina fumed. "If I did so, I'd have had to admit that I had sold them pornography. Anyway, what were my chances of winning against the Jesuits?"

Daniel looked at her affectionately. *You silly girl, why did you go and get yourself involved in men's business?* he thought. Did she really think that any man would take her seriously?

"If you allow me, I can help you," he said softly.

Nina closed her fan and folded her arms. "What do you want in return? I want things to be clear from the start to avoid any misunderstandings . . . like the last time."

"Do you not think my motives are unselfish?"

"No, I don't."

"Where's your telephone?"

They went to Nina's studio, and Daniel made two calls: one to the Consul General of France and the other to the Abbot in Siccawei.

Fifteen minutes later, Father Nicolas called Nina to tell her the good news that her calendars would be in print the next day. He apologized for the long delay and asked Nina to convey his warmest greetings to Mr. Bernard.

Nina hung up and stared at Daniel in amazement. "You're a miracle worker."

She left the room and returned soon after, holding a small ivory disk in her palm.

"This is the only thing left from Gu Ya-min's collection," she said. "I like this woman, sleeping on a chrysanthemum. Take it as a keepsake."

Daniel couldn't believe his eyes: it was a *kitsune,* a Japanese fairy tale fox. What Nina had thought were chrysanthemum petals were, in fact, the vixen's nine tails—the mark of its wisdom and magical power.

"Do you know what it is?" Daniel said.

Nina shook her head. "No, I don't."

"It's a *netsuke.* Japanese kimonos have no pockets, and they use the *netsuke* to attach special boxes for small personal belongings to their belts."

Daniel didn't tell Nina that the *netsuke* was also

considered to be an amulet. In the fairy tales, a mortal would never ask a *kitsune* for material riches—the coins and gold given would immediately turn into worthless rocks or wood bark. But as payment for a service, a *kitsune* could give a much more valuable gift, an amulet that grants love and the ability to read thoughts.

At their parting, Nina didn't directly invite him over again, but Daniel knew that she wouldn't be making him wait on her porch next time.

3

He was constantly on the lookout for a chance to see Nina, and every time they met she made it clear that there was to be nothing more between them than their brief conversations and the provision of an occasional favor.

Is she still mad at me? Daniel thought. *Can she really still be waiting for news from Klim Rogov?* Nina never mentioned him, and it was difficult to say for sure.

She released her new calendars, but the opportunity had been missed, and her business once again started going downhill. Her small publishing company was unable to compete with the big boys. They outbid her for the services of her artists and models, the cost of the posters was constantly on the increase, and her profits began to fall. Soon, Nina wasn't even able to pay her employees on time, and before long she had issued two promissory notes to Daniel, borrowing money for her expenses.

He was beginning to feel uneasy, too. His order to go back to Canton could arrive any moment, and then what would happen? Would he have to abandon Nina again? There was only one way out: to take her with him. But how on earth could he persuade her to drop everything and go to a half-ruined city full of Bolsheviks? And what were they going to do about Kitty? Send her to some boarding school? Nina would never agree to this. Daniel had watched Nina playing with the Chinese baby girl—and she was besotted with her.

He began to drop hints that her publishing business was not going to work out, and the sooner Nina gave it up, the better. "If you don't have a powerful patron, you won't last until the summer. Your competitors will eat you alive."

"Is that what you call 'friendly support'?" Nina snapped, frowning.

Intimidating her was a dangerous tactic, but reassuring her was even more so.

"I admire your tenacity," Daniel said, "but if a person close to me is about to make a mistake, I would always consider it my duty to warn them and let them know."

The business dilemma finally came to a head when the distributors point blank refused to accept Nina's posters anymore. The Heaven Peony, the largest publishing house in the city, could extend their payment schedule to six months, and Nina couldn't.

She was in utter despair, and Daniel didn't know what to do. In theory, he should have been happy, because if Nina didn't have any income, she would be much more compliant. But against all logic, Daniel acted quite to the contrary.

"I'll give you a loan so you can stay afloat," he said. "Tomorrow I'll be at the regatta. Come, and I'll give you the money."

4

The British expatriates in Shanghai had set up their own version of the annual Henley Royal Regatta, and it had become one of the highlights of the white community's social calendar. Grandstands were set up on the river banks, and the waterfront was lined with a fleet of sampans hired by keen spectators. Orchestras played and children screamed joyfully, while bluish smoke crept over the trampled grass where cooks were roasting lamb and pork.

Daniel tensely surveyed the ladies sitting under their parasols. Nina was nowhere to be seen. He had been invited to give out prizes at the competition, but was unable to concentrate on anything and asked Tony Aulman to stand in for him.

Once the regatta started, Daniel left his seat and began to amble between the tables. Nina hadn't shown up, and there was nothing to keep him waiting here any longer.

Daniel was puzzled. Had she decided not to deal with him and found herself another lender? Had something happened to her?

Suddenly he noticed a familiar hat in a white gazebo that stood apart from the crowd. Nina had come after all. Daniel almost ran to meet her.

"I didn't think you'd come," he said, sitting down next to her on the bench.

"I'm sorry I'm late."

She took a black satin fan out of her purse. It looked strangely mournful and out of place next to her white dress and its red belt.

"I brought you the money," said Daniel, pulling a wad of banknotes from his pocket. "Count it: there are five thousand dollars."

Nina smiled gratefully. "Thank you, but I don't need it. You mentioned you're going to Guangdong province soon. Would you be able to take me and Kitty with you?"

Daniel was dumbstruck; this was the last thing he had been expecting.

"Are you serious?"

"Absolutely."

He wanted to kiss her hand, but couldn't resist taking her into his arms instead. "I'm so glad that you're no longer angry with me."

She tried to pull away. "What if somebody sees us?"

"Who cares."

She freed herself from his embrace. "What's the best way to get to Canton? By steamer? I know that there's unrest in the south, and it's a bad place for a woman and a baby at the moment. But if you could help me when we get there, I'd be very grateful to you."

Daniel looked at her for a long time. "I'll think of something."

It was clear as day that Nina had decided to go to Canton to find Klim Rogov.

5

That night, Daniel couldn't sleep. Should he tell Nina that her husband was dead? But then she would start asking questions, and possibly even give up on her idea of going to Canton.

Daniel sat at the window, chain-smoking until he almost felt sick. He knew only too well how the *kitsune* fairy tales usually ended. Once wounded, a vixen would convince the man she had enchanted to share his vital energy with her; her strength would be restored but he would go crazy. Indeed, it was utter madness for him to sacrifice himself willingly for her sake.

The next morning Sam announced the arrival of Captain Wyer.

"I'm not at home," said Daniel and hurriedly went off to the stables.

It smelled of hay and horse sweat. Beams of light penetrated through the narrow windows under the ceiling.

The grooms took the golden-red horse from its stall, but as soon as Daniel put his foot into the stirrup, the tall figure of Captain Wyer appeared in the doorway.

"Get out," he snapped at the grooms, and they immediately disappeared.

Daniel dismounted and took the horse by the bridle.

"I didn't know you were here, sir."

"You did," Wyer said, cutting him short, "but I'm not interested in your pathetic attempts to avoid me. It's Edna that I want to talk about. As far as I'm concerned you may visit whores, like any other decent man, and I will think none the worse of you for it. But don't you dare go dragging my daughter's honor through the mud by getting yourself a mistress."

Daniel felt the blood rush to his face. He released the bridle, and the horse stepped back in its stall in fear.

"Mind your own business, sir," Daniel said quietly. "Otherwise you may live to regret it."

"Are you threatening me?" Wyer chuckled.

"If certain people in London get to know that you provide protection to smugglers and drug dealers, you'll find yourself out of office and straight into prison in no time."

"Listen, you sleazy son of a bitch, in this city the only person who makes threats that mean anything is me!"

Wyer took a stack of photographs from his map case and shoved under Daniel's nose. The images had been taken near Nina's house, and the photographer had taken a snap every time Daniel had visited her.

His meeting with Nina at the regatta has also been captured. The first picture showed Daniel offering her money, a second caught them locked in an embrace, while a third showed them getting into the same car.

"I've been following your mistress," Wyer said. "And if you're caught with her again, I'll show these pictures to Edna. Then, once she's divorced you, I think we'll have another look at the Czechoslovak Consulate case and re-examine the evidence Jiří Labuda told us about you. So think hard about it."

Daniel returned Wyer the photographs without saying a word.

"You'd better realize I'm deadly earnest," the captain said, and he went out into the street.

For a while Daniel stood there, tapping the top of his boot with his riding crop. *Things could be a lot worse,* he told himself. *Wyer evidently knows nothing about "Comrade Krieger."* But in any case, it would be best if he and Nina were to leave Shanghai immediately.

But what about the airplane? Would it be possible to take her to Canton by air? He needed a map and to refuel along the way. But to the south of Shanghai, there was nothing but endless Chinese countryside, where electricity was a rarity, let alone aviation fuel.

On his way to the house, Daniel met Ada.

"Good day, sir," she greeted him.

He looked at her inquisitively. Whatever happened, he would need to register his airplane with a front, preferably a person who knew nothing about military equipment. When Don Fernando got better, he would be able to bring the Avro to Canton by sea.

"Miss Marshall, I'll require your help tomorrow," Daniel said. "I'll pick you up at six in the morning."

"Are we going somewhere?" Ada asked.

"It's going to be a surprise. So don't tell anyone about it."

The poor girl was so confused that she was barely able to mumble, "Yes, sir, as you wish."

Daniel winked at her and went to his room.

An hour later, he passed the library and peeped in through the open door. Ada was dancing to a popular song, "I Was Waiting For You, Sweetheart."

20. THE STUDENT DEMONSTRATION

1

The opposition stronghold of Xiguan had been shelled by the mountain guns, killing about two thousand people, and the ensuing fire caused millions of dollars' worth of losses.

But Klim was very lucky. The Red Cross volunteers found him among the ruins, his head badly wounded by the gilded statue of Guan Yin. However, the goddess had covered him with her body and protected him from falling debris.

As a white man, he was taken to the Victoria Hotel on Shamian Island, which had been converted into a hospital. He was left unconscious in the hallway until One-Eye discovered him on his way to the Don's room.

Fernando insisted that the nurses put Klim next to him.

"Don't you dare die," he whispered to him. "You've saved my life and you're not going to croak on me now. Anyway, look at the room service, amigo! There's a bar, a balcony, and a gramophone with a full set of records. As soon as we're able to walk again, we'll make a trip to go and see the bathroom. I'm told the taps are gold-plated and the lamp brackets shaped like the most exquisite women."

Soon, a famous British surgeon arrived at the hospital.

"Please save my best friend," Don Fernando pleaded. "I'll give you every penny I have. I'll be in your debt for the rest of my life."

But the surgeon curtly replied he knew perfectly well what needed to be done without the Don's advice or inducements, and he ordered for Klim to be wheeled into the operating theater.

A little while later, at the Don's insistence, a nurse was explaining the finest details of Klim's medical notes to him. His friend had suffered a serious head injury, a stab wound to the chest, and an impressive list of minor cuts and bruises.

"That's bad that he's been hit on the head," One-Eye told the Don. "If Klim survives, he might start acting weird."

One-Eye had once been appointed an executioner and knew more about fatal wounds and injuries than any run-of-the-mill physician.

Much of the time, Klim was delirious, raving in Russian, Spanish, and English, and the Don was shocked to learn that his rescuer was married to Nina Kupina.

"You must be crazy to get involved with that sort of a woman," he said indignantly. "Her breasts are undoubtedly magnificent, but to marry her! Her sort is nothing but trouble. Did you know she had an affair with Daniel Bernard?"

"I did," Klim said in a quiet dangerous voice.

"Oh! You mustn't take anything I've said personally. I'm just worried about you, that's all."

When the Don received the telegram from Daniel, he replied that Rogov had been killed during the shelling. It was unlikely that Mr. Bernard was going to wish Klim a fast recovery.

In the meantime, Klim was getting sicker and sicker by the day.

"Send Nina a letter and tell her that I'm finished," he asked the Don on many occasions.

"Don't hex yourself," Fernando whispered fearfully. "Relax, I've already sent her five letters and ten telegrams." He was so superstitious he didn't even want to mention death.

All day long, the Don would pray to the Holy Virgin for Klim. "It won't cost you anything to save him. What do you want of me? I can recite the rosary a thousand times. How about I donate the consignment of leather that's been in my warehouse to the priests? I'm sure the soles of their shoes need saving."

Fernando even went so far as to promise the Holy Virgin that he would put himself on the path of righteousness and start a crusade against the criminal underworld. Not long after that, Klim miraculously began to get better.

"We are blood brothers now!" the Don yelled happily. "You've saved me from those Chinese butchers, and my prayers have saved you from death. Let's face it, you're not a Catholic and if it wasn't for me, you'd be burning in hell now. However, you'll be able to live and enjoy life for a while."

But enjoying his life was about the last thing on Klim's mind at that moment. He became taciturn and sullen, and every day after the letters were delivered, he would turn his face to the wall and refuse to talk.

Fernando knew that Klim was waiting for a letter from his wife, but didn't dare tell him that there would be no answer. He was good at counting but had no head for writing, and his message to Nina had been returned to sender with its misspelled address circled and underlined. Every day Fernando promised himself that he would ask Klim to rewrite the address correctly, but every day he would "forget" out of embarrassment.

In the meantime, the country was hit by a whirlwind of unexpected events. Sun Yat-sen died of liver cancer, and his adjutants began to argue about who would be his successor. The Kuomintang split into two wings: the Leftists gravitated towards an alliance with the Bolsheviks and the Chinese communists, while the Rights headed by General Chiang Kai-shek preferred to avoid changing one kind of foreign "patron" for another.

For Klim, these were matters of complete indifference.

"Is there any news from Shanghai?" he would ask absentmindedly each time Fernando started talking about politics.

However, the Don would pretend that he hadn't properly understood what Klim was really asking about.

"The city fathers want to prohibit child labor, to put up the fees for petty traders, and increase censorship in the Chinese press," Fernando said. "The students are protesting and fighting with the police every day, so we're pretty lucky to be out of that vipers' nest. I think we should stay in Canton and turn over a new leaf. We'll re-fit the *Santa Maria* and become honest fishermen. I hear there's a good trade to be had in octopuses."

But Klim was determined to return to Shanghai.

"What am I going do with him?" the Don complained to the Holy Virgin. "If I don't take him to Shanghai, he'll get into some rust bucket, pick up an infection from the other stowaways, and end up dying on me. You've seen him—he's just a bag of skin and bones. Without me, he'll be a goner for sure."

Fernando was constantly crossing himself and blowing kisses to the ceiling, but the Holy Virgin didn't answer his entreaties.

"All right, amigo, you win: I'll go with you to Shanghai," the Don decided. "But I warn you, don't expect my piety to last forever when we get there."

2

At dawn, as arranged, Daniel drove up to the House of

Hope and signaled three times with his car horn. A minute later, Ada appeared at the gate and flopped down on the front seat next to him. "Good morning, sir!"

It was impossible to look at her without an indulgent smile. She had no taste or appreciation of her youthful charm and was doing her best to imitate some showy movie actress. Her eyebrows had been plucked into two thin lines, her lips had been rouged with a stationery pencil, and a pink satin bow hung around her neck. Daniel recognized it from a gift box that some of Edna's friends had given to his wife.

Ada took a lollypop from her pocket and put it into her mouth. The air in the car began to smell of mint: a prudent girl, Ada was evidently making sure that she'd be prepared should Daniel surprise her with a kiss.

"Where are we going?" Ada asked.

"You'll see."

Despite the early hour, the streets were full of Chinese students in their traditional long-skirted coats. Some were carrying folded banners, while others were putting up posters. Many were gathered at the peddlers' kitchens, discussing something excitedly.

Daniel drove into a narrow street, which was bordered on one side by a neat hedge and the other by rows of Chinese houses with their tiled roofs.

Ada spied a taut canvas wing through a gap in the hedge and almost jumped out of her seat. "Goodness me, it's an airfield! Are you going to show me an airplane?"

"I'm going to do a lot more than show you one," Daniel said.

He drove the car up to a gate made of thin bamboo stems bound with wire. The guard ceremoniously opened it for them, and the car drove along the airfield, the gravel crunching under its wheels.

Ada's eyes nearly popped out of her head looking at the airplanes.

"Can we go a bit closer? Oh, I wish we could have our

photograph taken here."

"We can arrange that later," Daniel said with a smile. "Today we're going to fly to Suzhou."

"What?" Ada was lost for words. "We will . . . I mean—"

Daniel got out of the car and took her to a hangar.

"Are you sure this is going to be safe?" Ada said in a weak voice. "What if your airplane falls out of the sky? What if we get lost?"

She was overwhelmed by a combination of fear, mistrust, and excitement.

"Oh, you're probably just teasing me," she complained, forgetting herself. "How could you be so mean?"

The technicians removed the canvas cover from the Avro and wheeled it out onto the runway. Daniel helped Ada put on a helmet and a warm leather jacket—it would be cold up there in the heavens.

"I reckon I must look like a dragonfly." She giggled nervously as she adjusted her goggles.

"You do," Daniel replied bluntly and pointed to the back seat of the airplane. "Now get in."

He helped her into the cabin, sat down in the pilot's seat, and gave the orders for the engine to be started. The Avro coughed into life, bumping precariously along the airfield until finally with a mighty roar it soared into the sky.

"A-ah-ah!" Ada squealed excitedly.

Daniel made a turn and flew over the city, spotted with the shadows of the clouds. Its rivers stretched like rolls of exposed camera film glittering in the sun and its buildings like a set of multi-colored domino pieces that has been scattered over the ground by a fractious child.

As was his custom, Daniel flew over Nina's house, but this time he imagined he was dropping an invisible bomb that would destroy her past with all its bad memories.

"Don't worry darling," he whispered. "I'll arrange everything. You'll never need to worry again."

3

When they reached Suzhou, a city of humpback bridges and weeping willows, Daniel took Ada for a boat ride along the narrow canals that had been built the previous millennium.

The swarthy young boatman rowed slowly but deftly, each stroke of his oar creating small eddies in their wake.

The steps of the whitewashed homes ran down from the doors to the water's edge where carved, age-darkened boats were moored next to the banks. Children's voices and women's laughter wafted down from the open windows.

Weak with excitement, Ada was sitting in the prow near Daniel, his wrapped gifts at her feet—a silk robe, a hand mirror, and an embroidered fan which they had bought in a little shop on their way.

"This city is two and a half thousand years old," Daniel mused. "The same age as Confucius. Once Suzhou was the capital of the state of Wu, praised for its silk and beautiful women."

"Like her?" Ada smiled, glancing at a fat woman rinsing linen in the canal. "What sort of woman do you go for?"

He motioned towards Ada's reflection in the water, "I'm into this type. You know there is a piece of poetry:

Soft lilac twilight. I'm alone,
As I watch paper lanterns in the sky.
Again I'll stay awake till dawn
Observing boats go gliding by.
I wish for temple bells to sing you songs
About my heart so full, so high."

"I know what you're implying," Ada said, frowning, "but you're not going to leave your wife and business because of me. You've got too much to lose."

"One day you'll understand that this can all be easily exchanged for—"

"Would you even exchange it for your airplane?"

"If you want, I can give it to you," he said after a pause. "Did you never want to learn how to fly in your childhood? Let's make that dream come true."

The idea was so ridiculous that Ada just shrugged. "Oh, stop it! You're making fun of me."

"I'll make a gift deed out in your favor—now. The only thing I'm asking is for you to await my return. I'll be going on a business trip soon, and it will last for a few months."

Ada blinked in confusion. "You're either one heck of a liar or you're completely mad."

"I've gone completely mad and I'm very happy about it."

Ada was sure that he'd been joking until they went to a Chinese official and she received a document testifying that she was now the proud owner of an Avro 504.

4

Daniel persuaded Ada that it would be better to leave the airplane in Suzhou to keep their adventure a secret from Edna, and they hired a car to return to Shanghai.

"Mr. Bernard, I can't handle it," Ada said. "You keep doing good things for me, and I don't even know how I can pay you back."

Daniel smiled. "Don't worry about that."

They entered the city and drove along the Babbling Well Road, but as they went around the race track, the traffic ground to a halt because a crowd of students was blocking the Nanking Road. Drivers honked, rickshaw boys swore, but the young people didn't pay them the slightest attention, shouting their political slogans in one voice.

"What do they want?" Ada asked Daniel.

"Equality, justice, and the abolition of laws that worsen the living conditions for the poor," he said.

Daniel paid the driver and got out of the car.

"Let's go, Ada, or we'll be stuck here for a long time."

She followed him between the honking cars, holding the package with her gifts tight to her chest.

As they reached the police station, the crowd became denser.

"Make way!" Daniel snarled at the Chinese—students, monks, clerks, and coolies—but no one listened.

A puny young man gave a rousing speech standing atop a column covered with advertising. The crowd applauded him wildly.

By the time Daniel and Ada had reached the opposite side of the street, a fist fight had broken out near the gates of the police station. The students began to throw stones; someone was knocked down and kicked by the crowd.

Looking back, Daniel saw an officer in a pith helmet.

"This is your last warning!" the policeman shouted pointing at the line of Sikhs armed with rifles. "If you don't stop, I won't be responsible for the consequences!"

What's the point yelling? Daniel thought. *They don't understand English anyway.*

He grabbed Ada's hand. "Let's get the hell out of here."

It was then that the first volley exploded.

Startled, the crowd let forth an animal howl and scattered in all directions, smashing anything in its path.

"They'll crush us!" Daniel shouted, choking, as he was pressed flat against the wall.

He and Ada ran into a narrow doorway and found themselves in a small restaurant full of Chinese dressed in long blue robes. The steam was rising above their bowls, and an old ceiling fan was spinning with a quiet swishing sound.

A servant, as big as a wild boar, moved towards Daniel and Ada. "You are not allowed in here!"

He was about to kick them outside when a torrent of terrified people poured in through the door. Daniel noticed a disheveled white woman among them. She slid to the floor, holding her head in her blood-stained hands.

"Edna!" he yelled.

Forgetting about her gifts, Ada rushed to her. "Mrs. Bernard! What's happened to you?"

They dragged Edna into the kitchen.

"Give me a towel," Daniel snapped at the stunned cook. "Can't you see—she's bleeding!"

The cook threw him a damp cloth.

"What the hell are you doing here?" said Daniel angrily as he wiped a deep cut on Edna's forehead.

She looked at him, her eyes wild, her lips trembling, her bangs matted with blood.

"News is my job," she said.

"We need to get her out of here," Ada whispered. "What if the Chinese find out that she's Captain Wyer's daughter?"

They took Edna by her arms and carried her through the back door into a yard that was littered with garbage. Having wandered through a rat run of back alleys, they finally turned onto a nice-looking empty street.

The bright sun shone through the treetops. Police whistles and car horns could be heard nearby.

Daniel had never been on this street on foot, and only when he saw the familiar white house did he realize that they had arrived at Nina's.

Edna suddenly lost consciousness.

"She's dead!" Ada screamed.

"Be quiet, for God's sake," Daniel snapped at her.

They put Edna on the grass.

"Stay here, I'll be right back," he told Ada.

He ran up to Nina's house and banged on the door with his fist. A skinny dark-haired man appeared on the porch.

"What do you want?" he said with a Russian accent.

"Is Nina there?" Daniel asked, and only then recognized Klim Rogov staring at him.

5

SKETCHES

Klim Rogov's new diary

As a teenager, I often wondered what my own funeral would be like. In my mind's eye, I imagined there would be at least five hundred mourners, a military band, and a heartbroken fair lady at my coffin. Who would have turned up if I had given up the ghost in Canton? The best I could have hoped was Don Fernando, One-Eye, and a couple of coolies impatiently leaning on their shovels. Some send-off that would have been.

Perhaps it was this prospect that helped me survive, an act of protest against having the sum of my life marked in such an unseemly way. Besides, I had to find out what had happened to Nina and why she hadn't written to me after receiving so many of my letters via Don Fernando.

I tried to send her a cable before my departure but quickly came to an impasse. Canton was busy fighting spies, and they weren't allowing any Tom, Dick or Harry to send a telegram anywhere without authorization and ID.

On my way home, I prepared myself for the worst. Was Nina alright? Or perhaps she had found another admirer and forgotten all about my existence?

On May 30, 1925, the *Santa Maria* sailed into Shanghai, and Don Fernando generously agreed to drive me to Nina's.

"If you find your wife with a lover, come back and join me," he said as he left.

I was as tense as a coiled spring. The weather was clement, the sun shining, and the birds chirruping without a care in the world, but here I was feeling as if I was about to be read a death sentence.

When I came in, Kitty and her amah had just returned from a walk. My daughter had grown so much that I could hardly recognize her. When I left she couldn't even walk.

Kitty picked up a twig and gave it to me, saying, "Take this!" I squatted down, deeply touched, and asked her how she had been doing. She answered me in her baby language, which was absolutely incomprehensible to me.

The amah called Nina, and my wife ran to the porch, still in her white bathrobe, her hair dripping wet. Before I could say a word, she threw her arms around me and cried, "Why didn't you write to me?"

It turned out that Nina hadn't learned anything about my injury. Having received no news, she had decided to go to Canton to find me. The suitcases were ready and packed in her living room, and half a dozen different guidebooks were lying on the table.

We were both stunned and confused. In the months since our last meeting, we had conceived a thousand different plots of betrayal and death, and now it was hard to accept they had been completely unfounded.

Nina told me what had happened to her. The Jesuits had cheated her, her competitors had ruined her business, and she had little or no money to get by. I wondered how my brave girl had coped with it all?

I told her about my adventures and encounter with "Comrade Krieger."

"Daniel never told me a thing about it," Nina gasped.

I felt as though someone had just run a high-voltage through my entire body.

"Did he come here?" I asked.

Nina went deathly pale and began to explain in earnest that she didn't want to have anything to do with him. At that moment, there was a knock at the door, and there was the man himself at the doorstep, as large as life.

Nina was the first to pull herself together and began to shove the intruder out of the door. "Leave us alone. Please!"

I saw the way he looked at us and realized in an instant that my wife had broken his heart.

"Did you hear the gunshots?" he said. "The police have just dispersed a demonstration on Nanking Road. Edna has been wounded and lost consciousness."

"I'll tell the driver to take you to the hospital," Nina said.

She literally pushed him out and slammed the door behind him.

"We need to find out how Edna is," I said, but Nina stood in my way.

"Don't you dare go out there. The servants will take care of her. Don't you realize that you and Daniel will end up killing each other?"

Through the window, I watched Nina's car driving out of the gate. Daniel put Edna and Ada into it and they left.

"I'd better go," I said. "I don't want you and Kitty to get into any more trouble on my account. I'm sure Daniel Bernard will use every opportunity to rid himself of me, and Wyer isn't likely to have forgotten my past misdeeds either."

But Nina was confident that we still had a little time.

"The police won't come visiting just yet," she said. "They've got more than enough on their hands with the demonstration, and anyway Daniel will have already put two and two together that I know all about your encounter in Canton. There's nothing he can do about it now."

I really wanted to find out what had passed between her and Daniel, but I decided not to pry: the details would only lead to pain and recriminations. What we needed was to start all over again, from scratch, and right now the only thing I wanted to do was to play at happy families.

When we are children, it doesn't matter to us who we are in real life. A boy can play a brave hero, and a girl can be a beautiful princess. If everybody agrees to play their part then there is nothing to stop us making our fantasy a reality.

We feasted until well into the evening, played with Kitty, danced, and kissed, our lives and very essence melding into each other's. It was mind blowing how rapidly it all happened. The most trivial things, such as washing our faces next to each other at the sink, or me passing Nina a piece of soap behind the shower curtain acquired the most intense meaning. I never dreamed of being entitled to such joy.

It's now eleven-thirty at night, my body is exhausted but relaxed, however, I still can't get to sleep. I'm sitting in Nina's bedroom at her dressing table and writing my new diary, having moved her hairbrushes and perfume bottles to one side. My previous diary, "Receipts and Expenditures," has been lost in the vagaries of the Chinese mail service, but I don't regret it. There are some details of my life that I need to forget.

I constantly want to take a peek at my sleeping wife, to check that she is really here with me and that I haven't dreamt all this up. A mosquito net floats over her like a translucent cloud. My heart sings with hymns of praise, and my only regret is that I can't pick up a telephone to God and thank him for his sublime generosity.

21. THE GENERAL STRIKE

1

SKETCHES

Klim Rogov's diary

The Nanking Road massacre of May 30 claimed the lives of thirteen students with dozens more injured. The next day, the Chinese trade unions announced a general strike, and now the foreign concessions have found themselves left with neither telephone nor tap water.

Garage owners refuse to sell gas to foreigners, the trams have stopped working, and rickshaw boys no longer carry white passengers. I guess this must be the reason why nobody has come to kill us so far. Wyer's cutthroats are probably out on strike as well, and Daniel Bernard is feeling too lazy to go anywhere by foot in this heat.

Nina has come up with a new business idea. She

wants to set up a security agency and hire former White Army military men to guard us and her potential customers. The demand for these sorts of services is huge: everyone who has money is terrified of thugs coming to rob them. The rich who have come to Shanghai from the war-torn provinces are in a particularly difficult situation. They have neither friends nor relatives here. The police have gone on strike, too, and the prospect of hiring Chinese bodyguards, who might easily be gang members themselves, is a scary one.

Russians make perfect bodyguards in this situation: they have no ties with the local community and no connections with the Chinese underworld. They have combat experience, and they are eager to work, exhausted by their long-term unemployment.

Nina has learned the ins and outs of business the hard way, and now she is drawing up a proper plan and calculating how much money she will need to rent a new office and train her staff. I watch her and think that the act of setting up a business is, in its own way, a form of art, like creating a novel, a painting, or an invention.

I need to be ready for the day when my wife might start earning more than me. I guess I will flatter myself that I am a "gardener" who has spent many seasons tending to a rose bush that has produced into the most exotic blossom.

When I returned to Shanghai, I had mentally prepared myself for a long spell of unemployment, but the general strike has played into my hands: the demand for news from China has soared to the heavens, and now I have started writing for Reuters.

Previously, the world didn't care much about what was going on in China, but now it is obvious that we are all interconnected. The general strike in Shanghai caused immediate ripples in stock markets, and now the world is waiting for an explanation. What the devil is going on over here?

I have a difficult job: the Chinese are not very willing to talk to white journalists and often banish us from their meetings, claiming that we lie and distort what they say. The police are tough on us as well, dispersing demonstrations with horse charges and fire hoses. Several times I've returned home covered in bruises and soaked from head to toe.

The unions are prepared to call off the strike if the whites are ready to make significant compromises and reconsider the unequal treaties, but the Municipal Council is a local government and as such does not have the power to change international agreements. The strike ringleaders know this but they are doing their best to turn this small dispute into a major conflict, telling the people that the "white ghosts" are not interested in a peaceful solution. The more damage that can be inflicted on the colonialists, the harder the bargain the unions can negotiate for themselves at a later date.

White Shanghai is laying low, bristling and wrapped up in itself like a cornered porcupine. The mobilization of a Volunteer Corps has been announced, and marines from foreign ships have been summoned ashore to man the patrols. Rather than seeing these as protective measures, the Chinese mutter darkly about the foreign powers preparing for an occupation, and the situation only gets more heated.

The time and effort I spent on Wyer would now appear to be paying dividends. The small waves of discontent set in motion by my articles have grown into a tsunami of righteous wrath, and now the captain is possibly the most hated man in Shanghai. He is generally held to be the main culprit behind the events of May 30, although that Saturday he was actually out hunting ducks and only learned what had happened the next day. His very name has become synonymous with injustice, violence, and extortion, and the city is littered with leaflets calling for his death.

I don't crave Wyer's blood—after all, he is Edna's father—but I do want him out of Shanghai.

2

The International Settlement is full of rumors of Chinese workers stoning foreign foremen and pillaging the stores of their countrymen suspected of collaborating with the "white ghosts." In the wake of these rumors, Nina had no problems obtaining the license for her security agency and hired three dozen White Army men living in the Russian neighborhood along Avenue Joffre.

She is fully committed to her new business and has no time to deal with the calendars, leaving them to Binbin. She now spends all her time in negotiations with her new customers and signing security contracts for warehouses, shops, and weddings.

In the evening, tired and happy, we gather in Kitty's room to play with our daughter, to dance, and to invent plays with her plush toys.

I have learned to understand Kitty to some extent. She babbles in three languages: Russian words are meant for parents, English is associated with toys and the playground, and the Shanghai dialect she picked up from her amah is used while eating, bathing, and sitting on the potty.

No one could have convinced me three years ago that the awful events of that period could have marked the starting point for my new life. Now I find it funny to look back and remember what a fool I had been. Mistrust and resentment are like dust on the window; if you don't wash it off, the dirt makes it impossible to see what's going on both inside and outside the room. You make one mistake after another, the window gets increasingly smudged, the room gets darker, and you end up blaming everybody except yourself.

I feel sorry for Ada, who's making the same mistakes. I visited her at the House of Hope, but she refused to talk to me, didn't even open the door. "You left me behind, and I hate you," was all that she would say.

Ada won't even entertain the notion that she might have misinterpreted events, and I can't help her clean the window if she can't see that it's dirty. I've decided to let her be. She's a big girl now, and frankly, I have neither the time nor the inclination to get into an argument with her.

Nina and I are intoxicated by our happiness. I'm constantly astonished by such simple everyday miracles as finding Nina's hand on the pillow next to mine in the mornings. I stroke it gently in grateful wonder—just because it's there and I can.

Our life has become a joyful round of sweet and simple rituals. At night, Nina has got into the habit of putting her head on my chest. Within a minute my breathing lulls her into sleep, and I spend hours with my eyes open, unable to believe that it is her curls that I am running my hands through.

3

The Aulmans' servants left to join the strike, and Tamara and the children spend their evenings alone in the candlelight, waiting for Tony's return. Tamara's telephone was silent, and none of her friends offered her any help during the strike.

The bell at the front door rang.

"Daddy is back!" Roger shouted and rushed to open the door.

But it was Nina. Serious and practical as ever, she

entered the living room and put a small kerosene stove on the table.

"I thought you wouldn't have anything to boil water with," she said. "Now let's see about dinner, shall we?"

"Thank you for coming," Tamara said, deeply touched.

The boys followed Nina's every move as she deftly sorted out the pots and spoons. They had never seen a white woman cook before.

"Five minutes and everything will be ready," Nina announced. "Boys, bring the plates."

As they sat at the dinner table, Tony swept into the house, bringing with him the smell of horses, fires, and the sweet stiff pomade he used on his mustache.

"Oh, Miss Nina, glad to see you. Here, children, the ladies at the Anti-Strike Committee baked us volunteers some cookies today."

"How are things at the office?" Tamara asked.

Tony waved his hand. "We found a stock of counterfeit records, but the Chinese guards were on strike, and goods to the value of twenty thousand were left unguarded. I usually negotiate with the owners; they pay my clients and we return them the goods. But if the warehouse gets plundered, we all suffer losses."

"Do you want me to send my boys your way?" Nina asked. "They could keep an eye on your warehouse. By the way, there are a huge number of healthy unemployed men in the Russian community. They would be more than capable of solving our water and electricity supply problems if only someone could be persuaded to let them cover for the striking Chinese."

"Can you get your workers organized quickly?" Tony asked incredulously.

"If you post an ad at the Russian church, you'll have a whole crowd at your gate in an hour."

Tony leapt from the table. "Tamara, we need to go to the Municipal Council and talk to Mr. Sterling. Boys, take care of your mother. Miss Nina and I will be back soon."

4

SKETCHES

Klim Rogov's diary

Nina has acted as a mediator between the Municipal Council and the Russian community, and they have restored the water supply and got the post office working again. Our greatest success is that we managed to set free the Cossacks from the *Mongugai* steamer. The Anti-Strike Committee has distributed them out to the factories.

The strikebreakers have made our lives much easier. Shanghai hadn't exactly been the cleanest city in the world before the strike, but when the coolies stopped cleaning the cesspools, the heavy smell of rot spread like a pall over the entire city. Now, thank God, we can at least open our windows.

The Chairman of the Municipal Council, Mr. Sterling, has promised Nina a reward for her services to the International Settlement—he is going to help us get U.S. citizenship. We pray for everything to work out; with our backs covered by the American government, we will be able to defend ourselves against Wyer. However, thankfully, nothing has been seen or heard of the captain recently.

Our future looks bright, but of course there are always some clouds on the horizon.

Predictably, Nina's employees are ashamed to be working for a woman. She once told me that some of them have taken to giving her a nasty nickname and laughing at her behind her back.

She doesn't know how to react to it all. Should she ignore her detractors or should she fire the lot of them? Nina is in a constant state of self-doubt and often tries too hard to prove herself—much to the amusement of her critics and to her own chagrin.

She wants to share her fears and experiences with somebody, but her friends are not much help in this respect. Tamara thinks that a lady shouldn't be involved in business, and Binbin resents Nina not spending so much time with her at the publishing house.

The calendar business is like a weight around Nina's neck. "I've tried so hard, and everything I do there seems to fall on rocky ground," she complains. But she still expends a huge amount of energy trying to revive the business. If she were to let it fail completely, how would her employees feed their families?

She has taken so much upon herself, and the only solution she can see is to share her burden with me. But from the very beginning, Nina and I have had an agreement that we would never force each other to do things we are not interested in. Journalism by definition is not a particularly profitable profession, and Nina knows that this is a sore point for me. I have a hard time explaining to myself and others why my wife earns more than I do. Nina tries to avoid the subject, but I can see that deep down inside she believes that her business is more important. She's annoyed with the fact that I spend my time writing articles rather than going to the office with her.

Once Nina blurted out, "Daniel always used to help me." But as soon as she said it, she was mortified and asked me to forgive her. I replied that I'm smart enough not to take offense at a random slip of the tongue. But in reality, I am not.

As far as I know, Daniel left Shanghai after the strike, but I'm still overwhelmed by a gloomy melancholy every time I hear his name. For me, he has come to symbolize all the troubles and misfortunes that surround us: betrayal, sickness, and death.

22. MATERIAL EVIDENCE

1

Strangely, Edna was relieved when Daniel mysteriously disappeared again. At least she wouldn't have to wonder where he was and with whom. She had enough problems as it was: her father had been suspended on paid leave and his whole future was at risk.

When he was summoned to a meeting of the Municipal Council to answer about the events of May 30, Edna went there to provide her father with moral support.

The room was full of high-ranking officials, captains of industry, police officers, and foreign journalists. Naturally, no Chinese had been invited.

"My enemies deliberately organized the Nanking Road massacre," Wyer barked from the podium. "They bribed the protesters by giving them five dollars each. They are willing to do anything to undermine me and the defense of our settlement. But we'll never allow these street thugs to dictate terms to us."

Edna thought her father would be laughed out of the meeting. Did he really think they would believe his story that the students had surrendered their lives for a mere five dollars? But to her surprise, the captain's speech was greeted with a storm of applause.

"Don't expect the Chinese to be reasonable," said

Johnny Collor. "They were afraid that the ban on child labor would deprive them of an important source of income, but now they have nothing whatsoever other than the free rice distributed by charities. Is anyone even thinking about what is going to happen after the strike? If workers ruin their employers, where are they going to find another job after the strike is over?"

Mr. Sterling, the Chairman of the Municipal Council, took the podium.

"We conducted an investigation," he said, "and found out that all this was possible only because Chinese merchants are secretly financing the strikers. They think it will ruin their foreign competitors and increase the demand for local products. But their own factories rely on the electricity produced by our power station that they have conveniently 'forgotten' to shut down. Well, we're going to stop supplying our electricity to any factories whose owners support the strike. If they hate the West so much, let's see how they manage without our technical know-how."

Then Mr. Sterling thanked Captain Wyer for his excellent service and promised the audience that the white man will never leave China.

His speech was met with even more enthusiastic applause. Officials and businessmen patted each other on the back, laughing loudly and threatening to have the strike leaders strung up from lampposts as a lesson to others. Finding a compromise wasn't even on the agenda.

2

Wyer was confident that after his speech the Municipal Council would recall him to his position. But a week later Mr. Sterling, who had been such an ardent admirer of captain's merits and achievements, quietly announced to the press the arrival of a new Police Commissioner for the International Settlement. Captain Wyer, Sterling said, would be taking an early pension and returning to the mother country.

Enraged, the captain stormed into Edna's study.

"The scoundrel has organized a farewell dinner without even consulting me," he yelled. "That Nina Kupina is behind all this. She's made herself indispensable to him, and now that Russian vixen has turned him against anyone who has the true interests of the empire at heart."

Edna reluctantly lifted her head from her book. "You know perfectly well that Miss Kupina has nothing to do with it."

Wyer's face contorted with rage. "So, you're taking her side too now, are you?" He took a stack of photographs out of his map case and tossed them on her desk. "I showed them to Sterling, but he wasn't even remotely bothered. Perhaps you should be?"

Edna glanced at the photographs of Daniel and his mistress and threw the whole lot into the wastebasket.

"I'm past caring," she said.

3

Ada was secretly hoping that the Bernards' servants would join the strikers, giving her an opportunity to be promoted to maid or even housekeeper. But Yun called all the servants into his kitchen and in no uncertain terms told them that anyone upsetting Missy would become his personal enemy.

"One of my students works as a cook at the governor's, and the other at the house of the leader of the Green Gang," said the old man menacingly. "So I'll find a way to deal with you."

Ada had no choice but to wait for Mr. Bernard's return and dream about one day setting up her own restaurant or store with the seed capital he had promised to give her.

One day Sam rushed into the library and gave Ada a stack of photographs.

"Look what I've found! I was taking the trash out from Missy's study and found these pictures in the wastebasket."

At first, Ada thought these were old photographs that had been taken two years previously when Mr. Bernard was courting Nina Kupina. But then she noticed one of Daniel in a new hat he had recently bought.

"I wonder where these pictures came from?" Sam asked. "And what should I do with them now?"

"I'll keep them," Ada replied in a barely audible voice.

From that day on, she wasn't able to sleep a wink. If Mr. Bernard was in love with Nina, why on earth was he messing around with her, and why had he registered his airplane in her name?

The only explanation she could come up with was that the Avro had been stolen, and Daniel had decided to dupe her so that she would carry the can if anything were to happen. It was the perfect solution: Ada couldn't sell or use the airplane—she didn't even remember where they had left it.

If this was the case, she was in a pretty serious fix. She was so anxious that she began to lose weight, and Yun even started giving her an extra ladleful of soup at lunch.

"Are you pregnant?" he asked. "Or have you just get worms in your guts?"

"My great aunt is very good at curing all sorts of diseases," Sam said. "She even had a butcher as a client and removed all his warts."

"Leave me alone," Ada moaned and escaped into the library.

At night, she would look at the pictures Sam had given her and nearly weep with envy.

Why did the men she liked never fall in love with her? One of the photographs showed Daniel Bernard kissing Nina's hand, looking at her as if she were a queen. What was so special about her? She was ancient, almost thirty for goodness sake!

Chen the landlord told Ada that he had recently seen

Klim on the street. "Mr. Rogov is now living next to the racecourse with his wife and daughter. He seems to be doing all right, and said to say hello to you."

Does Klim know that Nina has cheated on him again? Ada wondered. *Apparently not.*

It was then that she came up with a new plan: what if Klim were to fall out with his wife and return to the House of Hope? They would become friends again, and he would be able to help her find a way to protect herself from Daniel Bernard.

4

Ada stood on the porch of Nina's house and was about to press the doorbell when she noticed that the front door was already slightly ajar. Her knees were shaking from fear, but she mastered herself and made her way into the hallway.

A slanting beam of sunlight from a semicircular window illuminated the disorder. Parasols, scarves, and gloves lay in a pile on the console table, and rows of children's leather sandals lay under the shoe rack. Ada was impressed and even envious of their quality next to her poor, rough canvas shoes.

She could distinctly make out angry voices coming from behind the sliding doors to the living room.

"Miss Nina hasn't paid us on time for months," a young woman with a Chinese accent was complaining, "but we said nothing because we wanted to help her to get back on her feet. We thought that she wasn't going to be like the other whites, but then she sent her Russian strikebreakers to the factories, and they've ruined everything we've achieved since the beginning of the protests."

"Nina is just trying to help her fellow countrymen find employment," Klim replied coldly.

"Do you seriously think that justifies what she's done?

The moment you Russians arrived in Shanghai, you began stealing our jobs. You have no right to interfere in our affairs. Tell Miss Nina that as of today she doesn't have a publishing house any longer. We all quit."

The doors were opened with a crash, and a Chinese girl, her face wet with tears, ran past Ada out into the street.

Klim entered the hallway and stared at Ada. "What are you doing here?"

She immediately realized she had come at a bad time.

"Oh, hi . . . Is Miss Nina at home?"

"No. Why?"

Ada took the photographs from her purse and handed them to Klim. He fanned them out and then put them back into the stack.

"Where did you get them?" he asked in a low voice.

"Miss Edna threw them away, and my friend Sam gave them to me."

"Go home," Klim said thrusting the photographs back to Ada and disappeared behind the sliding doors.

She stood in the middle of the hallway, confused. Klim had neither invited her into the house nor asked her how she was doing. He didn't even thank her for the information she had provided. Was he not even a little bit curious?

Annoyed, Ada threw the pictures on the floor and went out into the street, without even closing the door. Let thieves come and steal his daughter's shoes. What did she care?

5

Nina came home very late.

She entered the dark bedroom, took off her robe, and got into the bed, naked. Klim didn't move, but by the way he was breathing Nina could sense immediately that he was not asleep.

"Today we signed a contract to guard a parking lot for the municipal rickshaws," she said, snuggling up to him. "We should think about setting up a transport company of our own. I've already made some calculations: a rickshaw costs a hundred dollars and has a service life of about five years. We could rent it out to a coolie for a dollar a day, and if it breaks, he would be responsible for its repair. So that means that within under a year and a half we will have clawed back our capital outlay and from there on everything we make will be profit."

Nina ran her fingers over Klim's chest, but he brushed her hand away. Her heart sank; never before had he been so brusque with her.

"Are you mad at me for being so late?"

"No."

"What's the matter then?"

"Stay out of the rickshaw business," said Klim. "It's the most base form of exploitation. A rickshaw boy runs in all weather twelve hours a day for twenty cents a job. Almost none of them reach the age of forty before dying from overexertion."

"Nobody would be forcing them to work for me," Nina protested. "There are plenty of coolies in Shanghai who are desperate for any kind of job. Otherwise, they and their families would just starve."

Klim got up without a word. Frightened, Nina sat up in bed.

"Where are you going? Let's forget about the rickshaw business. I'm not interested in it if you're not happy about it."

"I've got a sore throat," Klim said. "I need to take something for it."

Nina could tell from the sound of his footsteps that he hadn't gone to the bathroom, where the cabinet with medicines was, but to Kitty's room. She waited for ten minutes, twenty, and then she picked up her robe from the floor and followed Klim.

A nightlight was on in Kitty's room, and soft toys were scattered all over the floor. Klim sat at the footboard of the bed, his back slumped, elbows pressed into his knees. He looked as though he had just learned about somebody's death and still couldn't believe it.

"Daddy, cover me," Kitty said in her dream.

Klim covered her swarthy little legs.

"And give me the bunny."

Obediently, he obliged.

Nina opened the door a little wider. She wanted to come in, but Klim waved her away with his hand. "Go, go. You'll wake her up."

He never returned to the bedroom and spent the night on the couch in his study.

In the morning, Nina found an envelope with the photographs on her desk. There was a note attached:

Hua Binbin told me that your publishing house was on the verge of bankruptcy and was kept afloat only thanks to Daniel Bernard.

I can see that you had to provide for Kitty and yourself, but I still need some time to process what has happened and decide what to do next.

6

SKETCHES

Klim Rogov's diary

As soon as the power to the Chinese factories was cut off, their owners sued for a negotiated settlement with the foreigners, and the strike came to the end.

The only beneficiaries of the strike have been the Russians who have managed to drag themselves out of abject poverty, and of course the Green Gang. The Chinese state is unable to protect the lives and property of its citizens, and organized criminal gangs have formed to fill the vacuum. They collect taxes from their territories, patrol them, and lay down the law. Their influence is growing by the day, and now the only branch of the state capable of coping with the Green Gang is the army. But our governor takes loans from the gangsters and is not going to pick a fight with them.

Nina and I are "fine." Wyer has left for London, and we no longer have the burden of the unsuccessful publishing business on our shoulders. Nina's security agency is flourishing, I still work for Reuters, and it seems that all our problems have been solved and we are finally settled.

But in reality, things have never been worse. Nina is constantly angry with me, one day crying then the next trying to explain that she and Daniel were just friends. But I can't bear it when she starts telling me where they went and what they did together.

If I pretend that everything is all right again, it won't change a thing. While I was dying in the hospital, unable to help Nina, she went running back to her sugar daddy to solve all her problems for her. She doesn't see anything wrong or remarkable about this because frankly there is more of the courtesan about her than the dutiful wife.

I'm surprised it took me so long to figure out that she wanted to go to Canton *with Daniel*. Her commercial venture failed, and evidently, he offered her the chance to be his kept woman. I returned in the nick of time to spoil Daniel's well-laid plans, and he was a bit unlucky. Or, maybe, on the contrary, I did him a favor, saving him from a load of unpleasant surprises in the future.

I need a home, a safe haven, a place where I can go back to knowing that my wife is waiting for me, accepting me for who I am. But living with Nina means being in a constant state of anxiety, wondering whether she is going to leave me for someone new. Today Nina's heart belongs to me, tomorrow it could be Bernard's, and the day after that anybody else who takes her fancy.

I ought to walk away from Nina and never look back, but I can't leave Kitty behind and I can't take her with me and deprive her of her mother and a home. Probably the wisest solution would be to stay calm, avoid conflicts, and not expect too much either from myself or Nina. Life is short, and we should enjoy what we have, instead of demanding the impossible.

Sometimes I wonder, what might have happened if I had never had the misfortune to chance upon Nina in Lincheng? I'd still be working at the *Daily News* and would probably have met another woman by now. There would have been no flight from Shanghai, and no near-death experiences in Canton. But, on the other hand, if everything had turned out differently, Kitty would have died the day she was born.

7

Unlike the public gardens in the International Settlement, the Chinese were allowed to visit the park in the French Concession—on the strict condition that they wore smart and tidy European-style clothes. An armed policeman was permanently stationed at the gates to ensure the rules were obeyed and the twenty cent tickets paid for and checked.

When Klim brought Kitty to the playground swings, the white moms would grab their children and move them away from her as if she had an infectious disease. Roaring with laughter, Kitty would chase after them and then come back and enjoy the deserted swings and slides all to herself.

"Let's go throw some pebbles in the pond," Klim told her, feeling uneasy.

Her delight knew no end when a flat pebble skimmed over the water to disappear under the branches of a willow tree.

"Now, look who's here!" came a familiar roar.

Klim turned to see the indomitable Don Fernando striding towards him, arms wide open. In one hand Fernando held his hat and in the other an ice-cream on a stick. One-Eye and the other bodyguards scurried after him, uncomfortable in their European style garb.

"Wow, who's this lovely little thing?" Fernando exclaimed as he noticed Kitty. "Hey, Klim, did you get yourself some Chinese piece with a child? Tut-tut! You're right, the Chinese are more reliable, and if you ever fancy a white girl, you can always go to Martha's. Her prices are outrageous but at least her hookers are checked by the doctor every week."

Klim took Kitty up into his arms. "I'd be grateful if you watched your language in her presence."

"Oh, come on!" the Don laughed. "We need to discuss business, amigo. Have you ever heard of Dame Nellie Melba?"

"No," Klim said, frowning.

The Don rolled his eyes. "The world famous soprano? In the past, only the very rich could get tickets to see her, but now any fool can enjoy her wonderful voice. Do you understand what I'm talking about?"

Klim looked at him, perplexed. God only knew what sort of crazy ideas inhabited that swarthy and irrepressible head of his.

"We need a radio station, that's what!" roared the Don. "Here, in Shanghai. And you know who's going to run it? You. I've already hired a room and installed the transmitter. We've got the technicians and what we need now is a journalist with the gift of the gab. It's a job with your name written all over it. What do you say?"

"I've already got—"

"Don't upset me, amigo. This is the future. From now on, ideas are going to be transmitted straight into people's homes and you're going to be in on the ground floor."

23. THE RUSSIAN MERCENARY

1

Daniel didn't send Edna a single letter, and gradually Ada realized that he wouldn't be returning to Shanghai. She found herself in a preposterous situation: on paper, she was filthy rich, with a real airplane to her name, but in reality, she had to scrimp and save for several months just to buy herself a new winter coat.

Edna had a radio in her living room, and Ada was surprised to hear Klim broadcasting over the airwaves. Soon he was famous throughout Shanghai with his funny comments on political issues and reviews of the latest record releases. Ada was so disappointed that she hadn't been able to win his affections that she began to lose faith in her feminine charms. She regarded her future and could only see herself becoming a dried-out, poor, old maid.

Meanwhile, Mrs. Bernard had gone quite crazy.

It all started when the Chinese actress Hua Binbin brought two teenage girls to see Edna. Sam and Ada were standing at the door and overheard their conversation. The girls were prostitutes who had escaped from a brothel. Binbin had met them in the temple, learned that they wanted to commit suicide, and had decided to save them.

She told Edna that she too had been contemplating suicide. She had lost her job, and during the strike, thieves had broken into her film studio and stolen all the equipment. So her dream of making a movie was also in ruins.

"But we have no right to complain," Binbin said to Edna. "These children's lot is a thousand times worse than ours, and they have no means of escaping their tormentors, while you and I have never experienced true poverty or starvation."

From that day, Edna and Binbin started a campaign raiding brothels that used underage prostitutes. With an ax in her hand and police officers behind her, Mrs. Bernard would break into the brothels, shattering the doors to the rooms where the children were imprisoned and frightening them to death in the process. Binbin would persuade them to go to a shelter at the church, where the girls were taught crafts and English. A few months later the former prostitutes would be able to earn their living with a respectable trade.

On more than one occasion, dogs' heads and threatening notes appeared on the porch outside the Bernards' front door.

"The Green Gang is behind child trafficking in Shanghai," said Yun with a sigh. "They are not to be trifled with."

Convinced that the gangsters would kill them all, he bought himself a coffin—just in case. Meanwhile, Sam bought an amulet from a traveling monk and gave it to Ada.

"I pray for you every day," he said in a serious tone, but it didn't make her feel any safer.

2

On her way home, Ada noticed a rough-looking man

tailing her. She stopped at a shop window to peer carefully behind her. He looked very suspicious with his cap pulled rakishly over one eye, his gray coat, and a map-case hanging from his shoulder.

Ada began to tremble like a rabbit. There was no doubt about it; he must be an assassin from the Green Gang. She increased her pace, but he kept up with her. She felt for her mother's manicure scissors in her pocket—recently she had made it a habit to never leave her apartment without a "weapon." Betty had told her that if someone is trying to attack you, you should hit his arm, leg, or butt with something sharp. This way you wouldn't kill him, but you'd have time to make your escape.

The man caught up with Ada when she was almost at her gate. She noticed his shadow on the wall, shrieked, and turned around.

"What do you want from me?"

The assassin took off his cap, gave a curt bow, and said: "Good evening! Do you remember me?"

He was skinny, wide-shouldered, and a good head taller than Ada.

"I'm Felix Rodionov," the man said, sniffling.

Ada flinched. That was the name of one of Klim's friends; he'd mentioned Felix in his diary.

"Do I know you?" she asked cautiously.

"I first noticed you in Vladivostok," Felix said, "when we were boarding the steamer. I helped you with your suitcase, and later we stood together in the queue for the field kitchen. You said that you came from Izhevsk, and your late father was an American."

"Oh yes, I remember now," Ada lied.

"Klim told me about you," Felix continued and fell silent, embarrassed. "Here, I have something for you."

He handed Ada an envelope with the rather grand inscription: "An Invitation to the Annual Shanghai Cadet Society Ball."

Ada was puzzled. "What is this?"

"The Corps graduates have clubbed together, rented a hall, and hired an orchestra."

"Are you asking me to go with you?"

"Will you?" Felix asked hopefully. "To be honest, I thought that you'd think I was completely mad and tell me to get lost."

They ended up standing at the gate for two hours, reminiscing about Russia and their journey to Shanghai.

Back in her room, Ada sat on her bed, unable to believe what had happened. Had Felix really taken a fancy to her? What if he were to court her, fall in love with her, and even propose to her?

Thinking about this made Ada giggle. Felix had only invited her to a dance, and here she was planning a wedding.

She took out the old creased paper icon and, with a sigh, kneeled in front of it.

"Holy Mother of God," Ada prayed, "please let me find someone who can love me."

3

At the Cadet Ball, Felix watched enviously as Ada waltzed with the other men.

"Why didn't you ask me for a dance?" she asked when they went outside.

Felix blushed and looked down at his feet in embarrassment. "I don't know how to dance. The teacher at the Corps died of cholera, and there was no money to hire a new one."

"But the other graduates can dance."

"They have a natural talent for it. I only bought the tickets for you. I know that you women like that kind of stuff."

Whenever Felix was not on duty, he would meet Ada at the gates of the Bernards' house after work. It felt strange to be treated like a princess. Since her mother's death, no one had cared for her in this way, and she wasn't used to it.

"Why don't you tell me a bit more about yourself?" Ada asked Felix. "What's on your mind most of the time?"

"Well, all sorts of stuff . . . Politics."

"What about your personal life?"

Will he confess that he wants to kiss me? Ada thought.

"Will you promise not to laugh at me if I tell you?" Felix said, blushing.

"Of course not."

"When I was a kid I read a book," he started. "It was about a seaman called Robinson Crusoe who ended up getting shipwrecked on a deserted island. I would like to do the same—as a way of testing myself. If I'm resourceful enough I'll find food and survive, if not, I'll die. I think I would be able to do it. I could get by on mice and lizards if I had to."

Ada looked at him, dumbstruck. A desert island? Mice? But what about kissing her?

Felix was a natural soldier, and his world was straightforward and down to earth. As he had been taught in the Cadet Corps, he saw everything in life in terms of good and evil.

Ada was not terribly pleased that he was working in a jail but he was an honest man who did good for others without demanding anything in return. When Father Seraphim was nearly beaten to death in the ring, Felix helped him get a job as a prison guard so that he would be able to recuperate.

Felix couldn't stand preening, materialistic women who could only think about themselves and their appearance. He had chosen Ada because he sincerely believed she was a modest and respectable girl, and now she recalled with horror how she had tried to seduce Klim and Daniel. Heaven forbid that Felix might ever suspect her of such depravity!

Ada was dying for him to propose. Felix was an ideal match. He would be able to support and protect her from any adversity.

He would even be able to deal with Daniel Bernard, Ada thought proudly.

4

Ada came up with a plan: she would convince Felix to emigrate with her to the United States. Betty had told her where she could get hold of a couple of U.S. passports stolen by stewards working on the cruise ships. With these, it would be easy for them to sail to Mexico, where nobody checked documents very carefully. After that, it would just be a question of starting a business in a frontier town, which would then give her and Felix the right to cross the U.S. border and settle wherever they wanted.

Ada decided to find and sell the Avro and use the money to buy their passage to America. She was sure Felix would agree to her idea, but couldn't think how she would explain to him her property rights on the airplane. What if Felix became jealous of Daniel Bernard? Or even worse, began to suspect that she was involved in her master's crimes?

She couldn't put things off any longer, and one day when Felix was walking her back to the House of Hope, she asked him what his plans for the future were.

His silence and hesitation were so long that Ada began to fear that he didn't want to marry her at all.

"I didn't want to scare you but I must tell you the truth," he said. "Very soon there's going to be a war here, in China."

Ada looked at him dumbfounded. "Why?"

"In the south, the Kuomintang nationalists are conspiring with the Russian Bolsheviks and Chinese communists. They have joined forces to create the NRA, the National Revolutionary Army, and this summer they are planning to advance north to take over China and destroy the foreign concessions."

"Shanghai is much too big for them to handle—" Ada began, but Felix raised his hand to stop her.

"Here in Shanghai, the local people are waiting for the NRA in the hope that they will free them from the evil 'white ghosts' for good. As soon as the army approaches the city, there will be an uprising and that will be the end of all of us."

"Emigrate with me to America!" Ada exclaimed.

Felix shook his head. "America isn't my home, Russia is. A lot of us Russian White soldiers have joined the army of Zhang Zongchang, the Dogmeat General, and we intend to fight the southerners. We have combat experience, and we'll show them what for. First we'll destroy Bolshevism in China, and then we'll take the fight to the Soviets. I resigned from the prison, and today I came here specially to say goodbye to you. Father Seraphim is also going to join up with me."

Felix had obviously gone completely mad, but Ada saw that it was useless to dissuade him.

"You have to understand," he simmered, "this is our big chance to rebuild the White Army. There is nothing for me to do in America. Do you want to condemn me to work as a jailer for the rest of my life?"

"We could start a hotel—" Ada protested.

"I'm not an innkeeper. I'm a soldier! I couldn't respect myself if I were to do anything else."

Ada didn't mention the airplane. Her dream of escaping to America had gone up in smoke.

Felix promised to send her a letter as soon as he joined his new detachment, and she promised to pray for him. It all happened very simply, almost casually.

"Well, good-bye then," Ada said as they reached the House of Hope.

She shook his hand and headed to the gate. Her head was buzzing, her eyes full of tears. It was all over.

"Ada, wait!" Felix caught up with her. "If you have any kind of problem, promise me you'll get in touch with my friend, Johnny Collor. He works at the International Settlement Police. His station is on Nanking Road."

"I will," she nodded.

"Ada . . . Sweetheart . . ." Suddenly Felix grabbed her by the shoulders and kissed her awkwardly and passionately. "Please don't be angry with me! You must remember that I have loved you from the moment I first set eyes on you."

"Me too!" Ada whispered.

She released herself from his arms and ran to the porch, sobbing.

24. THE ANCHORMAN

1

Klim invented a character called Anna for his radio show and showered this fictional woman with all the affection and attention that Nina craved. He told Anna jokes, amused and complimented her, and discussed what was bothering him with her on air. These monologues were so touching that soon he became an idol for thousands of listeners.

In a strange sort of way, Nina was jealous of Anna. To get back at Klim, she would tell him about her friendship with Mr. Sterling and hint at the major deals and negotiations she had taken part in.

"Do you really think you're going to make a half decent actor with your accent?" she railed at him on. "Why don't you find yourself a proper job?"

"I'm quite happy with my improper one," he replied. "I'm sorry, my dear, but I'm not going to change jobs just to impress that Mr. Sterling of yours."

It seemed to her that he only came home to spend time with Kitty. Klim shamelessly spoiled their daughter, and eventually, she began to see Nina as "strict Mommy" always putting a stop to any fun, while Klim was "fun

Daddy," her best playmate and fellow adventurer.

He thinks that I've been nothing but a pox on his life, Nina thought in despair. *The scars have remained, but otherwise, he has recovered just fine without me.*

The fact that he was "just fine" without her was the most unbearable part.

2

Klim decided to have a big birthday party that year.

"How are we going to accommodate them all?" Nina asked in surprise as she read the list of guests.

"Relax. I'll take care of everything," Klim promised.

On the appointed day, girls of every imaginable nationality, from Swede to Filipino, arrived at the house. Klim introduced them as his friends, and they set about laying the tables and decorating the rooms.

Nina tried to exert a modicum of authority but no one paid her the slightest attention. She felt like a stranger in her own house.

The telephone rang, and she picked up the phone.

"Miss Nina?" It was the Secretary of the Municipal Council. "Your papers have just arrived from Washington. You can come over and pick them up whenever you're ready."

Nina's heart skipped a beat. Several months ago, Sterling had promised her to find out if the Immigration Bureau could grant her family American citizenship—as an exception, outside the quotas and without entry into the United States.

Without a word to Klim, Nina got into her car and told the driver to take her to the Municipal Council. Her lips were parched with excitement and anticipation. Were they really going to grant her citizenship?

When she arrived, Sterling was busy with visitors, and Nina had to linger in the waiting room for a long time. The secretary brought her some coffee and the newspapers, but she couldn't concentrate on anything.

Citizenship! Those who are born with it never understand how vital it is to be a subject to the laws of a civilized country. Without it, you are quite helpless, like a mouse caught by naughty children. You have zero value as a human being, and your future depends on the sort of game the children decide to play with you.

Finally Sterling asked Nina into his office.

"Congratulations!" he said, standing up to greet Nina. "The question of your citizenship has been satisfactorily resolved."

"Thank you!" Nina said with emotion.

"But," Sterling frowned, "there's one setback. You applied for yourself, your husband, and your adopted daughter. According to the Immigration Act of 1924, people of Chinese origin don't have the right to receive citizenship, and I'm afraid I won't be able to help you there. So if you and Klim want to move to America, you'll have to leave your daughter behind. . . . I'm going to have dinner at Astor House. Do you want to join me?"

"Sure," Nina replied.

All the way to the restaurant she forced herself to smile, feeling in her heart like someone who has won the lottery only to have been robbed of her winning ticket outside the shop.

The more she thought about it the angrier she became with Sterling. Did he seriously think that she and Klim would abandon their daughter like a fondly regarded pet that is not allowed through quarantine?

Nina knew that Mr. Sterling didn't care about her that much. The real reason behind their friendship was that he needed her to make him look a little larger than life. There were rumors that he was homosexual, and he had to prove to everybody that he was "normal." Nina was the perfect foil. After her affair with Daniel Bernard, she had gained a reputation as a *femme fatale*, but she asked for little or nothing from Sterling in return and didn't poke her nose into his private life.

At dinner he chatted about politics, and Nina nodded mechanically.

Klim's party had already started. It was important to him as a celebration of his professional success. Ten years previously, in Argentina, he had also enjoyed a large following, and now, even out here in China, he had managed to get his life back on track. However, in a fit of petty resentment, Nina didn't feel like celebrating his achievement. She and Klim had got themselves into the bad habit of trying to prove to each other that they were past caring what the other thought. Of course, nothing could have been further from the truth, but the cycle of self-deception and self-destruction persisted.

Nina said goodbye to Sterling and got into her waiting car.

I'll apologize, she decided, *and tell Klim that I went to the consulate to get our documents. I'm sure we'll think of something for Kitty. There's no rule or law that doesn't have a loophole in it somewhere.*

3

When she returned home, the party was in full swing. The band was playing on the patio, couples were dancing, and the guests were proposing toasts to Klim's success and good health. However, the host himself was nowhere to be found.

Don Fernando, his face red, approached Nina.

"Is the pretty lady dancing tonight?" he roared above the hubbub, trying to whisk her off in his arms.

She wriggled out of his bear-like embrace. "Put me down and leave me alone!"

"As you wish, ma'am, but when you see your husband be sure to tell him I'm in love with his program."

Don Fernando grabbed a glass of champagne from the table, drank it down in one gulp, and rushed off to dance with a young woman standing nearby.

After much searching, Nina finally found Klim behind the house on a bench surrounded by a large bamboo thicket. Next to him was Tamara in her wheelchair. They were so engrossed in their conversation that they didn't notice Nina approach.

"Creating art and taking care of others are the two most important things in life," said Klim.

Tamara sighed. "I'm incapable of taking care of myself, and there's nobody who cares much about my art."

"Your art is important *for you*," he said. "When you create something significant out of nothing, you grow wings of your own and you make the world a better place."

Klim and Tamara barely knew each other, but she was happy to confide her innermost thoughts, and he was happy to listen to her sympathetically, despite all his guests waiting for him in the other room.

"Come over to our radio station," Klim suggested. "You have a nice voice, and nobody will care about your Russian accent. It's only bigots like Mr. Sterling and his cronies who worry about such trifles, and we at the radio station couldn't give a damn about their opinions."

Nina inwardly cringed. She knew who he had in mind when he had said "cronies." He was ready to help anyone except Nina, even a woman who was partly responsible for their daughter's death.

In her agitation, the package with the documents slipped from Nina's fingers and fell under the bench.

Klim spun round.

"Are you looking for something?"

Nina hastily gathered up the papers. "I . . . Well, we've both been granted American citizenship."

"Congratulations!" Tamara exclaimed.

But Klim wasn't remotely interested. "I hope you have a safe journey to America. Don't worry about Kitty and me. We'll be fine."

Nina was dumbstruck. Klim wanted her to leave, and

he had nonchalantly announced it in front of Tamara, of all people.

4

When the last guest had left, Nina joined Klim out on the patio where the dinner tables had been set. He took a peach from the vase, weighed it up in his hand, and offered it to Nina.

"Are you hungry? Probably not. The driver told me that you'd already eaten at Astor House with Mr. Sterling."

Nina was shaking with barely-contained rage.

"It's none of your business who I had dinner with. Get out of my house!"

Klim put the peach on a plate, slicing it into pieces with quick strokes of the knife.

"This is not your house," he said coldly. "I learned from Tamara that all this time you have been paying her a largely symbolic rent, although you would have no problem paying her a fair price now. I've told her we'll put that right."

"Are you crazy?"

"No, my dear, it's you who is crazy. You've become so materialistic that you think nothing of taking advantage of people, even those who are closest to you. You only play with Kitty when you're in the right mood, and you aren't even remotely bothered when she misses you. Jiří Labuda died because of you; you didn't pay your employees in the publishing house on time—while you could easily have pawned these dishes or all the other junk that you've filled the house up with!"

Klim hurled the knife into the fruit bowl, smashing it to pieces. Oranges jumped, unfinished wine glasses toppled over.

"Stop it!" Nina screamed, but Klim wasn't listening. He recalled all the fights she had had with her employees, her shady deals, her cozying up to unscrupulous clients—every single one of her transgressions, imagined and real.

Nina looked at him, shocked. She had thought that Klim was utterly indifferent to her affairs, but it turned out that he had been watching her every step, making a note of her every mistake.

"Do you know what you're doing now?" she said angrily. "You're trying to prove to yourself that I don't deserve your love. You've created a perfect hell for yourself and populated it with demons that don't even exist."

Nina slammed the door behind her and paused, startled with a strange thought: *No one wants me here—not because I've done anything bad, but because I'm not the person they want me to be. What on earth am I doing here?*

5

Klim wheeled Tamara into the radio station personally. His studio was a veritable Aladdin's cave of fantastic devices and cutting-edge technology. He would talk briskly to technicians in Shanghainese, polish new sketches for the program, and juggle apples while summoning up inspiration. As soon as he switched on the microphone, the entire team would gather on the other side of the soundproof glass, anticipating the riotous mayhem that was about to be let loose.

Even Don Fernando would be drawn into the carnival.

"He's my hero!" he would shout, shaking a newspaper with yet another complimentary review.

Klim was the only person in the world who didn't patronize Tamara with his sympathy. He had been absolutely right when he said that creative work gives people wings. Tamara was no longer seeking her friends' attention, and she had no time to invent ingenious ways of exacting her revenge on them.

The audience had no idea that Tamara was disabled. As far as they were concerned she was Klim's witty female side-kick, who was full of energy and kept them up to date with reviews of the latest movies and books. She and Klim would often act out comical sketches from Shanghai life. In one of them, Tamara cast herself as a grand White Lady and also played the part of a Beggar Boy, while Klim played the role of a Boyfriend.

"Hey, master," the Beggar Boy whimpered, "spare some change for an orphan? No papa, no mamma, no whiskey-soda."

The Boyfriend shooed him off, but the Beggar Boy only became more brazen. "Hey, master, is that your new missy? Or did you get the old one cleaned up?"

All the program's sound effects were created right there on the desk in front of the microphone. Tamara learned how to use police whistles, sacred bells, paper bags, and many other items to make the different sounds needed for their little plays. They imitated footsteps using an empty pair of boots; the electric fan was made to sound like an automobile engine; and the roar of the crowd was recorded onto a gramophone record.

When Tamara returned home, her children greeted her excitedly: "We were listening to your show! It was so funny!"

Tony kissed her hand and asked how Klim was getting on. "I'm so glad you're friends."

Tamara's happiness would have been complete, but on July 9, 1926, alarming news arrived from the south that the NRA, led by General Chiang Kai-shek, had launched an offensive against the northern provinces.

"If the war reaches Shanghai, we'll have to move to Japan," Tony informed Tamara. "Just in case, I've ordered for our most valuable possessions to be packed and sent to Nagasaki."

The prospect of being evacuated made Tamara feel sick to the stomach. She would have no job and no friends in Japan.

25. THE NORTHERN EXPEDITION

1

Daniel, his fellow pilots, and the air mechanics were among the first to head north, and very quickly they discovered that what they were involved in was not so much a war as a wanton waste of material and human resources.

The soldiers of the NRA marched barefoot through the green hills in the blazing sun, the columns stretching back for dozens of miles. Every piece of artillery had to be disassembled and carried by hand along tracks that were too narrow for even a handcart to pass through. The soldiers' brown heels packed the dirt and sweat poured from their straining bodies.

The troops crossed dizzying gorges spanned by ancient suspension bridges, and whole companies were lost when the crude ropes gave way under their weight. Cholera claimed the lives of hundreds of other soldiers—the doctors recruited by the NRA were often relatives of the high-ups, with no qualifications whatsoever. The best that most of them could do was to let off firecrackers in the superstitious hope that this would drive away evil spirits.

The only reason the NRA hadn't been completely

annihilated was because the northerners' forces were in an even worse condition and even more poorly equipped. The warlords held their people in such scant regard that they sent them into battle armed with swords against machine guns.

Daniel took refuge in cynicism. He convinced himself that a brutal civil war was the only way to cope with the country's gross overpopulation, and if the Chinese cared so little about their fellow countrymen, why should he? His duty was to serve Germany, and he was doing exactly that by keeping a close eye on his Russian "colleagues" and sending his findings back to Berlin.

In several months, the NRA seized the key industrial city of Wuhan on the Yangtze River, and Mikhail Borodin, the chief political adviser sent from Moscow, declared that he would turn it into a model communist city, free of all private property and exploitation. The poor applauded him wildly, but the Chinese officers and Chiang Kai-shek were markedly less enthusiastic about the Russians' ideas and popular support. The right wing of the Kuomintang began to openly question whether China had exchanged one kind of white overlord for another, and whether this was a cause that was worth fighting for.

Daniel did his best to increase the mutual mistrust between the Kuomintang and the Russians. After a busy day of talks and intrigues, he would come "home," to a requisitioned merchant's house. A timorous cook would hand him a pot of boiled beans, Daniel would have his dinner and retire to his broken bed in the master bedroom.

He would take the *netsuke* that Nina had given him out of his pocket and scrutinize the gleaming figure with its nine tails, wondering what had happened to Nina after his departure. No matter how things turned out, nothing good would come of her staying in Shanghai. When the NRA soldiers burst into the city, the mob would make short work of all the "white ghosts" in the foreign concessions.

However, since Nina had chosen Klim Rogov over

him, there was nothing Daniel could do to help her.

2

The hospitals were overcrowded and lacked medicine, so the commanders of the NRA ordered that a number of the trophies captured at Wuhan be auctioned to raise income for the Red Cross.

The auction was held in the former governor's mansion. Its gate gaped wide open and its floors were slick with the melted dirty snow that had been tramped in by taciturn officers in their military boots. They wandered around the tables where the auction items were arranged but no one dared open the bidding and let the others know that they had money. That would be tantamount to admitting that they had taken part in the town's looting.

A drably-uniformed official from the new communist government would occasionally peek into the auction rooms. They had already made a killing trading food and fuel on the black market, and now they were waiting for the Red Cross to drop their prices for the auctioned treasures.

Daniel Bernard wasn't there to buy anything; he had come to the mansion to meet up with an old friend from Shanghai. He moved from room to room admiring pale blue vases—the color of the sky after a downpour, works of embroidery as light as the breath of a child, and ancient lacquered jewelry boxes which had been privy to countless generations of secrets.

Daniel finally spotted Fernando accompanied by One-Eye and his other bodyguards.

"Hello comrade!" the Don yelled and he shook Daniel's hand. "How about treasure hunting today? I like this one," he said pointing his finger at a nearby painting on rice paper.

Daniel smiled indulgently. "That's 'The Noise of the Shadows Shaken by the Wind,' It's from the seventeenth century, the Ming Dynasty era."

"Wrap it up for me then," Fernando said. "And that statue with the red face too."

"That is Guan Yu, the Taoist God of war, camaraderie, and a good fight," Daniel said.

"Oh!" The Don frowned. "Better put it back, boys. I don't want any pagan gods, otherwise the Holy Virgin might get upset. I'd better take that one with the woman playing a flute. And please, don't tell me who she is."

After One-Eye had carried the purchases to the car, Don Fernando invited Daniel to the snow-clad courtyard which had a dark, neglected pond at its center.

"How are things going in Shanghai?" Daniel inquired, shivering. His thin coat didn't afford him much protection from the cold.

"Everybody is going crazy, like rats trapped in a bucket," Fernando replied. "Chiang Kai-shek's criminal record has mysteriously gone missing from the International Settlement police archive. Well, you can't blame them. Any day now they might need to enter into negotiations with him."

Daniel smiled. "What prudence!"

The Don told him that more than a hundred thousand refugees had entered Shanghai in the past few months. They were fleeing not only the NRA but the retreating northern armies. The influx of people and the summer drought had caused food prices to double, and the authorities were expecting riots any day.

"The Governor is out of his mind with fear," Fernando said. "He has ordered his soldiers to arrest anyone suspected of sympathizing with the communists or the Kuomintang. The prisons are so full that they are summarily executing suspects in the streets. Then they put their heads in bamboo cages and hang them from lampposts."

Don Fernando offered Daniel an Egyptian cigarette with a gold tip, a luxury even the top brass at the NRA hadn't enjoyed for several months.

"The Bolsheviks have learned their lessons from the general strike," the Don said, blowing the smoke towards his feet. "The Chinese will only fight the foreigners if there are civilian casualties. And if the authorities don't provide them with a massacre, the Bolsheviks will provoke them into one. They've formed a number of detachments of shock troops from the most loyal Shanghai workers, and they are ready to sack the foreign concessions at the first signal. In response, the Great Powers will kill thousands of Chinese—innocent and guilty alike—and this will lead to riots across the whole of the country. The Bolsheviks are hoping to ride this wave of unrest in order to seize power in China."

Don Fernando looked into Daniel's eyes. "I have a message for you from Big-Eared Du."

"The Green Gang ringleader?"

"The very same. We know that Chiang Kai-shek is not happy with his Russian advisers but can't oppose them openly because they are paying his bills. But if Chiang Kai-shek promises to leave the foreign concessions alone and purge the commies in his army, Shanghai will surrender without a fight, and your commander-in-chief will be provided with a different source of income."

"From the opium traders?"

"Not only them. The Great Powers want to negotiate peace, which could mean international support and loans for Chiang Kai-shek."

"I'll find out if he's ready to negotiate," said Daniel.

In the evening he sent a coded cable to Berlin, and the answer returned immediately: Daniel was to take part in the negotiations and gather as much intelligence as possible.

Soon after, he and Fernando paid a visit to the commander-in-chief's headquarters, and several days later the two of them returned to Shanghai with the news that Chiang Kai-shek was willing to listen to the representatives of the foreign concessions and the Green Gang.

3

Throughout dinner, Klim read his newspaper while Nina looked at him, feeling dejected and miserable. She had been waiting for him to ask her about her day in the office, but instead, he had been studiously ignoring her.

The candles flickered inside the carved lanterns on the table casting moving shadows onto Klim's newspaper. Its headline read: "Forty warships with reinforcements from the Great Powers expected to arrive by March."

It was highly unlikely they would reach Shanghai before the NRA.

"Did you hear that the Defense Committee commandeered all my employees?" Nina asked.

"Yes, I know," Klim said. "They need every man capable of bearing arms to guard the barricades around the concessions."

"But they've ruined my business! I have nothing left but an empty office, and my telephone is ringing off the hook. My customers are expecting their bodyguards to turn up for duty, and now they are threatening to sue me for breach of contract."

Klim didn't even look up from his paper.

"Don't you have anything to say?" Nina asked, her voice shaking.

"What do you want me to say?"

She snatched his paper from him and hurled it to the floor.

"Wake up, for Christ sake! There's a war on. We could die. Don't you realize that we have to patch up our quarrel and do something about our situation? For the sake of our own survival, if nothing else."

Klim took a coin out of his pocket and put it on top of one of the lanterns.

"Pick it up," he suggested.

297

Nina looked at him, puzzled.

"Go ahead, don't be scared," Klim encouraged. "It's solid silver. It's very valuable."

"But I'll burn my fingers."

"How do you know?"

"Because I know that's what's going to happen if I touch that coin."

"And I know exactly what's going to happen if we patch things up."

Klim stood up.

"I'll stay in Shanghai as long as possible," he said. "We have no other anchorman left, and someone has to read the news to the public. Tamara and her children are going to move to her other house in Nagasaki, and she has offered to take Kitty with her. I'm sure you can go too if you want."

4

The shop owners wanted to sell as much of their stock as possible before the war reached Shanghai, and Sincere Department Store announced a huge Christmas sale.

Nina wandered aimlessly from one department to another until she stopped in front of a display containing a big wrapped gift box tied with a red satin bow. To all appearances, it contained a valuable present, but Nina knew it was empty. It was the perfect metaphor for her own life.

No matter how hard she tried she couldn't save her marriage and business, and the only thing she had to look forward to was to return to the humiliating situation of living off Tamara's charity.

Nina went up to the second floor, where shelves with liquors stretched from the floor to the ceiling. A bottle of whiskey—that was all she wanted for Christmas.

She noticed a poster on the wall of a girl in a swimming suit about to dive into a wine glass. *Let's consider it an omen,*

Nina decided. She took a bottle from the shelf and turned to go to the checkout.

"Hello," said Daniel Bernard, who had been watching her, his arms crossed. His hair was close-cropped, his face had grown thinner, and gray streaks had appeared at his temples.

"What are you doing here?" Nina said in amazement.

"I was just following your every move and waiting for you to be good enough to notice me," Daniel said, smiling. "How are you?"

Nina didn't know what to say.

"I'm fine," she muttered finally and put the whiskey bottle back, blushing.

Daniel shook his head disapprovingly. "Let's find a place to sit and talk."

Klim had told Nina that this man was working for the NRA. It was clear that he had come to Shanghai for a good reason, yet she resisted the urge to call the police. Instead, she followed him to the third floor where there was a half-empty movie theatre.

The film started, and to the crackling sound of the projector and the accompaniment of an out-of-tune piano, Nina confided to Daniel everything that had happened to her over the last few months.

"It's all your fault," she whispered in despair. "You've ruined my life."

"Then it's up to me to fix it," Daniel said in a serious voice. "I have some business to see to in Shanghai, and then I'll go back to Wuhan. You should come with me."

"Are you kidding? It's a nest of communists. I know that Mikhail Borodin has his headquarters there."

"Believe me it would be better for you to stay away from Shanghai for the foreseeable future."

Nina went cold. "Is there going be a siege?"

"I just strongly recommend that you buy yourself a ticket on the *Pamyat Lenina*. It's a Soviet merchant ship. It will set sail for Wuhan next Thursday."

"But Wuhan is in the middle of a war zone!"

"There are no front lines in China," Daniel said. "Battles flare up wherever the opposing troops happen to run into each other. British and American warships are patrolling the Yangtze, and merchant ships are still free to sail up and down the river."

Nina stared blankly at the screen. Rudolph Valentino was fighting valiantly to win the heart of his fair lady.

If Kitty went to Nagasaki, there would be nothing to keep Nina in Shanghai. And she couldn't face having to swallow her pride and become Tamara's kept companion again. The very thought of it made Nina sick.

Klim had refused to mend their relationship and ended up turning his worst suspicions into a self-fulfilling prophecy. Daniel might be a man of extremely dubious honor, but at least he was ready to help Nina escape the trap that was enclosing them.

If I go with him to Wuhan, she thought, *I'll meet new people and find new opportunities. What does it matter that Daniel is working for the NRA? If he can get along with these people, then so can I. I just need a break, and then I'll be able to breathe again and think of something.*

She sensed Daniel's intense gaze.

"Well, will you come with me?" he asked.

"I . . . I don't know."

Nina took a deep breath. Should she leave everything behind? If she did, there would be no turning back. *But if I stay in Shanghai,* she thought, *I'll end up doing myself a mischief.*

"I won't promise you anything—" she began, but Daniel didn't let her finish.

"I'll see you on the ship."

Nina didn't wait for the movie to end but stood up and went outside. It would be better for both of them if no one were to see her with Daniel.

26. THE SECOND FLOOR

1

After Felix's departure for the war, Ada counted down each interminable day. These slowly turned into months and eventually half a year.

At night she would imagine what their reunion would be like. She would return from the Bernards', and he would be waiting for her at the gates of the House of Hope. These thoughts would rob her of her sleep, initially until midnight, then for an hour, and eventually just for a few minutes.

She had only received one letter from Felix; he had safely reached his detachment and joined his Russian comrades on the *Great Wall* armored train. She had no idea whether he was alive or dead by now.

To Ada, the very words "Battle for Shanghai" sounded like a doomsday knell. She timidly asked Edna if she was going to evacuate to the north, but her mistress didn't even want to think about it.

At Christmas, Edna decided that the orphans should be given fifty sets of underwear and set her servants the task of sewing them.

Ada had been sent to the department store to buy some thread, but she wasn't keen to return immediately and decided to take a look at the movie posters on the third floor.

Suddenly she noticed Mr. Bernard entering the cinema, and almost jumped out of her skin. Not so long ago, she had been visited by Felix's friend, Johnny Collor, who had told her that the new Police Commissioner had ordered an investigation against Daniel.

"We've found out that this man is behind weapon shipments to the south," Johnny told Ada. "If your master comes back, let me know immediately."

That day Ada had assured Johnny that Mr. Bernard would never return home, and now here she was staring at the revolving doors as they continued to spin after he had entered the cinema.

If I don't report him to the police, they might think I'm his accomplice, she thought and rushed straight to the police station.

2

"My master is back," she told Johnny after the guard on duty had called him down to the waiting room. "I saw Mr. Bernard entering the cinema in the Sincere Department Store."

Johnny grabbed the telephone. "I need a dozen armed men," he yelled into the receiver. "Stay here," he told Ada and he ran outside.

Soon Daniel was brought in, in handcuffs. They interrogated him for a long time and then asked Ada to identify him in a lineup. Then Mrs. Bernard arrived, almost dead with the worry and the shame of it all. She was also interrogated.

"Can I go now?" Ada asked Johnny when he walked hurriedly by.

He told her to stay in the waiting room.

Ada went back to her bench. She watched people rushing by and listened to the typewriters rattling away on the other side of the wall. A Chinese woman was sobbing quietly at the window, her baby tied to her back. It looked curiously at Ada and chewed on the hem of its swaddling clothes.

Ada heard Johnny shouting to someone, "Under martial law, we'd be within our rights to take him out and shoot him."

What if they do execute Daniel? Ada thought in horror. She felt so bad that it made her heart hurt.

Mad with anger, Edna slammed the door as she entered the waiting room.

"I trusted you!" she shouted at Ada. "I fed you, and now you have betrayed my husband."

"He's been—" Ada tried to defend herself but Edna wouldn't let her finish.

"Don't ever set foot in my house again!" she yelled. "You're fired!"

3

Dusk fell. Ada was sitting in her room, crying. She had no work, no money, and no family.

Maybe Klim might have been able to help her or at least give some advice, but it had been impossible to get into the radio station see him.

"Do you have an official invite?" the security guard had asked Ada.

"No."

"Then go away."

"But I'm his friend."

"That's what all his fans say. No one is allowed in, and that is that."

Ada didn't dare go to his house, afraid that she might meet up with his wife. Nina would definitely have worked out who had brought Klim those incriminating photographs.

Ada knew what she would have to do: she would have to sell all her possessions for food until she was left with nothing but the shirt on her back, and then the landlord would throw her out onto the street.

Behind the wall, she heard laughter and the strum of a guitar. Despite the war, everybody in the foreign concession was carousing and celebrating Christmas.

I need to go to the Havana, Ada decided.

Betty was most likely working tonight. A lot of the men had sent their wives to safety in the north, and she would have a lot of clients on her hands.

Anything was better for Ada than sitting on her own in the dark. She grabbed a coat and went out into the street. Huge snowflakes fluttered through the sky, melting the moment they touched the ground. Three frozen rickshaw boys shared a solitary cigarette. The gleam of the streetlights poured onto the road, diffusing with the shadows of the trees.

Two Japanese girls came around the corner, their wooden sandals clacking as they hit the road.

"Hey, ladies! Fancy a good time?" some sailors shouted.

The girls giggled, covering their mouths with their hands, and scuttled off in the opposite direction.

The closer Ada went to the Northern Sichuan Road, the thicker the crowds became. Drunken couples were dancing in the street. Boxers Café-Buffet, Crystal Garden, El Dorado—music and the crashing of dishes could be heard from every door.

I hate you all, thought Ada. *I hope General Chiang Kai-shek comes and slaughters the lot of you.*

The Havana was packed. There was a real Christmas tree in the corner and the air was heavy with the smell of fir needles and tobacco. A monkey wearing a red wig was chasing a clown on the stage. The audience roared with laughter.

Ada made her way to the bar.

"Where's Betty?" she asked the bartender.

"She's no longer working here," he said. "Some Italian businessman fell in love with her and took her away to Naples."

Ada didn't know why she headed upstairs to Martha's. To cry on her shoulder? On Christmas Eve?

She froze at the open door of the Madam's office. Martha was sitting behind her desk, looking through her bills. "Come and sit down," she said, nodding to Ada.

Without getting up from her chair, Martha reached for a cabinet, took out a small glass, and opened a bottle of cognac.

"Here," she said. "Drown your sorrows."

Ada downed the cognac, and the Madam brought her a dress, shoes, and a black velvet mask.

"Go change and get downstairs," she said. "Get drunk. Tomorrow you will have a cracking hangover and you'll have forgotten all your troubles."

"Why the mask?" Ada asked.

Martha laughed. "Look at yourself in the mirror. Your face is as blotched and red as a tomato."

Ada undressed and put on the gaudy, bright crimson dress with a bow at the hip.

Martha helped tie the mask and applied some lipstick to Ada's pale lips.

"There, that's much better," she said.

"Can I have another cognac, please?" Ada asked.

She drank the second glass in a single gulp and staggered downstairs.

"Don't forget to smile!" Martha screamed after her.

"What?"

"Smile! Men are not just after the wine and the women here. The Havana is a place where they can forget about their problems, and they're certainly not interested in yours."

Ada pinned a smile to her face and put her best foot forward.

4

Daniel had asked Fernando to bring his airplane from Suzhou, and the Don had spent the whole day out of Shanghai. The Avro was dismantled, packed into crates, and sent to the port. When Fernando returned to the city, he was greeted by surprising news: Daniel had been arrested.

The Don felt sorry for his friend but immediately realized that Destiny had given him a chance to play for high stakes. He paid a visit to Tony Aulman and told him that he urgently needed to see the chairman of the Municipal Council.

Within minutes, Tony had passed on the Don's message that Chiang Kai-shek was keen to avoid bloodshed and ready to negotiate.

Two hours later, an inconspicuous car arrived at Big-Eared Du's house. Out came Don Fernando, Tony Aulman, and Mr. Sterling.

The servant showed them past two armed men keeping guard and into the living room. The room was furnished in the European style—with a radio set, electric lights, and a telephone. But Big-Eared Du himself was a creature from another world, or rather another era—a tall, skinny man with a two-inch nail on his little finger. His shaved head was covered with a black satin cap, and a gray silk robe hung loosely from his bony round shoulders. The only element of his garb that matched the Western interior of his house were his leather shoes.

The guests sat in opulent chairs while the servants brought tea, and Aulman began to translate for Sterling.

"The main danger for us," Big-Eared Du said in a soft voice, "is not Chiang Kai-shek but the communists who are preparing an uprising in Shanghai. There are about four thousand armed workers, called the 'Red Guards,' in the northern outskirts, but the communist need three times as many fighters in order to capture the whole city. They do have reserves, but not enough arms."

"The commies are waiting for a steamer from Vladivostok, which will bring them all the smuggled weapons they need," said Don Fernando. "We have to strike the Red Guards first, or they'll destroy us. They have the numerical advantage, which is what matters."

Sterling turned visibly pale. "But we have an agreement with the Governor. He won't allow any rebellion here."

"If I were you, I wouldn't count on him," said Big-Eared Du. "The Governor wants to withdraw himself and his troops from Shanghai in order to fight another day. The Great Powers' warships are still a long way off, so we have no choice but to outbid the commies and persuade Chiang Kai-shek to become our ally. If he promises to purge the communists from his army and guarantee Shanghai's safety, the Green Gang will take care of the Red Guards. But my boys need five thousand rifles with ammunition and passes to cross the territory of the International Settlement. The Red Guards aren't expecting an attack from that side."

"I'll need to speak to my colleagues," said Sterling in a weak voice.

5

After bidding farewell to Tony and Sterling, Don Fernando went to the church to pray for the success of his venture. He felt he had played a masterly diplomatic hand. If he were to succeed in reconciling Chiang Kai-shek, Big-Eared Du, and the "white ghosts," Shanghai would be saved, and the Don would have connections at the very highest level in the city. No one would dare call him a bandit ever again. He would become a respectable gentleman, and the cream of Shanghai society would be happy to receive him.

I should marry a banker's daughter, at the very least, thought Don Fernando. *The kind that can play the piano, ride sidesaddle, and legitimize my earnings.*

Remembering Daniel, Fernando looked up at the statue of the Virgin Mary.

"I would ask you to have mercy on him," he whispered, "but if that were to happen he would replace me at the negotiating table, and that is not in my interests. You know me, I'm a good person and wish ill to no man. So please, just keep him in jail for a while and then grant that he be released."

Anyway, Daniel had no one to blame but himself. He should have gone to the Municipal Council immediately. Then he wouldn't be spending Christmas eve in a prison cell but in a good brothel surrounded by beautiful girls.

As for the Avro, Don Fernando decided that it would fetch a handsome price from the new government in Wuhan. The communists had an acute shortage of planes and would be willing to pay a lot of money for one.

6

Every room on the top floor of the Havana had been furnished in its own special style: a French boudoir, a ship's cabin, a stable with horse-collars on the walls and a heap of hay on the floor, and more.

In Don Fernando's room, all the available wall space had been covered with theater posters. Big chests sat on the floor filled with costumes, wigs, and hats, and the bed resembled a small stage with a velvet curtain. The young prostitute Don Fernando had picked at the restaurant, was a superlative actress. She was playing the role of the naïve innocent so realistically that the Don almost felt pity for her.

As though afraid of being recognized, she was wearing a mask. A clump of her hair was tangled in a knot from the ties on her mask and was sticking out awkwardly above the back of her head.

She wants to be a big girl, the Don thought in his drunken delight, *doing what the big girls are meant to do.*

The prostitute was to his taste with a tight, sleek tummy and prominent cheek bones. No waist, and breasts just beginning to take shape, as if she was just a thirteen- or fourteen-year-old girl.

Don Fernando made love to her tenderly. He looked into the dilated pupils of her eyes through the slits in her mask, kissing the dark lock of hair plastered to her forehead.

"Do you think I could be a high-class prostitute?" the girl asked when they had finished.

"You'll be the greatest whore in the world," said the Don pressing his hand to his chest.

Then he watched her get dressed. The dress she wore was beautiful, festive, but her underwear was worn out from endless washing. It was as though the girl wasn't even working here and had just come to Martha's to have some fun.

Oh, how wise and inventive these women are, Fernando thought. No one could beat them at the art of creating beautiful illusions.

Before leaving, he left a hundred dollars on the bed. The innocent little thing deserved something nice for Christmas.

27. GOOD-BYE, SHANGHAI!

1

Klim watched Nina as she packed her suitcase.

"Where are you going?"

"To Wuhan."

Nina slammed her suitcase shut and tightened the fasteners.

"Take my luggage to the car," she told the servant.

"May I ask *why* you're leaving?" Klim asked.

"Because I can't live with a man who doesn't love me."

"I assume that you have someone in Wuhan who *is* in love with you? Is his name Daniel Bernard by any chance?"

Nina left the room without even saying good-bye.

She went into the hallway and froze, listening. There was no hope for them. It hadn't even occurred to Klim to stop her.

As her car roared down the street, Nina stared indifferently at the bank of low-hanging clouds and the flags barely trembling in the wind.

"To Avenue Joffre," she commanded her driver.

For several years the citizens of the Great Powers had been looking down their noses at the Russian community in this backwater in the French Concession. The penniless refugees had disturbed the established way of life and shattered the myth of the superiority of the white race.

Now even Mr. Sterling had to acknowledge a basic unpalatable fact: It was not their race or knowledge but their circumstances that had given the whites their all-powerful reputation in China. A ticket on a steamer to the Far East was an expensive item and not an option for the poor of Europe or America. However, as soon as a big, randomly-formed group of white people had arrived in Shanghai, it became clear that there was nothing particular "superior" about being white. The differences between white and Chinese society weren't as great as everyone liked to pretend. White society was also divided into the educated and the illiterate, the simple-minded and the intelligent, those who contributed and those who didn't.

The outcome was visible here, in Avenue Joffre. Some of its inhabitants had vanished without a trace, but its libraries, schools, theaters, and shops were proof that the rest of the Russian refugees were a breed of survivors who had managed to rebuild their lives from the ashes.

What had Shanghai taught Nina? That fears are illusory and exist largely in your head. There was a time when the very idea of emigration would have chilled her heart, but in December 1922, she had taken a step towards the unknown and had succeeded. Now she was confident she would do the same.

Don't lose heart, Nina repeated to herself, but as the

funnel of the *Pamyat Lenina* hove into view, her heart sank. Armored steel panels had been riveted along the sides of the boat, and she could make out the shape of machine guns hidden under their canvas covers on the stern.

There was a war on, but it was too late to turn back now, and Nina stepped decisively onto the gangplank.

When she reached the upper deck, she saw Don Fernando, puffing on a cigar.

"What are you doing here?" he asked in surprise. "Does your husband know where you're going?"

Nina nodded reluctantly. She felt a pang of shame that Don Fernando should witness her affair with Daniel. However, maybe it was all for the best. Let him give Klim a blow-by-blow account. It was all he deserved.

Time passed, but there was still no sign of Daniel. Nina walked along the deck of the boat, looking askance at the Russian-speaking crewmen. It was incomprehensible: a couple of weeks ago, they had been in Soviet Russia, a completely different, parallel world.

Nina couldn't stand it any longer. "Do you know where Mr. Bernard is?" she asked Fernando. "He should be on this boat."

The Don looked at her in a strange way. "Oh . . . Mr. Bernard has already left."

"What? Where to?"

"To Wuhan. He . . . He's got some business there."

Nina looked at him, shocked. What was she to do? Go back home? That bastard Daniel had left her in the lurch again. She would be completely lost without him.

Rushing down the stairs, Nina caught her sleeve on the handrail and hit her elbow on a cast iron joist. The pain was so great that everything went dark for a moment.

There was a prolonged whistle, the anchor chain rattled, and the boat set sail.

Nina sat down on the step cupping her injured elbow in her hand. That was it; she was going to Wuhan. Her Shanghai adventure had begun with her being stranded on a boat with Don Fernando, and now history had repeated itself.

3

Nina tried to guess why Daniel hadn't told her that he had left early. Was he waiting for her now? Or were all the promises he had made back in the cinema some sort of practical joke?

To calm herself down a little, Nina leafed through a newly-printed Russian book she had found in her cabin. It had been published using the new Soviet alphabet and Nina found it difficult to read. However, the author's logic was even more baffling. The Bolsheviks regarded persecuting, robbing, and murdering the bourgeoisie as a justified means to their revolutionary ends. They seemed to believe that they would obliterate class barriers by destroying the exploiting classes and deciding who should live and who should die on the basis of their social origins.

Hasn't anyone noticed, Nina thought, *this ideology's similarity to racism?*

What kind of times did they live in when people around the world judged each other using such arbitrary categories as race or social origin instead of their personal merits?

She put the book aside, went to the window, and parted the curtains with the words "Glory to Labor!" printed on them. The steam engine was roaring, a muddy bow wave ran along the side of the boat. The river bank with its abandoned farmhouses was powdered with snow.

Is Klim worrying about me? Nina thought. *Or was he just glad to see the back of me?*

"Hey, Miss Nina!" Don Fernando banged on the wall. "Dinner is served. I ordered them to bring it to my cabin. Let's eat together to stave off the boredom."

Nina took her purse with her money and documents and went to visit the Don. One-Eye stepped aside, letting

313

her through the narrow cabin door.

"Come in and make yourself comfortable," Fernando told Nina.

She sat down at the table and immediately noticed an opium pipe next to her plate, its silver bowl intricately cast in the form of a demon's head. This was all she needed.

"Why aren't you eating with the other passengers in the dining lounge?" Nina asked nervously.

"Forget that," Don Fernando snorted. "Do you know who's sailing with us? Fanya Borodin, the harridan of a wife of Mikhail Borodin, Chiang Kai-shek's political adviser from Moscow. She and the other Soviet diplomatic messengers are also on their way back to Wuhan."

Fernando complained heatedly and at some length about Fanya, who had accused him of being a liar and a crook. "She's a fine one to talk when it comes to the truth. She just told the Shanghai authorities that she was a civilian, but in fact she was on a mission to help the communists."

Nina remembered Daniel telling her that it would be better to stay away from Shanghai.

"How do you know Mrs. Borodin?" she asked.

"I have a lot of acquaintances. I'm a useful man, you know."

The Don showed Nina the pipe. "Do you want a smoke? You look terrible, all pale and miserable. Don't worry, I won't offer you any opium; you'd get hooked in no time. Try some hashish instead. Have your dinner, relax, and then we can retire to my bed for a bit of fun."

Nina jumped up. "What the devil are you talking about?"

"Oh come on! You don't need to play the innocent with me. We're going to have to spend several days on this rust bucket before we reach Wuhan. Why not have a bit of fun before we get there? Klim doesn't want you anymore—everyone knows that you're not getting along with each other. And we don't need to tell Daniel anything."

Nina went cold at the thought that Fernando saw her merely as some cheap whore who was running away to her lover. In furious silence, she threw the napkin in Don's face and stormed outside.

Once back in her cabin, she could hear the Don's voice from the other side of the thin wall. "I can't guarantee you'll find Daniel in Wuhan, and I wouldn't recommend wandering around the streets on your own. A defenseless young woman like you could easily find herself with a big bump on her head, and without her astrakhan coat, stockings, and knickers, assuming you're wearing any of course."

Evidently, Fernando had decided that if he couldn't entice Nina into his bed, he would have fun harassing her with his dirty jokes and bawdy songs.

My soul is suffering so much,
You've set my heart and pants on fire.
The Holy Virgin knows full well
You have a butt that men desire.

Nina decided to ask the captain if she could move to another cabin, away from Fernando, but as soon as she went out into the corridor, she stumbled across One-Eye.

"Follow me," he said and pointed to Fernando's door. "The master is waiting for you."

Nina took a step back. How had she ever ended up on this steamer? She had already given up on the whole idea of going to Wuhan.

I'll ask the captain to drop me ashore at the nearest village, she decided. *Then I'll hire a carriage and return to Shanghai.*

One-Eye grabbed Nina by the arm, but she pulled herself away and ran down the corridor.

The light in the passenger lounge was on, and Nina could hear voices coming from behind the glass door. She entered the room and saw three men and a plump dark-haired woman sitting at the dinner table.

"Good evening," Nina said in Russian, with a forced smile. "May I join you?"

"Sure you can," the woman said. "Judging from your accent you're from Moscow, aren't you? My name is Fanya. What's yours?"

Nina guessed that Mrs. Borodin had taken her for a Bolshevik. Who other than a Bolshevik would be sailing up the Yangtze towards Wuhan in a Soviet steamer?

"Is that character bothering you?" Fanya asked as she noticed Nina's nervous glances at One-Eye's silhouette behind the door.

"He's been following me for some reason."

Fanya got up from the table and headed to the door, her worn-out shoes shuffling over the parquet floor.

"Who sent you here to eavesdrop on our conversation?" she snapped in her broken English. "Get lost!"

To Nina's surprise, One-Eye shrugged his shoulders and disappeared.

"I don't know how to thank you—" Nina began, but her new acquaintance just waved her hand.

"You need to play hard with types like him."

"If he keeps pestering you, tell us, and we'll sort him out," promised one of the diplomatic messengers, a strong young man with a luxuriant blond mustache.

The men tried to be as gallant with Nina as possible and treated her to cookies and candy with a portrait of— *Felix Dzerzhinsky, of all people!*—the head of the secret police.

"Why don't you just leave the poor woman alone?" Fanya exclaimed, laughing at her comrades' clumsy attempts to win Nina's favor.

Gradually Nina calmed down. The irony of it all: her enemies, the Bolsheviks whom she had feared more than anyone else, had taken her under their wing.

She stayed with them until the early hours of the

morning. They sang songs, told stories, and then played cards.

Finally, Fanya rose from the table and yawned. "It's already dawn—let's get some sleep."

At that moment an artillery shell whooshed overhead, and the entire company fell silent.

4

Felix sat on a log, smoking a cigarette, watching the scarlet sunrise over the Yangtze, while Chinese artillerymen tried to figure out how to take their guns across the river.

Things were really bad in the Dogmeat General's army. Russian and Chinese officers were constantly at one another's throats, many of them had taken to the bottle, and confusion in the rear was common place. Supply officers would only buy food from profiteers who paid them bribes, and half of the army was suffering from disease and illness. Medical care was almost non-existent, and Dogmeat's soldiers were so hungry that they were no longer as interested in attacking the enemy's position as they were in their logistical supply lines.

Father Seraphim approached, wearing a padded coat decorated with a Red Cross armband. His beard was completely wild and his eyes were red and bleary.

"Are they gonna give us our money or not?" he asked Felix. "They owe us five months pay and that's no laughing matter."

"Dogmeat probably thinks he's better off keeping us as cannon fodder, and then fodder for his army when the supplies finally run out. He's got no plans to pay us and let us go," Felix muttered.

Sadly, it was true: they had nowhere to go and no other choice but to fight to survive one day at a time. They knew that if they were taken prisoner, they would be horribly tortured before being executed.

Felix looked up and noticed a small steamer sailing round the bend of the river.

"Do you see that red flag on her stern?" a Chinese officer shouted as he ran past. "It's a Soviet ship! We must stop it. It's bound to be delivering food to Wuhan."

The Chinese discharged a warning shot across its bows, and the steamer anchored in the middle of the river.

As a Russian speaker, Felix volunteered to head the inspection on board, and along with other soldiers, he jumped in the rowing boat and rowed to the Soviet steamer.

Having ascended its rope ladder, he ordered the captain to hand him all his consignment notes. According to the ship's papers, the *Pamyat Lenina* was sailing to Wuhan to pick up a cargo of tea and was only carrying spare parts for a power plant in its hold.

"Tea?" Felix shouted angrily. "They're reduced to eating dogs and cats in Wuhan and you're planning to ship a cargo of tea!" He turned to his soldiers. "Search the steamer. Put the crew under arrest and bring all the passengers into the lounge."

5

The soldiers' impatient knocks shook the Don's cabin door to its timbers.

"Open up!" someone with a Russian accent shouted.

Fernando hadn't expected Dogmeat's soldiers to stop the *Pamyat Lenina*. There was a trade agreement between the Peking government and Moscow which allowed Soviet ships to freely navigate all Chinese rivers, despite the war.

The Don rushed around his cabin. If Dogmeat's men were to find out about the Avro, it would be curtains for him.

There was a heavy blow, and the door flew off its hinges. A tall, hook-nosed young man with a revolver in his hand burst into the cabin, followed by a number of

Chinese soldiers behind him.

Fernando hurriedly handed him his passport. "I'm a citizen of Mexico. I'm a neutral here."

The man looked through the Don's documents and grinned.

"Jose Fernando Burbano? Nice to see you."

The Don turned yellow. "How do you know me?"

"I used to be a policeman in the International Settlement. Your name regularly featured in our reports."

Fernando put his hand to his heart. "It's all lies and slander! I am an honest businessman. I have a radio station in Shanghai—"

But the young man wasn't having any of it.

"What are you doing on a Soviet boat?" he barked.

"I'm on a secret mission, under Mr. Sterling's orders. I have been told to negotiate the evacuation of foreign refugees from Wuhan—with Mikhail Borodin. By the way, did you know that his wife is here?"

"What are you talking about?" the man said, frowning. "We have reviewed the lists of passengers—"

"She is traveling with forged documents."

The man grabbed Fernando by the shoulder and dragged him to the lounge, where the other passengers were sitting, terrified.

"Stay here," the man ordered and left.

The Don leaned against the wall, casting glances at the white-faced Bolsheviks. Nina was there too. She was sitting on the couch, shaking like a leaf.

Now Fernando could hear the sound of iron hitting iron as the soldiers started searching the hold.

They're bound to find the airplane, Fernando thought, his heart skipping a bit.

A Chinese officer entered the lounge. "Which of you is Madame Borodin?" he asked the women.

Nina looked at Fanya, but she said nothing.

"No point denying it," Don Fernando whispered. "This way at least you become a bargaining chip. If the

319

Chinese think you're small fry, they'll just throw you overboard to feed the fish."

Fanya stepped forward. "I am Mrs. Borodin. Why?"

The officer looked at Nina. "And who is she?"

"She's my cousin. I warn you, sir: touch one hair of our heads, and you'll be in serious trouble."

"Do you confirm what this lady says?" the officer asked Nina.

"Yes," she replied hesitantly.

The hook-nosed young man came back into the lounge and, without a word, dragged Fernando out into the corridor.

"Who owns the airplane in the hold?" he hissed, grabbing the Don by his lapels.

"I . . . I don't know."

"Liar! The crewmen told me that you were in charge of it."

The man shoved a docket under the Don's nose.

"It says that the Avro belongs to Ms. Ada Marshall. I know that girl: she doesn't have enough money to buy a pair of decent stockings, let alone an airplane."

In a panic, Fernando looked back at the glassed door. Behind it, he could see Nina, hunched on the settee.

"It's all her fault," he whispered. "If you served in the police, you would know that Ms. Kupina has been engaged in arms smuggling before. I guess she used your friend as a front and put her name on the papers. Ms. Kupina is in cahoots with the crew and told them to blame it all on me if an emergency arose."

"Are you talking about Klim Rogov's wife?"

That was a bad idea, Fernando thought. *It seems that all these Russians know one another.*

"Klim kicked the whore out long ago," Fernando said in a muffled voice. "She cheated on him with Daniel Bernard. He was arrested a week ago for espionage, but she managed to escape. By the way, did you know that Ms. Kupina is Mrs. Borodin's relative? She just admitted it as much. Didn't she?"

The man swore in Russian. "How do you know all this?"

"Oh, I know a lot. I'm a very useful person." The Don forced himself to smile. "You can send a cable to the Municipal Council and ask Mr. Sterling whether he gave me the order to go to Wuhan or not."

"You can depend on that," the man muttered, releasing the Don's lapel. "If you're lying, I'll personally stove your head in with a rifle butt, but if Sterling confirms who you are, you can go wherever you want."

He paused, and his face softened a little.

"Thanks for the information about Borodin and her cousin. Without you, we would never have guessed who they were."

"My pleasure." Don Fernando looked into his eyes. "Can I give you a bit of advice? If you don't want that young friend of yours involved in the case, you'd better destroy all the Avro papers and present your report saying that 'The airplane was confiscated from an enemy spy, Nina Kupina.'"

The man nodded and escorted the Don back to the lounge.

Fernando felt weak from relief. He wished he could kneel down and thank the Holy Virgin for his miraculous salvation there and then.

Miss Nina has only got herself to blame, he thought, looking up at the ceiling. *She shouldn't have annoyed me. I feel sorry for her, of course, but what am I to do? I'll say a prayer of penance for her and donate some money to the church for a new sacristy. But holy Mother of God, please, don't desert me! I need you now more than ever!"*

28. THE ANCIENT CAPITAL

1

SKETCHES

Klim Rogov's diary

"Where's Mommy?" Kitty keeps asking me. "When will she come back home?" I tell her I don't know and that makes her angry: "You must know! You must!"

How can I explain to a three-year-old what has happened between Nina and me?

We met each other when the whole world around us was crumbling. Both of us were looking for a pure soul to love and to be loved by, a soul that would deliver us from every evil. Alas, ideal people, like distilled water, don't exist in the real world, and eventually our delight gave way to bewilderment. Far from behaving like guardian angels, we only brought trouble into each other's lives.

I have finally been acknowledged for my professional achievements, but what now? I go to work, read the latest bad news to my audience, and then try to cheer

them up with a new song, "I Hope You're Happy Now."
I no longer perform monologues to my fictional
girlfriend, Anna. Despite the constant demands from my
fans to bring her back, I don't have the heart.

Every day, my secretary drops a huge stack of letters
onto my desk from local young ladies declaring their
undying love for me. Who can honestly say that they
have never dreamed of being the object of such sincere
adulation and devotion? But now that I have achieved it
all, I couldn't care less.

The Chinese section of the city is full of armed
bandits who are constantly fighting turf wars with each
other, while here, in the foreign concessions, we are
busy dealing with the white refugees arriving from the
south-west. More than eight thousand of them poured
into the city in January 1927 alone.

The only good news is that reinforcements have
finally reached Shanghai, most of them colonial troops
from India. It's winter, and they arrived in short-sleeved
shirts and khaki shorts, and after one night in an
unheated barracks, almost all of them came down with a
chill.

The people in the foreign concessions do everything
they can to welcome the military. They try hard to be
hospitable in the hope that these foreign soldiers will be
more willing to fight for us and for Shanghai. The ladies
sew them warm pants and jackets; the Holy Trinity
Church has been turned into a lecture hall where the
officers can learn more about our city, and the twenty-
four-hour restaurant in the American Club welcomes our
saviors with the best food available at the cheapest
prices. Every night there are balls in the French Sports
Club, the Majestic Hall, and the Astor House. Girls flirt
with the officers, looking hopefully into their eyes and
silently imploring them, "You won't leave us to our fate,
will you?"

Frankly speaking, I don't care what happens anymore. If it weren't for Kitty, I would join the Russian crew on the *Great Wall* armored train. I'm pretty sure that eventually either the NRA or the Red Guards will blow it up, and that is a fate that sounds quite tempting at the moment.

2

Klim had finally been invited to become a member of the Shanghai Club, the most exclusive club in the city.

Its main staircase was made of white Sicilian marble; its restaurant boasted a menu with fine roast beef, saddle of lamb, and steak and kidney pie. It had an array of forty rooms at its disposal, an army of servants, and ironed newspapers—so they would feel pleasing to the touch.

The Club's main attraction was its famous mahogany Long Bar. The closer your place to the window, the higher your rank in the Club's hierarchy. According to tradition, the best seats were reserved for the pilots who sailed the Yangtze River. Top managers and bank directors would sit in the middle and the furthest, gloomiest end was reserved for new members like Klim Rogov.

The sad winter twilight descended swiftly, and a gray-haired waiter lit the candles in the thick-walled glass candleholders.

The bar was empty, and Klim was sipping his pink gin by himself, half-listening to the voices floating in from the next room: "To defend the city effectively, we need at least a division."

He pulled a coin out of his pocket and put it on the edge of the candleholder directly over the flame. The coin had a phoenix on one side and a dragon on the other, a symbol of the happy union between yin and yang, the male and the female.

When the coin was hot, Klim pushed it into his palm. The pain was as sharp as the blade of a knife, but he closed his eyes, punishing himself with his self-inflicted agony. *Let the scar be a souvenir,* he thought.

"Mr. Rogov!" cried Tony Aulman as he ran into the bar. "Thank goodness I've found you! I've just been talking to Don Fernando—he's informed me that Nina has been arrested by soldiers from the Dogmeat General's army and taken to a prison in Nanking."

Klim flinched, the coin rolled along the bar and jingled quietly as it hit the floor.

"They suspect your wife of supporting the communists," Tony added. "I just can't understand what on earth Nina is doing in Nanking?"

"I tried to warn her," Klim said, "but she never listens." He paused, trying to gather his thoughts. "Will you . . . will you come with me to Nanking?"

"The Dogmeat General's troops control the city now, and they are going crazy with the hopelessness of their situation. But, on the other hand, the Yangtze River is still controlled by the Royal Navy—"

"Will you come?" Klim repeated with a strained voice.

Tony threw up his hands. "Tamara would never forgive me if I let Nina down. And I wouldn't forgive myself either."

3

It would take several hours longer to reach Nanking by boat, so Tony and Klim decided to book a compartment for two on the night train.

At one of the stops hundreds of soldiers and coolies, who had been commandeered to build fortifications, crowded onto their train. The car was immediately filled with the smell of garlic, sweat, and cheap cigarettes. Within thirty minutes the lavatory was filthy, and in order to get to it, passengers had to pick their way past an obstacle course of shovels, mattocks, and sleeping workers.

Six armed soldiers joined Klim and Tony in their

compartment. As soon as they had sat down, they started to crush the lice in the folds of their clothes and play endless rounds of Rock-Paper-Scissors. Every few minutes, the sliding door flew open with a crash, and hawkers would appear at the door offering hot tea, watermelon seeds, and green slices of pickled eggs.

There was no point in protesting. Klim angrily watched the soldiers eating, burping, and spitting on the floor. One of them was sleeping with his mouth open, and another had the effrontery to take a small spirit lamp, an opium pipe, and a small lump of opium out of his travel bag. He placed a piece of the dark-brown resin in a spoon, heated it a little, and then put it into the pipe and shared it with his friends.

Tony pushed the window up to let the fresh air in. The wheels clanked, cinders from the engine's funnel flashed by the window, and the wind brought with it the smell of burning coal. Soon the soldiers were snoring, their heads lying at awkward angles on the headrests.

Klim sat, transfixed by the trembling sooty curtain and the thought of Nina.

He had talked to Fernando before leaving, and the Don had said that she had been going to Wuhan to see her lover, but the Dogmeat General's soldiers who had stopped her boat, looted her luggage, and handed her over to the Nanking authorities, along with the other passengers.

"She's a bitch," the Don had said, "but I feel sorry for her. I'll pay for Tony Aulman to get your Nina out of jail. I just hope the Holy Virgin takes all this into account when I get to the Pearly Gates."

When Don Fernando had heard that Klim was planning to go to Nanking, he went crazy.

"Are you out of your mind?" he yelled. "Hasn't she already done enough by breaking your heart?"

He had a point. What was Klim doing here, in this rocking, overcrowded car, listening to the soldiers' snores and looking nervously at the barrel of the rifle pointing directly at him in the hands of the young soldier sitting opposite him?

I can play the hero as much as I want, Klim thought. *But there will be no prize for my bravery. Even if I do rescue Nina, she'll still leave me for Daniel Bernard.*

Anyway, it was sheer foolishness to think in terms of what he would gain from all this. Klim had already received ten years of passionate love—not a bad prize when all was said and done really.

4

By 7:00 a.m. the train had reached the suburbs of Nanking, where the railroad station, the river port, and the trade company headquarters all converged. Klim and Tony hired a cycle rickshaw and told the boy to take them to the city.

At one time Nanking had been one of the great capitals of the world, but five hundred years ago, the imperial court moved to Peking, and the city gradually fell into decline.

Nanking, which had once boasted a population of two million, was now reduced to a mere two hundred thousand, and large areas of it that had once seen thriving neighborhoods were now covered with bare fields and rustling bamboo groves. The city's ancient canals had dried up long ago, and Klim marveled at the grand stone bridges adorned with ornately carved lions and dragons. The bridges led nowhere and served no purpose.

The majestic city wall, the longest in the world, was still standing too, almost untouched by time, its watchtowers embellished with colorful flags.

Tony noticed a column of enemy prisoners being marched past, their heads clamped into wooden cangues, and proceeded to tell Klim what the Chinese do to their criminals. Many forms of torture had been officially banned, but the judges still entertained and intimidated the people with public executions, from burying miscreants alive to cutting small chunks of flesh from their bodies, right down as far as the bone.

Klim felt cold, deaf, and unable to speak—his senses numbed. Only his eyes seemed to register anything, but then only annoying details like the thin thread of saliva that stretched between Tony's upper and lower lip every time he laughed.

An unbearable reek of smoked sausage rose from the basket nestled next to their legs. It contained Nina's essential provisions: a warm woolen blanket, three pairs of stockings, an English-Chinese phrasebook, and antiseptics. Oh God, this whole misadventure was so outlandishly unlike her!

"They also put their criminals into bamboo cages," Tony went on, completely oblivious to his companion's discomfort.

"For Christ's sake, shut up will you!" Klim snapped and squeezed Tony's hand so hard that he whimpered.

5

The prison warden informed them that the *Pamyat Lenina* had been scuttled in the middle of the Yangtze, its crew had been sent in chains to a dungeon, and that Fanya Borodin along with the other important prisoners had already been sent to Peking.

"We have nothing more to do here," Tony said and went out into the street. "Let's get back to Shanghai."

Klim remained pre-occupied all the way to the train station, where it turned out that the railroad company had been hit by another strike. He was silent when they reached the river port, with its huge, snow-dusted navy ships. The sky was low and gray, and it looked as if a soft felt blanket was about to fall onto the earth and smother it.

"It seems like we're stuck here for the time being," Tony grumbled as he returned from the ticket office. "The next steamer to Shanghai will set sail the day after tomorrow."

The only European hotel in the area, the Bridge House, was occupied by cavalrymen, and the Chinese inns were packed with refugees.

Tony and Klim went back to the prison and asked the warden if he had a spare cell that could provide them shelter for the night. The warden was surprised but nevertheless gave them a "room" with a stove and no bedbugs.

"We're much safer here than in the hotel," Tony began, but catching sight of Klim, he cut himself off midstream. "How are you? You look terrible."

"I'm fine," Klim replied rubbing his face.

They improvised a dinner of smoked sausage and some other supplies from the basket. Tony lay down and in a second was fast asleep, but Klim couldn't sleep a wink.

It felt strange that the person most dear to him might not be of any value to anyone else. It felt even stranger to suddenly realize that Nina *was* the dearest thing in the world to him—in much the same way that a drowning man values his last desperate gulp of air.

Before his wife had left him, or to be more precise, before Klim had emotionally abandoned her, there had always been an unspoken safety net between them: *I can always come back.* But now he felt as if a large chunk of flesh had been torn from his stomach, and there was no way of ever sewing it back in place.

6

In the morning, they were woken by the sound of artillery. Dressed in nothing but his underwear, Tony ran into the corridor demanding to know what was going on.

The warden rushed towards him. "Whatever you do, don't leave the prison!" the man yelled, his eyes full of horror. "It's the NRA! They've captured the city!"

29. THE GREAT WALL ARMORED TRAIN

1

Every day more and more warships sailed into Shanghai with reinforcements, and Martha's establishment was now working round the clock. The Madame would take the most promising clients aside and let them in on a "secret of the house": "Every night a mysterious young lady arrives at the Havana in a mask. Her dresses are the latest word in chic from Europe, her ears and neck adorned with the finest diamonds, but you wait until you see her dance."

"Who is she?" the client would ask, intrigued.

"A lady of quality. You can always tell a high society damsel by her manners. She is very discerning; she won't dance with just any man, but when one does take her fancy, she is his for the entire night."

"You don't say!"

"It's true. And the lucky man she chooses is in heaven. She orders champagne, and then they go upstairs. The rich have their own whims and fantasies—after all, they are in a position to make them a reality. She never ever tells anyone her name, but we call her Messalina after the Roman empress who liked to pretend to be a prostitute."

The clients were sure Martha was telling them tall stories, but none could resist the lure of the lady in the mask. And she would never disappoint, appearing at midnight on the dot—pale with blood-red lips, her dress slit up to the middle of her thigh—accompanied by a black attendant in a turban carrying a huge curved scimitar.

On her arrival, the orchestra would stop playing and all eyes would be drawn towards Messalina. And she— seemingly oblivious of the attention—would saunter around the tables, assessing each and every one of the customers. All of them would ask themselves with their heart in their mouths, *Will it be me?*

Eventually she would halt next to some confused and lucky individual, proffer her velvet-gloved hand to him, and greet him with a simple "Good evening."

Martha guarded Messalina's secret identity jealously. The taxi-girls and the rest of her staff were strictly forbidden to try to make her acquaintance, and the clients were told that anyone who tried to remove Messalina's mask would have their head chopped off. Whenever the *femme fatale* took a client to her room, her bodyguard would stand sentry at the door, his scimitar drawn.

Before dawn, Messalina would disappear, and Martha would stow the crumpled banknotes in her safe, thinking: *A girl in a mask—it's ingenious. If Messalina ever gets married or, God help us, slits her wrists, there will be no shortage of substitutes.*

2

At dawn the Madame invited Ada into her office, switched on the table lamp, and started calculating Ada's cut of the takings. "Twenty, thirty, forty . . ." Martha's plump hands deftly counted the banknotes, stacking them portrait side up.

"I don't know what these men are thinking about," she grumbled. "The NRA is at Shanghai's gate, the governor has fled, and the Red Guards are about to take control of the Northern Railway Station. But all our army boys can do is carouse their nights away in brothels. Of course, it's good for business, but all the same . . ."

She hadn't finished her sentence before a powerful rumble rattled the window panes.

"That's the *Great Wall* armored train!" Martha gasped, looking anxiously out of the window. "It must be in the North Railway Station fighting the rebels."

Ada went pale, scooped the money into her bag, and hastily buttoned her coat. "I have to go."

"Where? Wait!" Martha shouted, but Ada was already outside.

Despite the early hour, the street was crowded. Policemen blew their whistles, and fire trucks raced past. A huge cloud of smoke blotted out half the sky.

Ada spotted a vacant rickshaw.

"I need to go to the North Railway Station," she told the rickshaw boy, but he shook his head.

"I'm not going there. There's heavy fighting there."

Ada noticed a man walking past with a decrepit bicycle.

"Can I buy it from you?" she said. "How much do you want?"

She paid fifty dollars for the rusty piece of junk and rode it down the street, still in her smart dress, fur jacket, and heels.

3

The *Great Wall* and its crew were trapped on a short section of the railroad next to the North Railway Station. The Red Guards had dismantled the tracks and leveled the embankment on either side of the station. The train was forced to move back and forth, its heavy guns obliterating hundreds of shacks where the enemy was taking shelter. Soon a huge fire started, torching the entire neighborhood next to the railroad.

When the *Great Wall* returned back to the North

Railway Station to refill its boilers, the train's commander, Colonel Kotlyarov, summoned Felix to his staff car.

"The Red Guards won't dare make a direct attack until they're sure we've run out of ammunition," the colonel said. "Unfortunately, they don't have much longer to wait."

"If we surrender we'll be sure to die," Felix replied.

Kotlyarov nodded. "We need to send a messenger to the foreign concessions and ask for their help." He wiped a dirty sleeve on his perspiring forehead, leaving a sooty smudge. "You speak English well, Rodionov, and you know how to deal with the British. After dusk, you need to find a way through to the International Settlement."

"Yes, sir."

Felix left the staff car and stepped up onto a flatbed car protected by armored steel plates on its sides. On seeing him, the soldiers from his machine-gun detachment jumped up. "Permission to speak, sir. What's the plan?"

"We're going to make contact with the folks in the foreign concessions."

Smoke from the fires had turned the sky a brick-brown. Large flakes of ash settled on shoulders, caps, and hair.

A pair of heavy boots thudded along the platform.

"Felix, Ada's here!" Father Seraphim roared.

"What?"

"She's waiting for you over there, by the station platform."

Felix jumped out of the car and immediately recognized her, standing between a couple of soldiers.

"You're alive!" she shrieked and threw herself into his arms.

He held her tight, his arms trembling.

"You silly girl!" Father Seraphim sighed. "Why on earth did you come here?"

"I spotted her riding her bicycle along the platform," one of the soldiers reported excitedly. "I thought she was a spy or something and was about to shoot her. But then I heard her shouting in Russian."

Felix caressed Ada's slender fingers in his hands, looking perplexed. "What am I going to do with you now?"

"I couldn't wait," she kept saying. "I couldn't live without you."

Felix frowned at his comrades-in-arms who were crowding around them and eventually lost his temper, shouting: "Why don't you leave us alone, guys? This is a private matter."

Suddenly a machine gun barked somewhere nearby.

"Take cover!" Felix yelled and, grasping Ada's hand, he pulled her up into the car.

Panting, they leaned against the sandbags piled up along the wall of the car. The armored train jerked and moved forward, clattering.

"Why didn't you write to me?" Ada asked, sobbing. "I waited for so long!"

Felix pressed her to his chest. "I'm a military man. I could have been killed at any time. I didn't want you to worry about me. And if I managed to survive, then I knew I'd be coming back to you."

Felix's heart ached for Ada, for himself, and his comrades who were facing almost certain death within the next few hours. What were they fighting for? What were their deaths going to achieve? He could find no answer.

4

When darkness fell, Colonel Kotlyarov ordered Felix to prepare to leave the train.

"Good luck, son! Tell the British that we have sixty-four men, and we are experienced gunners, machine gunners, and military engineers. We can serve in the Russian Volunteer Corps and have a lot to offer the foreign concessions."

When the engine driver slowed down, Felix and Ada

leaped out of the car.

Rolling down the embankment, Ada cried in pain as something cold slashed her arm. Felix jammed his hand over her mouth, hissing, "Quiet!"

He bandaged the wound on her arm with a piece of fabric torn from the hem of her skirt, and they ran away from the railroad. Broken glass crunched under their feet, and they could feel the heat from smoldering embers through the soles of their shoes.

Several times Felix and Ada ran into the unknown detachments of soldiers. It was hard to tell whether they were Red Guards, police, or soldiers serving the governor.

"If we get arrested," Felix whispered, "we'll tell them that we got lost in the Chinese section of the city." He paused and added. "Do you . . . I mean, will you marry me?"

Ada squeezed his hand. "Yes. Then, we'll go to America."

Felix looked at her face, illuminated by the flames of the fire.

"We'll talk about all this later," he said and gave Ada a quick kiss on the cheek.

5

The checkpoint on the Boundary Road was besieged by a crowd of refugees shivering in the cold rain. From time to time a British officer with a megaphone and an umbrella would climb onto an armored car protecting the gates to the International Settlement.

"I repeat," he shouted, "Chinese policemen and soldiers are not allowed into the territory of the International Settlement."

Ada listened to him, wistfully looking at the gate draped in barbed wire. She was covered in soot from head to toe, her hair was dripping, and the wound on her arm was throbbing.

Felix hadn't had a chance to carry out Kotlyarov's order. He and Ada had spent two days rushing from one checkpoint on the cordoned boundary to the next, but all to no avail. As soon as people heard their Russian accent, they chased them away, threatening to shoot them on sight. "Get lost, you Bolshevik scum!"

In much the same way, abandoned soldiers from the governor's army ran from one gate to another—barefoot, bandaged, their epaulettes and insignias ripped off and in tatters.

The previous day, three officers from the *Great Wall* had joined Ada and Felix.

"It's all over," they had said. "The Red Guards blew up the train and slaughtered every single one of our men. We were the only ones to survive."

"What about Father Seraphim?" Ada asked.

"Caught a bullet in the head."

Here, on the Boundary Road, Felix eventually saw Johnny Collor patrolling the barricade, and his friend let him inside to talk to the officer in charge of the checkpoint.

"I'll get you passes," Felix had promised Ada and the officers, but now there had been no sign of him for over an hour.

Finally, Johnny Collor took the place of the British officer on top of the armored car.

"Whites will now be allowed to enter the International Settlement!" he shouted into the megaphone. "Including Russian military personnel."

The crowd stirred. Those Chinese who spoke English began to translate Johnny's speech.

Felix appeared at the gates. "Ada!" he called. "Come here!"

She rushed towards him, but a Chinese officer grasped her hand. "If you're going in, so are we."

The Russians started to argue with him. Felix tried to squeeze through the crowd to Ada, but dozens of hands grasped at him, pulling him back. The Chinese officer unsheathed his sword, slashed wildly, and Ada felt something hot spatter across her cheek. The crowd gasped and leapt back, and Felix fell with a gash to his neck.

Ada was deafened by the roar of a machine-gun shooting over the heads of the mob.

"To the gates!" shouted the Russian officer and manhandled Ada back through the cordon with him.

The crowd scattered, and the officers had a chance to drag Felix back into the cordoned area.

They carried him into an abandoned sweet shop. Ada struggled in Johnny's arms, screaming hysterically, but he wouldn't let her near the medics who had rushed forward and were now bent over Felix.

Their valiant efforts were to no avail, and he died an hour later.

30. THE NANKING INCIDENT

1

During the long months spent in solitary confinement, Daniel pondered many things. He was angry with himself for being arrested and with Nina for betraying him—he had no doubt she was to blame. But all this was soon subsumed by a very real fear of death after he contracted food poisoning. He sent Edna a note asking for help but received no reply. The warden who conveyed the message informed Daniel that he hadn't even been allowed into the house. With no doctor, no medicines, and without even the most basic human compassion from his family, Daniel was at his lowest ebb.

Fortunately, the poorly educated jailers hadn't confiscated his *kitsune netsuke*. They had thought it was a commonplace Chinese lucky charm, and Daniel asked his warden to take the *netsuke* to a pharmacist who collected antiques.

The pharmacist visited the prisoner and then sent him the medicine Daniel needed. By an irony of fate, Nina had saved his life without ever meaning to.

His case never went to trial. The prosecutors and investigators were too busy defending the city with the Volunteer Corps, and in any case, no one was quite sure which authority and which court was responsible for Daniel's trial.

Eventually, he was handed over to the Chinese

authorities, but when the NRA reached the outskirts of Shanghai, the guards unlocked the cells and fled.

In a daze, Daniel walked out of the prison gate and made his way through the crowded streets. He noticed banners and portraits of Chiang Kai-shek in the windows, and every other Chinese was wearing badges with the Kuomintang emblem—the white sun over a blue field. Even the cigarette packets for sale had the emblem emblazoned on their covers. It appeared that the tobacco factory owners had been hedging their bets long before the surrender of Shanghai.

People in the streets looked happy, their eyes were shining, and it was hard to believe that only a few weeks earlier Shanghai had been gripped in a paroxysm of fear at the prospect of the arrival of the NRA.

Nationalism changes people in the most peculiar ways, Daniel thought with a rueful grin. Chiang Kai-shek had made the "white ghosts" nervous and been transformed in the eyes of his people from a bandit into a prominent leader. Carried by a wave of national pride, no one cared now that the new father of the nation had slaughtered vast numbers of its sons and daughters.

Soon Daniel was in the apartment of his cryptographer, the son of a German pastor and a Chinese woman.

"Where have you been?" he asked, fussing over Daniel. "We've been looking for you everywhere."

Daniel explained what had happened to him—without mentioning Nina, of course.

The cryptographer brought him a piece of soap and a change of clothing.

"Here, clean yourself up and get a proper rest. I'll send a message to Berlin that you're back."

2

Daniel spent several days gathering information about what had been going on in the city while he'd been in jail.

Don Fernando told him about the seizure of the *Pamyat Lenina*: "Mr. Sterling sent the Dogmeat General's men a telegram, and they let me go. But Miss Nina was taken into custody."

"Did she really go to Wuhan after me?" Daniel asked, surprised. "I thought it was Nina who reported me to the police."

"Oh no!" exclaimed Don Fernando. "She's madly in love with you. When you were gone, she and I went to visit every morgue in the city. I was so sad that my heart physically ached—and all the while I still had to broker the deal to save Shanghai."

Daniel felt a rush of warmth inside. "Where's Nina now?" he asked.

"No idea," said the Don, sadly. "Probably she's finished."

Fernando informed Daniel that he had persuaded Chiang Kai-shek's representatives, Big-Eared Du, and Sterling, to come to an agreement that the Green Gang and the foreigners would provide the Kuomintang with funds in exchange for betraying the Chinese communists and their Bolshevik allies.

It had been promised that the NRA would sit tight until the Red Guards and the governor's soldiers had destroyed each other, and then enter the city unopposed. The foreign concessions were left untouched, Chiang Kai-shek came to a number of agreements with the "white ghosts" on mutual cooperation and some preferences to make the common people a little bit happier, and the International Settlement city fathers issued a resolution: "Chinese citizens may now freely visit all the city's parks."

Within a few days, there was a huge crowd in the Bund, waiting for their chance to try the forbidden fruit.

These developments were a bolt from the blue for the Bolsheviks and the Chinese communists. Trying to save the situation, Mikhail Borodin called for everybody to disobey Chiang Kai-shek's orders, but the Red Guards were in no position to resist the combined forces of the foreigners and the Kuomintang.

The result was a stalemate for Germany. Since Daniel hadn't been directly involved in the negotiations between Chiang Kai-shek and the "white ghosts," he hadn't been able to win any privileges for the Germans. Now they no longer enjoyed their favored status as the Kuomintang's sole Western ally, and German industrialists would see no rewards for their months of illicit support.

Berlin decided that the best strategy, for the time being, would be to keep pitting the Russians, Chinese, and the Great Powers against one another, and soon Daniel was ordered to go to Peking to conduct a large-scale secret operation there.

3

Tamara was about to depart for Nagasaki when the news spread like wildfire that Nanking had fallen just after Tony and Klim's arrival. The NRA soldiers had pillaged the local foreign concession, killed the vice president of Nanking University, and wounded the British Consul.

Every expatriate's worst nightmare had become a reality. Even the most unflappable and level-headed among them were soon busy packing their suitcases. Rumors spread that every boat ticket for Europe and America had sold out in a single day.

Tamara became sick worrying about Tony and Klim, and she couldn't stop reading newspapers and calling her friends to try and find out what was going on in Nanking.

"Mommy," Roger cried as he rushed into her room, "turn on the radio!"

Hurriedly she fumbled with the dial on the receiver.

"American missionaries who have lived in China for years," said an unknown anchorman, "are leaving the country in large numbers. Their churches are being burned down, and peasants are looting their houses."

"It would appear that it's not the messiah the Chinese have been waiting for but the NRA," said a voice remarkably like Klim's.

Tamara felt a flood of relief wash over her: he was safe after all.

"Tell us what happened in Nanking?" the anchorman asked.

"When the massacre started," Klim said, "a group of foreigners gathered at Mr. Hobart's house at the top of Sacony Hill. There were about thirty of us, including some marines with a radio transmitter."

"Where did they get it from?"

"The marines had been sent by the captain of a British ship—to observe the events that were unfolding in the city."

Please tell me, Tamara prayed silently, *please, tell me Tony is alive!*

"Looters started trying to break into the residence," Klim continued. "We threw all the valuables we could find out of the window to buy us time. While the soldiers were fighting over them, we let off a distress signal. Then the American and British ships opened fire on the city and forced the besiegers to let us go."

"How many Chinese were killed during shelling?" the anchorman asked.

"I don't know. I know that we lost eight people, and about a dozen were injured."

Tears were streaming down Tamara's face. Now she had no doubt that Klim would tell the audience that Tony was one of the victims.

"We made ropes out of sheets and climbed down the city wall," Klim said. "First down were the men carrying weapons, then the women and children. British seamen were waiting for us on the river bank with lifeboats."

"Are you sure you were attacked by Chiang Kai-shek's soldiers, not the communists?" the anchorman asked. "After all, we have a cease-fire now."

"Do you think the commander knows what all his troops are up to?" Klim answered. "In civil wars, men with guns are free to do what they like."

"Therefore the bombardment of Nanking was justified?"

Klim sighed wearily.

"I'm just grateful to be sitting here in Shanghai, chatting to you. I could just as easily be lying in a ditch with my throat slit open."

The anchorman thanked Klim and read the latest news. The new military commander appointed by Chiang Kai-shek had ordered the Red Guards, who had entrenched themselves in the northern districts of the city, to surrender their arms and give themselves up. But they had refused to obey him and organized their own communist government.

Tamara turned off the radio. *Without Tony,* she thought in horror, *I won't be able to save the children if street fighting breaks out here.*

She could hear the sound of an engine outside her window. Her mind went completely blank for a moment. *If they tell me that Tony is dead, I'll be dead, too,* she thought.

A floorboard creaked, the door hinge groaned, and a familiar figure appeared in the doorway.

"Tony!" Tamara gasped.

He walked into the room, his head wrapped in bandages.

"Humpty Dumpty sat on the wall, Humpty-Dumpty had a great fall," he said apologetically. "The rope that we used to climb the city wall snapped. I was lucky; Klim and a British lieutenant dragged me to the lifeboats. Otherwise, I'd never have made it."

"It's alright," Tamara sobbed. "We'll fix Humpty Dumpty."

4

Daniel went to see Don Fernando at the radio station to pick up his latest counterfeit passport. This one was in the name of a bogus Austrian businessman.

The Don was in his office listening to Klim Rogov, who was on the air talking about the massacre in Nanking.

"I'm sorry, but today is my last day here at the radio station," Klim said. "I have to go to Peking on personal business."

"What?" roared Don Fernando. "And who is going to present your show?"

Completely forgetting his guest, the Don ran out of the door, and a minute later Daniel heard a blazing row in the corridor.

"Are you crazy?" Fernando yelled at Klim. "Why are you going to Peking? To save your wife? She dumped you, and you're still ready to chase her to the ends of the earth like a damn fool?"

Daniel's heart skipped a bit. Was Nina in Peking?

He went into the corridor and saw Klim and Fernando, standing next to a brightly lit window.

"I've found out," said Klim, "that the Dogmeat General sold Fanya Borodin and other prisoners to the Peking warlord Zhang Zuolin. The northern border regions are plagued with infiltrators from the Soviet Union, and he's decided to arrange a show trial of prominent Bolsheviks to intimidate them."

"The sentence of the court has already been prearranged, don't you see?" said Fernando. "Zhang will simply execute his captives. How are you going to change that?"

"Don't even try to dissuade me," said Klim.

Daniel stared at him with an intense hatred.

"Nina needs help at the highest diplomatic level," he said walking up to Don Fernando and Klim. "I have contacts in the Peking Legation Quarter, and I'll do my best to get her out."

"Nina would never have been in this mess if it wasn't for you," Klim began in an icy voice.

"And who made her so miserable that she wanted to run away to Wuhan in the first place?"

Don Fernando stepped in between them. "If I were you, gentlemen, I'd concentrate on getting her out of prison first. Otherwise, the executioner will divide her up between the two of you. One of you will get the head, and the other the rest of her body."

In an instant, Daniel had taken stock of the situation. *I'll be needing someone who speaks Russian and who's prepared to take risks,* he thought. *Why not Klim Rogov?*

"Fernando is right," Daniel said in a conciliatory tone. "Let's join forces and go to the capital together."

He offered his hand. Klim paused and then reluctantly shook it.

"Do you really think you're going to save her? Really?" Don Fernando started, but then waved his hand in a gesture of futility. "O, Holy Virgin, please, just grant me that they don't kill each other before they get there. I'm not asking for you to make them see sense—I know that even your powers only have certain limits."

5

At four in the morning, the navy ships' sirens wailed, and army trucks raced through the International Settlement, full of armed soldiers. Edna jumped from her bed and peeked through her bedroom window.

"Who are they?" her amah asked in a terrified voice. "Who are they going to kill?"

The trucks disappeared as suddenly as they had appeared. Soon, shooting could be heard breaking out in the northern outskirts.

6

The newsboy didn't bring the morning papers, the phone was disconnected, and Edna waited in vain for her driver until noon.

"I'll walk to the *Daily News* office and see what's going on," she announced to her servants. "Who wants to come with me?"

All of them looked down, avoiding her intense gaze.

"You shouldn't go," said Yun. "It's raining cats and dogs, and there's shooting going on out there in the streets."

"Do as you wish, but I'm going," Edna said angrily, grabbing her umbrella and stepping out into the pouring rain.

As soon as she got out of the gate she saw Binbin, her coat unbuttoned and her lank wet hair hanging along her pale cheeks.

"The Green Gang killed all the Red Guards last night," Binbin sobbed. "The gangsters were able to drive through the concessions, past all the checkpoints. That means only one thing: the 'white ghosts' and Chiang Kai-shek planned the massacre in advance."

"That can't be true," Edna said in shock.

"The bodies were taken away in trucks," Binbin said. "I saw it myself. This morning, people came out onto the streets to protest in front of the NRA headquarters. There were a few thousands of us, and the soldiers began to shoot at us with machine guns."

Only now did Edna notice that Binbin's coat was spattered with tiny spots of blood.

Her umbrella dropped from her hands and was immediately whisked up by the wind into the rainy mist.

"Why did you go to this meeting?" Edna said, hugging her friend. "They could have killed you."

"I couldn't stay at home. We have been waiting for *our* army. We were hoping that Chiang Kai-shek would restore peace and justice—but he has conspired with the bandits and 'white ghosts' against us."

"Come to my house," said Edna. "Yun will take care of you, and I'll go to the *Daily News* office. I have to inform the world about what has happened."

7

Edna didn't recall how she got to the offices of the *Daily News* in the Bund. The elevator had just reached the ground floor, and Mr. Green came out into the lobby, dressed in a checkered coat and cap.

"Mrs. Bernard! Glad you're back—" he began, but cut himself off, alarmed. "What's the matter with you?"

"There has been a conspiracy between Chiang Kai-shek and Big-Eared Du's gangsters," Edna exclaimed breathlessly. "There was a massacre in the Chinese City—"

"Yes, I know," Mr. Green nodded. "I hope the communists will learn from their lesson."

Edna was stupefied. "Are you not going to publish anything about it?"

"We have already sent the special edition to the printing house. Chiang Kai-shek is a noble, resolute, and far-sighted politician who has saved our city from the horrors of Bolshevism."

"What are you talking about? Does killing without a trial sound 'noble' to you?"

Mr. Green looked at Edna strangely. "I thought you were good at politics."

Without a word, she went out into the Bund and stopped.

I have to go to the radio station to Klim, she decided. *It doesn't matter what's been between us in the past. He has to listen to me and publicize the massacre on air.*

The streets were now completely flooded, and Edna was up to her ankles in water, oblivious to the spray flying up from the passing cars.

347

When she reached the radio station building, Edna noticed a girl in a raincoat sitting on the steps by the entrance.

"Miss Marshall?" Edna called in amazement.

Ada looked up at her, misty-eyed. "My name is Messalina. I'm a prostitute at the Havana."

Edna grabbed her by the shoulders. "What are you talking about?"

"My fiancé has been killed, and Klim has left Shanghai."

Ada stood up and staggered away, her head hunched between her shoulders.

Edna watched her retreating back, and in horror realized that it had been she who had kicked Ada out onto the street. In the heat of her anger and shame, she had never even given a second thought to the consequences. It was obvious—how else would a girl like Ada be able to provide for herself? Edna, the great crusader against prostitution, had shoved the poor girl into the brothel with her own hands.

"Miss Marshall, wait!" Edna shouted, and she ran after the Ada. "We need to talk!"

31. PEKING

1

On her journey to the capital, Nina tried to escape twice. After the second attempt, the chief of the guards made her spend the night standing on the platform of the railroad car with her arms tied to the handrail. She tried to persuade the teenage soldier who was guarding her to let her go, but he pretended not to understand English and entertained himself all night by lifting Nina's skirt with the tip of his bayonet.

In the morning, she reported her tormentor to his superior officer, but he merely replied that this was her last warning.

"Next time you try to escape," he added, "I'll tell my boys to punish you as they see fit."

These men could rape or even kill Nina with impunity. Shooting someone "while they were trying to escape" was an easy matter.

But the worst part was that Nina couldn't see help coming from any quarter.

"Do you think your husband will try to save us?" she had asked Fanya when the guard brought her back into the compartment the two of them were sharing. "I'm sure the Dogmeat General will have informed your Mikhail that you've been captured."

Fanya shook her head. "Those bourgeois generals believe they can blackmail my husband into betraying the revolution for me. They have no idea there are more important things in this world than a single individual's devotion to his wife."

Nina felt utterly helpless, and it was something she found very difficult to accept. She didn't have a single foothold to cling to; she couldn't expect any justice or any respect, and her fate would be decided by an obtuse little sadist taking pleasure in her humiliation.

Nina was so crushed that she spent the rest of the journey to Peking in the corner of the compartment, her knees pulled up to her chest.

2

The train pulled into the station, and the prisoners were put into covered palanquins dragged by two horses, one in front and the other behind it. Guards with carbines were lined up on either side, and the convoy set off along the bumpy unpaved street. The palanquin rocked from side to side, and Nina held on to her seat for dear life.

Finally, the horses stopped, and the guards ordered the prisoners to get out.

"We will never surrender," Fanya told Nina when the warden separated and ordered them off into different directions. "Long live socialism!"

Nina was placed in solitary confinement, in a cell furnished with nothing but a bucket, a mug, and a rough bunk bed with two unclean blankets.

Her warden was an old crone with rotten teeth and unfeasibly long nails on her gnarled broken hands. She spoke some English: "Search, search . . ."

Nina set about undressing, but the warden made it clear that only she was allowed to take the prisoner's clothes off. When the cold claws started moving over her body, Nina could only close her eyes and repeat to herself, *This will all soon pass, it'll pass.*

Two younger female wardens checked through Nina's clothes and shredded all the buttons, which were wrapped in fabric, off her jacket. They left Nina her skirt, shirt, and shoes—everything else was taken away, including her underwear.

Nina got dressed and spent a long time sitting on her bunk, her hands clasped over her knees. She was sure that the wardens were standing outside the door, pushing each other like rats at the feeder, trying to sneak a curious peek through the peephole. "How's she coping? Is she afraid? Is she crying?"

3

That night Nina was interrogated. Three men sat in a smoky room; the area where the prisoner was meant to stand was clearly outlined on the floor.

"Stand in the center of this square," said a tall stooped translator. He looked like a heron waiting for a chance to catch something in the shallows.

An elderly investigator in a military uniform asked questions, and a scribe quickly drew columns of Chinese characters on the paper in front of him.

"What is your relationship to Mikhail Borodin?"

Nina looked at them from under her knit brows. "Look, this is a mistake. I don't know Borodin. I met Fanya on the boat. I lied that I was her cousin because I was hoping for leniency."

Nina demanded that they invite someone from the American Embassy and send telegrams to Klim and Tony Aulman in Shanghai.

The translator mumbled something, the investigator nodded, but the scribe put his brush aside and didn't even bother to write down Nina's words.

"Don't you believe me?" she asked, taking a step back.

Immediately a guard grabbed her arm roughly and pushed her back into the center of the square.

The investigator sighed. "Let's start from the beginning. What's your relationship with Mikhail Borodin and what was the purpose of your visit to China?"

He asked questions and proceeded to dictate the answers himself: Nina Kupina was a Soviet spy, she had been smuggling military equipment into the country and harboring an even more dangerous criminal, Fanya Borodin.

"What are you talking about?" Nina moaned. "What kind of military equipment?"

The investigator gesticulated towards a crumpled piece of paper, covered in writing in indelible pencil. "According to the search protocol, you were transporting an Avro 504 military airplane to Wuhan."

"That's not true!"

"Don't bother denying it. The evidence is in right in front of you."

The scribe scrawled endless tiny cobwebs of Chinese characters across the case notes with his spidery hand. Nina realized she was doomed.

4

Nina was allowed out once a day in the exercise yard, which was surrounded by white-washed stone walls. She was always alone and was forbidden to associate with any of the other prisoners.

On the second floor, there were narrow barred windows, and Nina could hear people talking and coughing, and occasionally a baby crying. But who the women in these cells were remained a mystery to her. She couldn't see their faces from the yard.

Nina discovered a little plant next to the wall that had tenaciously gained a foothold between the stone slabs. She brought water into the yard and began to water its withered stalk. Within a few days, it begun to sprout bright green leaves. But as soon as she was spotted, the warden guarding Nina marched over and stomped it into the ground. Nina felt so sorry for it, as though a small bird had been trampled instead.

During the day she was exhausted by the heat and the constant anxiety. What was going to happen next? Would there be a trial? Would she be imprisoned? And if so, how long would her sentence be?

During the night she was tormented by bedbugs, screeching iron doors, and the other prisoners' distant cries.

In the early mornings before sunrise, Nina would get up, walk to the window, and observe the pitched roof covered with black tiles. The city's roofs stretched away like giant scaly fish on their way to their spawning grounds.

The sky turned pink, the smoke began to rise from the chimneys, and the trees were transformed from dark gray to bright green. The birds performed a cheerful if chaotic chorus, and finally the rich, low sound of the signal bell swept over the city.

One day Nina watched an oncoming yellow cloud rapidly fill the morning sky. A minute later the window quivered as it was hit by a strong wind, and the room became as dark as night. A dust storm had rolled into Peking from the Gobi Desert.

The prisoners spent the next few days inside their cells. Nina could barely see the ridges of the roofs in the brown haze that had descended outside her window, and the prison was filled with an eerie silence. Sometimes Nina was under the impression that everyone had died and she was the only survivor.

She had tried to avoid painful thoughts about Klim, but

the dust clouds that swept past her window reminded her of the smoke from the fires during the Russian civil war. How had she and Klim managed to survive that nightmare only to destroy their lives once the worst had passed?

Nina was surprised to realize that despite everything, nearly all her best memories were associated with Klim.

One day she had casually mentioned that she was keen to read a book by an Italian opera singer called Lina Cavalieri. Nina hadn't even asked Klim to buy it, but a few weeks later she found the book on her dressing table.

Gifts like these meant much more to her than diamonds and furs. Klim remembered what Nina was interested in and had tried to make her happy, even though he personally could see no value in Mme. Cavalieri's writing.

Klim used to write little notes for Nina: "You are beautiful" next to the mirror in the lobby, "Look on the top shelf" in the pantry, where a bar of her favorite marzipan candy awaited her.

She remembered Klim lying in their bed and herself leaning over him to kiss him. He had pulled a white feather out of the pillow and blown it. It had floated through the collar of her blouse, out the other side and landed on his stomach. It had been silly but it had made them laugh at the time. Did he remember that?

Finally one night a storm broke over Peking. In the morning the roof tiles were shining like new, and a big tree behind the prison fence was in full blossom.

From that time on, Nina would admire it every morning and savor the memories of her precious but ill-starred love: that time when they had danced the tango and Klim had sung the words of the music to her in Spanish, that time when they had imagined what they would look like in their old age—a slim and sprightly couple at the head of a sparkling and talented family.

Initially, Nina thought she would soon run out of these kinds of reminiscences, but to her surprise, she had an amazing store of memories available to her from her ten years of married life with Klim.

Nina tried to recall similar memories of her time with Daniel. There had been a lot of witty talk, sarcastic remarks, excitement and emotions, but nothing that could compare with the kinship, freedom, and absolute trust that she had shared with Klim.

Like it or not, he had been the only man she had ever truly loved, even though they had experienced the most terrible and shameful ups and downs.

32. THE SOVIET EMBASSY

1

Daniel and Klim were driving each other mad but they had to put up with each other in order to get to Peking in safety. By sticking together it was much easier to keep an eye on their suitcases, find food, and deal with Chinese officers keen to take their seats in their compartment.

However, Daniel didn't miss a single opportunity to wind Klim up. He regaled him with the minutest details of his relationship with Nina and let him know that she had been ready to run away with him anywhere, to be as far away as possible from her lousy husband.

"The most ridiculous thing about this whole affair," Daniel said with a sigh, "is that your suspicions were totally absurd. We've never been lovers. So, what do you plan to do when you see her again? Are you going to beg for her forgiveness? Or perhaps you'll be more melodramatic and deliver your final ultimatum: 'It's me or him—you can't have us both.'"

Sometimes Klim felt an overwhelming urge to punch him in the mouth and be done with it. However, if he was going to save Nina, he knew he would need Daniel's help.

"Neither of us will get her," Klim said to Daniel. "You've had every opportunity to steal Nina away from me, but you didn't really want her, just like you never really wanted Edna or any of the women you've ever had for that matter. You have no interest in them as people. You want Nina just in order to prove to yourself that you're no worse than me."

Daniel laughed. "That's what celebrity does to people. With all your pathetic besotted fans, you think the whole world revolves around you, don't you? Well, sorry to disillusion you, old chap, but I couldn't give a damn about you. Although I have to say, I'm fascinated by your extraordinary ability to ruin your own life."

2

In Peking, Daniel and Klim rented a room in the Central Hotel, and Daniel immediately went to the Legation Quarter. He discovered that while they had been traveling up to Peking, Zhang Zuolin's soldiers had conducted a search of the Soviet Embassy under the pretext that the Russians were sheltering Chinese communists. Zhang had violated every diplomatic rule in the book, but nobody cared. During the search, his soldiers had discovered conclusive evidence that the Soviet Union was conducting subversive activities in China.

The Soviets had always claimed their actions had no bearing on the struggle of the local proletariat to liberate themselves from oppression, insisting that any uprisings were purely the initiative of local workers. But here were papers documenting the shipments of weapons and the supply of money and instructions to saboteurs, lists of secret agents, cyphers, and all sorts of other paraphernalia. Soviet agents had been directly instructed to organize provocations, robbery, and murder, in order to turn the Chinese masses against the West and their own government.

Newspapers around the world had published these documents proving the Bolsheviks' guilt and denouncing their perfidious actions. But it was all water off a duck's back for the Soviets—they were incapable of shame or embarrassment. Pretending to be offended, Moscow sent a formal protest to the Peking government, declaring itself a victim of a misinformation campaign directed against all the working people of the world.

Zhang Zuolin became even more incensed after this impudent reply and ordered that every Chinese person found on the territory of the Russian Embassy should be shot. However, he refrained from harming Soviet citizens, fearing that this could lead to direct military reprisals.

"Mr. Rogov, we are out of luck," Daniel declared on his return from another trip to the Legation Quarter. "Moscow has withdrawn its charge d'affaires and all its employees in protest. They only have a skeleton staff left, manning the consulate and working on the Borodin trial."

"So the Soviets are at least trying to defend them?" Klim asked hopefully. "Is there any chance of us making an appointment with the Russian Embassy?"

"Are you kidding? The Russians have been stripped of their diplomatic immunity, and they now see every stranger who comes to visit them as a spy or assassin. I need to think of a way of reaching them."

3

Klim found the city jail, but couldn't find out if Nina was being kept there or somewhere else.

Peking is a city of walls, he thought. The houses, office buildings, theaters, and entire neighborhoods were all surrounded by insurmountable barriers. As he wandered through the Chinese capital, Klim felt as if he'd entered a labyrinth of stone rectangles and squares.

One day he managed to make his way to the top of an ancient Bell Tower overlooking half of the city. A huge bell hanging from a wooden frame had been used to keep track of time for centuries.

"If you throw a coin at the bell and make a wish," the keeper hinted, "it will be bound to come true."

Klim knew that the keeper had invented the legend in order to trick the incredulous "white ghost" into throwing away his money, but nevertheless he still took his wallet out. To the bell keeper's great disappointment, Klim's coin vanished into the shadows under the ceiling and silently fell into the thick layer of dust on top of the bell.

"Time's up, the tower is closed," the keeper said angrily.

With a heavy heart, Klim trudged back to his hotel. While he'd been in the Bell Tower, a crazy idea had occurred to him. What if he were to overpower the keeper and use the bell to send Nina messages in Morse code to let her know that he was in the city and looking for her? Unfortunately, she didn't know Morse code.

When he reached the Central Hotel, Klim was met by Daniel.

"Get dressed for dinner," he told him. "I've figured out a way of making contact with the Russians."

Half an hour later Klim found himself in a small European restaurant next to the Legation Quarter. It was full of noisy foreigners gathered at round polished tables. Waiters ran to and fro with unimaginably large trays, dishes crashed, and the flags of the Great Powers swayed in the cigarette smoke under the high ceiling.

Klim and Daniel ascended the stairs to an open mezzanine area and sat themselves down at a tiny table near the railing where they had a clear view of the proceedings in the main room.

"China has become a magnet for every socialist from every country around the world," said Daniel looking at the crowd below. "Most of them are wealthy romantics who don't have to earn a living and can afford to travel to foreign countries. They have read rapturous and totally fictitious accounts of the Bolshevik coup in Russia and have now come here to witness the latest revolution, which, of course, is not going to happen now."

"What are we doing here?" Klim asked, perplexed.

Daniel gave him a mysterious smile. "Moscow believes that these gentlemen represent 'progressive opinion.' Half of them are freelance writers for leftist rags with a circulation of about five hundred copies, and when the Bolsheviks need to spread the word about something, they send their man here. See the curly-haired boy in the striped tie? That's Anatoly Levkin, a lawyer working for the Soviet Embassy. From time to time he invents another fake story, leaks it to the 'progressive press' here, and they dutifully file it as copy for their editorial offices. When their articles become mainstream news, Moscow is overjoyed. The world revolution is on course, the workers of the West are marching in solidarity with the great Russian proletariat, and the wise Soviet leader's great plan is running like clockwork."

"Is this lawyer working on the Fanya Borodin's case?" Klim interrupted impatiently.

"Exactly."

To Klim, Levkin had all the attributes of a mosquito. This small, long-nosed and bug-eyed young man would buzz from one table to another with his interpreter, fussing around, offering handshakes and cigarettes. Even up in the mezzanine, Klim could hear Levkin fervently arguing that the bourgeois press was publishing thinly-veiled lies about the recent raid on the Soviet Embassy.

"The only documents the Chinese found were harmless business papers," he said. "Then they swapped them for fakes in order to blacken the name of the world's first socialist state. It has never been the intention of the Soviet Union to meddle in the affairs of other sovereign nations."

How can he be such a shameless liar? Klim wondered. But, judging by the reaction in the main room, the "progressive press" were happy to believe him.

Levkin paid for his dinner, dismissed his interpreter, and was about to head for the exit.

"Go up to him and introduce yourself as a communist from Shanghai," Daniel whispered to Klim. "Tell him that you have connections with German diplomats and they have hinted that soon there will be similar raids on some Soviet embassies in Europe."

Klim stared at Daniel. That was all he needed—to make himself a pawn in Daniel's great game.

"Why don't you do it yourself?" Klim asked.

"I don't speak Russian."

Klim didn't budge, and Daniel became angry. "What are you waiting for? If you miss this opportunity, we won't be able to make contact with Levkin until it's too late. Why did you bother coming here to Peking if you're not prepared to stick your neck out?"

Klim got up, cursing, and walked briskly toward the stairs.

He overtook the Soviet lawyer just as he was about to get into his car, but Levkin appeared unimpressed by Klim's claims.

"Sorry, I have no time at the moment," he said dryly and told the driver to start the engine.

Daniel joined Klim just as Levkin's car was disappearing around the corner.

"The ball is well and truly in motion," he said, slapping Klim on the shoulder. "Give the bartender your address and wait. Soon Levkin will be calling on you."

4

Klim spent several agonizing days doing nothing but sitting in his room and reading the newspapers. With the Soviet Embassy scandal, Zhang Zuolin now had every justification he needed to start hunting down communists, and soon anti-Bolshevik hysteria began to spread throughout the whole of China. Chiang Kai-shek joined in, persecuting his former allies and claiming that the massacre of the Red Guards in Shanghai had been a cruel but necessary evil.

Mikhail Borodin, who was still in Wuhan, was

powerless to do anything to stop it. His social experiment had failed, and he had neither the money, nor allies to prevent the catastrophe that was unfolding before his eyes.

Russian political and military advisers were hastily evacuated from China. The Soviet Consulate in Tianjin was raided, and former White Army men laid siege to the consulate in Shanghai. In provincial towns, things were even worse: suspected communists were lynched in the streets by the mobs, and girls with short hair were accused of being Bolsheviks and summarily beheaded.

In these circumstances, there was little or no point in hoping for any leniency in Nina's case.

A week passed, and finally, a bellboy presented Klim with Levkin's card. "He's waiting for you downstairs, sir."

Klim dashed out into the lobby and almost collided with Levkin.

"I'd like to invite you to our embassy," the Soviet lawyer said. "Please get into my car."

Klim was desperate to ask Levkin about Nina, but he knew this was not the right time for questions.

The car drove up to the high walls surrounding the Legation Quarter. The guards checked Levkin's pass and opened a heavy gate covered with armored metal plates.

As they passed through, Klim could barely believe his eyes. As if by magic, they had left the sprawling Chinese city behind them and now found themselves in a neat European town with wide tree-lined streets of elegant mansions and imposing office buildings belonging to banks and insurance companies. The sound of splashing water emanated from the picturesque fountains, and elegantly dressed people dined calmly in the street cafes.

The only thing that reminded Klim that they were in China were the rows of rickshaws gleaming in the sun with their black lacquer and brass ornaments. The rickshaw boys stood to attention next to their carts in cleanly-laundered blue shirts and trousers, their heads covered with new straw hats.

Levkin's car drove through a latticed gate guarded by Red Army soldiers and stopped next to a large white house with a pair of fierce-eyed stone lions standing sentinel on the porch.

Klim got out of the car and looked around. The lawn was dotted with forlorn brown bald patches, and the flowers in their tarnished green bronze vases had long withered.

"We have no time for gardening here," said Levkin registering Klim's look of disapproval.

An old Chinese man in a faded tunic silently led them into a dimly lit lobby and immediately went back to his job of dusting a marble bust of Lenin that stood in the corner.

Klim followed Levkin along the corridor. The building appeared to be completely empty. The doors hung open; the carpets and curtains had been removed, and the sound of their footsteps echoed right up to the ceiling.

Levkin showed Klim into a small cheerless room that smelled of charred paper. "Stay here," he said. "I'll be right back."

There were empty folders piled up on the desk and a tin pail full of cigarette butts and scraps of burned documents.

Klim scrutinized an array of photographs of the most prominent members of the Bolshevik Party hanging on the wall. They were arranged in the form of a pyramid. Sitting at the apex was a portrait of a dark-haired mustached man called Stalin.

A moment later Levkin returned with a gloomy tall man in a traditional embroidered shirt.

"My name is Valdas," the man introduced himself. "Pleased to meet you."

His round head was shaved bald; he had a gray mustache, and his strong neck was red from sunburn.

"Unfortunately, your information about the attacks of the Soviet missions has been confirmed," Valdas said as he sat down on a creaky chair. "Yesterday, the British raided the Soviet trade mission in London. Their police acted in much the same way as Zhang's here and have seized documents, exposing our work in the United Kingdom."

"Has our foreign office sent a formal note of protest?" Levkin asked.

"The British government doesn't give a damn about our protests," said Valdas. "They have declared the Soviet Union a pariah state and will insist on an economic blockade. Our main task now is to prove them wrong, and it would be a great help if some third neutral party, for example, Germany, could do the job for us."

Valdas fixed his pale blue eyes on Klim.

"From what I understand, you have a friend in the German Embassy who is sympathetic and ready to help the Soviet Union. May I ask his name?"

Klim gave him one of Daniel's aliases.

"We appreciate your friend's intentions," said Valdas. "I assume that he is linked with their intelligence service since he knew about the raids in advance. Tell him that if the Germans can help us get out of this mess, military cooperation between our countries will move up to a new level."

Klim finally realized what was going on. People in the know at the Shanghai Club had mentioned that Moscow had invited the Germans to carry out weapon tests in the Soviet Union. Germany was craving revenge after its defeat in the Great War and was now doing everything in its power to develop new aircraft, armored vehicles, and chemical weapons—thus circumventing the Treaty of Versailles that prohibited it from rebuilding its armed forces. The Allies knew that something was going on, but they couldn't prove anything since the Soviet Union refused to allow any international commissions over its borders.

In all likelihood, Daniel was indeed working for German intelligence and trying to broker a military agreement with the Russians. But in order not to deflect the heat if something were to go wrong with the crazy Bolsheviks, he had sent Klim in his stead.

"What exactly do the Germans need to do in order to help you?" Klim asked.

"They could start by finding a printing press in Berlin," Valdas said. "For example, one run by former White Army officers, which has been producing the compromising documents found in our missions. There will need to be arrests, and the international press will need to be fed the spectacle of a couple of angry Russian immigrants who have been surreptitiously trying to harm and besmirch the good name of their former Motherland."

Speechless, Klim looked at Valdas and Levkin, who smiled calmly. He had always known that politics was a dirty business, but there were limits.

"May I ask how these 'fake documents' managed to find their way into the Soviet trade mission in London?" Klim asked sarcastically.

"Our enemies planted them there too of course," Levkin said grinning. "We'll arrest some recent returnees who will be only too happy to confess to the deed once we have finished with them."

They are true criminals, Klim thought in impotent rage. *Only they are acting on behalf of the state, not some Green Gang.*

The most ridiculous thing was that the "progressive press" will lap all this up because they would prefer to believe in mysterious conspiracy theories, rather than the blatant evil that was parading itself before their eyes.

Klim was tempted to leave there and then without even shaking Valdas' and Levkin's hands, however, he managed to master his revulsion.

"I will convey your words to my German friend," he promised.

Levkin accompanied him into the lobby.

"I was told that you will be defending Mrs. Borodin and her people," Klim said. "There is a woman, her name is Nina Kupina. She and I are old friends, and I'd like to know how she's doing—"

"I'll be seeing her soon," said Levkin. "Zhang Zuolin wants to keep up the appearance that justice is being served, so the accused have been granted lawyers."

Klim was relieved a little.

"Can I give you something for Nina?"

"I'm afraid not. The Russian prisoners are carefully guarded and searched. But if you want, you can write a few words for her. I'll try to show your note to Ms. Kupina."

Levkin produced a pencil and a blank sheet of paper.

"I'll get a power of attorney typed on the other side and take it with me to the jail," he said after Klim had written a short message for Nina. "Don't you worry about your friend. Comrade Stalin has ordered us to do everything possible to save our people."

Klim thanked him and went out into the street.

The sun was shining, the cicadas were singing, and the air was filled with the heady scent of jasmine and hot dust.

Don't get your hopes up, Klim thought trying to suppress his joy. What could a Soviet lawyer possibly do against the entire Chinese judicial system?

5

Back at the hotel, Klim told Daniel all about his negotiations with Valdas.

"Well done," Daniel said, beaming. "We'll rustle up the finest quality fake story about the production of fake documents."

"Why has Stalin decided to try and save Fanya Borodin?" Klim asked. "After all, her husband failed to seize power in China. Why would the Bolsheviks waste time and resources on the wife of a man who has failed the revolution?"

Daniel smiled condescendingly.

"You still don't understand what makes them tick, do you? By saving the Borodins, Stalin will be demonstrating to his supporters that he will never leave them in the lurch, even if they are superfluous to his needs. That way he plans to create a loyal and fanatical faction of his own within the Soviet communist party. These men will be completely devoted to him and help him get to the top. Do you remember Big-Eared Du? How do you think he became the top gangster in Shanghai? The same way; it's a time-honored formula."

6

The old woman with the claws escorted Nina to the visiting room, where she found a well-dressed, dark-haired young man waiting for her.

"My name is Anatoly Levkin." He introduced himself in Russian and shook Nina's hand. "I will be your attorney during your trial."

"Who sent you?" Nina asked in amazement.

"The Embassy of the USSR; I'm a legal advisor there. The investigation of your case is completed and has been submitted. You're being charged under article one hundred and one of the criminal code, and you're facing either a life sentence or the death penalty."

Levkin was glowing with pleasure at the prospect of the trial, like a trainee surgeon who has finally been entrusted with a life or death operation.

"You probably want to know how Fanya is," he said. "She's fine and asked me to say hello."

Nina could barely understand a word he was saying. *Dear Lord, the death penalty . . . What on earth for?*

"They are charging you with an attempted coup and the smuggling of weapons," Levkin explained. "Please sit down and make yourself comfortable. You shouldn't worry too much. The indictment is ridiculous, the prosecutor has no evidence, and I don't think there's going to be a public trial. We have hired the best Chinese lawyers for you, and we are hoping the judge will be willing to listen to their arguments. I'm going to need you to sign powers of attorney for Mr. Ma Dazhang and Mr. Guo Tingbao. It's good that they have agreed to represent you. They never take a case that they are not sure about."

"All my money is in Shanghai," Nina said. "How am I supposed to pay them?"

Levkin looked at her reproachfully. "The Soviet authorities will pay for everything."

He took some papers out of his briefcase and slipped them to Nina, but she was unable to make out the writing, which swam before her eyes.

Levkin pushed the inkwell towards her. "I'd appreciate it if you could be a bit quicker. I still have to go to the men's prison."

Nina signed the first copy, then the second, and finally the third, but then suddenly noticed an inscription in pencil on the margin:

I'm here. We'll figure something out.

It was Klim's handwriting.

The pen fell from Nina's hands.

"Is he really here?" she asked Levkin.

He motioned towards the guard standing at the door and quickly rubbed out Klim's words with an eraser.

"Well, I have to run."

Once he had left, Nina was taken to her cell and searched again. She could hardly wait to be left alone. She was brimming over with joy and, at the same time, disappointment that she hadn't had a chance to write anything to Klim in reply.

Everything was the same—the gray cell, the bunk bed, and the shabby door. Nina was facing the death penalty or an indefinite prison term, but a few words from Klim had given her life new meaning.

Nina covered her face with her hands and wept with happiness.

33. THE SENTENCE

1

Dear Kitty,

If you have received this letter, then that means that I have been arrested and, most likely, executed. It's frightening to have to write such things, and I know that I'm risking not only my life, but your future as well. But the Aulmans have promised to take care of you if something bad happens.

I must do everything possible to save your mother, and unless I do my utmost to help her, she has no chance. The Chinese authorities and foreign diplomats are out for her blood: they want to punish the Soviet Russia that Fanya Borodina and her cronies represent, and nobody cares that your mother has never had anything to do with it.

Unfortunately, I have no choice but to be a pawn in a dirty political game. I don't want to go into the details here but I will tell you the most important facts: as a result of the negotiations that have been started here, in Peking, Germany has lifted its support for the economic blockade of the USSR and in return received the right to test its chemical weapons in Russia.

A new leader, Joseph Stalin, is gaining momentum in the Soviet Union. In order to persuade him to become their ally, the Germans have decided to help release the Bolsheviks on death row here in Peking and send two hundred thousand dollars to bribe Huo Cong, the man judging their case.

Unlike most Chinese officials, Huo Cong is renowned for his probity. He has already had a number of people imprisoned who have dared to offer him a bribe, so no one from the Soviet Embassy staff is keen to approach him with this business proposal. We have also failed to find a local mediator, because, in the current political climate, everyone is afraid to have any dealings with Russians.

With each passing day, the court date looms ever closer, so I have volunteered to talk to the judge, and the embassy has agreed. Judge Huo Cong was born near Shanghai, and since I can speak Shanghainese, I can act without an interpreter, which spares us from looking for another person to get involved.

Once a week, Huo Cong goes to the Zhengyici Peking Opera Theatre, and I have decided to meet him there.

I've already been there on a scouting mission.

The actors were dressed in elaborate costumes playing scenes from ancient legends, and the auditorium was full of merchants and important officials drinking tea, along with curious foreigners who know nothing about Peking opera.

However, it wasn't the performance but the judge, the man who holds your mother's life in his hands, that I was watching. A beam of light from a dusty window fell right onto his table, and at times, I could see his parchment-thin, yellowing hand reach out to grasp his cup of tea. I desperately tried to get at least a glimpse of him, but every time he turned my way, his face was screened by a paper fan.

I'm going to try to approach him tomorrow. To say that I'm afraid would be a huge understatement. If I was faced with the prospect of a fight, I'd be inspired with rage or at least assessing my opponent's strengths and weaknesses, but I feel as if I'm about to jump into a well.

I don't know why I'm writing all this. You're only three years old, and when you grow up, you won't remember me. The idea that I might disappear from your life without a trace pains me intensely, but I have no other choice. I just want you to know what has happened to me.

Well, good-bye for now. It's time to go sleep or rather to toss and turn in my bed and pray for help from a God whom I find it increasingly hard to believe in.

Love you.
Dad

2

Levkin would regularly bring Nina new notes from her husband—words of encouragement and short silly poems that Klim had composed to keep her spirits up.

He never wrote about his feelings for her or made any mention of making up, and Nina still had no clue what his intentions were. Was Klim being so diffident because he didn't want Levkin to learn about his feelings? Or was Klim just supporting his wife out of compassion? He had, nevertheless, given up his beloved radio station for her sake, so surely that suggested that he was seeking a reconciliation.

If I'm released, what is going to happen next? Nina asked herself. She knew that once this major threat was over, Klim would always be prone to suspicion, and the round of jealousy and rejection would start all over again.

They seemed to find it much easier to love each other in times of trouble when they weren't faced with the small humdrum problems of everyday life. But Nina now realized that true happiness rested on the precious everyday trinkets that adorn our lives. Of course, a person could live without them, in much the same way as people could survive without books or music, but an existence without such things soon becomes a pale imitation of what life really should be.

Soon Levkin brought her another thing to ponder.

"Your Shanghai friend says hi to you," he whispered into Nina's ear during his next visit. "The one who helped you with the antiques. I saw him yesterday, and he asked me to convey his best wishes to you."

Nina gasped. "Does Klim know that this man is here in Peking?" she asked.

Levkin nodded. "Yes, they came to our embassy together. I think they are good friends."

Nina had no idea what it all meant.

3

Finally, the trial began. The recently renovated courtroom was empty except for the participants in the proceedings, the clerks, and the guards. As Levkin had predicted, it was essentially a closed hearing.

Before the session started, he gave the accused his instructions: "Please be sure to control your feelings— that's the most important thing. And we," he exchanged glances with his Chinese colleagues, "will see to everything else."

"All rise!" the interpreter intoned coldly.

To Nina, the old judge with his embroidered coat, silk

hat, and ethereal sallow complexion looked more like a dark spirit floating over the surface of the floor than a normal human being. His face was as blank and inscrutable as a death mask.

He interrogated the accused one by one.

"Declare your name and how long you've been living in China," he said. However, it was unclear whether he was listening to the Russian "white ghosts" or their lawyers at all.

Nina stared intently at his waxen face, with its barely visible apertures for eyes. For an instant she imagined that the judge didn't have any eyes at all and that she was staring straight into a black void. *The man is completely hollow inside, nothing more than an empty wrinkled husk,* she thought.

The hearing dragged on forever, like a school lesson taught by an uninspiring teacher.

Huo Cong told Fanya that her husband was an evil man. "From the documents seized in your embassy, it has come to light that Mikhail Borodin called Dr. Sun Yat-sen 'a simpleton who thinks too much of himself.' Here in China, we believe that only the greatest scoundrel would possibly condemn his master behind his back."

Fanya fidgeted on her bench, and Nina thought she was going to blurt out something terrible. But, thank God, Fanya managed to control herself and merely repeated what Levkin had told her to say: "I'm just a woman, and I don't interfere in my husband's business."

Nina was questioned about the airplane, where had it come from and who was the person she was going to sell it to.

"I was slandered!" she said passionately. "Ask the people who signed the search protocol. Let them prove that it was my airplane."

The judge mumbled something, and the interpreter shook his head. "These people are not here," he said. "The matter could take several more weeks if they are summoned. So it's not in your best interests."

Nina looked helplessly at her lawyers. What did the judge have in mind? Was he just hoping to close the case as soon as possible? Or was he really trying to help her?

The lawyers talked interminably in their incomprehensible Mandarin dialect.

If Huo Cong were to sentence me to death, what would happen to me? Nina thought. She had often had nightmares of being dragged to a place of execution through an angry, jeering crowd. She would try and fail to find Klim among the sea of hostile faces. She would scream his name, but he would never respond.

The judge finally announced that there would be an adjournment. Everyone stood up while he went out, and the guards escorted the exhausted prisoners out of the courtroom.

"It seems that Huo Cong might be willing to listen to Ma Dazhang," one of the diplomatic messengers whispered to Nina.

She nodded blankly. She still couldn't remember which of her lawyers was Ma and which was Guo.

4

On the night before sentence was to be pronounced, Nina couldn't sleep a wink. *I want to fall asleep and never wake up again,* she thought with a macabre shiver. *Although that might be exactly what happens to me once Huo Cong pronounces his verdict.*

Nina passed her hand over the back of her neck and caressed the dimple that Klim so loved to kiss. This was the spot that the curved blade of the Chinese executioner's sword would hit, and in a split second, everything that had once been Nina—everything that had been so warm, precious, and full of life—would be nothing more than a bloody mess.

How will Klim and Kitty cope with my death? she thought, trying to suppress the convulsive sobs that wracked her body. *Will they feel sorrow at my passing? Will they remember me at all?*

Never before, even during the war, had Nina experienced such a desperate fear of death.

She remembered herself as a child watching a baby deer with broken hind legs. Hunters had found it in the woods and taken it to the city to show to the children. It had been looking at little Nina, shaking with pain and terror, its face covered with dirt and snot smeared all over its matted fur.

Then the baby deer had been taken away, and later one of the hunters had brought Nina's mother a chunk of meat, still warm and bloody, with a clump of red fur hanging off it. "Here," he said, "feed your children."

Nina now felt as helpless as that little animal.

5

Nina found herself back in the courtroom again, intersected with dusty rays of sunshine and stuffy with the smell of fresh paint. Huo Cong began to read the introductory part of the sentence, and the interpreter translated, barely able to suppress his yawns.

Nina kept her eyes peeled on the judge, a single thought pulsating through her head: *This man is about to pronounce my death sentence.*

Huo Cong applied his seal to a piece of paper and said something quietly and impassively. *Here it comes,* thought Nina.

The interpreter scratched his cheek.

"On behalf of the Republic of China," he declared, "Judge Huo Cong declares you—not guilty."

Fanya and Nina burst into tears, and the diplomatic messengers hugged each other and shouted in relief.

Someone grabbed Nina by the shoulder. She turned and was surprised to see Levkin's tense and deadly pale face.

"Let's get out of here!" he hissed to her. "Hurry up if you want to live."

6

Huo Cong had decided that the two hundred thousand dollars that the Soviets had offered him would be sufficient to support him for the rest of his life. He and Klim had agreed that he would get half the money before the sentence, and the other half after the prisoners' release.

Klim was now waiting for him in a gas lamp repair shop used by Bolsheviks as a safe house. It was a stone's throw away from the courthouse, and it had been arranged that Huo Cong would come there immediately after pronouncing sentence to receive his second payment.

Klim stalked between the drawers and boxes, constantly glancing at his watch, anxious with anticipation. If all was going to plan, he would see Nina in less than an hour. According to the agreement, the judge would release her from the courtroom, and Levkin would immediately take her and the other prisoners to the Soviet Embassy.

Klim tried to imagine seeing Nina in person again. What would it be like? What would they say to each other?

He knew that Daniel had asked Levkin to pass on a message to Nina, too. Previously, Klim thought that he would nobly step aside and refrain from standing in their way, but now the very thought of doing so made his fists clench. *Nina is mine,* he thought. *I won't give her up.*

Now it was 11:00 a.m., and the judge should have already pronounced sentence.

Klim wanted to see what was going on up the street and approached the glass door with a "Closed" sign on it, but the master repairman, an old Polish communist named Janek, stopped him. "Stay inside."

Time crawled by so slowly that Klim thought that his watch had broken. Every time the shadow of a passerby flashed past the glass door, his heart skipped a bit.

Everything will be just fine, he kept telling himself. *The main thing is not to panic and to stick to the plan.*

Daniel had promised that he would bring a car that would take Klim and the judge to the Legation Quarter, but so far, there was no sign of him.

What if Daniel has lied to me? Klim thought. What if he had decided to get rid of his competitor and informed the police where they could find a corrupt judge and the Bolshevik agent, Klim Rogov?

At last he heard footsteps on the porch, and a bony finger tapped at the glass. Klim rushed to the door and was met by Huo Cong, who had already changed into a European suit and hat.

"Where's the money?" the judge asked.

Klim gave him the bundle of money, and Huo Cong dumped it on the workbench.

"Did you release the prisoners?" Klim said anxiously.

The judge nodded and began to count the bills.

Klim was so overwhelmed with joy and relief that he wanted to hug the old man.

"Thank you," he said quietly, but Huo Cong wasn't paying any attention.

There was still no sign of Daniel's car. Huo Cong lost count and began to start all over again.

"Hurry up!" Janek urged him as he looked through the blinds to the street. "If you two don't have a car, then you'll have to go on foot."

Suddenly his face turned an ashen gray. "Damn it!"

Klim rushed to the window and saw a policeman walking down the street.

"Do you have a back door?" Klim asked.

"I do," said Janek, his jaw shaking, "but it's a dead-end alley. The only way out is on to the main street."

Klim cursed and looked at the judge.

"Are the police after me?" Huo Cong asked, pressing the wads of money to his chest.

"They are," Klim said, grimly watching a man in the

distance talking to the policemen and pointing at Janek's shop. "I guess the neighbors must have spotted you coming in."

He noticed a number of rusty gas lamps standing along the wall.

"Are these carbide lamps?" he asked Janek.

"Yes," the repairman said. "Why?"

Klim pushed him aside and took the lid off an iron box labeled with the chemical formula CaC_2.

"Janek, I need a container—a jar or a vase—anything. We need to scare off the police. "

The repairman nodded, finally realizing what Klim was up to, and took a couple of empty beer bottles from under the table. Klim filled them with dull gray fragments of carbide, poured in some water, and shook the bottles.

"I'll be right back," he said running out into the street.

The policemen rushed towards him, blowing their whistles. Klim left the bottles on the sidewalk and ran back into the shop. Two explosions went off, one after the other, shattering the window, and the policemen scattered, shouting.

"They'll kill us all!" yelped the judge.

"Janek, do we have any more bottles?" Klim barked.

At that moment there was a roar of an engine, and a black car stopped at the back door.

"Get in!" Daniel shouted.

Klim, Janek, and Huo Cong got into the car, and it set off at top speed towards the main street. The policemen started to shoot at them, but it was already too late; the car had turned the corner and driven off, bouncing over the cobbled road.

Huo Cong was still clutching his money; Janek sat beside him, his hands pressed over his head.

"What happened back there?" Daniel asked.

Klim laughed nervously. "When I worked at the radio station, we used small amounts of calcium carbide to create the sound effect of explosions in our shows. I just repeated the performance for our police friends back there. Where's Nina?"

"With Valdas," Daniel said.

Klim was relieved. His mind was completely numb. How had they been able to make all this happen? He still couldn't believe that everything had worked out fine.

They entered the Legation Quarter, and the car drove up to the gate of the Soviet Embassy, where journalists and photographers had already gathered.

Daniel stopped and let Klim and Janek get out of the car.

"Find out what's going on here, and I'll take the judge to the German Embassy," he said.

His heart pounding, Klim approached the agitated crowd.

"Stand back!" the Red Army soldiers yelled at the crowd.

"Where are Fanya Borodin and her people?" someone shouted.

"We know nothing."

Klim and Janek pushed their way to the gate and showed the guards their passes.

As they reached the porch with the stone lions, they met a stranger in a military jacket.

"Comrade Borodin and her companions have already left," he said.

"Where to?" Klim asked in alarm.

"I'm sorry, sir, but I don't know."

"Where are Valdas and Levkin?"

"They have also left. All the embassy's employees have been evacuated back to the USSR."

Klim grabbed him by the shoulders. "Where are they?"

Pushing the man aside, Klim ran into the building, dashing from one room to another and throwing the doors open. A couple of guards chased after him. When they caught him, they pinned his arms behind his back and hurled him out of the gate.

Oblivious to the excited crowd around him, Klim stood frozen to the spot, staring at the embassy fence that looked as menacing and impregnable as a stockade of spears. How could they have taken Nina away, without even letting him say a word to her? Levkin must have realized a long time ago that he and Nina were more than "just friends."

Maybe we just missed each other, Klim thought. *Zhang Zuolin is bound to turn the entire city upside down to find Fanya Borodin and the other prisoners. They must be in hiding somewhere, I just need to figure out where.*

Klim rushed to the German Embassy but the guards wouldn't let him in. They told him they had never heard of Daniel.

7

Peking's walls and fences were covered with portraits of the traitor judge Huo Cong and the political criminals he had released. A huge reward had been promised, but they had disappeared without a trace.

Klim felt as if his entire misadventure in Peking had been some sort of delirious dream. Depressed, he would drink himself into oblivion and wander the city for hours with no idea of where he had been and why he had gone there. He would then return to his hotel room and sit there hoping against hope that someone would call him.

Finally, Daniel Bernard appeared at the door of his room, thin, unshaven, and haggard.

"Any news of my wife?" Klim asked hopefully.

Daniel shook his head. "When I learned that you were still here, I figured that you'd been unable to find Nina either. So here we are with nothing to do but to live in the past."

He took Klim's "Receipts and Expenditures" diary out of his pocket and opened it at the middle page. He tore out the second half that was covered in his own handwriting and handed the front half to Klim.

"You keep the Russian part," said Daniel, "and I'll keep the German."

Klim flipped through his mutilated diary. Its inside covers had doodles all over them—airplanes, cars, and portraits of Nina, some of them quite well executed.

"If you have something good to remember, then you have not lived your life in vain," Daniel said, and he left without so much as shaking Klim's hand.

A minute later a bellboy brought Klim a telegram from Tamara: "Kitty is missing you. Come back soon."

The next day, Klim bought a ticket to Shanghai.

34. BACK TO THE USSR

1

Klim was sitting in his studio in front of the microphone, reading the world news.

"In response to increasing tensions with Great Britain and the other Great Powers, the Soviet Union has organized a National Defense Week teaching the population how to shoot and use gas masks. There are continuing clashes between the police and socialists in Vienna."

After Klim had bid his audience goodnight, Don Fernando stuck his head around the studio door.

"Hey, Klim, have you heard the latest about your crazy friend Martha? Some respected figure in the local church community ran up a huge tab at her brothel and refused to pay it. So last Sunday, Martha went to his church, and when they handed the baskets out for the offertory, she put every one of his signed chits into the basket. 'The bearer of this note promises to pay for debts accrued in the Havana brothel.' What a mad scandal that was!"

Klim chuckled. "That's funny."

It was only then that he noticed a technician waving frantically behind the glass screen.

"Oh no, we forgot to switch the mike off!"

Don Fernando roared with laughter and then let loose a long list of profanities, before declaring that the whole mishap must have been decreed by Virgin herself: now people would be talking about his honest mistake in every tram, providing free advertising for his radio station and Martha's brothel.

Klim's secretary, Olga, knocked and entered the studio, a Russian newspaper in her hands.

"Klim, look! I thought there was something here that you might find interesting."

Klim took the paper. The front page headline read, "Escape from Chinese satraps: an interview with Fanya Borodin."

Fanya had reported that she, Nina Kupina, and the diplomatic messengers had been forced to hide for a whole month at a Russian orientalist's house in Peking. It had been too dangerous to leave the capital immediately: all the roads and train stations were being watched. Gradually, the dust had settled, and the fugitives managed to escape to the Soviet Union, along with diplomats, military advisers, and prominent members of the Chinese Communist Party.

Klim took a deep breath. So Nina was in Russia now.

He stood up decisively. "I have to go."

Don Fernando grasped his sleeve. "Where?"

"To Russia."

"Right now?"

"Yep. No time like the present."

2

Klim was only able to get a Russian visa in October, and he immediately bought tickets on the first Soviet ship sailing to Vladivostok. From there he hoped to get a train to Moscow. His plan was to find Fanya Borodin and ask her Nina's whereabouts.

He couldn't leave Kitty for an indefinite period and

decided to take her with him. All of his friends told him that he was crazy to return back to a country ruled by the Bolsheviks. The rumors coming from the USSR were frightening; in addition to military hysteria, the Russian economy had collapsed, stores were empty, and there were queues everywhere.

"If you want to commit suicide, why don't you ask One-Eye?" Don Fernando told Klim. "He'll give you some excellent advice on how to do the job properly."

Klim shook his head. "There are plenty of American tourists visiting the USSR every year. Kitty and I will easily mingle in with the crowd. I've already got her name on my American passport. Of course, it's illegal, but I don't think anyone in Russia will be any the wiser about that."

Klim prepared for his trip to his homeland as if he was organizing an expedition to the North Pole. The servants loaded twelve suitcases with canned food, soap, bedding, and other supplies for all events.

People who had previously visited the Soviet Union advised Klim to wear his best suit. Fine clothes provided travelers with good protection against the caprices of the local authorities, who were slightly in awe of "important foreign visitors."

Klim made sure that he and Kitty were fitted out with the most magnificent outfits for their trip. Tony Aulman, who saw them off at the dock, could barely suppress his laughter when he saw Klim in an elegant dark gray coat, a Homburg hat, and a crimson silk scarf.

"Did you see that Russian reporter taking a photograph of you just then?" Tony whispered, pointing at a young man with a portable camera in his hands. "Now your portrait will be plastered all over the Soviet papers with the caption, 'A typical capitalist running dog, looking to cash in on the honest labor of our brother workers.'"

"How do you know he's Russian?" Klim asked.

"He came to meet some of my clients, the sailors from the *Pamyat Lenina*," Tony replied, pointing to a group of men dressed in tattered clothes, who were also waiting to board. "Like a fool, I took up their case, and for half a year visited them in their prison. In the Shanghai Club, people have almost stopped talking to me. They're convinced I've sold out to the Bolsheviks. But there was no way I was going to let those people rot in a Chinese dungeon for the rest of their lives without a trial. No evidence of any crime was found, and I finally managed to talk the Chinese into deporting them back to the USSR."

"Say hello to Tamara for me," Klim said, shaking Tony's hand.

"I will," Tony replied, smiling.

The customs officer called Tony over, and he ran off to arrange his clients' boarding passes.

"So Mr. Rogov, you're leaving as well?" said a vaguely familiar woman's voice.

Klim turned round and was greeted by Ada, dressed in a traveling suit and a felt hat. Next to her stood a young Chinese man holding a suitcase in each hand.

"Sam and I are going to America," Ada announced. "Mrs. Bernard managed to get visas for us through her Moral Welfare League."

"So, your dream is coming true?" Klim asked in surprise.

Ada gave him a proud look. "All my dreams are coming true."

A steam whistle sounded on the little launch transporting the passengers to the big ocean liners.

Ada crossed herself. "That's us, we're off. God willing, we'll meet again."

Sam tightened his grip on the suitcases. "Where to?"

"Follow me," said Ada.

Sam followed her with adoring eyes, and Klim could tell that the young man was totally in love with Ada.

**Please support the *Russian Treasures* series
with your reviews on Amazon and Goodreads.**

It will help a lot—people make buying decisions on the
number of reviews, making every one of them precious.

THE RUSSIAN TREASURES SERIES

Russian Treasures. Book One

White Ghosts. Book Two

The Prince of the Soviets. Book Three

SUBSCRIBE TO A NEWSLETTER

The only way to know immediately when a new book by Elvira Baryakina comes out is to subscribe to her newsletter at www.baryakina.com/en/

Join and get *The Shaman*, a prequel to the *Russian Treasures* series, for free.

THE SHAMAN

A short story

Klim Rogov, the sole heir to the fortune of a noble family, has disappeared without a trace. Only his fifteen-year-old cousin has any idea what has happened, but she is keeping silent. There is little point trying to explain to adults the nature of the mysterious force that has commanded Klim to leave home, come what may.

If you'd like to talk about life and good books, please join Elvira Baryakina on her Facebook — http://facebook.com/elvira.baryakina

48543113R00238

Made in the USA
Lexington, KY
16 August 2019